Three men with a proud past;
three women with an uncertain future—
all in search of a perfect love.

Phillip Hunter. Sage Parker. Eric Hawk:
All have known the pride and pain of their
heritage. None has let a woman touch his
soul...until now.

Jennifer Marist. Megan McBride. Ashley Dane:
Three women thrust into a different world,
afraid to trust themselves to the passion of these

Relive the romance...

Three complete novels by your favorite authors!

About the Authors

DIANA PALMER

got her start in writing as a newspaper reporter, but fiction is her true métier. With over ten million copies of her books in print, she is the winner of seven national Waldenbooks Bestseller Awards and has been deemed one of the top ten romance writers in the country. A gift for telling the most sensuous tales with charm and wit is her trademark. Readers treasure her emotional style.

KATHLEEN EAGLE

saw her first novel published in 1984, following a long career as a high school English teacher. She's been writing for Silhouette and Harlequin ever since, and also writes bestselling mainstream novels. She has received awards from the Romance Writers of America, *Affaire de Coeur* and *Romantic Times*. Her husband, Clyde's, Lakota heritage has enriched her own life as well as her writing.

HEATHER GRAHAM POZZESSERE

is a *New York Times* bestselling author who has seventy titles to her credit and over ten million books in print. Her novels are published in fifteen languages in twenty-five countries. The author, who also writes under the names Heather Graham and Shannon Drake, has won numerous awards from the Romance Writers of America, Waldenbooks and *Romantic Times*. In addition to writing contemporary and historical romances, Heather is a full-time wife and mother of five.

BRAVE HEARTS

Diana Palmer

Kathleen Eagle

**Heather Graham
Pozzessere**

Published by Silhouette Books
America's Publisher of Contemporary Romance

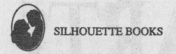

SILHOUETTE BOOKS

by Request

BRAVE HEARTS

Copyright © 1994 by Harlequin Enterprises B.V.

ISBN 0-373-20106-0

HUNTER
Copyright © 1990 by Diana Palmer
BUT THAT WAS YESTERDAY
Copyright © 1988 by Kathleen Eagle
BORROWED ANGEL
Copyright © 1989 by Heather Graham Pozzessere

Printed in U.S.A.

CONTENTS

A Note from Diana Palmer

Of all the books I've written, *Hunter* is at the top of my personal list of favorites. Many of you know that I minored in anthropology in college and that my husband, James (as well as James's younger brother and his wife), has a Native American heritage. *Hunter* was the result of some personal research into Western Apache culture, including the distinctive Apache language.

Many fine Native American actors served as inspiration for this book. Their roles have given us a new, strong image of Native Americans and their way of life. They are changing the obsolete image of their heritage and replacing it with vivid portrayals of very human people who were faced with an overwhelming European invasion of their land.

During those times, the tribal people of this nation fought with valor and surrendered with dignity. In this book, I honor them.

Diana Palmer

HUNTER

Diana Palmer

For Flo in Canada
and Ophelia in Augusta, GA,
with love

One

The silver-haired man across the desk had both hands clasped together on its surface, and his blue eyes were narrow and determined.

Hunter wanted to argue. He'd protested assignments before, and Eugene Ritter had backed down. This time the old man wouldn't. Hunter sensed Ritter's determination before he even tried to get out of the job.

That didn't stop him, of course. Phillip Hunter was used to confrontation. As chief of internal security for Ritter Oil Corporation for the past ten years, he'd become quite accustomed to facing off against all manner of opponents, from would-be thieves to enemy agents who tried to get the jump on Ritter's strategic metal discoveries.

"The desert is no place for a woman," he told the old man. He sat back comfortably in the straight-backed chair, looking as formidable as his Apache ancestors. He was very dark, with jet-black hair conventionally cut, and eyes almost black in a lean, thin-lipped face. He was tall, too, and muscular. Even his perfectly fitted gray suit didn't hide the hard lines of a body kept fit by hours of exercise. Hunter was ex-Green Beret, ex-mercenary, and for a short time he'd even worked for the CIA. He was an expert with small arms and his karate training had earned him a black belt. He was thirty-seven, a loner by nature, unmarried and apt to stay that way. He had no inclination to accompany Eugene's sexy field geologist out to Arizona on a preliminary survey. Jennifer Marist was one of his few ongoing irritations. She seemed to stay in hot water, and he was always deputized to pull her irons out of the fire.

Her last exploration had put her in danger from enemy agents, resulting in a stakeout at her apartment a few months ago. Two men had been apprehended, but the third was still at large.

Hunter and Jennifer were old sparring partners. They'd been thrown together on assignments more often than Hunter liked. Like two rocks striking, they made sparks fly, and that could be dangerous. He didn't like white women, and Jennifer was unique. Her soft blond beauty, added to her sharp intellect, made him jittery. She was the only female who'd ever had that effect on him, and he didn't like it. The thought of spending a week in the desert alone with her had him fuming.

"Jennifer isn't just a woman, she's one of my top field geologists," Eugene replied. "This is a potentially rich strike, and I need the new capital it will bring in. Jennifer can't go alone."

"I could send one of my operatives with her," Hunter replied.

"Not good enough. Jennifer's already been in danger from this assignment once. I want the best—and that's you."

"We don't get along, haven't you noticed?" he said through his teeth.

"You don't have to get along with her. You just have to keep anyone from getting his hands on her maps or her survey results." He pursed his lips. "The site's in Arizona, near the Apache reservation. You can go see your grandfather."

"I can do that without having to follow your misplaced ingenue around," he said coldly.

"Jennifer is a geologist," the older man reminded him. "Her looks have nothing to do with her profession. For God's sake, you get along with my other female employees, why not with Jennifer?"

That was a question Hunter didn't really want to answer. He couldn't very well tell Eugene that the woman appealed to his senses so potently that it was hard to function when she was around. He wasn't in the market for an affair, but he wanted Jennifer with a feverish passion. He'd managed to contain his desire for her very well over the years, but lately it was becoming unmanageable. The temptation of being out on the desert with her was too much. Something might happen, and what then? He had good reasons for his dislike of white women, and he had no desire whatsoever to create a child who, like himself, could barely adapt to life in a white world. White and Apache just didn't mix, even if he did frequently wake up sweating from his vivid dreams about Jennifer Marist.

"You can always threaten to quit," Eugene advised with a sharp grin.

"Would it work?" Hunter queried.

Eugene just shook his head.

"In that case," Hunter said, rising to his feet with the stealthy grace that was unique to him, "I won't bother. When do we leave?"

"First thing in the morning. You can pick up the tickets and motel voucher from my secretary. You'll need time to lay in some camping equipment, so the motel room will be necessary the first night. You and Jennifer will be pretending to be husband and wife when you switch flights in Phoenix to head down to Tucson. That's going to throw any followers off the track, I hope, and give you both time to scout the area before they discover their mistake and double back. Better get in touch with our operatives in Arizona and advise them of the plan.''

"I'll do that now."

"Try not to look so dismal, will you?" Eugene muttered darkly. "It's demoralizing!"

"Stop sending me out with Jennifer Marist."

"You're the only man in my corporation who could complain about that."

"I'm Apache," Hunter said with quiet pride. "She's white."

Eugene had been married twice and he wasn't stupid. He could read between the lines very well. "I understand how it is," he replied. "But this is business. You'll have to cope."

"Don't I always?" Hunter murmured. "Will you tell her, or do you want me to?"

"I'll enjoy it more than you would," Eugene chuckled. "She's going to go right through the ceiling. It may shock you to know that she finds you offensive and unpleasant. She'll fight as hard to get out of it as you just did."

That didn't surprise Hunter. He had a feeling Jennifer felt the same unwanted attraction he did and was fighting it just as hard. From day one, their relationship had been uneasy and antagonistic.

"It won't do her any more good than it did me," Hunter murmured. "But if she ends up roasting over a campfire, don't say I didn't warn you."

Eugene's blue eyes twinkled. "Okay. I won't."

Hunter left and walked along the corridor with an expression so cold and so fierce that one employee turned and went back the other way to avoid him. He had a fairly decent working relationship with some of Eugene's people, but most of them kept out of his way. The icy Mr. Hunter was well-known. He was the only bachelor who didn't have to fight off feminine advances. The women were too intimidated by him. All except for Jennifer, who fought him tooth and nail.

And now a week on the desert with her, he mused. He lit a cigarette as he walked and blew out a thick cloud of smoke. He'd just managed to give up cigarettes the week before. He was getting hooked again, and it was Eugene's fault. For two cents, he'd quit and go back and raise horses on the reservation. But that would bore him to death eventually. No, he'd just have to find some way to survive Jennifer. One day, he promised himself, he was going to walk out the door and leave Eugene with it.

Two

Jennifer Marist shared an office with several other geologists, a roomful of high-tech equipment, maps and charts and assorted furniture. On good days, she and the other geologists who worked for the Ritter Oil Corporation could maneuver around one another as they proceeded with their individual and collective projects. Unfortunately this wasn't a good day. Chaos reigned, and when the big boss himself, Eugene Ritter, asked Jenny to come into his office, it was a relief.

She took her time going down the long hall enjoying the glass windows that gave such a beautiful view of Tulsa, Oklahoma, and the lush vegetation that accented the walkway. Jenny was twenty-seven, but she looked much younger. Her long blond hair was soft and wavy, her deep blue eyes full of life and quiet pleasure. She wore a white knit sweater with simply designed gray slacks, but she still looked like a cover girl. It was the curse of her life, she thought, that men saw the face and not the personality and intelligence beneath it. Fortunately the men in her group were used to her by now, and none of them made sexist remarks or gave wolf whistles when she came into a room. They were all married except Jack, anyway, and Jack was fifty-six; just a bit old for Jenny's taste.

All told, though, Jenny had given up on the idea of marriage. It would have been lovely, but despite the modern world she lived in, the only two men she'd ever come close to marrying refused to share her with her globe-trotting career. They wanted a nice little woman who'd stay at home and cook and clean and raise kids. Jenny wouldn't have minded so much with the right man, but she'd spent years training as a geologist. She was highly paid and tops in her field. It seemed wasteful to sacrifice that for a dirty apron. But, then, perhaps she'd just never met the man she'd want to compromise for.

She glanced around as she entered the waiting room of Eugene's plush carpeted office, looking for Hunter. Thank God he was nowhere close by. She let out a tense sigh. Ridiculous to let a man get to her that way, especially a cold-blooded statue like Mr. Hunter. He was the company's troubleshooter and there had been a little trouble just lately. He and Jenny had partnered up for an evening to catch enemy agents who were after Jenny's top-secret maps of a potential new strike in strategic metals. It had been an evening to remember, and Jenny was doing her best to forget it all. Especially the part that contained him. They'd caught two men, but not the ringleader himself. Hunter had blamed her. He usually did, for anything that went wrong. Maybe he hated blondes.

She lifted her eyebrows at Betty, Eugene's secretary, who grinned and nodded.

"Go right in. He's waiting," she told Jenny.

"Is Hunter in there?" she asked, hesitating.

"Not yet."

That sounded ominous. Jenny tapped at the door and opened it, peeking around to find Eugene precariously balanced in his swivel chair, looking thoughtful.

"Come in, come in. Have a chair. Close the door first." He smiled. "How's the world treating you?"

"Fair to middling," she replied, laughing as she sat down in the chair across the desk.

He leaned forward, his silver hair gleaming in the light from the window behind him, his pale blue eyes curious. "Getting lonely since Danetta married my son and moved out?"

"I do miss my cousin," Jenny replied, smiling. "She was a great roommate." She leaned forward. "But I don't miss the lounge lizard!"

He chuckled. "I guess she misses him. Danetta's iguana is living with us, now, and my youngest son Nicky and he are best friends already. Cabe has promised Danetta a nice stuffed one for a pet anytime she wants it."

Jenny smothered a grin. Her employer's older son Cabe was well-known for his aversion to anything with scales; especially iguanas named Norman. Jenny had gotten used to the big lizard, after a fashion, but it was a lot more comfortable living without him.

"I've got a proposition for you," Ritter said without further preamble. "There's a piece of land down in Arizona that I want you to run a field survey on. I'll send down your equipment and you can camp out for a few days until you can get me a preliminary map of the area and study the outcroppings."

She knew she was going white. "The Arizona desert?"

"That's right. Quiet place. Pretty country. Peace."

"Rattlesnakes! Men with guns in four-wheel drives! Indians!"

"Shhhhh! Hunter might hear you!" he said, putting his finger to his lips.

She glared at him. "I am not afraid of tall Apaches named Hunter. I meant the other ones, the ones who don't work for us."

"Listen, honey, the Apaches don't raid the settlements anymore, and it's been years since anybody was shot with an arrow."

She glared harder. "Send Hunter."

"Oh, I'm going to," he said. "I'm glad you agree that he's the man for the job. The two of you can keep each other company. He'll be your protection while you sound out this find for me."

"Me? Alone in the desert with Hunter for several days and nights?" She almost choked. "You can't do it! We'll kill each other!"

"Not right away," he said. "Besides, you're the best geologist I have and we can't afford to take chances, not with the goings-on of the past month. And our adversary is still loose somewhere. That's why I want you to camp in a different section each night, to throw him off the track. You'll go to the target area on the second night. I'll show you on the map where it is. You aren't to tell anyone."

"Not even Hunter?" she asked.

"You can try not to, but Hunter knows everything."

"He thinks he does," she agrees. "I'll bet he invented bread..."

"Cut it out. This is an assignment, you're an employee, I'm the boss. Quit or pack."

She threw up her hands. "What a choice. You pay me a duke's ransom for what I do already and then you threaten me with poverty. That's no choice."

He grinned at her. "Good. Hunter doesn't bite."

"Want to see the teeth marks?" she countered. "He snapped my head off the night we lost that other agent. He said it was my fault!"

"How could it have been?"

"I don't know, but that's what he said. Does it have to be Hunter? Why can't you send that nice Mallory boy with me? I like him."

"That's why I won't send him. Hunter isn't nice, but he'll keep you alive and protect my investment. There isn't a better man for this kind of work."

She had to agree, but she didn't like having to. "Can I have combat pay?"

"Listen or get out."

"Yes, sir." She sat with resignation written all over her. "What are we looking for? Oil? Molybdenum? Uranium?"

"Best place to look for oil right now is western Wyoming," he reminded her. "Best place to look for moly is Colorado or southern Arizona. And that's why I'm sending you to Arizona—molybdenum. And maybe gold."

She whistled softly. "What an expedition."

"Now you know why I want secrecy," he agreed. "Hunter and you will make a good team. You're both clams. No possibility of security leaks. Get your gear together and be ready to leave at six in the morning. I'll have Hunter pick you up at your apartment."

"I could get to the airport by myself," she volunteered quickly.

"Scared of him?" Ritter taunted, his pale eyes twinkling at her discomfort.

She lifted her chin and glared at him. "No. Of course not."

"Good. He'll look after you. Have fun."

Fun, she thought as she left the room, wasn't exactly her definition of several days in the desert with Hunter. In fact, she couldn't think of anything she was dreading more.

Back in the office she shared with her colleagues, two of her co-workers were waiting. "What is it?" they chorused. "Moly? Uranium? A new oil strike?"

"Well, we haven't found another Spindletop," she said with a grin, "so don't worry about losing out on all that fame. Maybe he just thinks I need a vacation.'' She blew on her fingernails and buffed them on her knit blouse. ''After all,'' she said with a mock haughty glance at the two men, ''he knows I do all the work around here.''

One of her co-workers threw a rolled-up map at her and she retreated to her own drafting board, saved from having to give them a direct answer. They all knew the score, though, and wouldn't have pressed her. A lot of their work was confidential.

She'd just finished her meager lunch and was on her way back into the building when she encountered a cold, angry Hunter in the hallway that led to her own office.

The sight of him was enough to give her goose bumps. Hunter was over six feet tall, every inch of him pure muscle and power. He moved with singular grace and elegance, and it wasn't just his magnificent physique that drew women's eyes to him. He had an arrogance of carriage that was peculiarly his, a way of looking at people that made them feel smaller and less significant. Master of all he surveys, Jenny thought insignificantly, watching his black eyes cut toward her under his heavy dark eyebrows. His eyes were deep-set in that lean, dark face with its high cheekbones and straight nose and thin, cruel-looking mouth. It wouldn't be at all difficult to picture Hunter in full Apache war regalia, complete with long feathered bonnet. She got chills just thinking about having to face him over a gun, and thanked God that this was the twentieth century and they'd made peace with the Apache. Well, with most of them. This one looked and sometimes acted as if he'd never signed any peace treaties.

In her early days with the company, she'd made the unforgivable mistake of raising her hand and saying ''how.'' She got nervous now just remembering the faux pas, remembering the feverish embarrassment she'd felt, the shame, at how he'd fended off the insult. She'd learned the hard way that it wasn't politic to ridicule him.

"Mr. Hunter," she said politely, inclining her head as she started past him.

He took a step sideways and blocked her path. "Was it Eugene's idea, or yours?"

"If you mean the desert survival mission, I can assure you that I don't find the prospect all that thrilling." She didn't back down an inch, but those cold dark eyes were making her feel giddy inside. "If I got to choose my own companion, I'd really prefer Norman the Iguana. He's better tempered than you are, he doesn't swear, and he's never insulted me."

Hunter didn't smile. That wasn't unusual; Jenny had never seen him smile. Maybe he couldn't, she thought, watching him. Maybe his face was covered in hard plastic and it would crack if he tried to raise the corners of his mouth. That set her off and she had to stifle a giggle.

"Something amuses you?" he asked.

The tone was enough, without the look that accompanied it. "Nothing at all, Mr. Hunter," she assured him. "I have to get back to work. If you don't mind . . . ?"

"I mind having to set aside projects to play guardian angel to a misplaced cover girl," he said.

Her dark blue eyes gleamed with sudden anger. "I could give you back that insult in spades if I wanted to," she said coldly. "I have a master's degree in geology. My looks have nothing whatsoever to do with my intelligence or my professional capabilities."

He lifted a careless eyebrow. "Interesting that you chose a profession that caters to men."

There was no arguing with such a closed mind. "I won't defend myself to you. This assignment wasn't my doing, or my choice. If you can talk Eugene into sending someone else, go to it."

"He says you're the best he has."

"I'm flattered, but that isn't quite so. He can't turn anyone else loose right now."

"Too bad."

She pulled herself up to her full height. It still wasn't enough to bring the top of her head any higher than Hunter's square chin. "Thank you for your vote of confidence. What a pity you don't know quartz from diamond, or you could do the whole job yourself!"

He let his gaze slide down her body and back up again, but if he found any pleasure in looking at her, it didn't show in those rigid features. "I'll pick you up at six in the morning at your apartment. Don't keep me waiting, cover girl."

He moved and was gone before she recovered enough to tell him what she thought of him. She walked back to her own office with blazing eyes and a red face, thinking up dozens of snappy replies that never came to mind when she actually needed them.

She pulled her maps of southern Arizona and looked at the area Eugene had pinpointed for her field survey. The terrain was very familiar; mountains and desert. She had topographical maps, but she was going to need something far more detailed before Eugene and his board of directors decided on a site. And her work was only the first step. After she finished her preliminary survey, the rest of the team would have to decide on one small area for further study. That would involve sending a team of geologic technicians in to do seismic studies and more detailed investigation, including air studies and maybe even expensive computer time for the satellite Landsat maps.

But right now what mattered was the fieldwork. This particular area of southern Arizona bordered government land on one side and the Apache reservation on the other. The reservation was like a sovereign nation, with its own government and laws, and she couldn't prospect there without permission. What Eugene hoped to find was in a narrow strip between the two claimed territories. He had a good batting average, too. Old-timers said that Eugene could smell oil and gold, not to mention moly.

It was too short a day. She collected all her equipment to be taken to the airport and the charts and maps she ex-

pected to have to refer to. With that chore out of the way,
she went home.

Jenny cooked herself a small piece of steak and ate it with
a salad, brooding over her confrontation with Hunter and
dreading the trip ahead. He didn't like her, that much was
apparent. But it shouldn't have affected their working relationship as much as it did. There were other women in the
organization, and he seemed to get along well enough with
them.

"Maybe it's my perfume," she murmured out loud and
laughed at the idea of it.

No, it had to be something in her personality that set him
off, because he'd disliked her on sight the first time they
met.

She remembered that day all too well. It had been her first
day on the job with the Ritter Oil Corporation. With her
geology degree under her belt—a master's degree—she'd
landed a plum of a job with one of the country's biggest oil
companies. That achievement had given her confidence.

She'd looked successful that day, in a white linen suit and
powder-blue blouse, with her blond hair in a neat chignon,
her long, elegant legs in sheer hose, her face with just the
right amount of makeup. Her appearance had shocked and
delighted her male colleagues on the exploration team. But
her first sight of Hunter had shocked and delighted *her*, to
her utter dismay.

Eugene Ritter had called Hunter into his office to meet
Jenny. She hadn't known about his Apache heritage then;
she hadn't known anything about him except his last name.
He'd come through the door and Jenny, who was usually
unperturbed by men, had melted inside like warm honey.

Hunter had been even less approachable in those days.
His hair had been longer, and he'd worn it in a short pigtail
at his nape. His suit had been a pale one that summery day,
emphasizing his darkness. But it was his face that Jenny had
stared at so helplessly. It was a dark face, very strong, with
high cheekbones and jet-black hair and deep-set black eyes,

a straight nose and a thin, cruel-looking mouth that hadn't smiled when they were introduced. In fact, his eyes had narrowed with sudden hostility. She could remember the searing cold of that gaze even now, and the contempt as it had traveled over her with authority and disdain. As if she were a harem girl on display, she thought angrily, not a scientist with a keen analytical mind and meticulous accuracy in her work. It occurred to her then that a geologist would be a perfect match for the stony Mr. Hunter. She'd said as much to Eugene and it had gotten back to Hunter. That comment plus the other unfortunate stunt had not endeared her to Hunter. He hadn't found it the least bit amusing. He'd said that she wouldn't appeal to him if she came sliced and buttered.

She sighed, pushing her last piece of steak around on her plate. Amazing that he could hate her when she found him so unbearably attractive. The trick fate had played on her, she thought wistfully. All her life, the men who wanted her had been mama's boys or dependent men who needed nurturing. All she'd wanted was a man who was strong enough to let her be herself, brains and all. Now she'd finally found one who was strong, but neither her brains nor her beauty interested him in the least.

She'd never had the courage to ask Hunter why he hated her so much. They'd only been alone together once in all the years they'd know each other, and that had been the night they'd staged a charade for the benefit of the agents who were after Jenny's survey maps.

They'd gone to a restaurant with Cabe Ritter and his then-secretary, Danetta Marist, Jenny's cousin. Jenny had deliberately worn a red, sexy dress to "live down to Hunter's opinion" of her. He'd barely spared her a glance, so she could have saved herself the trouble. Once they'd reached the apartment and the trap had been sprung, she'd seen Hunter in action for the first time. The speed with which he'd tackled the man prowling in her apartment was fascinating, like the ease with which he'd floored the heavier man and rendered him unconscious. He'd gone after a second man, but that one had knocked Jenny into the wall in his haste to escape. Hunter had actually stopped to see that she was all right. He'd tugged her gently to her feet, his eyes blazing as he checked her over and demanded assurance that she hadn't been hurt. Then he'd gone after that second man, with blood in his eye, but he'd lost his quarry by then. His security men had captured a third member of the gang outside. Hunter had blamed Jenny for the loss of the second, who was the ringleader. Odd how angry he'd been, she thought in retrospect. Maybe it was losing his quarry, something he rarely did.

She washed her few dishes before she had a quick shower and got into her gown. The sooner she slept, the sooner she'd be on her way to putting this forced trip behind her, she told herself.

She looked at herself in the mirror before she climbed wearily into bed. There were new lines in her face. She was twenty-seven. Her age was beginning to bother her, too. Many more years and her beauty would fade. Then she'd have nothing except her intellect to attract a husband, and that was a laugh. Most of the men she'd met would trade a brainy woman any day for a beautiful one, despite modern attitudes. Hunter probably liked the kind of woman who'd walk three steps behind her husband and chew rawhide to make them soft for his moccasins.

She tried to picture Hunter with a woman in his arms, and she blushed at the pictures that came to mind. He had the most magnificent physique she'd ever seen, all lean muscle and perfection. Thinking of him without the civilizing influence of clothes made her knees buckle.

With an angry sigh, she put out the light and got under the sheets. She had to stop tormenting herself with these thoughts. It was just that he stirred her as no other man ever had. He could make her weak-kneed and giddy just by walking into a room. The sight of him fed her heart. She looked at him and wanted him, in ways that were far removed from the purely physical. She remembered hearing once that he'd been hurt on the job, and her heart had stopped beating until she could get confirmation that he was alive and going to be all right. She looked for him, consciously and unconsciously, everywhere she went. It was getting to be almost a mania with her, and there was apparently no cure. Stupid, to be so hopelessly in love with a man who didn't even know she existed. At her age, and with her intellect, surely she should have known better. But all the same, her world began and ended with Hunter.

Eventually she slept, but it was very late when she drifted off, and she slept so soundly that she didn't even hear the alarm clock the next morning. But she heard the loud knocking on the door, and stumbled out of bed too drowsy to even reach for her robe. Fortunately her gown was floor-length and cotton, thick enough to be decent to answer a door in, at least.

Hunter glowered at her when she opened the door. "The plane leaves in two hours. We have to be at the airport in one. Didn't I remind you that I'd be here at six?"

"Yes," she said on a sigh. She stared up at his dark face. "Don't you ever smile?" she asked softly.

He lifted a heavy, dark eyebrow. "When I can find something worth smiling at," he returned with faint sarcasm.

That puts me in my place, she thought. She turned. "I have to have my coffee or I can't function."

"I'll make the coffee. Get dressed," he said tersely, dragging his eyes away from the soft curves that gown outlined so sweetly.

"But..." She turned and saw the sudden flash of his dark eyes, and stopped arguing.

"I said get dressed," he repeated in a tone that made threats, especially when it was accompanied by his slow, bold scrutiny of her body.

She ran for it. He'd never looked at her in exactly that way before, and it wasn't flattering. It was simply the look

of a man who knew how to enjoy a woman. Lust, for lack
of a better description. She darted into her room and closed
the door.

She refused to allow herself to think about that smoldering look he'd given her. She dressed in jeans and a pink knit
top for travel, dressing for comfort rather than style, and she
wore sneakers. She left her hair long and Hunter could
complain if he liked, she told herself.

By the time she got to the small kitchen, Hunter was
pouring fresh coffee into two mugs. He produced cinna-
mon toast, deliciously browned, and pushed the platter toward her as she sat down with him at the table.

"I didn't expect breakfast," she said hesitantly.

"You need feeding up," he replied without expression.
"You're too thin. Get that in you."

"Thank you." She nibbled on toast and sipped coffee,
trying not to stare. It was heart-breakingly cozy, to be like
this with him. She tried to keep her eyes from darting over
him, but she couldn't help it. He looked very nice in dark
slacks and a white shirt with a navy blazer and striped tie.
He wore his hair short and conventionally cut these days,
and he was the picture of a successful businessman. Except
for his darkness and the shape of his eyes and the very real
threat of his dark skills. He was an intimidating man. Even
now, it was hard going just to make routine conversation.
Jenny didn't even try. She just sat, working on her second
piece of toast.

Hunter felt that nervousness in her. He knew she felt intimidated by him, but it was a reaction he couldn't change.
He was afraid to let her get close to him in any way. She was
a complication he couldn't afford in his life.

"You talk more at work and around other people," he
remarked when he'd finished the piece of toast he'd been
eating and was working on his second cup of coffee.

"There's safety in numbers," she said without looking
up.

He looked at her until she lifted her head and then he trapped her blue eyes with his black ones and refused to let her look away. The fiery intensity of the shared look made her body go taut with shocked pleasure, and her breath felt as if it had been suspended forever.

"Safety for whom?" he asked quietly. "For you?" His chin lifted, and he looked so arrogantly unapproachable that she wanted to back away. "What are you afraid of, Jennifer? Me?"

Yes, but she wasn't going to let him know it. She finished her coffee. "No," she said. "Of course not. I just meant that it's hard to make conversation with you."

He leaned back in his chair, his lean, dark hand so large that it completely circled the coffee mug. "Most people talk a lot and say nothing," he replied.

She nodded. Her lips tugged up. "A friend of mine once said that it was better to keep one's mouth closed and appear stupid than to open it and remove all doubt."

He didn't smile, but his eyes did, for one brief instant. He lifted the mug to his lips, watching Jenny over its rim. She was lovely, he thought with reluctant delight in her beauty. She seemed to glow in the early morning light, radiant and warm. He didn't like the feelings she kindled in him. He'd never known love. He didn't want to. In his line of work, it was too much of a luxury.

"We'd better get going," he said.

"Yes." She got up and began to tidy the kitchen, putting detergent into the water as it filled the sink.

He stood, watching her collect the dishes and wash them. He leaned against the wall, his arms crossed over his chest. His dark eyes narrowed as they sketched the soft lines of her body with slow appreciation.

He remembered the revealing red dress she'd worn the night they'd staked out her apartment, and his expression hardened. He hoped she wasn't going to make a habit of wearing anything revealing while they were alone together.

Jennifer was his one weak spot. But fortunately, she didn't know that and he wasn't planning to tell her.

"I'll get your suitcases," he said abruptly. He shouldered away from the wall and went out.

She relaxed. She'd felt that scrutiny and it had made her nervous. She wondered why he'd stared at her so intently. Probably he was thinking up ways to make her even more uncomfortable. He did dislike her intensely. For which she thanked God. His hostility would protect her from doing anything really stupid. Like throwing herself at him.

He had her bags by the front door when she was through. It was early fall, and chilly, so she put on a jacket on her way to the door. He opened the door for her, leaving her to lock up as he headed toward the elevator with the luggage. They didn't speak all the way to the car.

Three

Jenny was aware of Hunter's height as they walked to the car in the parking lot under her apartment building. He towered over her, and the way he moved was so smooth and elegant, he might have been gliding.

He put the luggage into the back of his sedan and opened the passenger door for her. He had excellent manners, she thought, and wondered if his mother had taught him the social graces or if he'd learned them in the service. So many questions she wanted to ask, but she knew he'd just ignore them, the way he ignored any questions he didn't want to answer.

He drove the way he did everything else, with confidence and poise. Near collisions, bottlenecks, slow traffic, nothing seemed to disturb him. He eased the car in and out of lanes with no trouble at all, and soon they were at the airport.

She noticed that he didn't request seats together. But the ticket agent apparently decided that they wanted them, to her secret delight, and put them in adjoining seats. That was when she realized how lovesick she was, hungry for just the accidental brush of his arm or leg. She had to get a grip on herself!

He sat completely at ease in his seat while she ground her teeth together and tried to remember all the statistics on how safe air travel really was.

"Now what's wrong?" he murmured, glancing darkly down at her as the flight attendants moved into place to demonstrate emergency procedures.

"Nothing," she said.

"Then why do you have a death-grip on the arms of your seat?" he asked politely.

"So that I won't get separated from it when we crash," she replied, closing her eyes tight.

He chuckled softly. "I never took you for a coward," he said. "Are you the same woman who helped me set up enemy agents only a few weeks ago?"

"That was different," she protested. She lifted her blue eyes to his dark ones and her gaze was trapped. Her breath sighed out, and she wondered which was really the more dangerous, the plane or Hunter.

He couldn't seem to drag his eyes from hers, and he found that irritating. At close quarters, she was beautiful. Dynamite. All soft curves and a sexy voice and a mouth that he wanted very much to kiss. But that way lay disaster. He couldn't afford to forget the danger of involvement. He had a life-style that he couldn't easily share with any woman, but most especially with a white woman. All the same, she smelled sweet and floral, and she looked so beautifully cool. He wanted to dishevel her.

He averted his face to watch the flight attendants go through the drill that preceded every flight, grateful for the interruption. He had to stop looking at Jennifer like that.

They were airborne before either of them spoke again.

"These people that you think are following us," she said softly, "is it the same group that broke into my apartment?"

"More than likely," he said. "You have to remember that strategic metals tend to fluctuate on the world market according to the old law of supply and demand. When a new use is found for a strategic metal, it becomes immediately more valuable."

"And an increase in one industry can cause it, too," she replied.

He nodded. She was quick. He liked her brain as much as her body, but he wasn't going to let her know that. "We didn't pick up the ringleader, you remember. He got away," he added with a cold glare at her.

She flushed. She didn't like being reminded of how helpless she'd felt. "I didn't ask you to stop to see about me," she defended.

He knew that. The memory of seeing her lying inert on the floor still haunted him. That was when he'd first realized he was vulnerable. Now he seemed to spend all his time trying to forget that night. The agents, his job to protect Jenny and the company, had all been momentarily forgotten when the agent knocked her down in his haste to get away. Hunter had been too shaken by Jennifer's prone position to run after the man. And that was what made him so angry. Not the fact that the agent had gotten away, but the fact that his concern for Jennifer had outweighed his dedication to his work. That was a first in his life.

"We're transferring to another flight in Phoenix, under different names," he said, lowering his voice. "With luck, the agents will pursue us on to California before they realize we're gone."

"How are we going to give them the slip? Are they on the plane?"

He smiled without looking at her. "Yes, they're about five rows behind us. We're going to get off supposedly to stretch our legs before the plane goes on to Tucson. We transfer to another airline, though, instead of coming back."

"What if they follow us?"

"I'd see them," he murmured dryly. "The rule of thumb in tracking someone is to never let your presence be discovered. Lose the subject first. This isn't the first time I've played cat and mouse with these people. I know them."

That said it all, she supposed, but she was glad she could leave all the details to him. Her job was field geology, not espionage. She glanced up at him, allowing herself a few precious seconds of adoration before she jerked her eyes back down and pretended to read a magazine.

She didn't fool Hunter. He'd felt that shy appraisal and it worried him more than the agents did. Being alone with Jennifer on the desert was asking for trouble. He was going to make sure that he was occupied tonight, and that they wouldn't set out until tomorrow. Maybe in that length of time, he could explain the situation to his body and keep it from doing something stupid.

It was a short trip, as flights went. They'd just finished breakfast when they were circling to land at the Tucson airport.

Hunter had everything arranged. Motel reservations, a rental car, the whole works. And it all worked to perfection until they got to the motel desk and the desk clerk handed them two keys, to rooms on different floors.

"No, that won't do," Hunter replied with a straight face, and without looking at Jennifer. "We're honeymooners," he said. "We want a double room.

"Oh! I'm sorry, sir. Congratulations," the clerk said with a pleasant smile.

Dreams came true, Jenny thought, picturing all sorts of delicious complications during that night together. The desk clerk handed him a key after he signed them in—as Mr. and Mrs. Camp. Nice of Hunter to tell her their married name, she thought with faint amusement. But it was typical of him to keep everything to himself.

He unlocked the door, waited for the bellboy to put their luggage and equipment in the room, and tipped the man.

They were alone. He closed the door and turned to her, his dark eyes assessing as he saw the faint unease on her face. "Don't start panicking," he said curtly. "I won't assault you. This is the best way to keep up the masquerade, that's all."

She colored. "I didn't say a word," she reminded him.

He wandered around the room with some strange electronic gadget in one hand and checked curtains and lamps. "No bugs," he said eventually. "But that doesn't mean much. I'm pretty sure we're being observed. Don't leave the room unless I'm with you, and don't mention anything about why we're here. Is that clear?"

"Why don't we just go out into the desert and camp?"

"We have to have camping gear," he explained with mocking patience. "It's too late to start buying it now. The morning's over. We'll start out later in the afternoon."

"All right." She put her suitcases on the side of the room that was nearest the bathroom, hesitating.

"Whichever bed you want is yours," he said without inflection. He was busy watching out the window. "I can sleep anywhere."

And probably had, she thought, remembering some of his assignments that she'd heard about. She put her attaché case with her maps on the bed, and her laptop computer on the side table, taking time to plug its adapter into the wall socket so that it could stay charged up. It only had a few hours' power between charges.

"Give me that case," he said suddenly. He took the case with the maps and opened it, hiding a newspaper he'd brought into the case and then putting it in a dresser drawer with one of his shirts over it. The maps he tucked into a pair of his jeans and left them in his suitcase.

Jenny lifted an amused eyebrow. He had a shrewd mind. She almost said so, but it might reveal too much about her feelings if she told him. She unpacked her suitcase instead

and began to hang up her clothes. She left her underthings
and her long cotton gown in the suitcase, too shy of Hunter
to put them in a drawer in front of him.

The gown brought to mind a question that had only just
occurred. Should she put it on tonight, or would it look like
an invitation? And worse, did he sleep without clothes?
Some men did. She'd watched him put his things away out
of the corner of her eye, and she hadn't seen either a robe or
anything that looked like pajamas. She groaned inwardly.
Wouldn't that be a great question to ask a man like Hunter,
and how would she put it? Isn't this a keen room, Mr.
Hunter, and by the way, do you sleep stark naked, because
if you do, is it all right if I spend the night in the bathtub?

She laughed under her breath. Wouldn't that take the
starch out of his socks, she thought with humor. Imagine,
a woman her age and with her looks being that ignorant
about a man's body. Despite the women's magazines she'd
seen from time to time, with their graphic studies of nude
men, there was a big difference in a photograph and a real
live man.

"Is something bothering you?" he asked suddenly.

The question startled her into blurting out the truth. "Do
you wear pajamas?" she asked, and her face went scarlet.

"Why?" he replied with a straight face. "Do you need to
borrow them, or were you thinking of buying me a pair if I
say no?"

She averted her face. "Sorry. I'm not used to sharing a
room with a man, that's all."

No way could he believe that she'd never spent a night
with a man. More than likely she was nervous of him.
"We're supposed to be honeymooners," he said with faint
sarcasm. "It would look rather odd to spend the night in
separate rooms."

"Of course." She just wanted to drop the whole subject.
"Could we get lunch? I'm starving."

"I want to check with my people first," he told her. "I've got a couple of operatives down here doing some investigative work on another project. I won't be long."

She'd thought he meant to phone, but he went out of the room.

Jenny sprawled on her bed, cursing her impulsive tongue. Now he'd think she was a simpleminded prude as well as a pain in the neck. Great going, Jenny, she told herself. What a super way to get off on the right foot, asking your reluctant roommate about his night wear. Fortunately he hadn't pursued the subject.

He was back an hour later. She'd put on her reading glasses, the ones she used for close work because she was hopelessly farsighted, and was plugging away on her laptop computer, going over detailed graphic topo maps of the area, sprawled across the bed with her back against the headboard and the computer on her lap. Not the best way to use the thing, and against the manufacturer's specs, but it was much more comfortable than trying to use the motel's table and chairs.

"I didn't know you wore glasses," he remarked, watching her.

"You didn't?" she asked with mock astonishment. "Why, Mr. Hunter, I was sure you'd know more about me than I know myself—don't you have a file on all the staff in your office?"

"Don't be sarcastic. It doesn't suit you." He stretched out on the other bed, powerful muscles rippling in his lean body, and she had to fight not to stare. He was beautifully made from head to toe, an old maid's dream.

She punched in more codes and concentrated on her maps.

"What kind of mineral are you and Eugene looking for?" he asked curiously.

She pursed her lips and glanced at him with gleeful malice. "Make a guess," she invited.

She realized her mistake immediately and could have bitten her lip through. He sat up and threw his long legs off the bed, moving to her side with threatening grace. He took the laptop out of her hands and put it on the table before he got her by the wrists and pulled her up against his body. The proximity made her knees go weak. He smelled of spicy cologne and soap, and his breath had a coffee scent, as if he'd been meeting his operatives in a café. His grip was strong and exciting, and she loved the feel of his body so close to hers. Perhaps, subconsciously, this was what she'd expected when she antagonized him...

"Little girls throw rocks at boys they like," he said at her forehead. "Is that what you're doing, figuratively speaking? Because if it is," he added, and his grip on her wrists tightened even as his voice grew deeper, slower, "I'm not in the market for a torrid interlude on the job, cover girl."

She could have gone through the floor with shame. The worst of it was that she didn't even have a comeback. He saw right through her. With his advantage in age and experience, that wasn't really surprising. She knew, too, from gossip that he disliked white women. Probably they saw him as a unique experience more than a man. She didn't feel that way, but she couldn't admit it.

"I'm not trying to get your attention. I'm tired and when I'm tired, I get silly," she said too quickly, talking to his shirt as she stiffened with fear of giving herself away. Odd, the jerky way he was breathing, and the fabric was moving as if his heartbeat was very heavy. Her body was melting, this close to his. "You don't have to warn me off. I know better than to make a play for you."

The remark diverted him. "Do you? Why?" he asked curtly.

"They say you hate women," she replied. "Especially," she added, forcing her blue eyes up to his narrowed dark ones, "white women."

He nodded slowly. His gaze held hers, and then drifted down to her soft bow of a mouth with its faint peach lip-

stick, and further, to the firm thrust of her breasts almost
but not quite touching his shirtfront. He remembered another beautiful blond, the one who'd deserted him when
he'd been five years old. Her Apache child had been an embarrassment in her social circles. By then, of course, her
activist phase was over, and she had her sights on one of her
own people. Some years back, he'd been taken in by a socialite himself. An Apache escort had been unique, for a
little while, until he'd mentioned a permanent commitment. And she'd laughed. My God, marry a man who lived
on a reservation? The memories bit into him like teeth.

He released Jennifer abruptly with a roughness that
wasn't quite in character.

"I'm sorry," she said when she saw the expression in his
dark eyes. She winced, as if she could actually feel his pain.
"I didn't mean to bring back bad memories for you."

His expression was frightening at that moment. "What do
you know about me?" he asked, his voice cutting.

She managed a wan smile and moved away from him. "I
don't know anything, Mr. Hunter. Nobody does. Your life
is a locked door and there's no key. But you looked..." She
turned and glanced back at him, and her hands lifted and
fell helplessly. "I don't know. Wounded." She averted her
eyes. "I'd better get this put away."

Her perception floored him. She was a puzzle he'd never
solved, and despite his security files, he knew very little
about her own private life. There were no men at the office,
he knew. She was discreet, if nothing else. In fact, he
thought, studying her absently with narrowed eyes as she
put away her computer, he'd never heard of her dating a
man in all the years she'd been with the company. He'd
never seen her flirt with a man, and even those she worked
with treated her as just one of the boys. That fact had never
occurred to him before. She kept her distance from men as
a rule. Even out in the field, where working conditions were
much more relaxed, Jennifer went without makeup, in
floppy shirts and loose jeans, and she kept to herself after

working hours. He'd once seen her cut a man dead who was trying to make a play for her. Her eyes had gone an icy blue, her face rigid with distaste, and even though she hadn't said much, her would-be suitor got the message in flying colors. Hunter wouldn't admit, even to himself, how that action had damned her in his eyes. Seeing her put in the knife had made him more determined than ever not to risk his emotions with her. There were too many hard memories of his one smoldering passion for a white woman, and its humiliating result. And, even longer ago than that, his mother's contempt for him, her desertion.

He turned away from Jennifer, busying himself with the surveillance equipment one of his cases contained. He redistributed the equipment in the case and closed it.

"Why do we have to have all that?" she queried suddenly.

He nodded toward her computer and equipment. "Why do you have to have all that?" he countered.

"It's part of my working gear," she said simply.

"You've answered your own question." He checked his watch. "Let's get something to eat. Then we'll have a look at camping supplies."

"The joy of expense accounts," she murmured as she got her purse and put away her reading glasses. "I wonder if Eugene will mind letting me have a jungle hammock? I slept in one when I was a kid. We camped next to two streams, and they were like a lullaby in the darkness."

"You can have a jungle hammock if you think you can find a place to hang it."

"All we need is two trees. . . ."

He turned, his hands on his lean hips, his dark face enigmatic. "The desert is notorious for its lack of trees. Haven't you ever watched any Western movies?" he added, and came very close to a smile. "Remember the Indians chasing the soldiers in John Wayne movies, and the soldiers having to dive into dry washes or gulches for cover?"

She stared at him, fascinated. "Yes. I didn't think you'd watch that kind of movie..." She colored, embarrassed.

"Because the solders won?" he mused. "That's history. But the Apache fought them to a standstill several times. And Louis L'Amour did a story called *Hondo* that was made into a movie with John Wayne." He lifted an eyebrow. "It managed to show Apaches in a good light, for once."

"I read about Cochise when I was in school. And Mangas Coloradas and Victorio..."

"Different tribes of Apache," he said. "Cochise was Chiricahua. Mangas and Victorio were Mimbreños."

"Which...are you?" she asked, sounding and feeling breathless. He'd never spoken to her like this before.

"Chiricahua," he said. His eyes searched her face. "Is your ancestry Nordic?" he asked.

"It's German," she said softly. "On my father's side, it's English." Her eyes wandered helplessly over his lean face.

Her intense scrutiny disturbed him in a new and unexpected way. Her eyes were enormous. Dark blue, soft, like those of some kitten. He didn't like the way they made him tingle. He turned away, scowling.

"We'd better go, Jennifer."

Her name on his lips thrilled her. She felt alive as never before when she was with him, even if it was in the line of duty.

She started toward the door, but he turned as she reached it, and she bumped into him. The contact was like fire shooting through her.

"Sorry!" She moved quickly away. "I didn't mean to...!"

He put a strong hand under her chin and lifted her face to his eyes. Her eyelids flinched and there was real fear in them at close range. "You really are afraid of me," he said with dawning comprehension.

She hadn't wanted him to know that. Of course she was afraid of him, but not for the reasons he was thinking. She

moved back and lowered her eyes. "A little, maybe," she
said uneasily.

"My God!" He jerked open the door. "Out."

She went through it, avoiding him as she left. She hadn't
expected the confession to make him angry. She sighed
heavily. It was going to be a hard trip, all the way, if this was
any indication. He was coldly silent all the way to the motel
restaurant, only taking her arm when they were around
people, for appearance's sake.

They were halfway through their meal when he spoke
again.

"It's been years since I've scalped anyone," he said suddenly, his angry eyes searching hers.

The fork fell from her fingers with a terrible clatter. She
picked it up quickly, looking around nervously to see if
anyone had noticed, but there was only an old couple nearby
and they were too busy talking to notice Jennifer and her
companion.

She should have remembered how sensitive he was about
his heritage. She'd inadvertently let him believe that she was
afraid of him because he was an Indian. What a scream it
would be if she confessed that she was afraid of him because she was in love with him. He'd probably kill himself
laughing.

"No, it's not that," she began. She stopped, helplessly
searching for the right words. "It's not because you're..."
She toyed with her fork. "The thing is, I'm not very comfortable around you," she said finally. She put down her
fork. "You've never made any secret of the fact that you
dislike me. You're actively hostile the minute I come into a
room. It isn't exactly fear. It's nerves, and it has nothing to
do with your heritage."

She had a point. He couldn't deny that he'd been hostile.
Her beauty did that to him; it made him vulnerable and that
irritated him. He knew he was too touchy about his ancestry, but he'd had it rough trying to live in a white world.

"I don't find it easy, living among your people," he said. He'd never admitted that to anyone before.

"I can imagine," she replied. Her eyes searched his. "You might consider that being a female geologist in an oil company isn't the easiest thing to do, either. I loved rocks."

His dark eyes conquered hers suddenly. The look was pure electricity. Desert lightning. She felt it all the way to her toes.

"I find you hard going, too, Miss Marist," he said after a minute. "But I imagine we'll survive. Eugene said we were to camp on the actual site the second night."

"Yes." Her voice sounded breathless, choked.

He found himself studying her hand on the table. Involuntarily his brushed over the back of it. He told himself it was for appearances. But touching her gave him pleasure, and she jumped. He scowled, feeling her long fingers go cold and tremble. His eyes lifted back to hers. "You're trembling."

She jerked her hand from under his, almost unbalancing her water glass in the process. "I have to finish my steak." She laughed nervously. "The stores will close soon."

"So they will."

The subterfuge didn't fool him, she knew. Not one bit. His chin lifted and there was something new in the set of his head. An arrogance. A kind of satisfied pride that kindled in his eyes.

He was curious now. A beautiful woman like Jennifer would be used to giving men the jitters, not the reverse. He let his gaze fall to her soft mouth as it opened to admit a small piece of steak, and he felt his body go rigid. Over the years, he'd only allowed himself the occasional fantasy about making love to her. As time passed, and he grew older, the fantasies had grown stronger. He could keep the disturbing thoughts at bay most of the time. But there was always the lonely night when he'd toss and turn and his blood would grow hot as he imagined her mouth opening for him, her hands on his back, her soft legs tangling with his in the darkness. Those nights were hell. And the next few, alone with her, were going to sorely test his strength of will. For her it would be a field expedition. For him, a survival course, complete with sweet obstacles and pitfalls.

He had to remember that this was an assignment, and enemy agents were following them. Strategic metals always drew trouble, not only from domestic corporations struggling to get their hands in first, but from foreign investors interested in the same idea. He had to keep his mind on his work, and not on Jennifer. But her proximity wasn't going to make that job any easier. He almost groaned aloud at the difficulties. There hadn't been a woman in a long time, and he was hungry. He wanted Jennifer and he was relatively sure that she was attracted to him. She was certainly nervous enough when he came close.

But, he thought, what if her fear of him was genuine and had nothing to do with attraction? Her explanation that it was because they were enemies didn't hold up. It was far too flimsy to explain the way she trembled when he touched her hand. Fear could cause that, he had to admit. And he had been unkind to her, often. He sighed heavily. Thinking about it wasn't going to make it any easier.

They went to a hardware store when they finished their meal, and Jennifer watched him go about the business of buying camping supplies with pure awe. He knew exactly what to get, from the Coleman stove to the other gear like sleeping bags and tent and cans of Sterno for emergencies. Jennifer had gone out into the field before, many times, but usually there was some kind of accommodation. She hadn't relished the idea of camping out by herself, although she loved it with companions. Hunter, though, was going to be more peril than pleasure as a tentmate. She had to get a grip on herself, she told her stubborn heart again. The prospect of a few nights alone with him was sending her mad.

He loaded the gear into the four-wheel drive vehicle he'd had waiting for them at the airport. It was a black one, and he drove it with such ease that she suspected he had one of his own at home. That brought to mind an interesting question. Where was home to him? She knew he had an apartment in Tulsa, but he spent his time off in Arizona. Near here? With a woman, perhaps? Her blood ran cold.

"We'll be ready to go in the morning," he told her when they were back in the motel room again, with their gear stowed in the locked vehicle outside. All except her computer and his surveillance equipment, of course. He wasn't risking that. "Do you want to shower first?"

She shifted uncomfortably. "If you don't mind."

"Go ahead. I'll watch the news."

She carried her things into the bathroom, firmly locking the door, despite what he might think about the sound. She took a quick shower and put on clean blue jeans and a clean white knit shirt. She felt refreshed and sunny when she came back out, her face bright and clean without makeup.

He was sprawled across a chair, his shoes off, a can of beer in his hand. He lifted an eyebrow. "Do you mind beer, or does the smell bother you?"

"No. My father likes his lager," she said as she dealt with her dirty clothes.

He finished his drink and stood, stripping off his shirt. "If you're finished, I'll have my shower. Then we'll think about something for dinner."

She was watching him as helplessly as a teenage girl staring at a movie star. He was beautiful. God, he was beautiful, she thought with pleasure so deep it rivaled pain. Muscles rippled in his dark torso from the low-slung belt on his jeans to the width of his shoulders as he stretched, and her eyes sketched him with shy adoration.

He was aware of her scrutiny, but he pretended not to notice. He got a change of clothes to carry into the bathroom with him and turned, faintly amused by the way she busied herself with her computer and pretended to ignore him.

Her helpless stare had piqued his curiosity. He deliberately paused just in front of her, giving her an unnecessarily good view of his broad, naked chest.

"Don't forget to keep the door locked," he advised quietly, watching the flicker of her lashes as she lifted her blue eyes to his. "And don't answer it if someone knocks."

"Yes, sir, is that all, sir?" she asked brightly.

He caught her chin with a lean hand and his thumb brushed roughly over her mouth, a slow, fierce intimacy that he watched with almost scientific intensity. She knew her eyes were wildly dilated as they looked into his, and she couldn't help the shocked gasp that broke from her sensitized lips or the shiver of pleasure that ran through her body.

His dark eyes didn't miss a thing. Her reaction, he decided, was definitely not fear. He couldn't decide if he was pleased about it or not. "Don't be provocative," he said softly, his voice an octave deeper, faintly threatening. "Get to work." He moved away before she could find anything to say that wouldn't be provocative.

She sat down at her computer, her fingers trembling on the keyboard.

He closed the bathroom door behind him. His action had been totally unexpected, and it made her even more nervous than she already was. If he was going to start doing that kind of thing, she'd be safer in the lion cage at the zoo.

She was uncertain of him and of herself. Being around him in such close quarters was going to be a test of her self-control. She only hoped that she wouldn't give herself away. She'd had some naive idea that because Hunter disliked women, he didn't sleep with them. But she was learning that he knew a lot more than she did, and the sultry look in his dark eyes really frightened her. If she didn't watch her step, she was going to wind up with more than she'd bargained for.

His motives were what bothered her most. He didn't like white women, especially her, so what had prompted that action? She didn't want to consider the most evident possibility—that he thought she was fair game, and he had seduction on his mind. She ground her teeth together. Well, he could hold his breath. She wasn't going to be any man's light amusement. Not even his.

Four

Four

When Jenny heard the shower running, she got up from her
computer and sat in the chair Hunter had occupied to watch
television. The chair still smelled of him. She traced the
armrests where his hands had been and sighed brokenly.
Jenny felt like a fool. She had to stop this!

She got out of the chair and went to work on her contour
maps, trying to pinpoint the best place to look, given the
mineral structure of the area. She'd begged time on Landsat earlier for another project, using the expensive computer time to study the satellite maps of this region of
southern Arizona. The terrain they were going to survey was
between the Apache reservation on one side and government land on the other. A narrow strip of desert and a narrow strip of mountain made up the search area, although
they were going to be camping in several different spots to
throw any would-be thieves off the mark.

She was deep in concentration when Hunter came back
out of the bathroom, wearing clean jeans and no shirt,

again. She had to bite her lip to keep from staring at him. He was unspeakably handsome to her, the most attractive man she'd ever known, but she couldn't afford the luxury of letting him know that. Especially not after the way he'd touched her mouth...

"Found what you're looking for?" he asked, placing one big hand on the table beside her and resting the other on the back of her chair. He leaned down to better see what she was studying. His cheek brushed hers and he felt her jump. His own breath caught. He wanted her. He should never have agreed to come on this expedition, because being close to her was having one hell of a bad effect on his willpower and self-control. He'd thought of nothing except the vulnerable look in her eyes when he'd touched her mouth so intimately, the yielding, the fascination. He wanted to grind his mouth into her own and make her cry out her need for him.

She was feeling the same tension. She knew he sensed her reaction, but she kept her head. "You startled me," she said breathlessly.

He knew better. His lean, warm cheek was touching hers as he stared at the map on the computer's small screen. She looked sideways and saw the thick, short lashes over his dark eyes, the faint lines in his cream-smooth tan. "Hunter..." His name was a soft whisper that broke involuntarily from her throat.

His head turned, and his eyes looked deeply into hers from scant inches away. She could taste his breath on her mouth, smell the clean scent of his body, feel the impact of his bare arms, his chest. He intoxicated her with his nearness, and she saw the hot glitter of awareness in those black eyes. She could see the thick dark lashes above them lower as his gaze suddenly dropped with fierce intent to her parted lips.

She shivered. All her dreams hadn't prepared her for the impact of this. Like a string suspended from a height, waiting for the wind to move it, she hung at his lips without breathing. A fraction of an inch, and his mouth would be on hers . . . !

The knock at the door startled them both. Hunter stared at her and cursed himself for his own vulnerability. She was intoxicating him, damn her. He was a new experience for her, that was all. He had to get himself under control.

He jerked erect and moved to the door. "Yes?" he asked as he opened it.

"Mr. Camp?" a feminine voice said loudly enough that anyone listening could hear. "I'm Teresa Whitley." A tall brunette moved into Jennifer's line of vision. The woman was smiling up at Hunter. "You requested some information about tour spots?"

"Inside," he said, holding the door open. He actually smiled at the woman, and Jennifer wanted to scream.

"Miss Marist?" Teresa smiled warmly, extending a hand as Jennifer came forward. They shook hands. "Nice to meet you. I'm with the corporation—under Mr. Hunter, in fact, so I'd better call you Mrs. Camp outside this room."

"Good idea," Jennifer replied absently. She was still vibrating.

"I've got some more information for you about the area. It's all here, on disk." She frowned. "I'm still learning about computers, I'm afraid. You do use the 3½ inch diskettes in your laptop?"

"I have a hard disk drive," Jennifer told her. "But I can use the diskettes as well."

"Thank goodness!" She handed the diskette, in its plastic case, to Jennifer. "I'm afraid I don't know much about science." She sighed, and her dark brown eyes sought Hunter's flirtatiously. "I'm just a security officer, so I deal with people instead of machines."

And, oh, I'll just bet you do it well, Jennifer thought. She didn't say so. She murmured something about checking out the new data and went back to her computer.

"If you'd like, we can run by the office and I'll give you the results of that security check you had us run," she told

Hunter. "We could have dinner afterward, if you haven't already eaten?"

Jennifer ground her teeth together. She knew now what Hunter had meant earlier when referring to his "other project." This was it, and it had brown eyes and a svelte figure. Jennifer wished she'd dressed to the hilt and put on her makeup. In full regalia, she could have given that exotic orchid a run for her money, but she'd thought dressing up might give Hunter wrong ideas about her.

"Fine," Hunter replied tersely. "Let me get my shirt on."

Finally, Jennifer thought. He hadn't bothered before, but perhaps he didn't want to drive Miss Security Blip out of her mind by flashing his gorgeous muscles.

Hunter glanced at Jennifer, watching the way she studiously ignored Teresa, not to mention him. He glared at her as he pulled a pale gray knit shirt out of his drawer and put it on. He ran a comb through his hair, with Teresa sighing audibly over him.

"You haven't met Teresa before, I gather, Jennifer?" he asked too casually.

"No," she replied, forcing a smile.

"She's Papago." He said it with bitter pleasure, knowing Jennifer would catch the hidden meaning. This woman was Indian.

"Tohono O'Odham," Teresa teased. "We changed our name from 'bean people' in Zuni to 'people of the desert' in Papago."

"Sorry," he said with a smile.

Jennifer hated that damned smile. She'd never seen it, but this woman was getting the full treatment. Of course, Teresa wasn't a blond scientist, she thought darkly. Well, he needn't think she was going to play third fiddle while he courted his secret agent here.

"I'd rather you stayed here...." he began as Jenny said, "I have a headache...."

He cocked an eyebrow and she cleared her throat.

"I'll order something from room service," she continued. "If I feel like eating later," she amended without
looking at him. "I've spent too much time at the laptop. The
screen bothers my eyes." God knew why she was trying to
justify her nonexistent headache. He and his brunette
wouldn't notice.

"I hope you feel better," Teresa said.

"Thanks."

"Shall we go?" Hunter asked as he pulled on his tan
sports coat over his knit shirt. He turned at the door. "Keep
the door locked. If you have room service, check creden-
tials before you let anyone in here."

"Yes, sir," she said with resignation.

He let Teresa out and started to close the door. He looked
back at Jennifer first, and the intensity of his stare made her
lift her head. His eyes held hers for one long moment before they went to her mouth and back up again.

"Don't wait up," he said, but there was another, darker
meaning in the casual remark.

"You can depend on me, sir," she saluted him.

He shook his head and went out the door.

She picked up one of her shoes and threw it furiously at
the closed door. It connected a split second before he opened
it again. The expression on his face was priceless, she
thought.

"I forgot my car keys," he said, watching her narrowly
as he went to the dresser to get them. On the way back, he
reached down and picked up her shoe, cocking an eyebrow
at it. "Target practice?"

She tried to look innocent. "Would I throw a shoe at
you?"

He studied her for a long moment before he dropped the
shoe on the floor. "I'll be back before midnight. You should
be safe enough."

"Definitely safer than Miss Whitley," she said, and could
have bitten her tongue clean through.

His head lifted. "That's true. Most men react to a deliberate invitation. Even me," he added, angry at his vulnerability and lashing out because of it.

Her face colored. "I did not—" she began.

"Invite me?" He let his eyes drop slowly to her mouth. "Yes, you did. But it won't work a second time. You're not my type, cover girl," he added with a mocking smile. "I like a woman with less experience than I have. Not more."

He went out without a backward glance, missing the fierce anger that burned in her cheeks. She hadn't invited him! She groaned. Yes, she had. She wanted him and it showed, but he thought it was because she was experienced and used to a full sexual life. What a laugh!

She went back to her computer. Anyway, he'd just warned her off, and maybe it was a good thing. He seemed to prefer Miss Whitley, and he could relate to her. She was from his world, and Jennifer was just a diversion that shouldn't have happened.

She glanced at her reflection in the mirror and sighed angrily. "You should have stayed home in Missouri and married a mountain man and had two point five children," she told herself. "Instead of joining an oil company and getting tangled up with Mr. Native American."

She refused to let herself think about that one weak moment she'd shared with Hunter. She ordered a fish dinner and coffee to be sent to the room, and she ate it in silence, hoping the fish would leave its scent and drive him crazy. She'd heard someone say that he hated fish. Good enough for him. She hoped his girlfriend gave him warts.

It was only ten o'clock when she put on her cotton gown—deciding to let Hunter think what he liked—climbed into bed and turned out the lights. She didn't mean to go to sleep, she was too fired up by the long day and longer evening. But she was tired and the day caught up with her. She closed her eyes and slept like a baby.

Hunter came in just after midnight, sick of Miss Whitley's too-obvious adoration, and found Jennifer sprawled on her bed in a gown that would have raised a statue's temperature.

The covers had been thrown off, and the gown was up around her thighs. She was lying on her back with one arm thrown over her head, and the bodice was half off, baring the exquisite pink curve of one firm breast. Her clothes hid most of her figure. She didn't seem to go in for revealing things, except for that one night when she'd sent him up the walls in a low-cut red dress that showed every man around just what he was missing.

She was no less lovely now in that white cotton gown with its delicate embroidery. With her long blond hair spread around her perfect oval of a face, her lips parted in sleep, her body totally relaxed, she made a picture that he was going to have hell forgetting.

He managed to turn away from her at last and stripped down to his shorts. He almost removed them, too, but her remark about pajamas came back to twist his lips into a smile. He turned back his covers and set one of the security devices, just in case. From what Teresa had found out for him, the agent had been misled by this "vacation trip" and had followed their flight on to California, not realizing that Hunter and Miss Marist had suddenly turned into Mr. and Mrs. Camp in Tucson. But it didn't pay to get careless.

He had to remember that, he thought, looking at Jennifer one last time before he turned out the light. It had been one close call tonight, when Teresa had interrupted them. Another few seconds, and he'd have taken Jenny's sweet mouth without one single thought for the consequences. She'd have let him. That memory haunted him until he fell asleep. For a woman who purported to hate him, she was remarkably responsive to his touch. He had to convince her that he wasn't interested, no matter what it took. Her responsiveness could have terrible consequences if he let himself take advantage of it.

* * *

The next morning, Hunter was awake and dressed and had breakfast waiting when Jennifer smelled the coffee and food and forced her eyes open.

She sat up, barely aware of her state of undress until she saw Hunter scowl and avert his eyes. She tugged down her gown, angry at having given him a show, and quickly got her clothes together to dress in the bathroom.

She fixed her hair and put on makeup this morning, and she was wearing a blouse for a change, one that buttoned up and emphasized the exquisite shape of her breasts and her narrow waist. It was red, to go with her white jeans, and as she looked at her reflection, she hoped Hunter had fits because of her outfit. Miss Whitley, indeed! This morning she was more than match for the security lady.

When she went back into the room, Hunter was dishing up eggs and bacon. "Coffee's in the pot, pour your own," he said curtly.

"Thanks." She took the plate from him, aware of her beauty and its effect, tingling when she saw his dark eyes glance over her body and away.

"We aren't going to a party," he informed her curtly.

Her eyebrows arched. "Jeans, a short-sleeved blouse and sneakers aren't exactly party gear," she pointed out.

He lifted his head, and his eyes made threats. "I'm not a eunuch. We're going out into the desert, where we'll be completely on our own for several days. Don't complicate things. You looked better yesterday."

"Did I? Compared to what?" she demanded coldly. "Or should I say to whom?"

He let out a heavy sigh and leaned back in his chair to study her. "Teresa is an operative. When she isn't trying to compete for attention, she's very good at her job. I'm not her lover, nor likely to be. Nor yours," he added with a cold stare.

She had to grit her teeth. "I wasn't inviting you to be my lover. I'm tired of knit blouses. It gets hot on the desert.

This blouse is cooler. So are the white slacks—they tend to reflect heat."

"God deliver me from scientific lectures before breakfast," he said icily, his narrow dark eyes making her nervous. "The fact is, Miss Marist, you saw Teresa as competition and you wanted to show me that you could beat her hands down in a beauty contest. All right, you have. You win. Now put on something less seductive and eat your breakfast. I'd like to get started."

She shook with mingled fury and humiliation and indignation, her fists clenched at her sides. No man had ever enraged her so much, so easily. She could have laid a chair across his skull with pleasure. Except that he was right. She *had* been competing for his attention. She just hadn't wanted him to realize it.

She grabbed up the same white knit shirt she'd worn the day before and pulled it on over her blouse, tugging her shirt collar through the rounded neckline. She didn't say another word to him. She sat down at the table and ate her breakfast. She was getting used to not tasting what she ate when she was with him. One way or another, he always managed to kill her appetite.

He finished his bacon and eggs and leaned back to sip his coffee, his gaze level and speculative. "Pouting?" he taunted. He wanted her and he couldn't have her. It was making him irritable. "You should know better than to throw yourself at men."

Her dark blue eyes flashed fire. She put down her coffee cup. "I don't pout," she said coldly, getting to her feet. "And I don't need to throw myself at men! Especially you!"

He got up, too, towering over her, his eyes dark with mingled frustration and anger. It got worse when she tried to step back and her cheeks flushed.

"To hell with it," he murmured roughly. He caught her waist and jerked her against his lean, powerful body, holding her there while his mouth bent to hers.

He didn't look in the least loverlike. He looked furious. "Hunter, no . . .!" she whispered frantically, pushing at his chest.

His lips poised just above hers, his dark eyes holding hers, his breath on her face. "You're going to push until you find out, aren't you?" he asked roughly. "Well, for the book, Apaches don't kiss their women on the mouth. But I'm no novice with your race or your sex. So do let me satisfy your curiosity."

The tone was smooth and deep, pure honey. She watched his hard lips part and then they were on her mouth, fierce and rough but totally without feeling. His breath filled her mouth with its minty warmth, his mouth moved with expert demand. But his body showed no sign of arousal, and he might have been holding a statue for all the warmth he projected.

She'd wanted this. She'd waited forever to be close to him like this, to feel his arms closing around her, enfolding her, to feel his hard mouth on hers. She breathed him, anguished pleasure racking her body at the taste of him, so intimate on her mouth.

But he was feeling nothing, and she realized it quite suddenly, with bitter disappointment. Almost at once he lifted his head. She opened her eyes and saw nothing in his face. No desire, nor need, nor love. There was nothing there except a cold curiosity. She was hungry, but he wasn't. Not a hair out of place, she thought with faint hysteria, Mr. Cool.

He let her go with a smooth, abrupt movement of his hands, putting distance between them effortlessly. "If you know as much about men as I think you do," he said quietly, "that should tell you exactly what I feel." He smiled, but it was a mocking, cold smile. "Bells didn't ring. Horns didn't blow. The earth didn't move. You have a pretty mouth, but I wouldn't kill for it. So now that we've breached that hurdle, can we go to work?"

She swallowed her pride and hurt. "By all means," she said. "I'll get my gear."

* * *

It was dark and they were camped on the peak of a small hill, under a palo verde tree. No jungle hammock, just a tent with two sleeping bags inside it. The bags were positioned as far apart as Jennifer could get them. Equipment was set up to monitor any movement for miles around. The computer was busy. There was no conversation. Jenny hadn't said one single word to Hunter since they left the motel, and if she had her way, she never would again. She didn't care about him, she told herself. She couldn't love a man who could be that cruel.

He was aware of her hostility, but he preferred it to those melting glances she'd been giving him. He'd deliberately been ice-cold with her when he'd kissed her. It had been imperative to show her that he felt nothing. Now he'd convinced her, and he wasn't pleased with his handiwork.

Jenny had withdrawn from him, into her work. Now it was she who was ignoring him, and it disturbed him to feel the distance he'd created. Not that it wasn't desirable. He couldn't afford the luxury of involvement with Ritter's top field geologist. It would complicate his own job, especially when the affair ended. And it would end. He and Jennifer were as different as night and day. He wanted her. She wanted him. But desire would never be enough to keep them together. He was old enough to know that, and she should be.

She was so different like this. They'd never been alone together on assignment, there had always been other people around. He saw a Jennifer that he hadn't known existed. A shy, uncertain woman with a keen analytical mind who actually downplayed her extraordinary looks. Or she had, he amended, until Teresa had tried her hand at upstaging Jennifer. Jennifer had tried to compete, to draw his attention. He should be flattered, he supposed, but it had made him angry to be the object of a female tug-of-war.

"Do you want anything to eat?" he asked when the silence became too tense.

"I had a candy bar, thanks," she replied. She was putting away the computer, her attention elsewhere.

"I brought provisions. You can have anything you like, including a steak."

"I don't want anything."

"Starve yourself if you like," he said, turning his back to fix himself a steak on the Coleman stove. "Pride doesn't digest well."

"You'll never know," she said under her breath.

He glared at her. "Do you have to have every man you meet on your string?" he asked. "Does your ego demand blind adoration?"

She closed her eyes. The pain was unbearable. "Please stop," she said huskily. "I'm sorry. I won't do it again."

He felt a strange empathy with her at times. He seemed to sense her feelings, her emotions. He was doing it now. She was wounded, emotionally.

He got to his feet and knelt beside her, his dark eyes enigmatic. "Won't do what again?" he asked.

"I won't . . . how did you put it? . . . try to get your attention." She stared at the darkening ground. "I don't know why I tried."

He studied the shadows on the ground. Night was coming down around them. Crickets sounded in the grass. A coyote howled. The wind caught her hair and blew it toward his face, and he felt its softness against his cheek.

"How old are you?" he asked suddenly.

"Twenty-seven," she replied, her voice terse because she didn't like admitting her age.

He hadn't realized she was that old. He frowned, wondering why on earth a woman so lovely should be so alone. "You don't date," he persisted.

"Checked the file, did you?" She pushed back her hair and glanced up at him and away as she closed the laptop and put it aside. "No, I don't date. What's the use? I was almost engaged twice, until they realized that I had a brain and wanted to use it. I wasn't content to be a room decoration and a hostess to the exclusion of my career. I've gotten used to being alone. I rather like it."

"Except sometimes on dark nights, when you go hungry for a man's arms," he added with faint insolence.

She stared at him with equal insolence. "I suppose you're in a position to know that," she agreed, nodding. "I've been alone too long, I suppose. Even you started to look good to me!"

He didn't answer her. He had to admit that he'd deserved that. He shouldn't have taunted her, especially about something that she probably couldn't even help.

She got up and moved away from him, tense and unnerved by his continued scrutiny.

"Come and eat something," he said.

She shook her head. "I meant it. I'm not hungry." She laughed bitterly. "I haven't tasted food since Eugene forced us on this ridiculous assignment. The only thing I want is to get it over with and get away from you!"

His dark eyes caught hers. "Do you, Jennifer?" he asked softly, his voice deep and almost gentle in the stillness.

She felt that tone to the soles of her feet and she turned away from him. It wasn't fair that he could do this to her. "I'd better get my equipment put away."

He watched her go. She seemed to bring out the very worst in him. "There's no need to run," he said mockingly, glaring at her through the growing darkness. "I'm not going to touch you again. I don't want you. Couldn't you tell?"

"Yes." She almost choked on the word. She turned toward the tent. "Yes, I could tell."

Her voice disturbed him. It seemed to hurt her that he didn't find her desirable. He drew in a slow breath, wondering what to do. It had seemed the best idea at the time, to put her at ease about his intentions. But he'd done something to her emotions with that cold, angry kiss. It hadn't been anything like the kiss he'd wanted to give her, either. Nothing like it.

He cooked his steak and ate it, feeling vaguely disturbed that he couldn't make her share it. He put out the fire, set his surveillance equipment, and went into the tent.

She was already in her sleeping bag, zipped up tight in her clothes, her eyes closed. But she wasn't asleep. He could hear her ragged breathing and there were bright streaks on her cheeks in the faint light of the flashlight he used to get to his own sleeping bag.

He put out the light angrily and took off his boots, climbing in fully clothed. He lay back on the ground, his eyes on the top of the tent, his mind full of thoughts, mostly unpleasant.

Jenny was crying. He could hear her. But to go to her, to offer comfort, would be the biggest mistake of all. He might offer more than comfort. Not wanting her was a lie. He did. He always had. But she'd want something more than desire, he thought. And desire was all he had to give.

She wiped at her tears, trying not to sniff audibly. She never cried, but she'd set new records tonight. Why did he have the power to hurt her so badly? She pushed the damp hair out of her eyes and stared at the wall of the tent, thinking back to camping trips with her parents and her cousin Danetta when they were girls. How uncomplicated and sweet life had been then. No career, no worries, just long lazy summer days and hope.

A coyote howled and she stiffened under the sleeping bag. Was it a coyote, or a wolf?

"It's a coyote," he said, giving it the Spanish pronunciation. "We call them songdogs. They loom large in our legends, in our history. We don't consider them as lowly as whites do."

"If you dislike white people so much, why do you work with us?" she asked angrily, her voice hoarse from the tears.

"It's a white world."

"Don't blame me. None of my ancestors ever served in the U.S. Cavalry out west. They were much too busy shooting Union soldiers."

"Was Missouri a southern state?"

"I'm not from Missouri originally. My parents moved there when I was seven. I was born in Alabama," she continued. "And that *is* a southern state."

"You don't have an accent."

"Neither do you."

He felt his lips tug into a smile. "Should I?"

"I wouldn't touch that with a pole, Mr. Hunter," she replied. "I've had enough of that big chip on your shoulder. I'm not aiming any more punches at it."

"Poles and chips and punches, at this hour of the night," he murmured gently.

"You don't have to talk to me, you know," she said wearily. "We can manage this assignment in sign language."

"Do you know any?" he asked in a dry tone as he crossed his arms over his head, stretching.

"A few phrases," she admitted, reluctant to confess it. "Eugene sent me up to Montana once and I had to parley with two Dakota Sioux. They spoke no English and I spoke no Sioux, so I learned to talk with my hands. It was very educational."

She was full of surprises. His head turned and he stared at her through the half darkness. "I could teach you to speak Apache."

She closed her eyes. "I don't want you to teach me anything, Mr. Hunter," she said huskily.

"Too bad," he replied, trying not to take offense. After all, he'd given her a hard time. "You could use a little tutoring. For an experienced women, you don't know much about kissing."

She couldn't believe what she was hearing. She sat up on the sleeping bag. "This from a man who already admitted that Apaches don't do it . . . !"

"That was back in the nineteenth century," he mused. He propped himself on one elbow and stared at her, his blood beginning to burn at the sight of her, so beautiful with her long hair around her shoulders. "How can you be twenty-seven and not know something so elementary as how to kiss a man properly?"

"You only did it to humiliate me...!"

"You didn't know that," he replied. He remembered her shy response, and it made him feel worse. Apparently the men in her life had been more interested in their own pleasure than hers, because no one had ever taught her about loveplay. He wanted to. His body went rigid as he realized how much he wanted to.

"I told you," she said, trying to salvage some of her pride. "I've been alone for a long time..."

"Have you? Why?" he asked.

She didn't want to go into why. He'd managed to cut her to the bone already with his cold manner, without the insult about the way she kissed. It hurt even more that he'd noticed, despite his lack of interest in her.

"Never mind," she said wearily. She lay back down and closed her eyes. "I just want to go to sleep. It's been a long day."

"So it has. We'll move camp tomorrow."

"Could we move it to Mars?" she asked. "It wouldn't make much difference, considering the lack of vegetation."

"You aren't seeing. The desert is alive and beautiful, if you know what to look for."

"You do, I suppose."

"I'm an Indian, remember?" he asked with rough insolence.

"How could I forget?" she muttered. "You never let anyone forget..."

"Go to sleep," he said shortly. He closed his own eyes, out of patience and totally out of humor. She was really getting to him. He turned his head on the sleeping bag and his eyes wandered slowly over the curve of her body under the quilted fabric. Damn Eugene, he thought furiously, closing his eyes against the sight of her. He'd never forgive him for this assignment.

Jennifer, meanwhile, was thinking much the same thing. He blew hot and cold, friendly one minute and hostile the next. She didn't know how to get along with him. He seemed to resent everything about her. Even the way she kissed, she thought bitterly. Well, hell would freeze over before she was going to kiss him again! She rolled over. Maybe in the morning, things would look better.

Five

But things didn't look better in the morning. Hunter was unapproachable. When he did glance her way, it was like an Arctic blast. Nothing she did was ever right, she thought ruefully.

She busied herself with getting her equipment together, trying not to let him know how hurt she was by his coldness. Worse, trying to forget the feel of him in intimacy, the hard expertness of his mouth on hers. Dreams had sustained her for so long. Now she had at least one bittersweet memory to tuck away. But like all memories and dreams, it wasn't enough.

They loaded the four-wheel drive and set off for the next site—the real one this time. It was back in a canyon, beside a stream under a nest of cottonwoods and oaks. Behind it was a mountain range, smooth boulders rising to jagged peaks high above and only a small rutted road through the dust to get to it.

"It's very deserted here," Jennifer murmured, thinking she wouldn't want to be here on her own. It was probably haunted....

"One of the old Apache camps," he said, looking around. "I feel at home." He glanced at her with faint menace. "But I can imagine that you don't. White captives were probably brought here."

She turned away. "If you don't mind sparing me your noble red man impersonation, I'd like to get my equipment."

He lifted an eyebrow. That was more like it. He'd grown weary of her attempts not to mention his ancestry or her embarrassment when she did.

"Apaches weren't the only tribe around here," he remarked as he lowered the tailgate and began removing equipment and sleeping gear. "Comanches roamed this far south, and Yaquis came up on raids from Mexico. There were bandidos, cavalry, cowboys and miners, gunfighters and lawmen who probably camped in this area." He glanced at her with a faint smile. "I hope that makes you less nervous."

Her eyebrows arched. "I'm not nervous... Oh!" She jumped when a yelp sounded somewhere nearby, and got behind Hunter, sheltering behind his broad shoulders.

He chuckled with pure delight, savoring that one surge of femininity from Miss Independence. "A coyote," he whispered. He glanced down at her as the yelps increased. "Fighting. Or mating," he added, his eyes burning into hers from scant inches.

She went scarlet, swallowed, and abruptly tore away from him with her heart beating her to death. It wasn't what he'd said, it was the way he'd said it, his black eyes full of knowledge, his voice like that of a lover.

"Could you set up the tent, so that I can get the portable generator hooked up to my laptop?" she said with shivering dignity.

He put down the sleeping bags and glanced at her. "What's wrong?"

"You're very blunt," she said stubbornly. "I wish you wouldn't go out of your way to make me uncomfortable."

His expression gave nothing away. He studied her curiously. "Did I embarrass you? Why? Mating is as natural as the rocks and trees around us. In fact," he added, his voice deepening, "some native tribes weren't that fanatical about purity in their young women. Adultery was the sin, not lovemaking."

She glanced at him angrily. "The Cheyenne were fanatical about maidenly purity, for your information," she told him curtly. "And the Apache were just as concerned with virtue . . ."

"Well, well," he murmured. "So you do read about Indian history?" A faint smile appeared on his dark face. "Do you find the subject interesting?"

Not for anything was she going to admit that she did because of him. She'd read extensively about the Apache, in fact, but she wasn't going to admit that, either.

Nevertheless, he suspected it. He pursed his lips. "Did you know that Apaches disliked children?"

"They did not," she said without thinking. "They even kept captive children when they raided, raising them as their own flesh and blood . . . Oops."

He laughed. His face changed, became even more handsome with the softness in his black eyes, the less austere lines of his face. "So they did," he murmured.

She turned away. "That wasn't kind."

"Why does it bother you to be curious?" he asked pleasantly. "I don't mind. Ask. I'll tell you anything you want to know about my people."

She put down her computer and her blue eyes searched his black ones. "I didn't want to offend you," she said. "You've always been reticent about your ancestry, especially with me. I know I got off on the wrong foot with you, right at the beginning," she added before he could speak.

"You frightened me, and what I did, I did out of nervousness. I never meant to offend you."

"That was a wholesale apology," he murmured, watching her. "I'll add one of my own. You frightened me, too."

"Me?" She was astonished. "Why?"

His eyes darkened and he started to speak, but the sudden beat of helicopter blades diverted him. He looked up, glad that he'd parked the vehicle under the thick cover of the cottonwood trees.

He caught Jennifer's arm and propelled her close to the Jeep, at the same time reaching behind him, into his belt, for the .45 automatic he always carried.

The sight of the cold metal in his hand made her nauseous. Sometimes it was easy to forget exactly what he did for a living. But this brought it home with stark clarity. He knew how to use the gun, and probably had, many times. She knew he'd been shot a time or two, and she'd seen one of the scars against his tanned shoulder, when he'd taken a shower two nights earlier. She shivered, remembering how he earned his living, what risks he took doing it.

He felt her tremble and glared toward the departing sound of the helicopter. He'd never known her to be afraid. This had to be a first.

"It's all right," he said, feeling unusually protective toward her. "I won't let anyone hurt you."

She looked up at him, glad he'd misjudged the reason for her unsteadiness. "Thanks," she said huskily. She looked toward the canopy of leaves. "Was that them, do you think?"

"Very likely." He put the safety back on the automatic and reholstered it with practiced ease. "We'll make a smokeless fire, just in case."

She smiled at him. "I suppose woodcraft, or the desert equivalent, was part of your upbringing?"

He nodded. "One of my ancestors fought with Cochise," he said. "When I was a boy, I knew how to find water, which plants I could live on, how to find my way in the darkness. Did you know that an Apache can go without water for two days by sucking on pebbles?''

"Yes," she said simply. Her eyes lingered on his dark face. "I . . . read a lot," she explained.

He let his gaze fall to her soft mouth. He had to stop remembering how silky and warm it felt, like a rose petal kissed by the sun. She wasn't a woman he could have, ever. Not as long as they both worked for the corporation. It would be the kiss of death to become involved on the job. One of them would have to go, and that wouldn't be fair. Jennifer was good at her job, and she loved it. He loved his, as well. Better to avoid complications.

She frowned slightly. "What are you thinking?" she asked.

He smiled faintly. "That a hundred years or so ago, I could have carried you off on my pony and kept you in my wickiup," he murmured. "My other wives might have beaten or stoned you when I was out making war, of course."

"Other wives, the devil," she said firmly. "Polygamy or no polygamy, if I'd lived with you, there would have been one wife, and it would have been me."

He smiled at her ferocity. Amazing that she could look so cool and professional, but under the surface there was fire and independence and passion in her. He could imagine her with a rifle, holding off attackers and defending her home. Children playing around her skirts on lazy summer days. He frowned. His eyes fell to her flat stomach and for one insane moment, he let himself imagine . . .

"Why are you looking at me like that?" she asked softly.

His gaze came back up to hers, the expression in his eyes unreadable. "We'd better get things set up. I'll pitch the tent."

He became unapproachable again, withdrawing deep into himself. Jennifer was sorry, because just for a few minutes it had seemed that they were on the verge of becoming friendlier. But Hunter was Hunter again when he had the tent up and the portable battery backup working. He left her to her computer and charts, busying himself with securing the parameters of their small camp and setting up his distance surveillance equipment.

She put on a pair of hiking shorts and long socks with her thick-soled walking boots and a button-up khaki blouse. She had a hat, an Indiana Jones one, in fact, that she used to keep the sun from baking her head. One thing she'd learned long ago was that a hat in the desert was no luxury. One case of sunstroke had taught her that, and Hunter had given her hell when he'd found her lying on the ground far away in the Middle East, where they were working on assignment one time, searching for oil.

He glanced up when she came out in her working gear, nodding at the hat. "You remembered, I see," he remarked.

"You gave me hell," she recalled, smiling.

"You deserved it."

"Yes, I did. All the same, you got me to a medic in short order. You probably saved my life."

"I don't want hero-worship from you," he said flatly, staring back at her. "We'd better get going. Keep to the trees if you can. We know we're not alone. It's best not to take chances."

"The stream bed is where I want to be," she said coldly. "And it isn't hero-worship."

"No?" He gave her a mocking appraisal. "Then what is it?"

"Fascination," she said with a mocking smile of her own. "You're different."

He didn't betray so much as a flicker of an eyelash, but the words hit home. She'd accidentally betrayed what he'd suspected all along, that she coveted him because he was a new experience for her. Like another white woman, years before, who'd been entranced not by who he was so much as what he was.

"Different," she emphasized. "Hardheaded, cold-eyed, bad tempered, unpredictable and totally exasperating!"

None of which had anything to do with being Apache, he mused, relaxing a little. He smiled with reluctant amusement.

"I could go on," she added. "But I do have a job to do."

"I'm not the only one here with a bad temper," he replied as they started out. "And you have a hard head of your own."

"I wouldn't have a bad temper if you'd stop stripping around me," she blurted out.

His eyebrows arched. "When did I do that?"

"At the motel."

"Oh." He chuckled as he strode along beside her. "I wanted to see if it would affect you." He glanced down. "It did."

"Most men your age are as white as dead fish and flabby," she remarked, refusing to let him get to her. "I can't be the only woman who's ever found you fascinating without your shirt."

No, but she was the only one it mattered with, he admitted to himself. He found her equally disturbing, but it wasn't a good time to say so. His eyes were alert, watching for signs.

"Look!" she exclaimed, bending down at the creek where tracks were visible in the wet sand. "A cougar!"

He knelt down beside her. "So it is. How did you know?"

"Big print, no claw marks," she explained. "Dogs and wolves can't draw their claws back in like a cat can, and they leave claw marks. Look at this. It's a buck deer—cloven hoof print. A doe's is rounded."

He met her eyes with grudging admiration. "Tracking interests you, I gather?"

"It always has. My father hunts deer every fall. He taught me."

"Kill Bambi?" he exclaimed with mock horror.

It was the first real flash of amusement she'd seen in him. She laughed delightedly and impulsively pushed him. He fell heavily onto his side, laughing, too.

"You hellcat," he murmured, reaching out with a lightning movement to drag her down heavily against him. He rolled her in the damp sand, pinning her, his face hard, his eyes glittering with excitement as he loomed over her. His gaze went down to her breasts, where the buttons of her blouse had parted during the struggle, leaving her cleavage bare. His breath quickened as he looked at her, his expression changing from humor to intent male appreciation.

The feel of all that hard muscle so close made her tremble with pure need. She could smell the scent of his clothing, the cologne that clung to his skin. She looked up into his black eyes and knew in that moment that he was everything she'd ever want. She wanted him to bend down, to pin her body to the damp sand. She wanted his hard, warm mouth to crush into hers and kiss her senseless. She wanted him.

And the ferocity of her desire made her ache. "Kiss me," she whispered, unbearably hungry for him. She reached up and touched his lean, hard face with hands that trembled, loving the warm strength of him. "Hunter...!" She managed to lift herself enough to reach his hard mouth, and hers touched it with helpless need.

He froze at the contact, his breath catching as he felt her lips so soft and warm against his own. For one insane second he almost gave in to his own hunger. But she was off-limits. She had to be, because there was no future in it for either of them. He forced himself to go rigid, despite the fact that his damned heart was beating him to death as he struggled with desire.

His lean hands caught her wrists and he pushed her down, tearing her mouth from his as he loomed over her, looking cold and dangerous. "Stop it," he said curtly, forcing the words out.

She felt the rejection right through to her heart. He didn't want her, so why couldn't she stop offering herself? She hated having him know just how vulnerable she was. How could she have done something so stupid? She flushed beet red. Yes, she was vulnerable, but not Hunter. Mr. Native American was steel right through.

"Let me get up, please," she said, her voice trembling.

Pure bravado, and he knew it. He could have her, right here, and she'd give herself with total abandon. But he knew, too, that once would never be enough. He'd have her and then he'd die to have her again. The fever would never be satisfied.

He let go of her wrists and got to his feet, turning away to keep his vulnerability from her as he stared up at the mountains with apparent unconcern. God, that had been close! He wondered if he could ever forget the way he'd seen her, the sound of her soft voice begging for his kiss, the petal softness of her seeking lips on his mouth...!

Jenny shivered with reaction, barely able to breathe. She got up and her eyes went helplessly to his back. Well, he'd made his lack of interest clear enough. Maybe her body would eventually give up, she thought with hysterical humor. Despite her beauty, he simply did not want her. It was the most humiliating lesson of her life.

She looked away, gathering her savaged pride. "I'm supposed to be working," she said in a thready whisper.

"The sun's getting high," he said without looking at her. "Get your samples and then we'll find something to eat."

She felt totally drained. She picked up her hat with a shaken sigh and retrieved the backpack with her tools. She didn't even remember dropping it, she'd been so hungry for the touch of him.

His dark face gave nothing away as he glanced once at her and turned away. "Where do you want to look? And for what?" he asked curtly. "Gold? Is that why this operation is so secretive?"

She glanced up at him, twisting her contour map in her hands. "I know what you must be thinking," she said. She could still taste him on her mouth and it made her giddy. "Gold and Indians don't mix. White man's greed for it has cost the Native Americans most of their land."

"There was a flurry here a year or two ago when someone found a very small vein of gold," he said. "There were amateur prospectors everywhere, upsetting the habitat, invading private property, some of them even came on the reservation to dig without bothering to ask permission. The Bureau of Indian Affairs takes a very negative view of that kind of thing, and so does the tribal government."

"I don't doubt it. But gold isn't what I'm after right now. I'm looking for a quartz vein, actually."

"Quartz?" He glared at her. "Quartz is a worthless mineral."

"Perhaps, but it can lead to something that isn't. I'm looking for molybdenite ore."

He frowned. "What?"

"Molybdenum is a silver-white metallic chemical element, one of the more valuable alloying agents. It's used to strengthen steel, which makes it of strategic worth. Like oil, it's a rather boom-or-bust substance, because its value fluctuates according to demand. Back in 1982, weak market conditions led to the closure of most primary molybdenum mines. Now there's a new use for it, so it's back in demand again. The United States produces sixty-two percent of all the world's moly, and that's why we've got competition for new discoveries."

"So you're looking for molybdenum," he murmured, trying to follow the technical explanation.

"I'm looking for its source ore, molybdenite, a sulfide mineral. It looks very much like graphite, but its specific gravity and perfect cleavage differentiate it from that. It's found primarily in acid igneous rocks such as granite in contact metamorphic deposits, and in high-temperature quartz veins. That's why I'm looking for quartz veins." She smiled at his confusion. "Don't look so irritated, Mr. Hunter. I couldn't fieldstrip an Uzi or set up surveillance equipment, either. If what I'm doing is Greek to you, what you do is another language to me, too."

That eased his bruised pride a little. He turned away. "Then we'd better get going. This area looks promising, you said?"

"Yes. The lay of the land and the mineral outcroppings I've found so far look very promising here."

"Moly. You say it's used to strengthen steel," he said, watching her.

She nodded. "A very profitable mineral to mine, too. There's already a deposit of it here in southern Arizona, another one in Colorado."

"But if you found gold instead, you'd put a real feather in your cap, wouldn't you?" he persisted, his eyes narrow and watchful.

"Oh, for heaven's sake!" She threw up her hands, her blue eyes blazing with hurt and anger. "You just love to think the worst of me, don't you? If I find gold, I'll take out ads in all the national tabloids and give interviews and send millions of people out here to harass the locals . . . !"

Involuntarily he put his thumb over her lips, stilling the words. "All right," he said quietly. "My mistake," he said, and his eyes fell to her mouth. His thumb moved caressingly over it, and his body began to tense. Her lips trembled under his touch. She was so vulnerable, and he hated hurting her. He wanted her, too, but it was simply impossible.

She couldn't bear to give herself away again. She drew back from him, still wounded from his earlier harsh rejection. "I'll just take some samples here," she said in a subdued tone, and without looking at him. "And get a few instrument readings."

He didn't say another word. But he was more watchful than ever for the rest of the day. He couldn't seem to take his eyes off her, and the more he looked, the more he wanted her. He almost groaned out loud when she stretched and he could see the sweet curves of her breasts outlined against the thin fabric of her blouse. She wouldn't deny him, and knowing it made the desire even greater. He had to get a grip on himself!

He prowled around his surveillance equipment, trying to get his mind off Jennifer's gorgeous body. When he couldn't prowl anymore, after dark, he stretched out on his sleeping bag and read by the light of the Coleman lantern while Jennifer rummaged in her suitcase.

Jenny was fascinated when she saw his books, the text indecipherable to her, despite her cursory knowledge of Spanish and French and a few words of Sioux.

"It loses something in the translation," he remarked when he noticed her interest. "I prefer the original language. This is Greek," he added, smiling faintly at her blush when she'd told him that what she was doing must seem like Greek to him.

She recovered quickly, though. "How did you learn Greek?"

"Overseas. I was CIA, didn't anyone tell you?"

She nodded, her eyes openly curious. "About that. And that you were in the special forces, and briefly a mercenary. You've done a lot of dangerous things, haven't you?"

"A few," he said, refusing to elaborate on it.

She gave up and busied herself getting a clean T-shirt and bra out of her suitcase. "It's dark. Do you think it would be all right if I bathed off a little of this dust? Are we safe here?"

"If you've got skinny-dipping in mind, I wouldn't advise it," he began.

"No, just my face and arms," she replied.

"Go to it. It's relatively protected here, and I've got sharp ears."

"Okay." She wanted some verbal reassurance that he wouldn't look, but he'd been withdrawn since they came back to camp. Probably she left him so cold that he wouldn't buy a ticket to see her totally nude. She felt terribly demoralized. Ironic, that men usually went crazy to have her, and Hunter wouldn't have her with cream and sugar.

The light from the smokeless camp fire gave her enough to see by. She pulled off her khaki blouse and, glancing behind at the half-closed tent flap, her bra. The cool water felt like heaven on her hot skin. She sponged herself off, thinking that Indian women must have bathed like this a century before, in this clean, cool glade with the sounds of crickets in the brush and the distant howl of coyotes or wolves and the faint swish of the trees when the wind blew.

Hunter tried to read his book, but the thought of Jennifer out there alone was too disturbing, especially after the chopper that had come so close. He didn't want to spy on her, but he justified his flash of conscience by telling himself that he'd been assigned to protect her.

He opened the tent flap and moved outside, silhouetted by the smokeless camp fire that was still burning under a pot of brewing coffee. Its dark, rich aroma filled his nostrils as he moved closer to the stream under the dark shadows of the trees.

Jennifer had her blouse and her bra off. He could see her smooth, silky back in the firelight, see the white lines where she'd sunbathed and the sun hadn't been able to reach. Odd that she didn't sunbathe nude, with a body like that, he thought stiffly.

He couldn't help looking. She half turned, her arms uplifted as she dashed water on her breasts, and his breath caught in his throat. They were full. Very full and very firm, and tip-tilted. Her nipples were hard from the cold water, dusky against the white streaks that cut across where her bra would have been. His body tautened and he felt himself beginning to tense with desire. He'd dreamed of seeing her this way, but the reality was devastating.

Jennifer, unaware of his scrutiny, finished her half bath and stretched, her body sensuously arched because the air was just cool enough to be delicious on her bare skin, and there was faint light from the nearly full moon. She sighed, brushing her long blond hair away from her freshly scrubbed face. The action lifted her breasts and they were high and firm and softly glowing in the light from the camp fire.

Hunter heard himself speaking, when he'd never meant to betray his presence. "In the old days, the penalty for an Apache warrior who spied on a woman at her bath was death. The risk seems worth it to me right now, Jennifer. I've never seen anything quite so beautiful."

His voice had startled her. She whirled from the big rock she was sitting on, her body poised for flight, so shocked by his eyes and nearness that she hadn't the presence of mind to cover her breasts.

He was looking at them, too, with blatant appreciation, without even trying to hide that he was studying her. "Your breasts are lovely," he said quietly, his voice a whisper of deep tenderness in the night. "Much fuller than I thought. Pink and mauve, like clouds on the horizon just at dawn when the sun touches them."

Poetry, she thought dizzily. He was wooing her with words and she wanted his eyes so badly that she couldn't even do the decent thing and pretend to hide herself. All day she'd felt him watching her. If only he felt as she did, shared the fiery attraction that made her too weak to deny him now. She stood, proud in her seminudity, letting him look, feeding on his eyes. If that wasn't desire in his face now, she thought, awed, then she couldn't recognize it at all. He wanted her! The knowledge took away her reserve, her inhibitions. She walked toward him, her heart in her eyes.

His jaw tensed. He watched her come toward him and he ground his teeth together in one last effort at sanity. Her lips were parted, her eyes soft and hungry, her breasts rising and falling jerkily with her unsteady breathing.

She stopped just in front of him, her cheeks faintly ruddy with embarrassment and excitement. She couldn't have imagined doing this, but it seemed the most natural thing in the world. She looked up at him, meeting his dark, fierce gaze, trembling a little, because he looked capable of anything at that moment. For all her loving bravado, she was innocent and he wasn't. The complications of her actions could be extreme.

His chin lifted as he watched her, his gaze a conqueror's, his face rigid. "You're asking for something you may not be able to handle," he said quietly. It was a warning.

She swallowed. "Would you...hurt me?" she whispered.

He nodded slowly. "Very probably," he said, letting his dark eyes fall to the perfect symmetry of her breasts. "I've gone a long time without a woman and I'm not particularly gentle even when I haven't. You don't have a lot of experience with men." His eyes shot back up, catching her surprise. "That surprises you? Didn't you know that sophistication is hard to fake?" He smiled gently. "You're blushing. You had to fight not to cover yourself when I looked at you. You're still fighting your primary instinct, which is to turn and run away before I give you what you think you want."

"What I think I want?" she asked in a shaky whisper.

He reached out and the backs of his fingers brushed very lightly over one taut nipple in a blatant, deliberate caress.

She gasped and jerked away, and his eyes reflected the smile on his firm lips.

"You see?" he asked softly. "You'd give yourself to me, with a little coaxing. But not in cold blood. You aren't used to this kind of intimacy with a man."

She did follow her instincts then, and folded her arms over her breasts, shivering as she lowered her eyes to his shirt.

"Twenty-seven. And so inhibited." He sighed heavily. "What happened, Jenny? Was the first time so traumatic that you didn't have the nerve to try again?"

"You don't have the right to ask me questions like that...."

He caught her by the shoulders. "You offered yourself to me," he said curtly. "That gives me the right. Was the first time difficult?"

She couldn't tell him that there hadn't been a first time. That was just too humiliating. "Difficult enough," she said unsteadily. "Please . . . I'm sorry. I'd like to go in, now."

It was what he'd guessed. She was probably afraid of being with a man intimately because some man had hurt her. It irritated him to think of someone hurting her. He wouldn't have. His hands stilled on her upper arms, feeling the silky warmth of them. He hesitated. He wanted her like hell, but his mind was in control—just barely.

With a rough sigh, he picked her up suddenly and carried her slowly back into the tent, his eyes holding hers. He laid her down gently on her sleeping bag and sat beside her, frowning at the way she crossed her arms over her breasts.

"Don't," he said softly, and moved her arms back to her sides. "Don't cover yourself. Let me look at you. God knows, that's all I can do now."

"You said you didn't want me. . . ." she whispered.

He sighed heavily, his expression sterner than ever, his dark eyes intent on hers. "Yes, I said it. My God, don't you have instincts about men? Don't you know . . ." He stopped, suddenly aware of the unblinking fascination of her eyes on his face.

Her blond hair was spread around her flushed face in glorious disarray, her small waist and flat stomach faintly visible where her shorts were a little large in the waistline. But he didn't touch her, yet. Only his eyes did, very slowly, very thoroughly, and she trembled all over from just that.

"You're helpless when I look at you," he said quietly. "When I touch you. Is there anything you'd deny me?"

She shook her head slowly, beyond denial. Her body trembled. "But you don't want to make love to me, do you?" she whispered.

"I can't," he said evasively. It wouldn't do to let her know how badly he did want her. His hand went out and she shivered with anticipation, but it was her hair he touched and nothing else, smoothing it away from her face. "I'm not prepared."

"Prepared?" she echoed the word blankly.

He wrapped a strand of blond hair around his forefinger and tugged it gently. "I could make you pregnant," he said simply. "Making love is one thing. Making a baby is something else. It shouldn't happen because two people are careless."

"No," she agreed. She couldn't tell him that to her it wouldn't be careless, that she wanted him and she wanted his child. Loved him, deathlessly. She felt warm all over. Her body arched gently, inviting his eyes. "Oh, please, couldn't you . . . ?" she whispered brokenly.

His breath came jerkily. His eyes slid down her, lingering on her taut nipples. "You ache for me, don't you?" he asked, and there was a kind of bitter compassion in the words.

"So . . . much," she whispered mindlessly. "More than you'll ever know!"

His jaw clenched. She was every man's dream, lying there like that. She was his dream, surely, and it took every ounce of willpower he possessed to hold back.

Despite the hurting tautness of his body, the fever in his blood, he controlled the urge. He bent and gently brushed his lips against hers in the soft stillness of the tent. "Go to sleep," he whispered.

"Hunter," she moaned, her body on fire. Her arms locked around his strong neck, trembling, her eyes frantic. "Please!"

He groaned. "Jenny, you don't understand . . . God!" His mouth opened and crushed down on hers suddenly, and he allowed himself the pleasure of one long, endless kiss. His lips twisted against hers, his chest levered down over her bare breasts. He could feel them through the thin fabric of his shirt, the nipples biting into his skin and he shivered with reaction. She smelled of flowers. Her arms held him, her fingers in his thick, dark hair, caressing him. His hands slid under her bare back and brought her even closer, his tongue starting to probe her lips. She stiffened, surprising him, because her ardor had been so headlong and eager.

He lifted his dark head, breathing unsteadily. "Don't you like deep kisses?" he asked huskily.

"I . . . I didn't," she said, her own voice shaking. "Not with anyone else." She moved her fingers down to his mouth and touched it hesitantly. "Could you . . . teach me how?" she breathed at his lips.

The words kindled something explosive in him. It glittered in his eyes. "Yes," he said roughly. "I can teach you."

She was as close to heaven as she'd ever dreamed of being. His mouth bit hers gently, lifting and probing, delicately coaxing. His breath became ragged, and so did hers. He heard her soft gasp as his tongue probed her lips softly, felt her fingers tangle, trembling, in his thick hair.

"Are you ready for me?" he whispered deeply, and felt her shiver. "Open your mouth, and I'll let you feel me . . . inside you."

She cried out. The sound of her voice, the eager parting of her lips sent him over some vague precipice. He groaned, too, as his tongue penetrated her roughly, deeply, in thrusts that lifted her against him and made her weep with reaction. He made a sound deep in his throat and for feverish seconds, he gave her the weight of his body, the unrestrained ardor of his devouring mouth. His hands slid over her bare, silky back, feeling the warm softness of it with blind pleasure, savored the trembling hunger of her mouth. But then he became slowly aware of her uncontrollable shivering, felt the tears in his mouth. Her very abandon was what brought him to his senses. God, what was he doing?

He dragged himself away and sat up, ripping her hands away from his head, her wrists turning white under the involuntary pressure of his lean, dark fingers.

"No!" he said fiercely.

She looked at him through a sensual daze, her eyes smoky with desire, her face expressionless with it. "Hunter," she whispered weakly.

His hands tightened. "I'm Apache," he said harshly. "You're white. My God, don't you understand? We belong to different worlds. This whole damned situation is impossible, Jennifer!"

She realized belatedly that he'd stopped. Her mouth throbbed from the drugging contact with his, and she only began to realize how close he'd come to losing control. So had she. He'd wanted her for those brief seconds, and she gloried in the way he was loving her until he came to his senses. She looked at him hungrily, loving him, awash in sweet pleasure.

"Do you hear me?" he asked, his voice a little less cutting. "Jenny?"

"Yes, I ... hear you." She caught her breath, her eyes searching over his dark face. "I can't stop shaking," she whispered, surprised by the reactions of her body—new reactions, although he wouldn't realize that. She was a newcomer to raging, abandoned desire. "Oh ... my!" she whispered, moaning a little with frustration.

"Shhh," he whispered. His voice sounded actually gentle. "I know. It hurts. But I can't take the risk." He brought her hands to his mouth before he put them down and gently pulled the sleeping bag over her taut breasts, covering her. She was crying. He bent and kissed away the tears, his lips tender on her wet face. "Breathe deeply, little one. It will pass."

He moved away and she watched him through her tears. "My things," she remembered. "I left them by the stream."

"I'll get them." He looked back at her. "I'm going to have a cup of coffee before I come to bed. Do us both a favor and try to be asleep when I come back," he added quietly. "This was a moment out of time, this whole damned trip. But reality is waiting back in Tulsa, and we've got a job to do here. Let's try to get it done and put this behind us."

She swallowed, tugging the sleeping bag closer around her. "You're right, of course," she managed shyly, embarrassed now that her heated skin had cooled. She couldn't meet his eyes. "I'm sorry about what...what I did. I...I can't think what came over me..."

He could feel her embarrassment. Odd, that, when she was twenty-seven and so beautiful. But she'd admitted herself that she'd been hurt, and it had been a long time for her. "Abstinence," he replied. "I know how it feels. You get to the point where you can't bear it any longer. I don't think less of you for wanting me, Jennifer," he added quietly. "I'm rather flattered," he confessed.

She relaxed a little. At least he wasn't ridiculing her. He couldn't know that her abstinence had been lifelong. And through it all, despite that shattering tenderness he'd shown her, he'd kept his head. He said she was beautiful, and he'd looked at her and kissed her. But he knew how badly she'd wanted him, so it might just have been pity. She didn't want to think about that, it hurt too much. She stared at him with soft, quiet eyes.

"How long has it been for you?" she asked gently. "Is it all right, if I ask you that?"

He drew in a slow breath, his broad chest lifting and falling, making his muscles ripple. "Two years," he said.

She searched his hard face. "Is it because I'm white that you won't take the risk?" she asked, her voice barely above a whisper. She had to know.

He stared at her for a long moment. Better to end it here, and temptation with it. "Yes," he said. "I want no possibility, ever, of a child coming from my desire for a woman with white skin."

Desire. Only desire, she thought miserably, and he'd just admitted it. She felt shamed, somehow. "Desire," she whispered.

He schooled his features not to give him away. He nodded his head, very slowly. "Isn't that what you felt for me?"

He turned away. "I'll check the perimeter. Good night, Jennifer."

It would have hurt less if he'd hit her, but she didn't say a word. She lay down and closed her eyes. So now she knew. He felt nothing for her, nothing at all, except a desire that was so mild it couldn't even affect his control. And no way was he going to risk the possibility of creating a child. And she wanted nothing more, because she loved him. What a laugh!

Jenny shivered with mingled shame and bitter disappointment. It might have been better if he'd never touched her at all. She wouldn't be able to forget the expert touch of his hands, his mouth, the things he'd whispered to her. He was no novice, and now she was going to spend years remembering that. Tormenting herself with what might have been.

Jenny got up and managed to get another blouse from her suitcase and put it on. Her breasts were still sensitive from the rough contact with his chest. For such a torrid interlude, it had been remarkably innocent, she thought. He'd looked at her, he'd kissed her. But there had been no deep intimacy at all. Because he didn't want her enough, she supposed, and forced her eyes to close.

Outside, Hunter was lighting a cigarette. Smoking might calm his nerves. He looked at the hand holding the cigarette and watched it shake. Jennifer unclothed was a sight to do that to a stronger man than himself. He wondered how he'd ever managed to let her go. His body was burning and throbbing with need of her. She wanted him. He could go back into that tent right now and she'd open her arms for him.

But it would be a mistake. Despite her blatant desire for him, she was somehow less experienced than he'd expected. Shy and even a little afraid, but so hungry for him. He remembered her voice, whispering to him to teach her about deep kisses, the sight of her breasts in the light of the camp fire . . .

He groaned out loud. Another beauty. Another white woman. She wanted him because he was someone out of her experience, and he'd better remember that. He'd already had a taste of being used for his uniqueness. Jennifer was beautiful enough to choose her own man. He couldn't believe that she'd keep him for long, once her desire was satisfied. Hilarious, really. It was usually the man who pressed the woman for physical satisfaction. Now he was the hunted, and Jennifer the predator. Other men might take what she offered. He couldn't. There was more to it than physical desire. He respected her, as a woman, as a scientist, as a person. He couldn't use her, even without the cultural barriers separating them. But it didn't make the night any easier for him. When he finally gave in to sleep, it was almost dawn.

Jennifer forced herself to work the next two days without thinking back. Hunter himself managed to keep his mind on his job, scouting the periphery, watching for signs of interest as they moved camp twice more. He hadn't been unkind, either. But his attitude toward her was suddenly impersonal. Employee to employee, with no personal comments of any kind. Only once, when she caught him staring at the stream where he'd seen her bathing, did any emotion show in his lean, hard face. She pretended not to see, because her own control was precarious. She wanted him still, now more than ever.

Because of that, she pushed herself, working at breakneck speed to do the samples of the outcrops and decide where seismic tests would have to be made by the geological technicians. Sound technology was the oilman's best friend, because it could save him millions by telling him where to drill. It was of the same benefit to the miner. Modern technology was invaluable when it came to determining underground mineral locations.

In no time, Jennifer had her fieldwork done and was ready to go back to Tulsa, back to sanity. It was almost a relief to have temptation out of the way, not to be alone with Hunter anymore, even if her heart was breaking at the thought of never having the experience again.

Hunter had registered her silence, her withdrawal. He'd thanked God for it during the past few days, because his desire for her had grown beyond bearing. Lying beside her in the tent at night had kept him sleepless. All he could think about was the way she'd looked in the firelight, the sweet vulnerability in her eyes when she'd offered herself to him, the ardent sweetness of her mouth under his. He wished he could forget. He had a feeling the memory was going to haunt him until he died. But if she even remembered what had happened, she gave no indication of it. She wouldn't look him in the eye anymore, as if her behavior had shamed her. He hated doing that to her, making her ashamed of such glorious abandon. But he couldn't give in. He'd fought his own need and won. But it was a hollow victory.

"Glad to be going home?" he asked when they were on the plane.

It was the first remark he'd made in two days that wasn't related to the job.

"Yes," she said without looking at him. "I'm glad."

"That makes two of us," he said with a rough sigh. "Thank God we can get back to normal now."

Normal, she thought, as if her life would ever be that again. Now that she knew his ardor, she knew the touch and feel and taste of him, she was going to starve to death without him. But he seemed completely unaffected by what had happened. And why not? He was experienced. Probably these interludes were part of his work background, and the encounter they'd had was a fairly innocent one. She shivered, thinking what might have happened if he'd wanted her back, if he'd been prepared. She'd never have gotten over him if they'd gone that far. She closed her eyes and tried to sleep. They'd be back in Tulsa soon, and they wouldn't be doing any more traveling together, thank God.

* * *

That peaceful thought lasted only until she was sitting in Eugene's office, giving her report. The land containing the potential moly strike was dead on government land, and Eugene cursed roundly.

"They're trading that tract. Look here," he muttered, showing her the area on the map. "They're trading it for a tract they like in Vermont. Damn! All right, there's only one thing to do. Pack an evening gown and some nice clothes. You and Cynthia and I are going to Washington to do some quick lobbying with one of our senators. I went to school with him and he's very Oklahoma-minded. Don't just sit there. Get going! I'll want to leave first thing in the morning."

"Yes, sir." She went home and packed. So much for her idea of staying at home for a while so that she could get over Hunter.

And there was one more unpleasant surprise waiting. When she got to the airport, to board Eugene's corporate jet, who should be waiting with Eugene and his blond wife, Cynthia, but Hunter, looking as irritated and put out as she felt.

Six

Cynthia saw the flash of antagonism in Hunter's dark eyes as Jennifer approached, and she smiled to herself. "You look lovely, Jennifer," she told the younger woman, and linked her arm with Jennifer's. "Let's get buckled up while they finish the walkabout. How have you been?"

Hunter spared Jennifer one brief glance. His expression was as hard as stone. He'd spent days trying to forget her, and fate had thrown him a real curve today. He wanted to go off into the desert and spend some time alone. Maybe that was the answer, when Eugene could spare him. Maybe civilization was getting to him.

"You're brooding," Eugene muttered, glaring at him. "What's the matter?"

"I was just getting used to peace and quiet," Hunter murmured with a dry smile.

"God help us," Eugene shuddered. "Peace and quiet is for the grave, man. No good for healthy humans. Come on. I'll see if I can light a fire under the pilot."

"Better let him do his job," Hunter cautioned. "More than one plane has gone down because its owner was too impatient for the final check."

Eugene glared at him again, but that level stare intimidated even him. "Okay," he muttered. "Have it your own way."

Hunter smiled at the retreating figure, and all the while he was wondering how he was going to survive being close to Jenny without reaching for her.

The flight seemed to take forever. Hunter alternately read and glared at Jennifer, who pretended not to notice. Things had been so strained between them that she was uncomfortable with him. Her behavior in the desert and his reaction to it embarrassed and inhibited her. She sat with Cynthia, only half listening to the older woman's comments about clothes and Washington society while she wondered how she was going to cope with several days of the stoic Mr. Hunter.

They got off the plane at the airport in Washington at last, and Jennifer was momentarily left behind with Hunter while Eugene and Cynthia paused to check times for the return flight with the pilot.

She didn't know what to say to him. She averted her eyes and stared toward the other planes, with her purse and makeup case clutched tightly in her hand.

Hunter was smoking a cigarette. He glanced down at her impatiently and finally stopped and just stared at her until he made her nervous enough to look up. But when he saw her embarrassment, he was sorry he'd done it.

"Don't make it any harder than it already is," he said, his deep voice slow and terse. "What happened that night was just an interlude. I lost my head and so did you. Let it go."

She swallowed. "All right."

He scowled through a cloud of smoke as he searched her deep blue eyes. Involuntarily his gaze slid to her blouse and his eyes darkened with memories.

She turned away. That look was painful, and despite his assertion that it was over, it didn't seem as if he'd forgotten a single thing. Neither had she. The feel of his eyes on her, his mouth on her lips, haunted her night after lonely night. She didn't even like being near him because just his proximity made her shiver with need. It was a reaction unlike anything she'd ever experienced before in her life, a mad hunger that she could never satisfy.

Hunter was having problems of his own. God, she was lovely! Just looking at her hurt. He turned away to help get the luggage off the plane and carry it to the waiting limousine. He had to stop remembering.

The hotel they stayed at was four-star, very plush and service-oriented. Eugene had reserved two suites of rooms. Unfortunately, Jennifer was relegated to one with Hunter, which surprised and inhibited her.

Eugene noticed her uneasiness and averted his eyes before she could see the faint glimmer of amusement in them. "You'll survive it, Jenny," he said. "I want you where Hunter can watch you. You're the most important part of this enterprise. I can't have enemy agents trying to spirit you off under my nose, can I?"

"We have other security people...." she began hopefully.

"But Hunter's the best. No more arguments. I hope you brought an evening gown. There's an embassy ball tomorrow night."

"I did," she said reluctantly. It was a year old, but still functional, and it fit her like a second skin. She frowned bitterly, thinking of the exquisite white confection and regretting that she didn't still have the little red number she'd knocked Hunter's eyes out with a few months back. She'd thrown it away in a temper after that one bitter date with him.

Eugene had arranged appointments all over Washington, and he went alone, leaving Jennifer to go sightseeing with Cynthia and Hunter.

Cynthia was enchanted with everything she saw, from the Lincoln Memorial to the reflecting pool outside it, the spire of the Washington monument and the White House and the nation's Capital. But Jennifer was enchanted with Hunter and trying so hard not to let him see. She wore tan slacks with a colorful pink blouse and sandals for the sight-seeing tour, and Cynthia wore a similar ensemble. Hunter wore a suit.

He escorted them around the city with quiet impatience, and Jennifer knew without being told that he hated the noise and traffic, and that he would have preferred to be doing something else. But he didn't complain. He pointed out landmarks and hustled them in and out of cabs with singular forbearance. All the same, Jennifer noticed how relieved he looked when they were back at the hotel.

Eugene returned in time to go to supper, phoning Hunter to give him the time and place they were to eat. Hunter hung up, glancing at a nervous Jennifer poised in the doorway to her bedroom.

"You've got an hour to get dressed," he said. "Time for a shower, if you like. We're to meet him and Cynthia at the Coach and Whip for dinner."

"All right," she said. "I'll be ready."

He stared at her with quiet, steady dark eyes. "What are you going to wear?"

"Why?" she asked, startled.

He pursed his lips. "I hope it isn't something red," he murmured, turning away with an involuntary smile on his hard mouth.

"Oh!" she burst out.

But, he didn't look back or say a word. He just went into his own room and closed the door.

Except for that one unexpected incident, dinner went off without a hitch. But if she'd hoped for anything from Hunter, she was doomed for disappointment. He ate and excused himself, and she didn't see him again for the rest of the night or most of the next day. She and Cynthia amused themselves by going to a movie while Eugene had one last talk with someone on Capitol Hill. Then, almost before she knew it, Jennifer was getting ready to go to a real ball.

Jennifer felt like a girl on her first date as she put on the white satin gown to wear to the ball. She'd never been to anything really grand, although she'd come close once when she and Hunter were on assignment overseas. She put her long blond hair up in an elegant coiffure with tiny wisps of hair curling around her ears. She had a pair of satin-covered pumps that she wore with it, but the dress itself was the height of expensive luxury. She'd bought it on impulse, because at the time she'd had no place at all to wear it. It had a low-cut bodice and spaghetti straps that tied on each shoulder. The waist was fitted, but the skirt had yards and yards of material, and it flared gracefully when she walked. It covered all but the very tips of her pumps. She put on her makeup last, using just a little more than she usually did, but not too much. She looked in the mirror, fascinated because she looked totally different this way. Her whole face seemed radiant with the extra touch of rouge and the pale gray eye shadow with a tiny hint of light blue.

She looked at herself with faint satisfaction. She'd never been glad of her looks before, but tonight she was. She wanted Hunter to be proud of her, to want to be seen with her. She closed her eyes, imagining the music of a waltz. Would Hunter ask her to dance? She smiled. Surely he would. They'd waltz around the ballroom and all eyes would be on them . . . That jerked her back to reality. Attention would be the last thing Hunter would want, and probably the only dances he knew were done with war dances around a camp fire.

She grimaced mentally. That would be just the thing to say to him, all right. It would put them quickly back on their old, familiar footing and he'd never speak to her again. Which might not be a bad idea, she told herself. At least if he hated her openly he wouldn't be making horrible remarks about the red dress she'd worn that one evening they'd gone out together.

On the other hand, why had he mentioned it at all? That was twice, she realized, that he'd made a remark about that particular dress. She smiled to herself. Well, well. He remembered it, did he? She'd go right out and find herself another red dress, one that was even more revealing, and she'd wear it until he screamed!

The sudden hard rap on the door made her jump. "Yes?" she called out.

"Time to go," Hunter replied quietly.

She grabbed her purse, almost upending the entire contents on the floor in the process, and rushed to their joint sitting room.

She stopped short at the sight of Hunter in a dinner jacket. It could have been made for him, she thought as she stared at him. The dark jacket with its white silk shirt and black tie might have been designed for his coloring. It made him look so elegant and handsome that she couldn't tear her eyes away.

He was doing some looking of his own. His dark eyes ran down the length of her body in the clinging white dress, growing narrower and glittering faintly as they lingered on her full breasts and worked their way back up to her soft mouth and then her dark blue eyes.

"Will I do?" she asked hesitantly.

"You'll do," he said, his voice terse with reluctant emotion. He met her eyes and held them, watching her cheeks go pink. "Oh, yes, you'll do, Jennifer. And you know it without having to be told."

She dragged her gaze down to his chest, to the quick rise and fall of it under the shirt. "You don't have to sound angry," she muttered.

"I am angry. You know it. And don't pretend you don't know why. I wouldn't buy that in a million years." He moved toward the door while she was still trying to puzzle out what he meant. "Let's go," he said, without looking at her again. "Eugene and Cynthia are waiting for us."

She started past him and paused without knowing why. Slowly she lifted her eyes to his and looked at him openly. Her heart ran wild at the fierce warmth she saw there, at the visible effort he made at control. "Is it all right if I tell you that you're devastating?" she asked softly.

He lifted his chin without replying, but something flashed in his dark eyes for an instant before he turned away with a faint smile. "Come on."

He was quiet when they joined the other couple, which was just as well, because Eugene monopolized the conversation—as usual. It was exciting to go to a ball in a big black limousine, and Jennifer wished her parents could see her now. She almost looked up at Hunter and said so, but he wouldn't find it interesting, she knew, so she kept her silence.

The big Washington mansion where the ball was being held was some embassy or other. Jennifer had been too excited about being with Hunter to care which one it was, or even where it was. She was trembling with contained excitement when Hunter helped her from the car and escorted her up the wide steps that led to the columned porch, which was ablaze with light. The faint sounds of music poured from the stately confines of the mansion.

"What a piece of real estate," Cynthia said mischievously, clasping Eugene's hand tightly in her own. "And I thought we had a nice house."

"We do have a nice house," he reminded her. "And we could have had one like this, but you seemed to think that it would be—what was the word you used?—pretentious."

"And it would have," she reassured him. "I was just admiring the pretentiousness of the embassy," she added, tongue-in-cheek.

Jennifer grinned. "Do you suppose the staff wear roller skates to get from room to room with the trays?"

"I wouldn't be a bit surprised," Eugene said, "but for God's sake don't make such a remark to our host. You can take it from me that he has absolutely no sense of humor."

"Can I ask why we're going to a ball at a foreign embassy to talk about land out West?" Jennifer asked.

"Sure!" Eugene assured her.

She glared at him.

He chuckled. "All right. There are two senators I have to see, and I was tipped off that they were both going to be at this shindig. You and Hunter go socialize until I need you— if I need you. I may be be able to pull this one off alone."

"Then why are we here?" Jennifer persisted.

Eugene forcibly kept himself from glancing at Hunter. "Because I wanted to make sure you weren't abducted and held for ransom or some such thing while I was talking terms," he said. "Go and dance. Can you dance?" he taunted.

She drew herself up to her full height, an action that made her firm breasts thrust out proudly, and Hunter shifted a little jerkily and moved away. "Yes, I can dance," she told him. "In fact, I studied dancing for three years."

"So go and practice." His blue eyes narrowed on Hunter's averted face. "You might teach Hunter how."

Hunter cocked a thick eyebrow down at him. "My people could teach yours plenty about how to move to music." A wisp of a smile touched that hard face and his dark eyes twinkled. "We have dances for war, dances for peace, dances for rain, even dances for fertility," he added and had to grit his teeth to keep from glancing deliberately toward Jennifer.

"How about waltzes?" Eugene persisted.

"Ballroom dancing isn't included in the core curriculum for CIA operatives," he said, deadpan.

"Jennifer might be persuaded to teach you..." Eugene began.

But before he could even get the words out, Jennifer was suddenly swept away by a tall, balding man with a badge of

office on the sash that arrowed across his thin chest. She was
dancing before she knew it, and from that moment on, she
didn't even get a peek at the hors d'oeuvres on the long, elegant table against the wall. She was dying of thirst, too, but
one partner after another asked her to dance, and she was
too entranced by the exquisite music of the live orchestra to
refuse. Especially since Hunter didn't even bother to ask her
for a dance, whether or not he knew how. When her first
partner swept her off onto the dance floor, he'd walked
away without even looking back and she hadn't seen him
since.

She pleaded fatigue after a nonstop hour on the dance
floor and found her way to the powder room upstairs. By
the time she came down, Hunter had apparently come out
of hiding because an older socialite had him cornered by a
potted plant against one wall. He looked irritated and half
angry, and Jennifer felt a surge of sympathy, although God
alone knew why she should.

She started toward him, hesitated, and he looked up at
that moment and his eyes kindled. He even smiled.

That had to mean he was desperate for rescue. He never
smiled at her. Well, he was going to get his rescue, but she
was going to enjoy it. She moved toward him with pure
witchery in her movements, patting her hair back into place.

"Here I am, sweetheart!" she called in a rich exaggerated Southern drawl. "Did you think I'd gotten lost?" She
draped herself over his side, feeling him stiffen. A mischievous sense of pleasure flooded through her. Well, he'd asked
for it. She smiled thinly at the older woman, who was
watching her with narrow, cold eyes. "Hello. I don't think
we've met. I'm Jennifer Marist. Hunter and I work for an
oil corporation in Oklahoma. It's so rarely that we get to
enjoy a fabulous party like this, isn't it, darling?" she asked,
blinking her long lashes up at him.

"Rarely," he agreed, but his eyes were promising retri-
bution. He was already half out of humor from watching
her pass from one pair of masculine arms to another. Then

this social shark had attacked. He'd been desperate enough to encourage Jennifer to rescue him, but he hadn't exactly expected this type of rescue. Fortunately his expression gave nothing away.

"I was just telling Mr. Hunter that I'd love to have him join me for a late supper," the older woman said, blatantly ignoring Jennifer's apparent possessiveness. She smiled at Hunter, diamonds dripping from her ears and her thin neck. "I want to hear all about his tribe. I've never met a real Indian before."

Hunter's jaw clenched, but Jennifer smiled.

"I know, isn't it fascinating?" Jennifer confided. "Did you know that he rubs himself all over with bear grease every night at bedtime? It's a ritual. And he keeps rattlesnakes," she whispered, "to use in fertility dances outside during full moons. You really must get him to show you the courting dance. It's done with deer heads and pouches full of dried buffalo chips...."

The older woman was looking a little frantic. "Excuse me," she said breathlessly, staring around as if she were looking for a life preserver. "I see someone I must speak to!"

She shot off without another word and Jennifer had to smother a giggle. "Oh, God, I'm sorry," she whispered. "It was the way she said it..."

He was laughing, too, if the glitter in his eyes and the faint uplift of his lips could be called that. "Bear grease," he muttered. "That wasn't the Apache, you idiot. And the dance a young girl does at her very special coming-of-age ceremony is done with a pouch of pollen, for fertility, not dried buffalo chips."

"Do you want me to call her back and tell her the truth?" she offered.

He shook his head. His dark eyes slid over her body in the clinging dress, and there was a definite appreciation in them. "If I have to suffer a woman for the rest of the evening, I'd prefer you," he said, startling her. "At least you won't ask embarrassing questions about my cultural background."

"Thanks a lot," she murmured. "And after that daring rescue, too."

"Rescue, yes. Daring?" He shook his head. "Hardly." He chuckled deeply. "You little terror. I ought to tie you to a chair and smear honey on you."

"You have to do that in the desert, where you can find ants," she reminded him. "You asked to be rescued, you know you did."

"This wasn't exactly what I had in mind," he muttered.

"Was she trying to put the make on you?" she asked, all eyes.

He glared at her. "No. She was trying to find out how many scalps I had in my teepee."

"Apaches didn't have teepees, they had wickiups," she said knowledgeably. "I hope you told her."

His eyebrows rose. "Who's the Indian here, you or me?"

"I think one of my great-grandfather's adoptive cousins was Lower Creek," she frowned thoughtfully.

"God help us!"

"I could have just kept on walking," she reminded him. "I didn't have to save you from that woman."

"No, you didn't. But before it happens again, I'm going to stand on the balcony and hope I get carried off by Russian helicopters. I hate these civilized hatchet parties."

"Mind if I join you?" she asked.

His eyes narrowed. "What for? You're the belle of the ball. You've danced every damned dance!"

"Only because you walked off and left me alone!" she threw back at him, her blue eyes flashing. "I thought we were together. But I suppose that's carrying the line of duty too far, isn't it? I mean, God forbid you should have to survive a whole evening in my company!"

"I said I was going outside," he replied with exaggerated patience. "If you want to come along, fine. I don't like being the only Indian around. Where were all these damned suicidal white women over a hundred years ago? I'll tell you, they were hiding behind curtains with loaded rifles! But now, all of a sudden, they can't wait to be thrown on a horse and carried off."

"You're shouting," she pointed out.

His dark eyes glittered down at her. "I am not," he said shortly.

"Besides, you don't have a horse."

"I have one at home," he replied. "Several, in fact. I like horses."

"So do I. But I haven't ridden much," she replied. "There was never much time for that sort of thing."

"People make time for the things they really want to do," he said, looking down at her.

She shrugged. "There are plenty of places to ride around Tulsa, but I think it's a mistake to get on a horse if you don't know how to control it."

"Well, well." He stood aside to let her precede him onto the balcony, past the colorful blur of dancing couples. The balcony was dark and fairly deserted, with huge potted plants and trees and a balustrade that overlooked the brilliant lights of the city.

Seven

Jennifer couldn't believe he'd actually allowed her to invade his solitude without a protest. It was sheer heaven being here beside him on the balcony, without another soul in sight.

She leaned forward on the balustrade. "Isn't it glorious?" she asked softly.

He studied her hungrily for a moment before he turned his gaze toward the horizon. "I prefer sunset on the desert." He lit a cigarette and smoked it silently for several seconds before his dark eyes cut sideways to study her. "Did you really want to dance with me?" he asked with a faint smile. Actually he danced quite well. But having Jenny close was a big risk. She went to his head even when they were several feet apart.

"Wasn't it obvious that I did?" she asked ruefully.

"Not to me." He blew out a cloud of smoke and stared at the distant horizon. "I won't dance, Jennifer. Not this kind of dancing, anyway." He was careful to say *won't* and not *can't*—lying was almost impossible for him. Apaches considered it bad manners to lie.

"Oh. I'm sorry. You do everything else so well, I just assumed that dancing would come naturally to you."

"It doesn't," he replied. "Where did you learn?"

"Dancing class," she said, grinning. Odd how comfortable she felt with him, despite the feverish excitement his closeness engendered in her slender body. She could catch the scent of his cologne, and it was spicy and sexy in her nostrils. He was the stuff dreams were made of. Her dreams, anyway.

"You studied ballroom dancing?" he persisted.

"Tap and ballet, actually. My mother thought I should be well-rounded instead of walking around with my nose stuck in a book or studying rocks most of the time."

"What are your parents like?" he asked, curious.

She smiled, picturing them. "My mother looks like me. My father's tall and very dark. They're both educators and I think they're nice people. Certainly they're intelligent."

"They'd have to be, with such a brainy daughter."

She laughed self-consciously. "I'm not brainy really. I had to study pretty hard to get where I am." She smiled wistfully.

"You know your job," he replied, glancing down at her. "I learned more about molybdenum than I wanted to know."

She blushed. "Yes, well, I tend to ramble sometimes."

"It wasn't a criticism," he said. "I enjoyed it." He looked out over the horizon. "God, I hate society."

"I guess it gets difficult for you when people start making insulting remarks about your heritage," she said. "It's hard for me when I get dragged on the dance floor by men I don't even know. I don't particularly like being handled."

He frowned. He hadn't thought of her beauty as being a handicap. Maybe it was. She'd had enough partners tonight. Enough, in fact, to make him jealous for the first time in memory.

"I don't like being an oddity," he agreed. "I've never thought of you that way."

She smiled. "Thank you. I could return the compliment."

He turned away from her, leaning against the balcony to look out at the city lights. "I suppose I'm less easily offended than I was before you joined the company. Maybe I'm learning to take that chip off my shoulder," he added, glancing at her with a rueful smile. "Isn't that what you once accused me of having?"

She joined him by the balcony, leaning her arms on it. "Yes. It was true. You got your back up every time I made a remark."

"You intimidated me," he said surprisingly. He lifted the cigarette to his firm lips, glancing down at her. "Beautiful, blond, intelligent...the kind of woman who could have any man she wanted. I didn't think a reservation Indian would appeal to you."

"I suppose you got the shock of your life that night by the creek," she remarked, a little shy at the admission.

"Indeed I did," he said huskily. His eyes darkened. "I never dreamed you wanted me like that."

"It wasn't enough, though," she said sadly, her eyes moving to the dark landscape. "Wanting on one side, I mean." She pushed back a loose strand of blond hair that had escaped her elegant upswept coiffure. "You didn't smoke while we were camping out."

"You didn't see me," he corrected. "It's my only vice, and just an occasional one. I have the infrequent can of beer, but I don't drink." His eyes narrowed. "Alcoholism is a big problem among my people. Some scientists have ventured the opinion that Indians lack the enzyme necessary to process alcohol."

"I didn't know. I don't drink, either. I like being in control of my senses."

"Do you?" He looked down at her quietly.

She wouldn't meet his eyes. "I always have been. Except with you."

He sighed angrily, lifting the cigarette to his mouth again before he ground it out under his heel. "So I noticed," he said gruffly. Her nearness was making him uncomfortable. He didn't like the temptation of being close to her, but he didn't want to spoil the evening for her by saying so.

She moved a little closer so that she could see his lean, dark face in the light from the ballroom. "Hunter, what's wrong?" she asked softly.

He hated the tenderness in her voice. It tempted him and made him angry. "Nothing."

She wanted to pursue the subject, but his expression was daunting. She smoothed down the soft material of the dress. With its sleeveless bodice that dipped almost to her waist, and the clingy chiffon outlining her narrow waist and full hips, she was a vision. She knew she looked pretty, but it would have made her evening to hear Hunter say so. Not that he would. She glanced back toward the dancers inside. "I guess this is familiar territory to you," she murmured absently. "High society, I mean."

He frowned. "I beg your pardon?"

"Well, you do a lot of work for Eugene, and this is his milieu," she explained, glancing up at him. "And I know you've had to look after politicians for him, so I suppose it entails a certain amount of socializing."

"Not that much." He folded his arms over his chest. "I don't care for this kind of civilized warfare. Too many people. Too much noise."

"I know how you feel." She sighed, staring toward the ballroom. "I'd much rather be outdoors, away from crowds."

He studied her with renewed interest. She wasn't lying. He remembered her delight in the desert those days they'd spent together, her laughter at the antics of the birds, her quiet contemplation of dusk and dawn. That pleasure hadn't been faked. But with her beauty and education, surely this was her scene.

"You look at home here, nevertheless," he said. He lit another cigarette and blew out a cloud of smoke. She was making him more nervous by the minute. Her dress was pure witchcraft.

"That's funny," she murmured, and smiled. "The closest to this kind of thing I ever got in my youth was the high school prom—or it would have been, if I'd been asked. I spent that night at home, baby-sitting the neighbor's little boy."

The cigarette froze en route to his mouth. "You weren't asked?"

"You sound surprised." She turned to look up at him. "All the boys assumed that I already had a date, because I was pretty. There was one special boy I liked, but he was just ordinary and not handsome at all. He didn't think he had a chance with me, so he never asked me out. I didn't find out until I was grown and he was married that he'd had a crush on me." She laughed, but it had a hollow sound. "Women hate me because they think I'm a threat to them. Men don't take me seriously at work if they don't know me because pretty blondes aren't supposed to be intelligent. And if I'm asked out on a date, it's automatically expected that I'll be dynamite in bed. You mentioned once that I don't date anybody. Now you know why."

"Are you?" he asked.

Her eyebrows lifted. "Am I what?"

"Dynamite in bed."

She glared up at him. There was something like amusement in his tone. "Don't you start, Hunter."

He tossed the cigarette down and ground it out under the heel of his dress shoe, but his eyes didn't leave hers. "Why not?" he asked, moving closer with a slow sensual step that made her heart beat faster. "I'm human."

"Are you, really?" she asked, remembering that night on the desert when he'd seen her bathing. She almost groaned. His restraint had overwhelmed her, then and since.

He caught her hands and slid them up around his neck. "Stop dithering and dance with me," he said quietly.

His voice was an octave lower. Deep, slow, sensuous, like the hands that, instead of holding her correctly, slid around her, against her bare back where the low cut of the dress left it vulnerable.

She gasped. "You said... you didn't dance," she whispered.

"You can teach me," he whispered back.

But it didn't feel as if he needed any instruction. He moved gracefully to the music, drawing her along with him. The feel of him this close, the brush of his warm, rough hands against her silky skin, made her tremble. When he felt the trembling, he drew her even closer. She shivered helplessly, feeling his hands slowly caressing her, his lips in her hair, against her forehead, as he made a lazy effort to move her to the rhythm of the slow bluesy tune the orchestra was playing. But it wasn't as much dancing as it was making love to music. She felt his chest dragging against her breasts with every step, his long, powerful legs brushing against hers at the thigh. She remembered his eyes on her bare breasts, his arms around her, the feel of his hard mouth. And she ached for him.

She tried to move back, before she gave herself away, but his hands were firm.

"What are you afraid of?" he asked at her forehead.

"You," she moaned. "What you make me feel." Her hands grasped the lapels of his jacket. Twenty-seven years of denial, of longing, of loneliness. Years of loving this man alone, of being deprived of even the most innocent physical contact. And now she was in his arms, he was holding her, touching her, and she couldn't hide her pleasure or her need.

"Jenny." He bent closer, his mouth tempting hers into lifting, his eyes dark and quiet and intent in the stillness. He stopped dancing, but his hands smoothed lazily up and down her back, and he watched the rapt, anguished need color her face, part her lips. She looked as if she'd die to have him make love to her. It was the same look he remembered from the night he'd seen her bathing, and it had the same overwhelming effect on him.

"Please," she whispered, and her voice broke. She was beyond hiding it, beyond pretence, totally vulnerable. "Would it kill you to kiss me again, just once? Oh, Hunter, please . . . !"

He lifted his head with a rough sigh, looking around them. He eased her into a small alcove, hidden to the rest of the balcony, and slowly moved her until she was against the wall. His hands rested on either side of her head against it, his body shielding hers, and then covering hers, trapping her between it and the wall in a slow, sensual movement.

"Lift your mouth to mine," he whispered.

She did, without a single protest, and had it taken in a succession of slow, brief, tormenting bites. She whimpered helplessly, shaking all over with the need to be close to him. He tasted of cigarette smoke and expensive brandy, and the kiss was almost like a narcotic, drugging her with slow, aching pleasure. She clung to him with something akin to desperation, so out of control that she couldn't begin to hide what she was feeling. Her body throbbed with it, trembled with it. Twenty-seven years of denial were going up in flames, in his arms.

"My God, you're starving for me," he said huskily, his voice rough with surprise as he looked down at her. "It's all right, little one," he breathed as his dark head bent again. "It's all right. I'll feed you . . ."

His mouth covered hers then, slowly building the pressure into something wild and deep and overwhelming. As if he understood her need for passion, he pushed down against her and his mouth became demanding, its very roughness filling the emptiness in her.

She slid her arms around his lean waist and pressed even closer, tears rolling down her flushed cheeks as she fed on his mouth, accepting the hard thrust of his tongue with awe, loving the feel of his aroused body bearing hers heavily against the wall. She wept against his hard lips and he lifted his head.

"Oh, don't . . . stop," she whispered brokenly. "Please, please . . . don't stop yet!"

He was losing it. His mouth ground into hers again, tasting the softness of her parted lips, inhaling the exquisite fragrance of her body into his nostrils. His body was rigid with desire, his hips already thrusting helplessly against hers with an involuntary rhythm. His mouth crushed hers roughly, his teeth nipping her full lower lip in a pagan surge of fierce need.

"I want you," she whispered into his mouth. All her control was gone, all her pride. She was beyond rational thought. "I want you. I want you so much!"

He dragged his head up. His hands gripped her upper arms hard while he fought for control. She'd already lost hers. Her eyes were dilated, wild with need, her body shaking helplessly with it. She was his. Here, now, standing up, she would have welcomed him and he knew it. It was all he could do to back away. But he had to remember who they were, and where they were.

"Jennifer," he said quietly. His voice sounded strained. He fought to steady it. "Jennifer!" He shook her. "Stop it!"

She felt the rough shake as if it was happening to somebody else. She stared up at him through a sensual veil, still shivering, her body throbbing with its urgent need of his. He shook her again, fiercely, and she caught her breath. The world spun around her and she suddenly realized where they were.

She swallowed hard with returning sanity. Her face went scarlet when she remembered begging him...

His hands tightened and released her arms. "Come on, now," he said, his voice gentle where it had been violent. "Come on, Jenny. Take a deep breath."

He knew she was vulnerable. He knew it all now. Tears ran down her cheeks, hot and salty, into the corners of her swollen mouth.

He drew her head to his jacket, his hands soothing at her nape. "It's all right, little one," he said quietly, his teeth clenched as he fought his own physical demons. He was hurting. "It's all right. Nothing happened."

"I want to die," she whispered brokenly. "I'm so... ashamed!"

"Of what?" he asked, frowning. He framed her face in his lean, warm hands and lifted it to his eyes. "Jenny, there's no shame in being a woman."

She could hardly see him through her tears. "Let me go... please," she pleaded, pushing at his chest.

He didn't like the way she looked. Desperate. Horrified. As if she'd committed some deadly sin. He couldn't let her leave in this condition.

"Calm down," he said firmly, taking her by the shoulders to shake her again. "I'm not letting you out of my sight until you're rational."

She bit down on her swollen lower lip, hard, tasting him there. She closed her eyes. She couldn't bear to see his face.

"What in God's name is wrong with you?" he asked, leaning closer. "You wanted me, that's all. I've felt that kind of desire before, I know how helpless it can make you."

Yes, he'd felt it, but not with her. That was what hurt so much, that she felt it and he didn't. He'd kissed her because she'd begged him to, but she was sure there hadn't been anything else. Just pity and compassion. If only she knew more about men...

She lifted her cold hands and wiped at her tears. "I need to wash my face," she whispered. "I can't go back in there ... like this."

He bent and brushed his lips tenderly against hers, but she jerked away from him, her blue eyes wide and terrified.

His head lifted and he studied her, realization kindling belatedly in his mind. So that was it. The hidden fear. She'd lost control. He'd made her helpless and she was going to fight tooth and nail to keep it from happening again. Was that why she didn't date anyone? Had she lost control before and was afraid of giving rein to her passionate nature? Or was it just years of denial catching up with her? Her violent desire for him had weakened his resolve painfully.

"Do you want me to do something about this?" he asked, his voice deep and quiet, posing a question he'd never meant to ask.

"What?" she asked numbly.

"A need that violent should be satisifed," he said matter-of-factly. "I know you want me. I've known that for a long time. But now I understand how desperate the need is."

She couldn't believe he was saying this. Her face was scarlet, she knew, but she stared up at him helplessly while he offered her the fulfillment of every dream she'd ever dreamed.

"Do you want me to take you back to the hotel and satisfy you, Jenny?" he asked quietly, his expression giving away nothing, although his body was still keeping him on the rack. He wanted her obsessively. He could taste her in his mouth. He wanted to taste all of her the way he'd savored her soft lips. He wanted to strip her and kiss every pink inch of her, from head to toe.

"I ... might get pregnant," she whispered, too shaken to be rational, too hungry to refuse. "You said ..."

He didn't like remembering what he'd said. "I'll take care of you," he said firmly. "In every way. There won't be consequences of any kind. Least of all the risk of a child torn between your culture and mine," he added bitterly.

She was twenty-seven, almost twenty-eight. She'd never known intimacy with anyone, but she wanted, so much, to know it with this man. She'd loved him forever, it sometimes seemed. He was offering her untold delights. She knew without asking that he was expert. The way he'd kissed her had told her that. He wouldn't hurt her. With luck, he'd never know that she was a virgin.

"I . . . want you," she whispered helplessly.

His chest expanded jerkily while he searched her eyes, curious about the faint fear and melancholy there. But one didn't question a gift like this. He caught her soft hand in his and led her back into the ballroom.

She remembered very little about the minutes that followed. They left. She said something polite to their host and hostess and to Eugene and Cynthia. There was a cab ride back to the hotel, she was at the door of his room. He put her inside without bothering to turn on the light.

Then she was in his arms. It was heaven. Pure, sweet heaven. He took her hair down and buried his face in it before his mouth slowly, inevitably, found her lips. She clung to him, tasting him, while he kissed her and kissed her until she couldn't stand. She felt his mouth and his hands on her bare skin as he removed her dress, her underthings, her hose. Then he lifted her and carried her to the bed.

"I want to look at you," he said huskily.

"Yes." She didn't flinch as the bedside light came on, although her cheeks reddened, even though he'd seen part of her like this before. He looked and she shivered at the bold hunger in his dark eyes as they went over her slowly, with fierce possessiveness.

"Pink satin," he whispered, his voice deep and slow in the stillness of the room. "I wanted to look at you like this that night you were bathing, at all of you. I wanted to touch you, but I didn't dare. I couldn't have stopped." He reached down and spread her hair on his pillow, his eyes darkening. "Exquisite," he whispered, his eyes sliding down her.

She shivered. She hadn't expected him to say things like that.

He sat down beside her, still fully clothed, not touching her. His eyes searched hers. "This is the first time," he said.

Her heart jumped. He knew!

"The first time," he continued, "that I've been with a white woman in years. This is something I never meant to happen."

She couldn't help the relief she felt that he hadn't guessed about her innocence. But what he was saying finally got through to her and she realized what it meant.

"You don't have to," she said uncertainly, because now that it was about to happen, she was nervous.

He reached out and traced one soft, firm breast, watching her body react helplessly and instantly to his touch. "I'm Apache," he said, studying her face. "There are places inside me that you can't see, can't touch. Different beliefs, different customs, different life-styles. I live in your world, but I prefer the stark simplicity of mine." He traced around one dusky erect nipple, hearing her soft gasp. "I've spent years trying not to see you, Jennifer," he said, his voice barely above a whisper. "Years of dreams that kept my body in anguish..." He bent to her breasts, his mouth slow and ardent.

She couldn't believe he'd said that. She shivered and arched toward his lips, holding his face to her. "You mean...you want me, too?" she asked, fascinated.

He lifted his head and looked down into her eyes. "Yes," he said simply. "But only this once," he added, his voice stern. "Only tonight. Never again."

She swallowed. She wanted so much more than that, but it would have to do. She could live on this for the rest of her life. "All right," she whispered.

He stood with a long sigh and began to remove his own clothes. He did it with lazy grace, with a complete lack of inhibition that told her too well how familiar this was to him. She hated the other women in his life because they'd given him that expertise.

His keen eyes caught her expression and he lifted an eyebrow as he bent to remove the final barrier. "What was that hard look about?" he asked.

He turned back to her and the hard look was utterly forgotten as she stared blatantly at his nudity. He was all bronzed muscle and powerful etched lines and curves, so beautiful that she sat up and caught her breath at the perfection of his body.

"What is it?" he asked, frowning curiously.

"There was a statue in the Louvre," she stammered. "I saw photographs of it...Greek, I think. I remember being awed by the power and beauty of it and thinking that, well, that no mortal man could come close to that kind of perfection." She averted her eyes to the bed. "I didn't mean to stare. I guess you've been told ad nauseum how ... beautifully masculine you are."

He felt the impact of that breathless adoration in her voice. He'd never heard himself described that way by anyone. His conquests had been sporadic, and even then more animal than sensual. He'd given in to his needs only when he couldn't bear them any longer, and in his later years, it hadn't been that often. With Jennifer, it was different. He was touched by her headlong, helpless need of him. He'd thought that it was purely physical, but her eyes were telling him otherwise. A woman didn't look at a man like this when her only concern was fulfillment, and her shy blushing face made him uneasy.

He slid onto the bed beside her, turning her so that she was lying against him. He felt her flinch at the first touch of his aroused body, and he tilted her face so that he could see it.

"It's frightening for a woman with every new man, isn't it?" he asked absently. "Not knowing if he'll be gentle or cruel, demanding or brutal?"

"Yes. Of course," she lied. She could feel the heat of him, the threatening masculinity in a way she'd never dreamed of feeling it. She had to be careful. If she gave herself away, he'd never touch her. She wanted this with him so badly, refusing to admit even to herself that pregnancy was a very big part of the wanting, that her need of him included that faint possibility.

"I'm not cruel," he said, moving her so that she was completely against him. He felt the soft little tremors in her body as she stiffened in reaction before she relaxed and let him hold her closer. "I'm not brutal." He slid one lean hand along her side, over the curve of breast and waist and hip down to her smooth, soft thigh. He eased his leg between both of hers and brought her into intimacy. "And for your sake, I'll try not to be too demanding."

She gasped at the sudden stark contact.

"Shhhh," he whispered, smoothing the hair at her nape. "Lie still. It's better like this, lying on our sides. It's more intimate. Lift your leg over mine."

She blushed scarlet, praying that she wouldn't blow her cover. She did as he told her, but her hands were gripping his shoulders for dear life, biting in, and her stiffness was making him curious.

"Haven't you ever done it like this?" he whispered at her ear as his hands began to touch her intimately.

"No," she choked. It was true. But she'd never done it any way at all, including like this.

"Look at me."

She had to force her shocked, frightened eyes to meet his, and then she saw the curiosity narrowing them. He touched her where she was most a woman and she clenched her teeth to keep from crying out.

His firm lips parted as he probed delicately, holding her eyes. He scowled, because something was different here. Very different.

"Are you . . . are you going to use something," she managed, trying to divert him.

But it didn't work. He was experienced enough to recognize what was different, because this particular difference was so blatant that he didn't have to be a doctor to know what it was.

"My God," he whispered explosively. His hand stilled, but it didn't withdraw.

"Hunter..." she began, passion growing cold at the look on his face.

He searched her eyes and his hand moved. She bit her lip and tears threatened.

"Does this hurt, little one?" he whispered softly, and did it again. She tried not to flinch, but the intimacy and faint discomfort defeated her. "Yes," he answered his own question. His face mirrored his shock. He looked at her as if he'd never seen her before, and still that maddening hand didn't move away. He couldn't believe it. A woman with her beauty, at her age. A virgin.

"I didn't think you'd know," she stammered. "The books say that even a doctor can't tell..."

"That's true," he replied gently. "But you're intact, little one. Do you understand? Almost completely intact."

She swallowed, lowering her embarrassed eyes to the jerky rise and fall of his bronzed chest. "The doctors said that it would be uncomfortable, but that I wouldn't have to have surgery when the time came," she said finally. "It's mine to give," she added, lifting her face back to his.

"And you want to give it to me?" he asked gently.

"Yes."

He eased her over onto her back, his eyes soft and quiet and very dark. "Then give it to me this way, for now," he whispered. His mouth touched hers so tenderly that her heart ached, and his hand began to move very slowly, expertly, on her.

She tensed at the sudden shock of pleasure and tried to get away, but he threw a long, powerful leg across both of hers.

"No," he whispered into her mouth. "I'm going to take you up to the stars. Don't fight me," he said softly.

She trembled as the pleasure bit into her body. It came again, and again. And all the while he kissed her, his lips tender on her face while he made magic in her body. He saw the fear and smiled reassuringly, his voice coaxing, softly praising. He felt the urgency, felt when it reached breaking point. He knew exactly what to do, and when. Her back arched and she gasped, weeping as the pleasure took her, convulsing her under his delighted, fascinated gaze. Heat washed over him, blinding fire exploding, racking him even as he heard her cry out. Then, ages later, she relaxed, her tears hot and salty in his mouth as he kissed them away. He relaxed, too, because in the midst of her own explosive fulfillment, her movements had triggered his. He kissed her closed eyelids, thinking that never in his life had he experienced anything quite so perfect. And from such relatively innocent love play.

He lifted his head, turning hers toward him to search her drowned, shamed eyes.

"Is sex a sin for you?" he said softly. "Is that why you're a virgin?"

"There was never anyone I wanted enough," she whispered, sobbing. "I wanted you so badly. So much that I would have died to have you..."

He brushed her mouth with his, feeling humble. "Virginity is a rare gift," he whispered. "Yours to give, certainly. But not outside marriage. I have my own kind of honor, Jennifer. Taking your innocence without a commitment would violate everything I believe in." He lifted his lips from hers and searched her eyes quietly. "I won't take you. And, yes, I want to. I always have."

She swallowed the tears, wiping them away with the back of her hand. "I'm sorry if I hurt you," she said, avoiding his bold gaze.

"Hurt me how?"

She flushed.

He laughed gently. "Oh. That. No. I had as much pleasure from it as you did." He rolled over onto his back lazily and stretched, feeling years younger and full of life. He sprawled, aware of her fascinated eyes on his body, drinking in that feminine appreciation. "God, that was good," he said huskily. "Good! Like the first sip of water after the desert."

She sat up, a little self-conscious of her nudity, but his eyes were warm and admiring and she forgot her shyness. "But we didn't do anything, really," she said.

He brought her hand to his chest and caressed it. "I felt exactly what you did. The same need, the same sweet release." His head turned toward her. "Sleep with me."

She colored. "You just said . . ."

"That I wouldn't have sex with you," he agreed. "That isn't what I asked. Stay the night. We'll lie in each other's arms and sleep."

Her breath caught. "Could we?"

He drew her to his side, pillowing her head on his broad shoulder. "Yes. We could." His hand reached for the light, and he turned it out, folding her closer. "For tonight," he whispered at her ear, "we're lovers. Even if not conventional ones."

She closed her eyes with ecstasy, wanting to tell him everything, how she felt, how deeply she loved him, needed him. But she didn't dare. He thought it was just desire, and she had to let him keep thinking it. If he knew how involved she was emotionally, his pride wouldn't let him near her again. He wouldn't want to hurt her.

She flattened her hand on his chest and sighed. "This is heaven," she whispered.

He didn't echo the words back, but he could have. He'd never spent an entire night in a woman's arms. The need to keep Jennifer here kept him awake long after she relaxed in sleep.

The next morning, he kissed her awake. He was already dressed, but his eyes were enjoying the sight of her with the covers pulled away in a purely masculine way.

"Nymph," he murmured, sweeping a possessive hand down her body. "How can you be a virgin?"

"Pure living," she said, and laughed delightedly.

He brought her to her feet and kissed her softly. "You'd better get dressed. Morning is a bad time for men, and all my noble scruples aren't going to protect you if I have to look at you this way much longer."

She sighed and leaned against him. "There won't be a man," she whispered. "Not now."

His teeth ground together. Why in God's name did she have to say things like that? "Get dressed," he said tersely.

She was shocked at the sudden change in attitude, at his fierce anger. She pulled back from him, wounded, and searched for her clothes.

He didn't turn his back. He couldn't. He watched her dress, his heart pounding, his body aching for hers. It had taken all his willpower to drag himself out of bed this morning, when he wanted her to the point of madness. It had taken a cold shower and a self-lecture to get himself back in control.

"I wanted you last night," he said huskily. "I want you even more this morning. I'm not trying to be cruel, but the risk is just too damned great, do you understand?"

She was back in her gown now, everything under it in place. She nodded without really understanding and without looking at him and went to get her purse off the dresser, where he must have put it this morning. She took out a small brush and made some sense of her disheveled hair. She shouldn't feel like a fallen woman, she told herself. But she did. She'd thrown herself at him, and he hadn't wanted her enough to take the risk of involvement. It had been just a pleasant interlude to him. But to her, it had been everything.

He stood behind her, in dress slacks and shirt and tie and sports jacket, very urbane and sophisticated. His lean hands held her shoulders and he looked at their joint reflection, his eyes narrowing at the contrast.

"Dark and light," he said curtly. "Indian and white. If I gave you a baby, it would belong to both worlds and neither world. We could never have a child together."

So that was why he was so afraid of not being prepared with her. Because he didn't want her to have his child. It was so final...

She broke down and cried. He whipped her around and held her, rocking her, his arms fiercely possessive, the tremor in her body echoing in his.

"I could love you," he said roughly. "You could become the most important thing in my life. But I won't let it happen. We can't become involved. You have your world, I have mine." He tilted her mouth up to his and his dark eyes were frightening as they searched hers intently. "Kiss me. This is goodbye."

Her mouth opened for his, inviting it, giving him everything he asked for, everything he didn't. He groaned, lifting her into an intimate, exquisite embrace, and she whimpered because the pleasure was overwhelming. She clung to his powerful shoulders, breathing him, while the kiss reached its climax and left them both shaking. He let her slide to the floor, letting her feel his stark, urgent arousal. She was the cause of it; he was proud that he was such a man with her.

She took a slow breath, her mouth red from the aching kiss, and stepped back from him. Something died in her soft blue eyes as she looked up at him, but she managed a smile.

"Do you have a first name?" she whispered.

He nodded. "Phillip. I don't think I've ever told it to anyone else."

She fought back the tears. "Thank you." She turned away from him, picking up her purse with hands that shook. "I'd better go back to my room." She glanced back at him. "It was the best night of my life. I'll live on it forever."

She opened the door and ran out, blind and deaf, almost stumbling in her haste to get across the parlor of the suite to her own room. Such a short distance, yet it was like moving from one life to another, she thought, blind to the tormented face of the man she'd left behind.

Hunter watched her door close, and he leaned heavily against his door facing. It was for the best, he kept telling himself. But the memory of Jennifer in his arms was going to take years to fade. Maybe more years than he even had left.

Eight

Back in her own room, Jennifer changed from her evening dress into slacks and a short-sleeved red silk top, put her blond hair in a ponytail and tied it with a colorful red patterned scarf. But her heart wasn't in how she looked. Hunter had said goodbye, and what he meant was that they could work together for another ten years, but it would never again be more intimate than two colleagues.

She hoped that Eugene would be through with his politicking so that they could go home to Tulsa. She couldn't spend much more time around Hunter without going mad, especially after last night. He knew things about her now that no one else in the world did, and it was faintly unnerving.

His tenderness had surprised and delighted her, despite the circumstances. She wished she knew a little more about men. It occurred to her that a man who'd worked himself into a frenzy wanting a woman would have every right to be furious when he had to draw back. But Hunter hadn't been

angry with her. He'd been kind. Did that mean that he
hadn't wanted her very much in the first place, or did he care
enough to put her feelings before his? She'd never been so
confused, or so embarrassed. It was humiliating to have him
know not only that she was on fire for him, but that she was
a virgin to boot. If he wanted a weapon to use against her,
he had a great one now. She dreaded facing him again. She
had a feeling that last night wouldn't make any difference in
his public treatment of her.

As it turned out, she was right. When she got downstairs
to the restaurant for breakfast, Hunter stood, as did Eugene, for her to be seated, but his expression was stony and
it gave away absolutely nothing.

"Good morning," Eugene said with a smile.

"You look very pretty," Cynthia added.

It wasn't a good morning, and Jennifer didn't feel pretty,
she felt sick all over. She didn't quite meet Hunter's eyes as
she sat down, mumbling something polite.

"Wasn't the ball wonderful?" Cynthia asked with a sigh.
"I've never enjoyed anything quite as much."

"It was super," Jennifer said, staring blankly at her
menu.

"I noticed that you were getting a lot of attention,
Hunter," Eugene murmured dryly. "Especially from our
host's sister."

"She wanted to see my scalps," he explained with a faint
smile. He glanced toward Jennifer, his dark eyes giving
nothing away. "Jennifer rescued me. We both had enough
popularity to suit us by then, so we went back to the hotel."

"Sorry," Eugene said, sobering. "I hadn't realized I'd be
putting you on the spot like that."

"I can handle social warfare," the younger man said im-
perturbably. "How did things work out?"

Eugene grinned. "Great. I got my deal. All we have to do
is wait for the paperwork, and they're going to shoot that
through. We should be able to send you two back down

there to finalize the exact location within a month. I want to talk to two more people today. We'll fly home first thing in the morning.''

At the mention of sending them back to the desert, Jennifer's face went paper white. Under the table, Hunter's lean hand caught hers where it lay on her lap. He enfolded it and his fingers contracted gently, sending a fiery thrill through Jennifer's body.

''I thought you knew where to look,'' Hunter replied.

Eugene nodded. ''Oh, we do. What we're going to need you to do is camp out at a false location, to make sure our friends are led off the beaten track while we're running our seismic survey and doing flyovers.''

''You don't think the agents will be able to hear dynamite blasts going off over the hill when our geologic technicians set up the seismic equipment to register the sound waves?'' Jennifer asked with a smile. Hunter's strong fingers were warm and reassuring around her own, but they were making it hard to breathe normally.

''We'll work something out,'' Eugene said. He studied Jennifer's face with an intensity that made her nervous, especially when his calculating blue eyes went to Hunter. ''Uh, you don't have any problem with spending a few more days out on the desert together?''

''Of course not,'' Hunter said easily.

''No,'' Jennifer agreed, and even smiled.

''You're both lying through your teeth.'' Eugene nodded slowly. ''But I can't help it. You started this for me, you'll have to finish it. I'll try to work things so that we keep the field time to a minimum. Now. What shall we eat?''

Breakfast seemed to take forever. Jennifer still couldn't puzzle out Hunter's behavior. That lean hand wrapped around hers before breakfast had knocked half the breath out of her, even if his expression hadn't revealed anything.

While Eugene and Cynthia stood at the counter, Hunter caught Jennifer's arm and pulled her gently to one side.

"There's no need to look like that," he said softly, his dark eyes searching her shy ones. "It's all right."

"How do I look?" she asked.

"Embarrassed. Shamed." His hand dropped from her arm. "We did nothing last night that would have consequences. You understand?" he added, his dark eyes probing.

She turned red and swallowed hard. "Yes, I know," she said huskily. She couldn't meet his eyes.

"But it still embarrasses you to look at me?"

"Yes," she whispered.

His lean hand touched her long ponytail and he felt at a loss for words for the first time in recent memory. He didn't quite know what to say to her. She was nothing like the woman he'd thought her. He could hardly make himself believe that such a beautiful, desirable woman was totally innocent. And in so many ways. He looked at her mouth and felt again its soft, hungry response, felt the fierce need in her body that he'd wanted so desperately to satisfy. He still ached for her, but the shock of her chastity had spared him the shattering loss of honor he would have felt had he compromised her.

"You were a surprise, little one," he said half under his breath.

"And a big disappointment, I imagine, too," she replied.

"No." He gently tugged her ponytail until she looked up at him. "You don't have to worry about being alone with me on the desert. I'll take care of you. In every way."

She forced a smile. "I'll try not to be too much of a trial to you," she said quietly. "I'm...sorry...about what happened at the ball. I guess you know it all, now, don't you?"

"I know that you're vulnerable," he replied, his eyes soft and very dark. "I won't take advantage of it."

She searched his eyes with helpless attraction. "It's never been like that," she whispered worriedly. "Not ever..."

"We all have an Achilles' heel," he said. "Apparently I'm yours." He smiled gently. "It's all right. We'll muddle through."

"Do you have one?" she asked shyly.

"One what?"

"An Achilles' heel."

He chuckled softly. "Of course. Haven't you guessed yet what it is?"

"Your ancestry," she said with sudden insight.

"Smart lady." He noticed Eugene gesturing toward them and slid a careless arm around her shoulders. He couldn't help but feel the shiver that ran through her slender body, and he felt a little guilty at encouraging her physical infatuation for him. But it flattered his pride and touched his heart. If he didn't put some distance between them pretty soon, she could become a worse Achilles' heel even than his ancestry.

The day wore on, with Jennifer trying desperately not to look at Hunter with equal amounts of possession and wonder, and failing miserably. Eugene stayed in meetings until dinner, so Hunter escorted the women to all the places they hadn't seen before. Nothing had changed on the surface in Hunter's relationship with Jennifer. He didn't touch her except when it was necessary, and he didn't pay her any more attention than he paid Cynthia. Jennifer noticed that, and it made her feel even worse than she already did. The night before had been a revelation to her. But Hunter, even though he seemed a little less rigid with her, betrayed no sudden passion for her. By the time Eugene rejoined them and they had dinner at the restaurant that evening, Jennifer was more depressed than ever.

Hunter noticed her lack of spirit, and he was sorry. It had been equally difficult for him to pretend that nothing had happened. But for his sake as well as Jennifer's he had to keep things on a business basis from now on. He didn't dare risk a repeat of the night before. Having found Jennifer virginal had kept him awake all night. He wanted her more now than he ever had. It was agony to look at her and know that she'd give in to him with hardly any coaxing; to know that she'd give him what she'd never given another man.

He watched her all through dinner, hungry to get her alone, to kiss her until she was too weak to stand up. He didn't dare, of course. He was going to have to think of something to keep him occupied tonight and out of trouble.

Fate did it for him. He went with the women upstairs while Eugene had a drink with another contact. He'd suggested that they go by their suite first, to drop off Jennifer, trying not to notice the wounded look on her young face. But just as they rounded the corner off the elevator, they spotted a man coming out of Jennifer's room.

"Stay here," he said tersely, jerking out his .45 automatic. He was off in one single graceful movement.

Jennifer wanted to scream after him to be careful, her heart in her eyes, her pulses jerking wildly as he pursued the other man down the corridor and around another corner.

"Oh, Lord," Cynthia said huskily, putting a protective arm around Jenny.

"He was in my room," Jennifer said. "I hope he doesn't hurt Hunter! It's got to be some of that same group who broke into my apartment before. They're after my maps!"

"But you didn't bring them, did you?" Cynthia asked worriedly.

"Hunter has them," Jennifer said huskily. "But he hides things well. I suppose my room was the natural one to search."

"Risky for them to come here," Cynthia commented.

Jenny's thoughts were occupied with the man chasing the prowlers. She didn't hear the other woman's words. "I wish Hunter would come back!" She stared down the corridor worriedly.

He did, a minute later, pushing his automatic back into its holster on the way. He looked and felt furiously angry.

Just the thought that the agent could have broken into Jenny's room while she was in it, asleep, made him crazy.

"He got out on a fire escape. There was a car waiting, damn the luck," Hunter said angrily. "We'll have to arrange something for tonight."

"Jennifer can stay with me, and you can stay with Eugene," Cynthia volunteered.

"No." Hunter didn't look at Jennifer. "You're safer with Eugene. I'll be in the suite with Jennifer. Nobody will get in."

"You could sleep on the sofa," Jennifer volunteered with downcast eyes, thrilled that he was being so protective.

"We'll discuss it after we leave Cynthia at her door. I'll post an operative outside it tonight. You'll be safe until Eugene comes up," he promised Cynthia.

"You're very efficient," Cynthia said with a smile, and a teasing glance at Jennifer.

Jennifer didn't say a word. She went along to drop Cynthia off and then minutes later she was alone with Hunter in her room. He had some odd instrument and he went over the entire apartment with it, careful to check everywhere. He discovered two tiny metal devices, which he dealt with before he said a word.

"I've sent a man down to my room to play possum," he told her, shucking his jacket. The shoulder holster was firm around his broad chest, the dark butt of the handle stark against his white shirt.

She shivered at the sinister outline of the gun, at the memory of how Hunter earned his living. Sometimes she could forget it altogether, but not at times like this, and she feared for him.

He saw that nervous scrutiny and lifted an eyebrow. "I won't shoot you by mistake," he murmured dryly.

"It's not that." She wrapped her arms around his chest. "They never give up, do they?"

"From what you've told me about strategic metals, I'm not surprised." He moved closer, his lean hands smoothing over her shoulders. "Lie down and get some sleep, if you can. In the morning we'll go home. A couple of weeks in the desert while things are finalized, and we'll be home free. No more danger."

"Yes." And no more interludes like this. She thought it, but she didn't say it.

His dark eyes held hers. "Go on," he said gently. "I told you last night, there won't be any more close calls."

"I know. I'm a little nervous about the intruder, that's all," she lied.

"Of course." He knew she was lying. He watched her put away the clothes that had been disarranged, seeing the way she grimaced at the thought of strange hands on her things. But she packed them before she got out a nightgown. He was standing in the doorway, and his expression was grim.

"Are you...going to stay there while I change?" she asked huskily.

His jaw tautened. "If I did, you wouldn't spend the night alone."

He turned away and closed the door, trying not to picture Jennifer's soft, nude body in that room.

It was a long night, but there were no incidents. The next morning when Jennifer got up and dressed, Hunter was on his way out of the suite.

"Marlowe's outside the door," he said tersely. "We leave for the airport in thirty minutes."

"I'll be ready," she said quietly.

He nodded curtly and closed the door behind him.

They flew back to Tulsa that morning, but Jennifer barely had time to get settled back in her apartment before she and Hunter were on a plane heading to southern Arizona all over again.

"Same song, second verse," she murmured as they took the camping equipment back out to the desert, having gone through the process of renting a four-wheel-drive vehicle and buying camping equipment all over again.

He glanced at her, a smoking cigarette in his hand. "Well, it's not quite so bad. This time you don't have to do any real prospecting. We're only camping out."

"No television, no movies. Just the two of us and a handful of enemy agents, right?" she mused, trying not to give away how miserable she was.

"It won't be that bad," he said with a faint smile. "I'll teach you how to track and all about Apache customs. We'll get by."

She nodded. "With bullets whizzing around us and people trying to kill us for a mineral strike, right?"

"Stop that. Nobody's going to try to kill you. They want the land, not bodies."

She wished that was reassuring, but it wasn't.

They pitched the tent at the site they'd occupied the first night when they were here before. It was a good six miles from the actual site, but still close enough that seismic tests could be detected with the right monitors. But Eugene was an old fox, and her rock samples had been assayed by now. He used seismic tests extensively when he was searching for oil deposits, but moly was a different element and there were all sorts of detecting devices he could use to search out deposits.

"Nervous?" Hunter asked as they pitched camp.

She nodded. "A little."

He built a fire and proceeded to prepare food, a process Jennifer watched with fascination.

"Hunter, did you grow up around here?" he asked suddenly.

He nodded. "I used to wander all over this country as a boy. Within limits, of course. I kept to the reservation."

She studied him across the camp fire. "And now?"

He looked up, studying her face in the flames. Even in jeans and a floppy T-shirt she was gorgeous, he thought. "Now I live in Tulsa."

"You said you kept horses."

"Yes. On the reservation. I own a small homestead. The house is my refuge. Actually I should say that the tribe owns the land, and ownership is overseen by the tribal council. We aren't allowed to sell any land without approval from the Bureau of Indian Affairs. The reasoning for that is a long story, and one I'd rather not go into right now," he added when she started to speak.

"All right," she said easily. He handed her a plate of stew and a cup of black coffee, adding a couple of slices of loaf bread to her plate. She ate hungrily. "Something about the night air gives me an appetite," she sighed when she finished. "Look at the stars. They're bigger here. And it's so quiet... Well, except for the coyotes and an occasional four-wheel-drive vehicle and the sound of rifle fire as people shoot road signs for amusement."

He glanced at her ruefully. "You're poetic."

"Oh, very." She wrapped her hands around her knees and stared at them.

He watched her for a minute, remembering another night alone, at another camp site, and her bare breasts in the moonlight. He got up suddenly.

"I'll have a look around. You might go ahead and turn in. It's been a long day."

"Yes, I think I will," she agreed easily. She went into the tent and got into her sleeping bag. Amazingly she was asleep when he finally came to bed.

The days went by all too slowly, and by the end of the week, Jennifer's nerves were raw and she was snapping at Hunter. He wasn't in any too good a humor himself. Jennifer lying beside him in the tent night after night was driving him out of his mind. The scent of her, the sound of her, the sight of her were so firmly imbedded in his brain that he felt part of her already.

The memories didn't help. He'd come so close to possessing her, and now his body knew the reality of hers and wanted it. The hunger kept gnawing at him, making him impatient and irritable.

"Must you keep turning those scanners on?" Jennifer asked when the police scanner began to get on her nerves the Friday night after they'd arrived.

"Yes, I must," he said tersely. "They're reporting an incident near here—presumably at the test site where Eugene's geologic technicians are working. I'm going to have a look. Stay close to the tent. Have you still got that .22 rifle I gave you?"

"Yes, and I can use it," she replied. "Was anybody hurt?" she asked.

"If I knew that, why would I be going to check it out?" he asked curtly. "What a damned stupid question!"

"Well, I'm not a trained agent, so you'll have to forgive my ignorance!" she shot back. "Go ahead and get shot! I won't cry over you!"

"I never expected that you would," he returned. He got into the four-wheel drive and took off without looking back.

Jennifer's nerve deserted her the minute the Jeep disappeared. She sat down beside the scanner and listened to it uneasily, glancing around with the rifle across her legs. She didn't know what had happened, and the fact that the agents were the most likely people to be bothering the technicians was unsettling news. What if they came here and tried to shake the information they wanted out of her while Hunter was gone?

That was ridiculous, of course. She laughed out loud. Of course they wouldn't come here . . .

The sound of a Jeep alerted her and she jumped up. Hunter, she thought with relief. She ran toward the rutted road with the rifle in time to be caught in the headlights of the vehicle that was approaching. There was an exclamation and a shot as the vehicle suddenly reversed and rushed off in the other direction.

Jennifer felt something hot against her arm, like a sudden sting. She touched it and her fingers came away wet.

She looked down at her arm. She could see a dark stain in the faint light from the camp fire. She lifted her fingers closer and the unmistakable smell of blood was on her hand!

I've been shot, she thought in astonishment. My God, I've been shot!

She sat down heavily next to the camp fire, with the rifle still in her shaking hands. If only Hunter would come back! She was alone and afraid and she didn't know what to do. Obviously the agents had come roaring into camp with the intention of seeking information. They hadn't expected her to come running toward them with a rifle. They'd shot at her in apparent self-defense and had raced away before she could get a shot off at them. It might be funny later. Right now, it was terrifying.

Her arm hurt. She grimaced. The sound of a vehicle approaching came again, but this time, she didn't run toward it. She raised the rifle, wincing as her arm protested, and leveled it at the dark shape spurting into camp.

"That's far enough!" she called out.

The engine and lights were cut off. The door opened. "Shoot and be damned," Hunter's deep voice replied.

Nine

Jenny thought that as long as she lived, she'd never forget the expression on Hunter's face when she collapsed in his arms and he discovered that she'd been shot.

She managed to explain what had happened while he laid her gently on her sleeping bag inside the tent and moved the Coleman lantern closer to check the wound.

"I must have passed them coming back. Damn it!" he burst out, adding something in a very gutteral language that seemed to raise and lower in pitch and stop suddenly between syllables.

"Is that... cursing?" she asked.

"Yes, and thank your stars you can't translate it," he added icily. He glanced down at her. "They raided the other camp, but they were a little too late. The technicians flew back to Tulsa this afternoon with the data. They left the tents and other gear, just as Eugene had instructed, to give them time to get away. They were supposed to contact us, but apparently they were being watched too closely."

"Eugene will kill them," she murmured, groaning when his fingers touched around the gash in her soft skin.

"If he doesn't, I will," he returned. "Which is nothing to what I intend doing to the man who shot you."

She stared up at him through waves of pain. His eyes were frightening, and at that moment he looked pagan, untamed.

"It isn't bad," she said, trying to ease the tension she could almost taste as his hard, deft fingers searched around the cut. They seemed just slightly unsteady. Imagine anything shaking the stoic Mr. Hunter, she thought with hysterical amusement.

"I can't see properly in this light. Come on." He helped her to the vehicle and helped her into the passenger side. He turned on the overhead light after he'd climbed quickly in beside her, and once more his eyes were on the cut. "You can manage without stitches, but it needs an antiseptic."

"There might be a drugstore . . ." she offered.

He turned off the light and started the engine. He never seemed to feel the need to answer questions, she sighed to herself. Amazing how he expected her to read his mind.

"But what about our things?" she asked.

He cursed again, turning around. "Wait here." He left the engine running, put out the camp fire, got her case and his out of the tent along with the technical gear, and left the rest of it.

"But the tent, the sleeping bags . . ." she began. He glanced at her and she stopped when she saw his expression. She cleared her throat. "Never mind."

He set off into the desert and drove for what seemed forever until he came to a small house, set against the jagged peak of one of southern Arizona's endless mountain chains. He pulled into the dirt driveway, and Jenny wondered whose home it was. The house was livable, just, but it needed painting and patching and a new roof.

"Come on." He opened the door and helped her out.

"It's a beautiful setting," she murmured as she drank in the sweet, clear air and looked around the yard at the ocotillo and cholla and agave that surrounded the yard. "Like being alone in the world."

"I've always thought so," he said stiffly. He escorted her onto the porch and produced a key to unlock the door. He didn't look at her as he opened it and pulled the screen door back to let her enter the living room.

It was nothing like the exterior of the house, she noticed as he pulled a long chain and the bare light bulb in the ceiling came on. The living room was comfortable and neat, with padded armchairs and cane-bottomed chairs, Indian rugs on the floors and spread over the backs of the chairs. There was some kind of furry round shield with tiny fur tails hanging from it, and basketry everywhere.

Hunter was watching her, waiting for disgust or contempt to show on her soft face. But she seemed fascinated; almost charmed by what she saw.

She turned back to him, her eyes shining despite the faint throb of the wound on her arm. "It's your house, isn't it?" she asked.

His dark eyebrows arched. "Yes."

"You're wondering how I knew," she murmured dryly. "It's simple. You're the only person I know who would enjoy living totally alone in the world with no nosy neighbors. And this," she gestured toward the living room, "is how I'd picture your living room."

He managed a faint smile. "Come on. I'll put a patch on the injury, then I'll find something to cook."

"All right."

"No comment about the cooking?" he added, leading her into a stark white bathroom with aging fixtures.

"I'd be surprised if you couldn't cook. You seem so self-sufficient."

"I've always had to be," he said simply. He stripped off his jacket, rolled up his sleeves and got out medicine and bandages from the cabinet over the sink. "My father died when I was small. I lived with my grandfather, on the reservation, until I was old enough to enlist. When I got out of the Green Berets, I kicked around for a few years doing other things. Eventually Ritter offered me a job and I've been there ever since."

"No wife, ever?" she asked hesitantly.

His dark, quiet eyes met hers. "Women don't fit in a place like this," he said. "It's stark and bare-bone comfort, and it's lonely. In case you haven't guessed, this is part of the reservation, too." He waited for her reaction, but there wasn't one. He shrugged and continued. "I'm away most of the time. I've never asked anyone to share it because I don't think a woman could. My job would be an immediate point of contention and my heritage would be another. I live on the reservation," he added with a mocking smile. "I can see how that would go over with most in-laws. And I believe in some of the old ways, especially in family life."

"A woman's place is three steps behind the man..." she began.

"A man should behave as one," he returned simply. "And a woman has her place—a very special place—in the order of things. She gives life, nurtures it. She gives warmth and light to her man, her children." He ran a basin of water, found a cloth and bathed the wound on Jenny's arm. "But, no, I don't think her place is three steps behind her man, or that she becomes property when she marries. Perhaps you don't know, but in the old days, many Apache women fought right alongside their men and were as respected as the warriors."

"No, I didn't know," she confessed. The touch of his fingers was painful delight. Her eyes glanced over the hard lines of his dark face with pure pleasure. "You're proud of your ancestry, aren't you?"

He looked down at her. "My people are like a separate state, under federal jurisdiction," he replied. "We have our own laws, our own reservation police, our own code of behavior. When we live in your world, we seem alien." He laughed coldly. "I wish I could tell you how many times in my life I've been called Tonto or Chief, and how many fights I've been into because of it."

She was beginning to understand him. He'd grown a shell, she supposed, because of the difficulties. And now he was trapped in it and couldn't find his way out.

"I know a little about prejudice," she said, surprising him. "I'm a female geologist and I work in the oil business." She smiled. "Equality is all the rage in accounting and law firms back east, and even in corporations. But out in the boondocks in the oil exploration game, there are Neanderthal men who think a woman goes to those lonely places for just one reason. I wish I had a nickel for every time I've had to threaten someone with a suit for sexual harassment."

"Looking the way you do, I can understand your problem," he mused, glancing at her with dancing dark eyes. "How does this feel?" he added when he'd put antiseptic on the wound and lightly bandaged it.

"It feels much better, thank you," she said. Her eyes searched his dark face while he put away the medicine. "What do you mean, the way I look?"

He closed the cabinet and gazed down at her. His face was expressionless except for the dark, disturbing glitter in his eyes as they slid down her body and up again. "Is it important to hear me say it?" he asked. "You know how lovely you are."

Her breath caught. "I've been told I was," she corrected. "It never meant anything. Before."

His jaw clenched. He stared at her until she flushed and still his eyes didn't waver or even blink. "Be careful," he said quietly. "I still want you very badly."

"I'm twenty-seven years old," she whispered. "If it isn't you, it won't be anybody. Ever. I said that once. I meant it."

His breath expelled roughly. He caught her around the waist and pulled her up from the edge of the bathtub where she'd been sitting. His arm was steely strong, and the feel and scent of him so close made her almost moan with pleasure.

"How much do you know about birth control?" he asked bluntly.

"I know that babies come if you don't use any," she replied, trying to sound sophisticated with a beet-red face.

His eyes were relentless. "And do you think I'm prepared for casual interludes with women all the time?"

"Most men are," she faltered.

"I'm not most men," he returned. "These days I think of sex as something that goes hand in hand with love, respect, honor. It used to be a casual amusement when I was a young man. I'm thirty-seven now, and it isn't casual or amusing anymore. It's serious business."

She could have reminded him that for a few minutes one night, he'd forgotten all those reasons, but she didn't. Her eyes fell to his firm chin. "It isn't casual with me, either," she whispered "But I'd give anything . . . !" She bit her lip. "I'm sorry."

His hand came up, framing her own chin, lifting her eyes to his. "You'd give anything . . . ?" he prompted slowly.

She closed her eyes so that he wouldn't see the longing. So that she wouldn't throw herself at him again, as she had that night in Washington. "Nothing. I'm just tired. I wasn't thinking."

"I know you're infatuated with me," he said out of the blue.

Her eyes flew open, startled. "What?"

"It isn't something you hide well," he replied. His eyes narrowed. "I've had hell trying not to take advantage of it. I'm a new experience for you, something out of the ordinary, and I know already how you seek the unusual. But since you don't know, I'll tell you. Sex is the same with an Apache as it is with a white man, in case you—"

He broke off because she slapped him, with the full strength of her arm behind the blow. Tears welled in her eyes; her face had gone white with shock and grief.

He didn't flinch. He let her go, very gently, and moved away. "I'll see about something to eat," he said, with no inflection at all in his voice as he started toward the kitchen.

Jenny cried. She closed the bathroom door and cried until her throat hurt. If he'd tried for months to think up something hurtful, he couldn't have succeeded any better. She knew he was aware of her desire for him, but she hadn't known he was aware of her feelings, too. It made her too vulnerable.

Finally she dried her eyes and went out without looking in the small mirror. She could imagine what she looked like without having to see herself.

He glanced at her and his expression hardened as he proceeded to fry steak and eggs. "I'd expected to spend the weekend here, so I loaded up on supplies yesterday," he said. "You can set the table."

She took the dishes from the cabinet he gestured toward and set two places, including a mug for the coffee that was brewing in the modern coffeepot. She took her time meticulously folding two paper towels to go at each place.

"Utensils?" she asked in a totally defeated tone.

"Here." He opened the drawer beside him, but as she moved closer to reach inside it, he turned suddenly and pulled her to him. His mouth eased down over hers with a gentle, insistent pressure that caught her completely off guard. She felt his strong teeth nipping tenderly at her lower lip until her mouth opened for him. Then she felt his tongue inside, touching her own, his arm contracting, the sound that echoed out of his throat, deep and gruff and faintly threatening.

Her nails bit into his back where her arms had gone under his and around him, and she bit off a short, sharp little cry as the pleasure cut the ground from under her feet. The injury to her arm was still throbbing, but she held on for dear life, uncaring in the thrall of such aching pleasure. She didn't want him to stop, not ever!

All too soon, he lifted his head. His eyes were dark with emotion, his jaw clenched. "Finish setting the table," he said huskily, and abruptly let her go to concentrate on the Spanish omelet he was making.

She couldn't help the trembling of her hands as she complied with that request. It wasn't until they were halfway through the impromptu meal and the strong, fresh coffee that she was able to get some kind of control over herself.

"To continue what I started to say when we were in the bathroom, I'm not prepared for an intimate encounter," he said when she laid down her fork. He didn't look at her as he said it. His eyes were on the coffee cup in his hand. "And as I told you in Washington that night, half-breed children belong in no one's world."

Her eyes searched his face. A suspicion at the back of her mind began to take shape. He looked Apache. There was no doubt about that part of his heritage. But the way he felt about mixing the races, wasn't it violent if he'd never had experience of it?

"Which one of your parents was white, Phillip?" she asked softly.

His head jerked up. His eyes flashed at her. "What did you say?" he asked in a tone that should have backed her down. It didn't.

"I said, which one of your parents was white?"

"I'd forgotten that I told you my given name," he said softly. "You've never used it."

She began to realize, belatedly, that it was her use of his first name that had rattled him, not her reference to his parentage. She hesitated. "I didn't realize I had," she said after a minute.

He leaned back, troubled, the coffee cup still in his lean, dark hand. He watched her intently. "My mother was white, Jennifer," he said finally.

"Is she still alive?"

He shrugged. "I don't know. She couldn't take life on the reservation, and my father was too Apache to leave it. She left when I was five and I haven't seen her since. My father died a year later. He gave up. Life without her, he said, was no life. I always consider that I lost both my parents when I was five, so I don't qualify the statement. I don't know where my mother is." His face hardened. "I don't care. Her family put me through school and supported me while I was younger. I didn't find out until I was much older. My grandfather never would have told me, but I found a check stub. He was a proud man." He looked down at his hands. "Life on the reservation is hard. Unemployment, infant mortality, poverty... It's no one's idea of the American dream. He took the money for my sake, not for his. What he didn't spend on me, he sent back."

She stretched her hand toward his free one, lying on the table and abruptly stopped. He wouldn't want sympathy, she supposed.

But surprisingly, his own hand slid the remaining distance and enveloped hers, his thumb softly stroking her palm. "White and brown," he observed, staring at the differences in color. "I'm still Apache, Jenny, despite my white blood. But if I had a child with a white woman, he'd be a lost soul, like me. Caught between two worlds. My own people have a hard time accepting me, even though I look more Apache than white."

Her eyes adored him. "I can't imagine a more handsome man of either race," she said quietly.

His face went a ruddy color, and she wondered if it was possible to embarrass him.

She smiled wickedly. "My, my, are you *blushing*?"

He let go of her hand with an outright laugh. "Compliments are difficult for me," he said gruffly. "Eat your omelet."

She picked up her fork with a sigh, wincing a little as the movement made her arm uncomfortable. "Can I ask why we aren't having bacon or sausage with our eggs?" she murmured.

"Apaches don't eat pork," he said. "Or fish. Ever."

"Why?" she asked, astonished.

"Beats me. We just don't."

"I thought I knew something about your people. I suppose I don't know much at all."

He smiled to himself. "You know more than most whites."

"I guess that operative of yours who's Papago knows more," she murmured without looking at him. "She's the kind of woman you'll marry one day, isn't she?"

He frowned down at his omelet. "I don't know that I'll marry at all," he said. He lifted his eyes to her sad face and felt a wave of grief that almost knocked him flat. She was infatuated with him, but she could never endure life here. She was beautiful and sweet and he wanted her until she was all but an obsession. But his mind kept insisting that he couldn't risk having her turn out like his mother. His mother hadn't been able to take living in an Indian world.

She sighed wearily. "I've had the same feeling lately. I'm almost twenty-eight. Despite the fact that women are becoming mothers later and later in life, I don't really like the risk factors after thirty-five." She smiled at her omelet as she cut it. "Funny. I always thought I might make a pretty good mother."

"You've had the opportunity to marry," he said stiffly.

"Oh, of course. Soft, carefree city men who have affairs and look upon marriage as slow death. I had one proposal from a man who was twenty years older than me and wanted to live in Alaska." She glanced up. "I hate polar bears."

He smiled. "So do I."

"My other proposal was from a boy my age when I was eighteen, and he only wanted to marry me to get away from his parents. He was rich and I wasn't—it was a sort of rebellion." She put down her fork. "I've never been asked to marry anybody because I was loved. Wanted, yes. But that wasn't enough."

"You're not over the hill," he reminded her.

"It doesn't matter." She looked up at him, her eyes wide and soft and gentle. "I'm sorry you stopped that night in Washington," she said huskily. "I wouldn't have regretted it, ever."

His jaw tautened. He finished his steak and washed it down with coffee. "It would have hurt like hell."

She traced the rim of her plate, her heart beating madly at the memory of his arms around her, his body intimately over her own. "It wouldn't have hurt long," she whispered. "I wanted you too badly to care."

"God, yes, you did," he said through his teeth. The memories were driving him crazy. "Shaking in my arms, and I'd barely touched you. By the time I put my mouth on yours, you were trembling all over with the need. I never dreamed that women felt it like that."

"Maybe most women don't feel it like that," she said uneasily. "Maybe there's, well, something wrong with me...."

"There's nothing wrong with you that a night in my arms wouldn't cure," he said curtly. His dark eyes caught her blue ones and held them hotly. "But it would only be a night, and we'd have the rest of our lives to regret it."

Her lips parted as she searched his eyes. "No, we wouldn't," she whispered. "And you know it. You want me just as much as I want you."

He nodded slowly, his gaze dropping to her full breasts and back up again to her mouth and her eyes. "You can only give your chastity once."

"I know that, too," she replied. "I meant what I said. If it isn't you, it won't be anybody." Her breath sighed out raggedly. "I love you," she said achingly.

He let out a long, weary sigh. After a minute he got up and held out his hand. She took it, feeling his lean fingers enfold hers, wrap gently around them.

He led her into his bedroom without speaking and closed the door. "Do you want the light out?" he asked.

She bit her lower lip. She wanted to be sophisticated and worldly, but she was already blushing.

He smiled with bitter irony. "Never mind." He reached up and turned off the light, leaving the room in almost total darkness, except for the half moon that left its yellow shadow over the patchwork quilt on the bed.

"What do we do now?" she whispered, her voice husky with excitement and faint apprehension.

"What we did in my hotel room that night in Washington," he murmured as his hands reached for her. "Except that this time I won't pull back when I feel the barrier..."

"Phillip." She moaned his name into his mouth as it came down on hers, gasping when she felt him pull her hips roughly into the already aroused thrust of his.

"This is how badly I want you," he whispered, his breathing mingling with hers. "It happens the minute your body touches mine. Magic."

"Yes." She pulled his shirt out of his jeans and slid her hands up against his bare back, feeling the taut muscles, the rough silk of his skin. It was cool, and seconds later when her bare breasts melted into the hard wall of his chest, that was cool, too, against the heated warmth of her own skin.

When he had every scrap of material away from their bodies, he lifted her, with his mouth gently moving on her own, and laid her on the quilt. His hand went to the bedside table. He opened a drawer and removed something. Seconds later, he placed it in her hand and taught her how to put it in place. Even that was exciting and sensual in the hot darkness.

"This is so we won't make a baby," he whispered, his voice deep and slow as he moved over her. His teeth nibbled softly at her upper lip. His lean hands smoothed down her body, lingering on her soft thighs, making her tremble with the pleasure of his touch.

Her body was shivering. He kissed her tenderly, and then his mouth moved down to her breasts and caressed their hard tips until she was writhing under him.

"You like that, don't you?" he whispered. "I like it, too, little one. You taste of satin here, and of desire here," he breathed against a taut nipple, his lips pulling at it with sensual tenderness.

She clung to his muscular arms, her breath coming in jerks while he kissed and touched and tasted, the darkness like a warm blanket over her fears.

When she was shuddering, he eased her trembling legs apart and levered himself down between them, his mouth poised just above her own, his eyes glittered into hers in the darkness. He probed tenderly and felt her tense.

"When I push down, try not to do that," he whispered. "If you tense up, it's going to hurt more."

She shivered with delicious anticipation, her body throbbing with a heat it had never felt before. Her legs moved to admit him even closer and her nails bit into his shoulders. "I'll try," she breathed.

His chest rose and fell deeply. His hips moved down, and she made a noise deep in her throat as she felt the burning pain. She tensed involuntarily. "I'm... sorry," she gasped.

"It can't be be helped," he said quietly. "I'm going to have to hurt you. Cry out if you want to. I'm sorry...!"

She did, because it was worse than she'd imagined it would be. But she didn't fight him or try to push him away even then. She bit her lip and moaned, trying to force her body to relax as it protested the invasion of his.

"Only a little longer," he whispered. His mouth came closer. "Kiss me. It will help."

She let him take her mouth, opened it to admit the slow, deep penetration of his tongue that imitated what his body was doing to hers. It was so erotic that it tricked her taut muscles into relaxing, and suddenly what had been almost impossible was easy and smooth.

He heard her intake of breath and lifted his head, smiling down at her through his own fierce excitement. The act of possession was almost enough to trigger his fulfillment. He had to stop and breathe himself to keep control.

"Phillip," she whispered achingly. Her eyes sought his, and she could barely believe it was happening, at last.

"How does it feel?" he whispered at her lips.

"Incredible," she managed, her voice shaking.

"And we haven't begun," he breathed as his mouth began to open on hers. His hips lifted and moved and she shivered, because the surge of pleasure she felt shocked her.

The sound of the car roaring up outside was an interruption that froze them both in incredulous shock.

"My God," he ground out. "No!"

But the car was stopping. Worse, there were lights flashing, so it had to be a police car.

He lifted himself away from her, shuddering as he fell onto his back and arched. He groaned and stiffened, while Jennifer tried to weather the frustration and anger she felt.

There were footsteps on the porch and a loud, heavy knock at the door.

"Just a minute!" Hunter shouted. He got up, pulling on his jeans with hands that shook. "God almighty, I'll kill someone for this!" he muttered. He leaned over Jennifer's shivering body and bent to kiss her with rough hunger. "Get dressed, quickly."

He left the room and she turned on the light, hurrying to get back into her clothes and make some kind of order in the room. She brushed her hair with his hairbrush and, satisfied that she looked as presentable as possible, she opened the bedroom door.

Hunter was talking to another man. They had to be speaking Apache, because Jennifer couldn't understand a word.

"This is Choya," Hunter introduced the shorter man. "He's chief of the reservation police. I've been telling him what happened. Since the incident occurred on Apache land, he'll be responsible for the investigation and any arrests."

"In other words, I get all the headaches," the newcomer grinned, perfect white teeth flashing. "My God, Hunter, I go home to a wife with buck teeth and you have her." He shook his head. "I need to change medicine men."

Hunter chuckled. "You know Maria's the prettiest woman around, so shut up. Is there anything else you need to know?"

"Not tonight," Choya said, and exchanged a knowing glance with Hunter. "Sorry about my timing. I'll get back on the road now. Good night."

"Good night," Jennifer said, blushing all over.

Hunter closed the door behind him and turned to Jennifer. He didn't move until the car drove away, his dark eyes sliding over her, his dark, bare chest lifting and falling slowly.

"Come here," he said curtly.

She went to him without hesitation. He lifted her, but instead of carrying her back into the bedroom, he carried her to the rocking chair and sat down with her across his lap.

"Thanks to Choya, we can't finish what we started," he said, smiling into her heated face. "I was prepared, but only for one time." He bent and drew his mouth slowly over hers. "Still burning?" he breathed.

His hand was on the buttons of her blouse, which she put on without her bra, and now he knew it. She arched, letting him look, letting him touch.

Her fingers tangled in his dark hair and pulled, tugging his face toward her bare breasts.

"All right," he whispered. "Is this what you want?"

It was. Oh, it was, she thought in sweet anguish, loving the touch of his mouth on her velvety skin. She lay in his arms and made no protest when he stripped off her jeans and underwear. His hand found her and moved, and his mouth reached up for hers. He rocked the chair and touched her rhythmically, and the combined force of the sensual movements very quickly brought an explosive culmination in her taut body.

She cried out and shivered and was still. He gathered her close beside him, her breasts brushing his bare chest, his cheek against her hair.

"It isn't enough," he whispered. "But it's safe. One day, so help me, I'll put you under me in bed and fill you until you scream."

She bit his shoulder in anguished need, and he shuddered and brought her even closer. "What about you?" she asked huskily.

"Don't worry about me," he said, ignoring his own need. He could handle it. He'd have to, he couldn't take the risk.

"You're no longer a virgin, technically," he said, lifting his head to search her eyes. "Despite the fact that we were barely together, I had your virginity tonight."

She smiled up at him with awe. "Yes."

He touched her mouth, tracing her lips with a finger that wasn't quite steady. "And you don't regret it?"

"No," she whispered.

His jaw clenched as his eyes fell to her bare breasts. "Neither do I," he said. "You belong to me."

"I know."

His eyes flashed as they met hers. "There won't be another man."

"I know that, too."

He stared into her eyes for a long moment, then he stood and carried her back into the bedroom. He stripped himself before he turned out the light and put her under the covers. He drew her body against his and pressed her cheek into his bare shoulder with a long, rough sigh.

"In the morning, get up as quickly as you can," he said at her ear. "A man awakens aroused and his wits are dulled by it. Don't be tempted to take chances. I won't forget and I won't forgive."

She sighed. "All right," she said reluctantly. She closed her eyes, pressing her hand flat on his chest and curling into his taut body. "Good night, Phillip."

His hand covered hers. "Good night, little one." He brushed a careless kiss against her forehead and then her eyes, lingering on the thick, long lashes.

"I'm sorry," she whispered.

"For what?"

"You had nothing."

His body was taut but he tried to ignore it. "I'll live," he murmured, trying to keep his voice light.

But she heard the stress in it. Hesitantly she slid her hand down his body and felt him tense. She waited for him to stop her, but he didn't. She heard his breathing change and felt his body arch in a slow, delicate rhythm. Her fingers moved down and he arched into them.

"Yes," he whispered, his eyes closed.

She stroked him, feeling him throb, feeling him tauten, hearing the anguished groan that broke from his lips as her hand explored him.

"Do it," he bit off.

He taught her, kicking the covers off, his eyes glittering in the darkness. She heard his breathing become tortured, watched his body react to her shy, loving touch. He watched her until it became impossible and then he arched up, crying out, and she learned things about men that all her reading hadn't prepared her for.

Eventually they slept. She supposed that she should regret what had happened. If she ever did marry, even if she hadn't been totally seduced, she was no longer completely chaste. But it was Hunter she'd given that privilege to, and she had no regrets. She loved him so deeply that she could live on tonight, forever if she had to.

She got up the next morning and went into the living room with shy reluctance. She never quite knew what to expect from Hunter, because he was so unpredictable.

He was putting food on the table. He glanced up. "I was about to call you," he said politely. "Sit down."

It was as if nothing had ever happened between them. She stared at him curiously as she sat in the chair.

He poured coffee with a straight face. "How's the arm?"

"It's sore, but I think it will be all right."

"We'll get you to a doctor before we leave for the airport. We're going home today."

"So soon?"

"It's past time," he returned tersely, and the eyes that met hers were angry. "Last night should never have happened. You have a very disturbing effect on my willpower, and I'm tired of it. I'm taking you back to Tulsa. If there's another assignment like this, I'll send one of my operatives with you instead. There aren't going to be any repeats."

She lowered her eyes to the table. "You can't bear to lose control in any way, can you?"

"No," he replied honestly. "You're becoming a liability, and I can't afford one. My job requires total concentration. What I feel when I'm around you could get us both killed. I made a mistake last night that could have been fatal. I left you alone. If we hadn't been at each other's throats out of simple physical frustration, I'd have had the presence of mind to take you with me. But I didn't."

"I'm all right," she said quietly.

"You could have died. Or I could have. I've had enough emotional stress to last me a lifetime, Jennifer," he said, his voice final. "From now on, I'll stick to women who can give out and get out. No more lovesick virgins."

She went scarlet. She couldn't even deny it. "I'll do my best to stay out of your way," she said.

"That would be appreciated," he replied. He couldn't look at her. It was hurting him to cut her up like this, but he had to make her angry enough to keep away from him. Wanting her was becoming an obsession that could cost him his job or his life under the right circumstances.

She dragged her eyes up for one brief instant. "Are you sorry we made love?" she asked huskily.

"Yes, I'm sorry," he said without a flicker of emotion. "I told you I'd been without a woman for a long time. You were handy, and you must know how beautiful you are." He forced a mocking smile. "It would have been a unique experience. I've never had a willing virgin before. But the newness would have worn off before morning, I'm afraid. I prefer an experienced woman in bed. Someone who knows how to play the game without expecting declarations of love and proposals of marriage."

Her face was very pale, but she smiled. "Well, no harm done," she said gamely. "Thanks for the instruction." She lowered her eyes to her coffee cup. "What time do you want to leave?"

He couldn't repress admiration for her bravery. No tears, no accusations, just acceptance despite her pain. That made it worse somehow. But he had to be strong.

He got up. "In half an hour," he said. "Leave the dishes. I'll be coming back here when I've put you on the plane."

"You aren't coming?" she exclaimed.

"No. I've got some leave due. I'm taking it now. I'll phone Eugene from the airport. Get your things together, please."

It was so hurried—the trip to the doctor's office, the antibiotic and tetanus shots, the rush to get to the airport in time to board a plane for Tulsa. She was en route before she realized how shocked and hurt she really was. It was a good thing that he hadn't let her say goodbye, so that she didn't break down. He'd given her the ticket, said something about having someone meet her at the airport, and then he'd left her at the right concourse gate without a goodbye or a backward glance.

She got off the plane in Tulsa and there was a car waiting. It whisked her back to her apartment. Once she got into it, she threw herself on her bed and cried until her eyes were red. But it didn't take away the sting of knowing that Hunter

had only desired her. She'd given him everything she had to
give, and he'd still walked away without a backward glance.
She loved him more than her own life. How was she going
to live without him?

Ten

Jennifer couldn't decide what to do. She was so miserable that she only went through the motions of doing a job that she'd once loved. Her co-workers noticed the quiet pain in her face, but they were too kind to mention it.

Eugene got his molybdenum mine. The deal went through with flying colors, and the enemy agents went home in disgrace, having pursued the wrong site and gotten themselves in eternal hot water with their furious superiors.

Hunter stayed on vacation for a couple of weeks. When he came back into the office, he pointedly ignored Jennifer, refusing to even look her way when he passed her in the hall.

His attitude cut her to the bone. She lost weight and began to give in to nerves. She jumped when people approached unexpectedly. She made mistakes on her charts—the kind that she never would have made before. Eugene called her on the carpet for her latest error, which had cost the company a good deal of money drilling in what turned out to be a dry hole.

"Everybody hits a dry hole once or twice," he raged at her in the privacy of his office. "And under normal circumstances, it's excusable. But, damn it, this isn't! This was carelessness, Jennifer, plain and simple."

"Yes, it was. And I'm going to turn in my resignation," she said, amazed to hear the words coming from her lips.

Apparently Eugene was, too, because he stopped in mid-tirade to scowl at her. His blue eyes narrowed and he studied her. After a minute, he leaned back in his chair with a long sigh.

"It's Hunter, of course," he said out loud, nodding at her shocked expression. "He tried to quit a couple of weeks ago, too. I refused his resignation and I'm refusing yours. You don't have to see each other. I've already made arrangements to transfer him to our Phoenix office for a few months. He leaves at the end of the week."

She didn't know what to say. It wasn't going to do any good to deny it. But it puzzled her that Hunter had offered to resign. She knew how much he loved his job.

"Surprises you that he tried to quit, doesn't it?" he asked her. "He wouldn't give a reason, but he keeps trying to get assignments out of the country. You, on the other hand, keep refusing any assignment that would require him to look after you. Interesting, isn't it?" He leaned forward abruptly. "What happened out on the desert? Did he make a pass?"

She lowered her eyes to the floor so they wouldn't give her away. "We had some differences of opinion," she replied. "And we agreed that it would be better if we kept out of each other's way in the future."

"Is that why you're losing weight and making one mistake on top of another?" he asked pleasantly.

She lifted her face proudly and stared him down. "I cost you a lot of money, so I guess you're entitled to know. I'm in love with him."

"How does he feel?"

"Mr. Hunter doesn't tell anyone how he feels," she replied. "He said point-blank that he doesn't want to get mixed up with a white woman in any emotional or physical way, and he told me to get lost."

Eugene whistled through his teeth. "Well!"

"I'm trying to get lost, except that I keep bumping into him and he stares right through me." Her voice revealed the pain of the experience all too well. She averted her face. "If you'll send him to Phoenix, I think I can get over him."

"Do you? I wouldn't make any bets on it. And if his temper is any indication, he's having some problems of his own. He was livid about letting you get shot. I gather that he feels responsible."

"It was my fault as much as his," she replied. "I don't blame him. My arm is as good as new."

"Too bad we can't say the same of your brain," Eugene mused. "It's a very good brain, too. I'll send him off. We'll see how you both feel in a few months. If this blows over, he can come back."

"Fair enough." She got to her feet. "Thank you."

"Have you tried talking to him?" he asked as she started to leave.

"He won't," she replied. "Once he makes up his mind, nobody gets a chance to change it."

"Just a thought," Eugene said with a smile. "It would be one way of finding out if he shares your feelings."

Jennifer tormented herself with that thought for the rest of the day. But it would do no good to throw herself at him again, she mused bitterly. He'd already shown her that he wanted her physically. It was every other way that he was rejecting her.

Still, she couldn't resist one last try. So when he came down the hall the morning before he was to leave for Phoenix, she deliberately stepped into his path.

"Eugene says you're being transferred," she said, clutching a stack of topo maps to her breasts to still the trembling of her hands.

Hunter looked down at her. She was wearing gray slacks with a white pullover knit blouse, her blond hair long and soft around her shoulders. He drank in the sight of her without letting her see that it was killing him to leave her.

"I'm going home for a few months, yes," he replied, staring down at her with no particular emotion in his dark face. "It's been a long time since I've had the opportunity to see my grandfather and my cousins and visit old friends."

She wondered if any of the old friends were female, but she didn't dare ask. She looked up into his eyes with her heart in her own, with no idea of how powerfully she was affecting him.

"I'll miss you," she said softly.

He lifted an eyebrow and smiled mockingly. "Will you? Why?"

She bit her lower lip without answering.

He stuck his hands into his pockets and the smile left his face as he looked down at her. "Sex is a bad basis for a relationship," he said bluntly. "I wanted you. Any man would. But common ground is something we never had, and never could. I don't want a white lover, any more than I want a white wife. When I marry, if I marry, it will be to one of my own people. Is that clear enough?"

Her face went very pale, so that her blue eyes were the only color in it. "Yes," she said. "You told me that before."

"I want to make sure you get the message," he replied, forcing the words out. "It was a game. I play it with white women all the time. A little flirting, a little lovemaking, no harm done. But you're one of those throwbacks who equate sex with forever after. Sorry, honey, one night isn't worth my freedom, no matter how fascinating it was to have a virgin."

She dropped her wounded eyes to his sports jacket. "I see," she said, her voice haunted.

His fists clenched inside his pockets. It was killing him to do this! But he had to. He was so damned vulnerable that he wouldn't have the strength to resist her if she kept pursuing him. It had to end quickly. "Now go back to your office and stop trying to fan old flames. I've had all of you that I want...."

She whirled and ran before he finished, tears staining her cheeks. Nothing had ever hurt so much. She went into her office and slammed the door, grateful that her co-workers were still at lunch. She dried her tears after a while and forced herself to work. But she knew she'd never forget the horrible things Hunter had said to her. So much for finding out how he really felt. He'd told her.

Hunter was on his way to the airport, feeling like an animal. Tears on that sweet, loving face had hurt him. It had taken every ounce of willpower he had not to chase her into the office and dry them. But he'd accomplished what he set out to do, he'd driven her away. Now all he had to do was live with it, and he'd never have to worry about the threat of Jennifer again.

Simple words. But as the weeks turned into months, he grew morose. Not seeing Jennifer was far worse than having her around. He missed her. His grandfather noticed his preoccupation and mentioned it to him one evening as they watched the horses prance in the corral.

"It is the white woman, is it not?" Grandfather Sanchez Owl asked in Apache.

"Yes," Hunter replied, too sad to prevaricate.

"Go to her," he was advised.

Hunter's hands tightened on the corral. "I cannot. She could never live here."

"If she loved you, she could." He touched the younger man's shoulder. "Your mother never loved your father. She found him unique and she collected him, as a man collects fine horses. When his uniqueness began to pale, she left him. It is the way of things. There was no love to begin with."

"You never told me this."

Grandfather's broad shoulders rose and fell. "It was not necessary. Now it is. This woman . . . she loves you?"

Hunter stared out over the corral. "She did. But I have done my best to make her hate me."

"Love is a gift. One should not throw it away."

Hunter glanced at him. "I thought that I could not give up my freedom. I thought that she, like my mother, would betray me."

"A man should think with his heart, not his head, when he loves," the old man said quietly. "You do love, do you not?"

Hunter looked away, wounded inside, aching as he thought of Jennifer's soft eyes promising heaven, remembered the feel of her chaste body in his arms, loving him. He closed his eyes. "Yes," he said huskily, fiercely. "Yes, I love!"

"Then go back before it is too late."

"She is white!" Hunter ground out.

The old man smiled. "So are you, in your thinking. It is something you do not want to face, but you are as comfortable in the white man's world as you are here. Probably more so, because your achievements are there and not here. A man can live with a foot in two worlds. You have proven it."

"It wouldn't be fair to a child," he said slowly.

The old man chuckled. "A man should have a son," he said. "Many sons. Many daughters. If they are loved, they will find a place in life. This white woman . . . is she handsome?"

Hunter saw her face as clearly as if she were standing beside him. "She is sunset on the desert," he said quietly. "The first bloom on the cactus. She is the silence of night and the beauty of dawn."

The old man's eyes grew misty with memory. "If she is all those things," he replied, "then you are a fool."

Hunter looked over at him. "Yes, I am." He moved away from the fence. "I am, indeed!"

He caught a plane that very afternoon. All the way to Tulsa, he prayed silently that he wasn't going to be too late. There was every chance that Jennifer had taken him seriously and found someone else. If she had, he didn't know how he was going to cope. He should have listened to his heart in the first place. If he'd lost her, he'd never forgive himself.

To say that Eugene was shocked to see him was an understatement. The old man sat at his desk and gaped when Hunter came into the office.

"I sent you to Phoenix," he said.

"I came back," Hunter returned curtly. "Jennifer isn't here. Where is she?"

Eugene's eyebrows arched. "Don't tell me you care, one way or the other?"

The dark face hardened visibly. "Where is she?"

"At her apartment, taking a well-earned vacation."

"I see."

Eugene narrowed one eye. "Before you get any ideas, she's been seeing one of the other geologists."

Hunter felt his breath stop in his throat. His dark eyes cut into Eugene's. "Has she?"

"Don't hurt her any more than you already have," the old man said, suddenly stern and as icy as his security chief had ever been. "She's just beginning to get over you. Leave her alone. Let her heal."

Something in Hunter wavered. He stared down at the carpeted floor, feeling uncertain for the first time in memory. "This geologist . . . is it serious?"

"I don't know. They've been dating for a couple of weeks. She's a little brighter than she has been, a little less brittle."

Hunter's hands clenched in his pockets. He looked up. "Is she well?" he asked huskily.

"She's better than she was just after you left," Eugene said noncommittally. He eyed the younger man quietly. "You've said often enough that you hated white woman.

You finally convinced her. What do you want now—to torment her some more?"

Hunter averted his face and stared out the window. "My mother was white," he said after a minute, and felt rather than saw Eugene's surprise. "She walked out on my father when I was five. I thought she didn't love him enough to stay, but my grandfather said that she never loved him at all. It...made a difference in the way I looked at things. To ask a woman to marry a different culture, to accept a foreign way of life, is no small thing. But where love exists, perhaps hope does, too."

Eugene softened. "You love her."

Hunter turned back to him. "Yes," he said simply. "Life without her is no life at all. Whatever the risk, it can't be as bad as the past few months have been."

The older man smiled. He picked up a sheaf of papers and tossed them across the desk. "There's your excuse. Tell her I sent those for her to look over."

Hunter took them, staring at the old man. "Have I killed what she felt?" he asked quietly. "Does she speak of me at all?"

Eugene sighed. "To be honest, no, she doesn't. Whatever her feelings, she keeps them to herself. I'm afraid I can't tell you anything. You'll have to go and find out for yourself."

He nodded. After a minute, he went out and closed the door quietly behind him. He wondered if Jennifer would even speak to him. Whether she'd be furiously angry or cold and unapproachable, remembering the brutal things he'd said to her when they parted.

All the way to her apartment, he refused to allow himself to think about it. But when he pressed the doorbell, he found that he was holding his breath.

Eleven

Jennifer left her dishes in the sink and went to answer the doorbell, a little irritated at the interruption. She'd spent the past few months in such misery that she was only beginning to get her head above water again. Missing Hunter had become a way of life, despite the fact that she'd started dating a very nice divorced geologist in her group. And if he did spend the whole of their evenings together talking about his ex-wife, what did that matter? Didn't she spend them talking about Hunter and things they'd done together?

She opened the door, and froze. So many lonely nights, dreaming of that hard, dark face, and here he stood. She felt her insides melting at just the sight of him, feeding on it like a starving woman.

She stared up at him with a helpless rapture in her eyes, the old warm vulnerability in her face. It had been so long since she'd seen him. The anguish of the time between lay helplessly in her face as she looked at him. He watched her with equal intensity. His dark eyes held hers for an endless, shattering moment before they slid down her thin body and back up again. She looked as if she was shattered to find him on her doorstep, but at least she wasn't actively hostile. He measured her against his memories for one long moment.

"You can't afford to lose this kind of weight," he said softly. "Are you all right?"

His concern was almost her undoing. She had to fight tears at the tenderness in his voice. She forced a smile. Act, girl, she told herself. You can do it. You did it before, when it was even harder. He's surely here on business, so don't throw yourself at his feet.

"I've been on a diet," she lied. "Come in and I'll brew some coffee. How are you?"

He stepped into the apartment, looking and feeling alien in it. His eyes were restless, wandering around. Her apartment reflected her personality and her life-style. There were souvenirs from her travels everywhere, along with the sunny colors that echoed her own personality, and the numerous whimsical objects she delighted in. Potted plants covered every inch of available space, and ferns and green plants trailed down from high shelves. There were Indian accents, too, including a war shield and some basketry. His eyes lingered on those. Apache. He smiled gently.

She saw where his gaze had fallen and tried to divert him. "My dad says it looks like a jungle in here, but I like green things," she said, leading him into the kitchen. She tugged nervously at her yellow tank top. "How have you been? Is this a business call? Did Eugene want me for something? I'm just off for this week, but I guess . . . !"

"Eugene wanted me to drop some papers off for you," he said, drawing them out of his inside jacket pocket. He dropped them onto the kitchen table. "Something about a new rock formation one of your colleagues wants to check out." He pulled out a chair and straddled it, his eyes narrowing as he watched her make coffee. "I thought you might go back into the field after I left. What happened?"

"I've decided I like desk work," she said. It was a bald-faced lie, but he couldn't be told that. "I'm getting too old for fieldwork. Twenty-eight next birthday," she added with a smile.

"I know." He leaned his chin on his dark hands, clasped on the high back of the chair. "Still alone?" he pursued.

"There's a nice man in my office. Divorced, two kids. We...go out together." She glanced at him. "You?"

The geologist made him angry. Jealous. His dark eyes glittered and he found a weapon of his own. "There's a widow who lives next door to my grandfather, on the reservation. No kids. She's a great cook. No alarming habits."

"And she's Apache," she said for him on a bitter, painful laugh.

"Yes," he bit off. "She's Apache. No complications. No social barriers. No adjustments."

"Good for you. Going to marry her?"

He pulled out a cigarette and lit it without answering. The snub made her nervous.

She got down coffee cups and filled them. "Are you going to take off your coat, or is it glued on?"

He chuckled in spite of himself, shedding the expensive raincoat. She took it from him and carried it into the bedroom, to drape it carefully over the foot of her bed. A few minutes, that was all she had to get through. Then he'd go away, and she could again begin to try to get over him.

She went back into the kitchen, all smiles and courtesy and they talked about everything in the world except themselves. No matter what tactics he used to draw her out about her feelings, she parried them neatly. He was beginning to believe Eugene, that she had no feelings left for him. And he had only himself to blame, he knew. He'd deliberately tried to hurt her, to chase her away. The fact that his motives had been good ones at the time counted for nothing. He felt empty and alone. He knew he was going to feel that way for the rest of his life. He'd almost certainly lost her.

She talked about the fellow geologist as though he'd become her world.

He put out his second cigarette and glanced at his watch. "I've got to go," he said in a voice without expression.

"Another overseas assignment, no doubt," she tried to sound cheery.

"Internal," he replied. He glanced at her. "I've given up fieldwork, too. I lost the taste for it."

That was surprising. He didn't seem the type to thrive on a desk job. But then, she'd thought she wasn't the type, either. She managed. Probably the widow didn't want him in a dangerous job anymore, and he'd given it up for her sake. The thought made her sick.

"I'll get your coat," she said, smiling. Her face would be frozen in its assumed position by the time he left, she thought ruefully.

She picked up his coat from the bed. This would be the last time. He'd marry the widow and she'd never see him again. She'd lost him for good now. She drew his coat slowly to her breasts and cradled it against her, tears clogging her eyes, her throat. She brought it to her lips and kissed it with breathless tenderness, bending her head over it with a kind of pain she'd never felt before in her life. It held the faint scent of the cologne he wore, of the tobacco he smoked. It smelled of him, and the touch of it was precious. She was losing him forever. She didn't know how she was going to live.

She straightened, feeling old and alone, wondering how she was going to go back in there and pretend that it didn't matter about his widow. That the past few months had been happy and full. That her life was fine without him in it.

In the other room, the man who'd happened to glance toward her bedroom had seen something reflected in the mirror facing the door that froze him where he stood. Her lighthearted act had convinced him that she didn't care, that she never had. But that woman holding his coat loved him. The emotion he saw in her face would haunt him forever, humble him every time he remembered the anguish in those soft blue eyes. She wasn't happy without him. He knew now that she'd been pretending ever since he'd walked into the apartment. She'd only been putting on an act about not caring, to hide her real feelings. He grimaced, thinking how close a call it had been. If he'd taken her act for granted and left, his life would never have been the same.

He caught his breath and turned away. All his former arguments about the reasons they were better apart vanished in an agony of need. If he walked out that door, she was going to die. If not physically, surely emotionally. She loved him that much. He loved her that much, too. It was vaguely frightening, to love to that degree. But even with the obstacles, they were going to make it. He'd never been more certain of anything in his life.

He took the coat from her when she rejoined him, her mask firmly in place again. She couldn't know that he'd seen her through the mirror, so he didn't let on. He wanted to see how far she was willing to go with the charade, if she could keep it up until he walked out. Now that he knew how she felt, it was like anticipating a Christmas present that was desperately wanted.

"It was nice to see you again," she said as she went with him to the door.

"Same here." He opened the door and stood silhouetted in it, with his long back to her, looking alien and somehow unapproachable. "You haven't said whether you were glad to see me, Jennifer," he said quietly, without turning.

She lowered her eyes to the floor. "It's always good to see old . . . friends, Phillip."

He drew in his breath sharply. The sound of his name in her soft voice brought back unbearable memories. "Were we ever friends?"

"No. Not really. I'm . . . I'm glad . . . about your widow, I mean," she said, unable to conceal a faint note of bitter anguish in her tone.

He sighed, still with his back to her. "The widow just turned eighty-two. She's my godmother."

Her heart jumped. She took a steadying breath. "The divorced man only takes me out so he can talk about his ex-wife. He still loves her."

He turned. He shook his head, the light in his eyes disturbing, humbling. "Oh, God, what a close call we had! You little idiot, do you really think I came here on business?" He held out his arms and she went into them. And just that quickly, that easily, the obstacles were pushed aside, the loneliness of the past gone forever.

He bent to her mouth and hers answered it. She moaned, shuddering, her control gone forever.

He lifted his head, and had to fight her clinging arms. "I'm going to close and lock the door, that's all," he whispered shakily, reaching out to do it. "I don't want the neighbors to watch us make love."

"Are we going to?" she asked helplessly.

He nodded. "Oh, yes," he said fervently. He bent, lifting her in his arms. "I love you," he whispered at her lips, watching the soft, incredulous wonder grow in her face as he said it. "And now I'm going to prove it physically, in the intimacy of lovemaking. At least I won't have to hurt you, will I, little one?" he asked, smiling gently at the memory of that night in his house.

She clung to him, shivering helplessly, her face buried in the heated skin of his throat. "You won't give me a child, ever, will you?" she whimpered.

His breath caught. He paused at the bedroom door, meeting her sad, hungry eyes. He started to speak, failed. He looked down at her mouth. "I won't . . . use anything, if you like," he whispered. His eyes went back up to hers, lost in their shocked delight. "It's all right," he said, his voice tender. "A child . . . will be all right."

She was crying. He undressed her gently, but she couldn't even see him through her tears. She loved him. He loved her. There would be children and years of being together, wherever they chose to live. On the reservation, off it, in the desert, anywhere at all.

She said so, seeing him come down on the bed beside her, a blur of mahogany skin and lean muscle.

"Say the words while I'm loving you," he whispered, his lips slow and tender on her yielded body.

"The...words?" she echoed, arching as his mouth pressed down on her flat belly.

"That you love me," he said lazily. "I said it, but you didn't."

"How could you not know?" she moaned achingly. "I offered myself every time you looked at me. I did everything but wear a button.... Oh!" She stiffened as his mouth touched her in an unexpected way.

He lifted his head, his eyes darkly smoldering. "Do you want that?" he whispered.

She almost didn't answer him. She had a feeling that the experienced women he'd known had expected it, and an equally strong feeling that it was something he'd do for her sake, but never for his own.

She sat up, touching his lean face lovingly. "If you want it," she whispered. "I..." Her eyes fell to his chest, and further. She caught her breath at the sight of him. "I'll do anything you want me to."

He tilted her eyes back up to his. "Is it something you want?"

She shook her head. "I'm sorry..."

"Sorry!" He laughed with soft delight and caught her close, his mouth rough on her bare shoulder. "I'm as old-fashioned as you are, in some ways. Not really modern enough for this day and age. But if you want that kind of intimacy, you can have it."

"Maybe someday," she whispered. "When I'm less inhibited." She flushed. "Right now, all of it is a little scary..."

He lifted his head and his dark eyes searched hers. "We'll sit up this time, and you can control when it happens."

She went scarlet. He brushed her mouth with his. "Don't be shy," he whispered into her lips. "It's as new to me as it is to you, to make love and be in love. I don't want to make it disappointing for you."

"It could never be that," she said gently. "Not with you."

"Try to remember that it's an art, like any other," he said, brushing back her hair. "It isn't perfection at first. It may be uncomfortable despite what we did in my bed that night, and there may not be much pleasure in it for you. I can make it up to you afterward." He drew in a slow breath. "I've been without a woman for a long time, and my body isn't always mine to control. I'll hold back as long as I can...."

His anguish made her feel protective. She lifted her lips to his face and kissed his eyes closed, loving the newness of being in love, of being loved in return, of being wanted. "Whatever you do to me will be all right," she whispered. "Love me, now, please. Teach me."

"God, what a thing to tempt a man with," he groaned. He eased her down on the bed, and his mouth found her with aching expertness. He kissed and touched and teased until the flames were blazing in her slender body, until she was crying and twisting up to his mouth and hurting with her need of him.

She was only dimly aware when he moved, sitting back against the headboard with her body over his. He lifted her, his hands faintly tremulous, and positioned her so that she felt him suddenly in stark, hot intimacy.

Her eyes dilated, looking straight into his. He took her hands and placed them on his hips.

"Now," he whispered.

She hesitated, but the strain in his face made her realize the torment he was enduring for her sake. She bit her lower lip and pushed. To her amazement, there was only a little discomfort, but not pain. She gasped.

He smiled gently, even through his excitement. "Yes," he whispered. "I thought it might be so. There's nothing to be afraid of now."

His hands settled, warm and hard on her hips. He whispered to her, something that made her body shiver, something so intimate that she gasped and her blood surged in her veins. And at that moment, his hands jerked mercilessly and she felt the white-hot fury of sudden pleasure biting into her.

He rolled over with her, still a part of her body, his voice whispering, coaxing. His mouth brushed against hers, his lips tender, his hands touching her. His mouth settled gently on hers and he began to move, very slowly.

She jerked helplessly. "Phillip!" she exclaimed as the sudden pleasure made her rigid.

"Hold on," he murmured against her mouth. "I'm going to make you want me so badly that you'll fly in my arms. Bite me. That's it, bite me!" he whispered fiercely.

She'd dreamed of a tender, slow initiation with moonbeams and pink clouds. Instead, it was like a vicious fever with pleasure so throbbing and fierce and merciless that she became wanton.

Her nails bit into him, like her teeth. He pushed her down into the mattress with the rough thrust of his body and she arched up to receive it, her legs tangling in his. She looked up at him, her eyes fastened to his, her breath gasping out as his face moved closer and then away, and the mattress rose and fell noisily.

"Look down," he said under his breath.

She did, too lost in him to be shy anymore. He looked, too, and when her eyes met his, passion was smoldering in them.

"Show me where, Jennifer," he whispered, moving her hands to his hips. "Teach me where you feel the most pleasure when I move."

She flushed, but she obeyed him, guided his body, and cried out when he followed her lead. And then it all seemed to explode at once. His movements were rough and quick, his powerful body strong enough for both of them, his hands controlling her wild thrashing, holding her down, making her submit. His mouth crushed into hers and she heard his tortured breathing, his harsh groans, as the pleasure arched him into her body.

Incredibly she went with him. Soaring. Up into the sun. Shivering with cold and heat so intricately mingled that she was only living as part of him. She was saying something, but she couldn't hear her own voice.

When she opened her eyes again, there was a new kind of lassitude in her limbs. They felt numb and boneless, like the rest of her body. She could breathe again. Her heartbeat was almost normal.

A dark, loving pair of eyes came into view above her. "That," he whispered, "is the sweetest expression of love I'll ever experience in my life. You're my woman."

"Yes." She said it with shy pride, because now it was over. The mystery was gone, but the magic remained. She touched his mouth, fascinated. "Will I get pregnant from it?" she whispered.

He smiled lazily. "I hope so," he whispered. "Creation should be like this, from seed so exquisitely planted in love. Now do you understand what I meant, about not making a casual entertainment out of something so profound? The ultimate glory of lovemaking is the act of creation." He bent and kissed her with rapt tenderness. "I want to plant my seed in you. If we can make a baby together, even if he is a product of two worlds, I want to."

She clung to him, her mouth ardent and loving. "So do I," she whispered huskily. "Oh, so do I! I love you."

"I love you just as much," he said with fierce possession. He was surprised at how quickly his body responded when he kissed her, at the kindling passion that bound them together almost at once.

"No, don't stop," she whispered when he hesitated.

"It's too soon . . ."

"No!" She pulled him down to her and put her mouth hungrily against his and felt him shudder. She opened her eyes as his body slid over hers and they melted together with delicious ease.

"You see?" she whispered shakily. "It's so easy now."

"So easy." He smiled tenderly and his mouth bent to hers. He bit at it, very gently, and his body echoed that tenderness, his arms enfolding hers. He rolled abruptly onto his side and smiled at her surprise. "That night in Washington, I wanted to do it like this, remember? Now we can. Put this leg over mine, here," he guided softly. "Now, like this . . . !"

She watched his face contort as his hand brought her hips suddenly against his. It was fascinating to watch him, to see the passion kindle and ignite.

"Jennifer, you're staring," he whispered.

"I know. I want to watch you," she whispered back, her eyes wide and soft and curious. "Is it all right if I look?"

He shuddered. Her fascination with his pleasure brought it all too soon. His body buckled and began to shudder. He felt the familiar tension building to flashpoint, hamstringing him, racking him. He looked into her eyes and felt her hands shyly tugging at his hips and he cried out.

Convulsions of unbearable pleasure ripped through him. He was aware at some level of her stare, of her scarlet face as she saw him experience fulfillment. It made it all the more shattering. He was helpless and she was seeing him this way, but it didn't matter. Nothing mattered. He was burning. Burning. Burning!

He cried out, his body rippling beside hers. She pressed into his arms and helped him, loving the fury of his hands gripping her hips, loving the unbridled pleasure she saw in his face. He was truly hers, now. Completely hers. She shivered, amazed that his own satisfaction caused her body to fulfill itself in one long, hot wave of shuddering pleasure.

Long afterward, they slept. When she woke at last, it was to the smell of something delicious cooking in the kitchen. She got up and dressed, slowly, with the memory of what had happened like a candle in her mind.

Phillip was standing at the stove cooking steak. He was wearing only the trousers from his suit. His chest and feet were bare. He glanced up as she joined him, and his eyes were warm and tender.

"Are you hungry?" he asked, opening one arm to draw her to him and kiss her softly.

"A little," she whispered. Her eyes met his. "Do you really love me?"

"With all my heart," he whispered back, his eyes punctuating the words. "Life without you is no life, Jennifer. You'll have to get used to having an Apache husband."

"You want to marry me?" she asked, holding her breath.

He put down the fork he was using to turn the steak and brought her against him, bending to kiss her with fierce hunger. "Of course I want to marry you!" he said impatiently, when he lifted his head. "I always did. But the memory of how it was for my mother colored my whole life. Until my grandfather told me the truth—that my father was only a conversation piece for her; that she never loved him. He sent me to you," he added huskily. "He said that I was a fool."

She smiled gently. "No. Just a man afraid to trust. But I'll never hurt you, my darling," she said, sliding her arms around him, laying her blond head on his bare chest. "I'll give you children and live with you anywhere you say."

"Your job . . ." he began.

"Geology isn't something you forget. I'll have babies for a few years, then when they're in school, I'll work out of the Tucson or Phoenix offices. Eugene won't fire me completely."

His lean hands stilled on her back. "I can't let you make that kind of sacrifice for me."

She lifted her head. "You gave up fieldwork," she replied. "And I know how much you loved it. You did that because of me, didn't you?"

"Yes," he admitted finally. "I didn't want the risk. I was thinking about how it would be for you and the children while I was away."

She smiled with pure delight. "Me and the children," she mused. "And yet you went away swearing that you wanted nothing to do with me."

"Lying through my teeth," he added with a dry chuckle. "I drove my grandfather crazy."

She reached up and touched his thick, dark eyebrows. "We're so different in coloring. I wonder if our children will look like you or me?"

"I hope they'll look like both of us," he replied. "My grandfather said that I was living proof that a man can have a foot in two worlds." He smiled at her. "He doesn't like whites, as a rule, but he'll like you."

"My parents will like you," she returned.

He frowned. "Are you sure?"

"Well, I did just happen to tell them about you a few thousand times over the past few years, and I had this picture that I begged out of the personnel files. My mother thought you were striking, and my father was sure you'd be able to keep me out of dangerous places if I ever married you."

"They don't mind the cultural differences?" he stressed.

"They raised me with a mind of my own and let me use it," she replied. "They're not rigid people, as you'll see when you meet them. They're very educated people with tolerant personalities. Besides all that, they want grandchildren."

"I see. That was the selling point, was it?" he murmured.

"Yes, it was. So we'd better set a date and get busy."

He bent and kissed her, ignoring the smell of burning steak. "How does next Friday suit you?" he asked.

"Just fine." She kissed him back, smiling. The steak went right on burning, and nobody noticed until it was the color of tar and the texture of old leather. Which was just as well, because they were in too much of a hurry to get to the courthouse for a marriage license to worry about food, anyway.

* * * * *

A Note from Kathleen Eagle

Many people have considered *But That Was Yesterday* to be a ground-breaking book, but it is first and foremost a love story. If I've done my job, Sage and Megan will quickly come alive for you and you'll find yourself caring for them as flesh-and-blood people right from the start. As *people*, not stereotypes. That's important because this story deals with alcoholism—an issue that has long been a source of stereotyping for Native Americans. But it's honestly a source of pain for the whole human family and a problem that destroys too many relationships. In a letter, one reader told me that she recommended *But That Was Yesterday* at an Al-Anon meeting and the group ended up reading it both for insight and enjoyment. While it offers no easy answers, here's a story that celebrates the light at the end of the tunnel and the leavings in Pandora's box—hope.

All rolled up in a love story? You bet!

Kathleen Eagle

BUT THAT WAS YESTERDAY

Kathleen Eagle

For Clyde,
because I love him.

Prologue

Sage Parker hated being locked up. He clenched his teeth when he heard the steel door clank shut behind his back. More than one judge had said that just the sound was enough to convince a man to mend his ways. It was a sound that chilled the blood, all right. That sound combined with the taste of stale cigarette smoke and the smell of dirty socks to start his gut churning. But neither the sound nor any part of this place had ever convinced him to do anything.

Sage glanced over his shoulder at the man in uniform, who jangled the keys on the big key ring and jerked his chin toward the cot near the far wall. "He's got ten minutes before he goes to court, Sage. You know the routine."

Sage knew it well. He nodded as he shoved his hands into the pockets of jeans faded honestly through years of wear. No matter how many times he'd been here, no matter what the circumstances, it never got any easier. He dragged his boot heels against the cement floor as he approached the cot.

"How're you doing, Jackie?"

The man sitting on the cot had heard the sound of the cell door, too, but he hadn't looked up. He hung his head and stared at the patch of floor between his feet as he hugged himself around the middle. The question went unanswered.

Sage looked down at the top of the man's head and struggled against the urge to turn around and walk out. This was the drunk he most hated seeing—the one who had fallen off the wagon after a period of sobriety. It disgusted him first, but he recognized that feeling as a cover-up. Truly, it scared the hell out of him. Finally, it humbled him. He laid a hand on Jackie's shoulder and sat beside him on the cot.

"Got the shakes, huh?" Jackie didn't have to answer that question, either. Sage felt the man's tremors under his hand. The tribal judge would commit Jackie to a detoxification program, but shock was an imminent danger now. "Are you going to make it, Jackie?"

Jackie shook his head slowly. "I dunno, Sage. I dunno. I don't feel too good. I just dunno." The litany became a hoarse whisper.

Sage acknowledged the watchful eye of the closed-circuit camera. The officer at the front desk had seen the bulge of the two ounce bottle Sage carried in his breast pocket when he made calls like this. Nothing had been said. There was a tacit understanding that Sage Parker knew what he was doing. He drew a deep breath and exhaled slowly.

"You think a shot would straighten you out enough to get you to detox?"

Jackie turned his head and let Sage see the hope those words had sparked in bleary, blood-shot eyes. Sage scorned that false hope, but he couldn't help sympathizing with the man for being sucked in by it. He pulled the airline-size bottle from his breast pocket and broke the seal. It was a good brand, Sage thought, but then, he'd always bought the best when he was buying. He tipped the bottle to Jackie's lips and administered the gin carefully, as though it were a dose of medicine. Jackie reached up, but Sage held the bottle tightly, pulling it away as Jackie swallowed.

"Thanks." Jackie wiped his mouth with the back of a shaky hand. "The rest of that's just gonna go to waste, Sage."

"Yeah, well..." Sage lifted a shoulder as he capped the bottle. "Better to waste the gin than get wasted ourselves." He slipped the bottle back into his pocket and gripped Jackie's shoulder again. "Right, friend?" Jackie nodded dumbly. "You'll stop shaking in a minute."

"For a while, at least."

"Yes," Sage said quietly. "For a while."

The keys rattled in the lock again, and both men looked up. "Time to face the music, Jackie," a police officer announced.

Sage helped Jackie to his feet. The handcuffs were always the worst part, he thought. The clicking sound pinched his heart.

"Think he'll be okay for an hour or so?" the officer asked Sage.

"He won't make it through any lectures from the judge."

"You've heard 'em all, anyway," said the policeman with a laugh. "Haven't you, Jackie?"

Jackie ignored the question as he cast a soulful look over his shoulder. "I'm sorry, Sage. I met up with some old buddies, and I thought I could handle it. Six months down the tubes now, huh?"

"You'll start over." Sage gave a nod toward the open door. "First things first, Jackie. We'll be waiting for you."

"I was doin' good, though, wasn't I?"

"You were doing great."

Jackie squared his shoulders and crossed the threshold with his escort. "See? I was doin' great."

"You weren't doing so great when they picked you up last night," the officer reminded him.

Sage was glad to walk out of the cell. He put his hand over his breast pocket as he watched the man in uniform lead

Jackie down the hall. He could feel the heat of the liquid burning his hand through the glass and the cotton cloth. No matter how vehemently he denied it, there was a distant longing out of the past that nagged at the weaker part of his brain. He gave the men's room door a hard shove and strode to the sink to pour the rest of the stuff out. He never carried a bottle with a broken seal, and he never tossed a bottle for someone else to find. He even rinsed it out before he dropped it in the trash can. If he'd left any "corners," it was only water, which couldn't hurt anybody. Sage was thorough. He had to be. He was responsible for his own actions, and he had the weaker part of his brain to consider.

Chapter 1

Sun-bronzed and bare to the waist, the man wielding the jackhammer was an arresting sight. His flesh vibrated as though charged by the power he held in his grip. A red bandanna kept the sweat out of his eyes, but his body was beaded with it, and the moisture glistened in the South Dakota sun like the mica in a granite road cut. Small beads gathered in the central valley of his chest to form a rivulet, which made a quick run to his abdominal plane and disappeared into his jeans.

Megan's gaze skittered over the power tool that was framed by the man's flexed-knee stance. Its bit gouged without mercy at the face of rockbed that had been gauged, sampled and declared by Megan McBride to be in the way of progress. She wondered how this man felt about changing the face of the earth. After all, he was an Indian—Native American, she amended mentally—and traditionally they resented the kinds of changes she was in the business of making. Perhaps it didn't offend him too much. He was doing his job and doing it well. If he had any sense that he was being watched, he gave no indication of it as he concentrated on his work.

"Sage Parker." Megan jumped at the words shouted close to her ear. She turned a questioning look at the older man who stood behind her shoulder. Didn't Bob think she knew the names of the men on her crew by now? "Good man," Bob added. "Let's go back to the trailer where we can talk."

The noise level wouldn't be much better in Megan's mobile office, but at least it would be possible to talk there. The machine-gun rattle of the jackhammer became distant as they made their way down a steep grade, turning their feet sideways to keep from sliding. Bob Krueger was a gentleman of the old school, prepared to offer Megan a hand despite the fact that her young body handled this activity far more gracefully than his older one did, but he curbed the impulse. The old school wouldn't have allowed a woman on a road construction site, certainly not as the engineer in charge of the project. Offering her a hand in front of her all-male crew would have been a disser-vice.

Megan noted the progress of the big yellow earth movers. She knew the operators would be watching one another, each challenging himself to move more dirt than the other. It was a form of competition that kept an otherwise tedious job interesting. They would blast through more rock before the day was out, and, if all went well, they would remain on schedule.

"How're you getting along with Taylor?" Bob offered the question after they'd closed the trailer door and left at least a portion of the dust outside.

Megan eyed her foreman's desk. He wasn't much of a record-keeper, and the desk showed little sign of organized use. "So far, so good," she said. "But, in his mind, I think the project is yours, and I'm just a messenger."

Bob sat on the corner of Megan's desk, which was clear of all but two file folders and a clipboard. She was careful to protect her work from the fine dust that was always in the air on a construction site.

"Has he challenged your authority in any way?" Bob asked. He was a veteran of the Highway Department and a man with enough experience to know that skill, not gender, was the measure of a good highway engineer.

"Not yet," Megan said as she pulled out a file drawer. "But I think he'd like to. Whenever we talk, I get the feeling there's one more thing he wants to say, but he decides he hasn't quite got me figured out well enough to risk it."

"Are you ready with a response?"

She withdrew a folder and gave the older man a smile that lent a hint of feminine sophistication to her startlingly blue eyes. "How long have you known me, Bob?"

"Since you started with the highway department. What was it? Five—six years ago?"

"Eight, if you count my summers on the survey crew." She raised an eyebrow as she slid the drawer shut. "I'll admit I didn't always have a ready response in those days, but I've made a habit of updating my repertoire."

"Loaded with classics, I'm sure."

Megan laughed. "Whatever brings the most respect. With these guys, that's likely to be honky-tonk rather than classical."

Bob nodded as Megan handed him the folder. He flipped it open. "Anyone else causing you any problems?" She was his protégé, and he wanted this project to go well almost as much as she did.

"Not really. Not . . . seriously." Bob glanced up from the first page of the report she'd handed him and waited for her follow-up. She folded her arms and rested the backs of her thighs against the edge of the desk. "A couple of the men seem to have trouble getting themselves to work sometimes."

"Transportation problems?"

She lifted her shoulder. "They've offered that as an excuse once or twice."

"Are they buddies with Taylor or something?"

Megan chortled. "Hardly."

"It doesn't matter. A lot of guys are looking for work, Megan. Don't put up with any—"

"Taylor would like to fire them, but—" The look in her eyes told him how uncomfortable she was with the problem. "We had very few applications from Native Americans, and I don't want to fire the ones we've got. They're good workers, but there are two men—well, one in particular—"

"Not Parker, I hope."

Megan shook her head quickly. "No, Parker's completely reliable."

Bob smiled, apparently relieved by the news. "Parker's the best man on your crew. I'd hate to hear he wasn't making it to work."

Visions of the man flashed through Megan's mind. She'd learned that he could handle almost any job on the site, from heavy equipment to explosives. In her business she saw brawny, sweaty men all the time. It was Sage Parker's versatility that caught her attention, not his virility. Reliability, versatility—those attributes should not go unnoticed.

"So why don't you see if he can help you with the others?"

The question reclaimed Megan's attention. "Who? Parker?"

"If you're not ready to fire these guys, you might get some ideas on how to handle them from Parker. I hear he's got some kind of recovery program going on the reservation."

"Recovery program?" She pronounced the words as though they were part of a foreign tongue.

"For alcoholism."

"Nobody said these men had a drinking problem, and I'm not jumping to any conclusions just because—"

"Of course you're not," Bob said calmly. "Neither am I. I'm suggesting you let Parker in on your concern and see what he's got to say. I've worked with him off and on over the years. He's put down a lot of miles."

"You don't think he'd . . . take offense?"

"You're the boss here, Megan. And you're the only woman." Bob nodded toward the door and offered a conspiratorial grin. "To a man, those guys are all worried about offending *you*."

Whenever Karl Taylor went to the office there were bets taken. One of these days he was bound to make the same kind of remark to McBride's face as he made behind her back, and one of them was going to come flying out the door. Some said the lady would flee in tears. Others thought she'd kick Taylor out on his butt. Either way, the crew enjoyed the suspense. They were disappointed once again when Taylor emerged at quitting time and closed the door behind him.

"Hey, it's time to knock off for the day!" he announced. "What's everybody standing around here for? How about a stop at the Red Rooster?"

Sage only half-listened as he buttoned his shirt, calculating the distance between himself and a shower. He tossed his leather work gloves on the seat of the pickup and dug in his pocket for his keys. He lifted the corner of his mouth in a smile as he noticed the way the stiffened gloves had landed, with the fingers curled and clawing at the air. Great for a movie, he thought. *Ravaging Gloves*.

"Hey, Sage." Sage turned his head toward the hand on his shoulder, then looked up at Scott Allen's friendly, sunburned face. "Come on over to the Rooster with us. I'll stand you a game of pool."

"Some other time, Scott. I've got horses standing around a dry stock tank right about now."

"Gotta take some time off once in a while." Scott gave Sage an amicable parting pat on the shoulder. "You work too hard, buddy."

"Making up for lost time," was the reply Sage regularly gave to that comment, although he knew few people really understood what it meant.

"Parker!" Taylor's voice brought Sage around again, this time more slowly. He needed the extra seconds to prepare his patience. "Boss lady wants to see you before you take off." Taylor snatched off his cap and wiped his forehead with his sleeve. He chuckled as he put it back on and adjusted the bill. "Ain't that a crock? My wife's the only 'boss lady' I ever expected to answer to, and there's no way in hell she'd take on a job like this."

"Thought you said your wife used to flag," one of the men reminded him.

"Way back when. Now she's home raising kids."

Sage stuffed his shirttails into his jeans and slammed his pickup door. He'd heard enough of Taylor's "wisdom" on women. He wanted to tell the ruddy-faced foreman that spouting that nonsense on this particular job was a sure sign of his incompetence, but Sage needed the work. The fact that the engineer on the project was a woman didn't bother him. Being summoned to the boss's office was another matter.

"Hey, Sage, why don't you stop in for something cold to drink?" another man asked as he walked by.

"I already asked him, Randy. He's gotta get home."

Sage offered the two young men a smile and lifted a forefinger as he walked past their pickup. "You have one for me, Randy. Just one."

"The legend lives on," Scott teased. "You entered up in the bronc riding this weekend, Sage? I'd like to have a chance to beat you out, just once."

Sage laughed. "You wish! The legend lives on because I know when to quit. You guys take it easy."

Sage lifted the bandanna from his head and raked his fingers through his hair as he wadded the cloth and stuck it in his back pocket. The metal steps wobbled under his work boots as he took a deep breath and reached for the doorknob. He'd turned this summons over in his mind several times, and he couldn't come up with a reason for it. He'd been doing his job. He'd done every task Taylor had tossed at him, and he'd never been late for work. But experience told him that being called to the office generally meant he was about to be reprimanded, and he'd never handled that well.

When she looked up from the chart on her desk and smiled, his first thought was, Don't do that lady. It makes you look too damn cute. "Taylor said you wanted to see me."

"Yes. I know it's time to go home, and I promise not to keep you long." She rose from her chair and moved to the front of the desk.

Sage stood about as close now as he'd ever been to her, and it occurred to him that he hadn't really noticed how small she was. She wore her honey-blond hair cropped short in back and styled longer on top. He detected little makeup, and the clarity in those deep blue eyes made him uneasy. It wasn't a look he could deal with. There was nothing hazy, or frosty or even provocative about it. Her eyes were simply bright and clear.

"Bob Krueger was here today. He's pleased with our progress." She folded her arms and leaned back against the desk. There was nothing feminine about her khaki jumpsuit—except, perhaps, for the way she had the collar turned up in the back—or her lace-up work boots, besides the fact that they were the smallest pair he'd ever seen. Sage shoved his hands in his pockets and waited for her to come to the point. "He had high praise for you."

But? "I've worked on a few of Bob's projects."

"So he said. You seem to be trained for every job on the site."

"I've had a lot of years' experience in highway construction." She'd read his application. She knew that.

"Are you an engineer, too?"

He returned her level gaze. "I've had some vocational training, but I've never been to college." He jerked his chin toward a cabinet. "That's all in your files. Somebody decided I was qualified for this job, and they hired me."

"I think you're *overqualified*, Sage. You should have applied for foreman."

Sage scowled. What was this all about, anyway? "We've got a foreman on this project, and you're the engineer. My paycheck's the same whether I set charges or operate a blade."

"I just want you to know the opportunity's there the next time you apply. Bob thinks very highly of you."

Sage drew his hands out of his pockets slowly as he struggled to fit the pieces of this conversation together. That clarity he'd seen in her eyes might have been misleading. "Am I being fired from *this* project, or what?"

"Of course not. I just wanted to pass Bob's compliment on to the person who should hear it, and then I—" She raised her eyebrows in a kind of confession. "I wanted to ask for a favor."

"A favor?"

She braced her hands on the desk at either side of her hips. The suit she wore gave no hint of the shape of those hips, but the crisp cotton fabric had stretched across her thighs when she leaned back. It wasn't the first time he'd caught himself wondering about those thighs.

"Advice, really," she said. "I don't know what to do about Jackie Flying Elk. He hasn't been to work for two days, and Karl wants to fire him."

Sage drew a long breath and released it slowly. He had to remind himself that, yes, Jackie was his business. He'd taken four hours' leave on Jackie's account. But the man was responsible for his own job. This woman had called him in here to talk about one of her employees just because he was Indian.

When Sage made no comment, Megan continued. "Jackie is very good at his job, and I don't want to fire him. I'd like to give him another chance. He's got to get back here tomorrow or have a good excuse, Sage. I can't—"

"Why are you telling me this?"

"Well—" She knew it was a good question, and she wasn't sure she had a good answer. "I can't find a phone number for him."

"He doesn't have a phone. I can tell you where he lives." He saw the reluctance in her eyes, and he knew then that he hadn't been wrong about them. They hid nothing.

"I thought maybe you could talk to him. You're friends, aren't you?"

"Of course. Jackie Flying Elk, Gary Little Bird, Lawrence Archambault. Who else have you got? We're all buddies. I even get along with some of the white guys on the crew."

Megan pushed her fingers through her hair and cast a glance at the ceiling. "I'm going about this all wrong." She braced her hands against the desk again. "I was hoping you'd talk to Jackie. Tell him to come back to work tomorrow. I don't know what else to do."

"If Jackie's run out of chances, you do what you have to."

"I'm trying to be fair." Cornered, Megan always bristled like a cat. She knew she was doing it now, and she made a conscious effort to control her voice. "I've wondered... it's possible that Jackie has a drinking problem, and if he does—"

"It's also possible that *I* have a drinking problem."

"If you do, it doesn't interfere with your work." Her fur was up again. "In Jackie's case, it will mean the loss of his job. He's definitely letting it get out of hand if it's... if it's what I think it is."

"You're very perceptive, Miss McBride. It does sound like Jackie might have a problem." Sage was beginning to enjoy this conversation. She was every bit as uncomfortable now as he'd been when he'd first come through the door. "I can't solve it for him."

"All I'm asking you to do," she said carefully, "is *talk* to him. Tell him to be here at eight tomorrow morning."

"Jackie won't make it to work tomorrow, and no amount of talk is going to change that."

Megan's shoulders sagged, and she looked as though he'd just surprised her with a totally unexpected checkmate. "Why not?"

"Because he's sick, Miss McBride."

"Why didn't you tell me that in the first place? If he's sick—"

"He *was* drunk. Now he's sick. It takes a while to dry out."

She should have kept the desk between them, Megan decided. He was standing there telling her things that somehow scared her, and there was no emotion whatever in his dark eyes. If she had her desk and her charts and her aerial photographs spread out between them, she would feel stronger. She thought of Jackie, who worked like a beaver and kept the crew laughing at his jokes. "Is he in . . . jail?"

"He's in a detoxification unit."

She wasn't sure what that meant, but she nodded. "Could we call that a hospital?"

"You can call it whatever you want. It's staffed by medical people."

"Would they be able to give me any indication—"

"Look, you're not gonna know what they can tell you unless you call and ask." He lifted one corner of his mouth in a humorless smile. "You don't have to risk actually setting foot on Pine Ridge soil, Miss McBride. The detox unit has a phone."

"I have been to Pine Ridge," she said patiently. "Please understand that Jackie's problem bears no reflection on the Native American members of our crew. Anyone who misses work without calling in gets a warning, a reprimand, and then—"

"And then he gets fired. If you have a policy, why aren't you sticking to it?"

Megan came away from the desk and took a stance that said she might be willing to square off with this man, despite his size, in defense of the poor man she'd hoped Sage would defend.

"I believe the circumstances might be mitigating," she said.

"In what way?"

"He—" Pick something, she told herself. "You said yourself that Jackie doesn't have a phone."

"So I did."

"And you said he was sick."

He'd said it once. No confirmation was necessary.

"Illness is a valid excuse for missing work."

"So there you have it." He appeared to toss the issue off with a casual shrug. "Your problem is solved."

"But for how long?"

"Good question." Sage had been standing over a jack-hammer most of the day. He decided Taylor owed him a seat, so he sat on the foreman's desk. "What are you going to do about Gary Little Bird?"

"He's not as bad. He's had a warning."

"You must have forgiven the day he came to work an hour late."

"He had car trouble."

"Did he?" He folded his arms across his chest. "Did you know that before this weekend, Jackie hadn't had a drink in six months?"

"But he's—"

"Missed work. I know. Because he drives an Indian car." He lifted one shoulder. "Or should I say *Native American*? Probably came out of Detroit. We buy American made, American used. Before the summer's over, my pickup will be sitting along the road halfway between my place and here, and I'll be tinkering under the hood for most of the morning. It's heated up on me twice in the last week."

"If that happens—"

"You'll dock me. That's the policy." He stood up and tucked his thumbs in the pockets of his jeans. "Look, Miss McBride, I'm sure you mean well. You know, by rights it's

Taylor who runs the crew. I'll do what I can for Jackie, but that doesn't include taking care of him on the job. I suggest you make that call and talk to the doctor."

On impulse, Megan offered a handshake. "Thank you for your time, Sage. I've learned a great deal." Her hand disappeared in his, but he was captivated, too—by her eyes. "Bob Krueger *did* say you were the best man I had on this crew. I thought you should know that."

Sage nodded, released her hand and turned to leave without another word. She was a bit stunned when he shut the door behind him.

His family had lived on the western side of Pine Ridge Indian Reservation for at least four generations. Before that, they had been part of the nomadic band of Lakota people known as the Oglala. They were not related to the Commanche Parkers, but he was often asked if the famous Quannah Parker had been an ancestor. So far as he knew, he had no famous ancestors. His great-grandmother had married a mixed-blood named Parker, who had given her his name and his child and then wandered away.

Sage turned his battered blue pickup at the approach to his part of Parker land and drove between the two huge posts that had been set there in better days. The crossbar had fallen some time ago. Sage had set a goal for himself. When he owned a hundred head outright, he would put up another crossbar and hang a sign. With a hundred head of cattle, he could call this a ranch again.

His place bordered some of the most scenic land east of the Black Hills—the South Dakota Badlands. The government had once ceded all this land to the Lakota, including the Black Hills, but gold had been discovered, and the Hills had been seized once white occupation had become an accomplished fact. The Lakota had been assigned to various Dakota Territory reservations, which shrank in size over the years. The Oglala had been given this site within teasing reach of the sacred Hills. The Badlands had been a farcical substitute.

Later the government decided that the Badlands were unique in their own way, and Badlands National Park was created. It had the look of terrain from a science fiction film. Tourists remarked that it certainly was stark, beautiful, *bad* land, and they traveled on to the Black Hills to see the faces of the presidents. Now Sage leased government land, the land that had once been part of Pine Ridge but was now called "public domain," and his stock grazed it. Even through his darkest days, he had managed to salvage his claim to the land.

He'd lost the house, but he was replacing it board by board. He parked the pickup near the barn and peered between the corral rails. There stood the five horses for whom the roar of the blue pickup was a call to dinner. Sage was glad to see them, too. He remembered the day six years ago when he'd sold the last of his horses. It had been like selling his soul. His uncle Vern had bought the last two and had given Sage a terrible look of pity as he'd led them away. Sage never wanted to see that look again, and he'd vowed to feed his horses at least as well as he fed himself.

He balanced himself on the top of the corral, anchoring his boot heels on the second rail. At his back the five horses ground their oats with teeth that were as efficient as any millstone. It made good music. In Sage's ears, it was a rich sound. His father had measured his own success by the number of horses he'd owned. Sage lifted his head toward the eastern horizon and watched his cows amble over the hill in single file, following the well-worn path their predecessors had made for them. He kept them close while the calves were new, and the stock tank was their watering hole for now. Later he would move them out to the hills for better grazing.

Here was more wealth, Sage thought. Fourteen cows, and all but one had calved successfully. The dry cow would be sold and replaced. Not many ranchers would consider fourteen cows a measure of wealth, but few had learned as Sage had. The cows represented his effort to rebuild his life. The house was a symbol, as well. Even in its skeletal state, it was a beginning. It stood on the spot where the old house had been. Not the one the bank had built when he'd started out—the one they'd auctioned off and hauled away on a semi when he'd given up. Not the one the government had built for his parents some twenty years before that—the one they'd called a six-fifty house because the government had allocated six hundred and fifty dollars to each tribal member to build the little three-room structures. No, the new house would stand where the cabin his family had occupied when he was a young child once stood.

He was putting it there because he needed to recall that time. He needed to reconnect himself with those good memories. The tent the family had lived in during the summer they'd built the log house had stood near the grove of cottonwoods—only the cottonwoods hadn't been there then. They'd made a baseball diamond where the corral now stood, and his family had been its own team. His father's cousin had lived with his family, the rival team, four miles away. Those had indeed been good times, and it was worth digging back through all the baggage of what his life had been in the interim to recall them.

He might have pitched a tent for himself for the summer, but he wouldn't finish the house before winter. The little trailer he lived in served his needs adequately. It provided enough hot water for a quick shower, with which he was about to pamper himself, along with a refrigerator large enough to preserve the hamburger he was about to cook and a bed that held all of him but his feet if he slept corner to corner. He worked hard enough during the day so that the size of the bed didn't matter when he finally fell into it at night. Nor did the fact that he slept alone bother him.

He eyed the trailer and thought of Megan McBride. She worked in a little trailer, but he was sure she didn't live in one. In the last few weeks he'd permitted himself one foolish indulgence. From a safe distance he'd watched Megan McBride at work. It hadn't troubled him that a woman was engineering the construction project. In his culture, women took charge as a matter of course, though they spoiled their men in the way of women everywhere. It *had* disturbed him when he realized he'd begun to fantasize about her, but he continued to indulge himself. He watched her assert her authority on the job, and he wondered about the shape of the legs she hid under her jumpsuits. He wondered how strong they were, how agile, how smooth. He knew those heavy work boots must house slender ankles and small, feminine toes.

There were other women in his life—those he met with at least twice a week in the recovery group he'd christened Medicine Wheel. The difference was that Megan McBride was unattainable, which made it safe to think about her. Safe, perhaps, but unwise. He'd come to grips with that fact earlier that day when she'd turned the tables on him. *She'd* watched *him* work. She'd observed his skill, the progress he was making, the way his piece of work fit into the scheme of the project. Those things she'd seen through the eyes of an engineer. But she'd lingered, and he'd felt the scrutiny of a woman's eyes. Later she'd asked him to discuss problems that were human and not mechanical, and another barrier had been ripped away. He saw through her. She was a caretaker, a do-gooder, pure and simple. That was the characteristic that drew them to one another, and the one he had to avoid.

Still, he wondered what she had seen when she'd looked at him through a woman's eyes.

Chapter 2

South Dakota's chain of jewels was the Black Hills. Megan loved her job because it took her outdoors, and this was her favorite part of a state that boasted a wonderful variety of terrain. She had worked her science in all corners of it. Nearly flat farmland stretched over the eastern portion of the state. Heading west, the land began to pucker into rolling hills and buttes that were harbingers of what one would find nearly two hundred miles from the wide Missouri, the river bisecting the state from north to south. But the hint did little to prepare the traveler for that first glimpse of the Hills, which appeared in the distance as a blue-black uprising against a sky that had thoroughly dominated the vista over hundreds of South Dakota miles.

Megan's project involved paving a stretch of gravel running east-west in the southern portion of the Hills. To the east was the Pine Ridge Sioux Indian Reservation. The town of Hot Springs was to the southwest. The tourist's hills, with granite sculptures, gold mines and little towns still rowdy enough to be called Western, stood to the north. Beneath this land lay a maze of caverns, an underground world built by subterranean water and as yet largely unexplored. This tourist's dream could become a highway engineer's nightmare. The initial survey and sample work for this project was proving unreliable.

Karl Taylor straightened slowly as he looked up from the charts that were spread across his "boss lady's" desk. Megan stood on the opposite side, arms folded, waiting for a response. "So how much deeper you think you're gonna go?" he finally asked.

His tone made it clear that he intended to object to her answer, whatever it was. He'd been waiting for a good place to draw the line, and this would be it. Like the South Dakota buttes, his regularly scheduled objections to her decisions had been harbingers of the inevitable uprising.

"I'm projecting ten feet, but it might be more."

"Ten feet! That's a major change in the plans."

"I realize that."

The door opened, and both of them turned as Sage Parker stepped in and closed it behind him. Taylor lifted an accusing eyebrow at Megan as he planted his fist at his waist, which became a hip without the slightest change in contour.

"I sent for Parker because he's running the scraper," Megan said.

"So what? I'm running Parker, along with the rest of the crew."

"*I'm* running the *project*. This stretch has turned out to be a slough." Megan pointed to the map, indicating the area with a closely trimmed fingernail. "We'll dig out the goop even if we have to go down fifteen or twenty feet, and we'll backfill it. I also want to raise the grade so we get better—"

"Raise the grade! You're talking major changes, McBride. Look at this, Parker." Like an anxious woodpecker, Taylor tapped his finger against a spot on the map. "She's talking ten-twenty feet down here, which calls for 'dozing. That scraper by itself won't cut it."

The scene was one Sage would have preferred to walk out on. Taylor was the construction foreman, and McBride was the engineer. It was up to them to have this out, then let him know how to set up his equipment. He would move as much dirt as he was told to move. Against his own better judgment, he stepped closer to the desk and glanced at the fingerprint Taylor had made on the map. He didn't need a picture. He'd been out there digging in it.

"This is a big job, McBride," Taylor said. "And you're making it bigger. Have you checked with Krueger?"

"He's out on a site." Megan thrust her hands into the pockets of her jumpsuit. "The changes are necessary," she said quietly. "There's no question."

"There's plenty of question." Taylor gave the map a final tap with his knuckles and turned to Sage. "Wouldn't you say, Parker?"

Sage eyed Taylor's red, round face, then Megan's, which was smooth and tanned that golden shade that only a true blonde seemed to be able to achieve. He figured this threesome could line up two ways: two whites and one Indian, or two men and one woman. For some reason, Taylor had chosen the latter. Tough. Sage glanced down at the map again. "I've paved over this stuff before, Taylor. You have, too. In another year you'll have more potholes than blacktop, and you'll have to resurface."

"So we resurface," Taylor said. "That's not our problem right now. The problem is that the specs don't call for all this digging and backfilling. I say get Krueger out here and see what he says before we make any decisions."

"*We* don't have a decision to make. It's my design," Megan insisted. "It needs to be changed, and I'm changing it."

"Fine." Taylor reached out and snatched the pencil that was perched above Megan's ear. He grinned as he handed it to her. "You go right ahead and change your *design*. Let me know if Krueger approves it." He turned to Sage and nodded toward the door. "Shut the equipment down, Parker. We're knocking off for the day."

Her eyes turned icy, and her jaw became rigid. Sage felt the heat of her humiliation. Out of respect, he did not permit himself to pity her as he told her with a brief look that her self-control had not gone unnoticed. Her glance was just as quick and no less communicative. In good time she would make her point without losing her temper. It was not her knowledge at issue; it was her authority.

Bob Krueger upheld her decision, and the digging proceeded. Krueger warned Taylor against giving Megan any problems, and Taylor cheerfully accepted both the warning and the order to proceed with the changes. Both had come from a man. If they wanted to drag this job out, it was fine with him.

Megan had hoped to see the digging completed before the first inevitable June downpour, but two days later she knew it wasn't to be. Between the subterranean water and the deluge from the sky, the crew was up to its knees in water, and they were again two men short. Taylor's cheer was short-lived.

"I tell you what," Taylor shouted over the roar of a compressor used to power the water pumps. "If those two Indians aren't back on the job tomorrow, I'm gonna ship 'em both off to an equal opportunity cannery."

Megan glanced at Sage, who was busy arranging a compressor hose and had no visible reaction to Taylor's remark. She hoped he hadn't heard it. "Gary called in," she told Taylor. "He couldn't get out to the highway, and he said Jackie's road is pure gumbo."

"Yeah, well, *we're* here." He gestured widely at the men sitting in their cars and pickups. "These guys are here."

The sky was gunmetal gray, and the hilltops were lost in the thickness of it. Megan adjusted the collar of her yellow slicker as another runnel of rainwater slithered down the back of her neck. "This isn't going to break today," she said. "We just need someone to stay and man the pumps."

"Parker!"

Parker, Megan thought. As always, it was Parker. She watched Taylor shout orders into Sage's face. Water dripped from the brim of Sage's orange hard hat as he offered a calm reply. Taylor slogged over to a blue pickup, and Megan heard him tell Randy Whiteman to relieve Sage on the pumps at two o'clock that afternoon.

Heading for his own pickup, Taylor backpedaled a few steps as he announced to Megan, "I'm outta here. If this lets up, I'll see you tomorrow." As he turned on his heel, he slipped, flailed wildly and narrowly missed planting his rump in the mud. "Damn moon dung," he muttered as he took more care trekking across the slick organic goop that was also known to road builders in coarser terms.

Tires spun and threw gravel in their wake as, one by one, the crew members' vehicles took to the road. The unimproved cutoff was closed to through traffic, forcing other drivers to use the longer paved route, which was about a twenty mile jog to the south. On a day like this Megan figured the paved route was certainly preferable, although the plan she was formulating for herself would take her over a long stretch of gravel road within the hour.

The thunk of a closing door drew her head around. Sage had taken shelter in his old blue pickup. She had intended to offer him the office. The gently falling rain tapped on her hard plastic hat. The mud sucked at her work boots as she made her way to the passenger side and rapped at the window. The other door opened, and he did a chin-up over the roof of the cab.

"Come around this side," she was told. "That door doesn't work."

She could hear the seesaw moan of a steel guitar playing on the radio, but he flicked it off when she reached his side. He pushed the door open, and she stuck her head inside. Water dripped from her hat onto his jeans.

"Would you like to use the office?" she asked.

Her face was inches from his, and she was dripping all over him, but he found himself ignoring any inclination to move away. "I need to stay close to the pump in case it clogs up."

"May I speak with you for a moment?"

"Come on in." He slid over.

"I'll get your seat wet."

He laughed and nodded at the puddle she was making under the steering wheel. "You'll get *your* seat wet." He grabbed a faded blue towel from the dashboard and took a swipe at the water. "Give me your slicker. I'll stick it over here with mine."

The wet slickers were piled next to the broken door, and Sage wiped at the seat once more, pulling his hand back just before Megan settled down and pulled the door shut. She dropped her hat to the floor and tossed her head, flinging droplets like a lawn sprinkler. He blotted his face with the towel.

"Oh. I'm sorry."

"Let's face it—" He smiled and tossed her the towel. "We're wet. Should I turn on some heat?"

"Not for me. I'm fine." She gave the hair cropped close to her nape a brisk rub with the terrycloth. "Do you mind doing this?"

"What?"

"Staying to man the pumps."

"It's better than losing a day's pay."

She turned to find that he was watching her. His hair dangled across his forehead and curved over his damp collar like wet, black fringe. The chambray and denim covering his shoulders and his thighs were soaked, and she imagined that his socks were as wet as hers. "I'm glad it's your choice," she said. "Everybody else seems to have specialized, while you're always doing something different. I wondered if Taylor was assigning you whatever nobody else wanted to do."

"Taylor might have a bad mouth on him, but he knows his dirt." Sage raked his fingers through his hair in a vain attempt to push it back from his forehead. "I've got a lot of experience, and he doesn't mind making use of it. Neither do I."

The rain pattered against the roof of the pickup. Megan peered through the windshield at the big yellow bulldozer sitting idle only a few yards away. "Still, nobody likes to sit around all day in wet clothes."

"Then maybe somebody oughta go home and change." He smiled when she turned to him again. "I've been ranching most of my life," he said. "I spend a lot of time in wet clothes."

"And I've got a stop to make before I can go back to Hot Springs, so I'll be wet a while longer, too."

She had yet to give him a hint regarding her purpose for being in his pickup, but he decided it was her prerogative to lead up to whatever it was any way she wanted. She was the boss. "Want some coffee?" he asked. He leaned toward her and reached under her legs, smiling at the wary look she gave him. "It's under the seat."

"Coffee would be great," she said. She tried to stem the shiver that crept along her spine, but it won out, spreading in ripples to her extremities.

Sage tossed the Thermos bottle into his left hand and reached for the keys with his right. "Hit the accelerator," he said as he turned on the ignition. "A little heat wouldn't hurt, either."

"I guess not. I hate it when my socks get wet."

"So do I." He spun the cap on the silver-colored Thermos and stuck it between his knees while he unscrewed the stopper. "Take them off and let them dry out." As he poured, he glanced past the rising steam at the gauges behind the steering wheel. "I've got enough gas to keep the heat on for a while."

"But you have to be able to get home. How far is it?"

"From here to my place? About thirty-five miles." He handed her the coffee he'd poured. "We'll have to share. I don't have an extra cup."

Megan held the cup close to her nose and inhaled the rich aroma of strong, black coffee. The steam warmed her face as she sipped. "Mmm," she murmured between sips. "Perfect."

"I'm gaining a reputation for making good coffee."

"Really? On a day like this you could set up a stand."

He chuckled. "I don't see too many prospective customers."

"Which leads you to wonder why I'm still here." Without meeting his eyes, she handed him the cup.

"Yeah, the thought did cross my mind." He tasted the coffee and decided it wasn't his best. He'd been in a hurry that morning after he'd had to fix a gate the horses had knocked down. But he'd made it to work on time.

She turned toward him and rested her elbow on the steering wheel. "Taylor was gunning for Gary and Jackie again this morning."

"I heard."

"I was afraid you might have." She drew a deep breath and gave a sigh. "I don't want you to take offense at the things he says, Sage."

"Why?"

"Well, because you're doing such a good job. Taylor has such a—"

"No, I mean what's with *you* not wanting *me* to take offense? If I take offense, it'll be between me and Taylor. Why does that concern you?"

"Because Taylor's a bigot, and the project could suffer from his attitude. If he keeps this up and we lose all our Indians—I mean our Native—"

Sage's laughter cut her short. "Lose all our Indians?" He wondered why he was laughing instead of bristling and decided it was either because she looked so pretty sitting there in her wet jumpsuit or because she was trying so damn hard. "Is that anything like losing all our marbles? You're gonna lose yours just trying to figure out what to call us."

"Native Americans." She folded her arms and lifted her chin. "I *meant* to say Native Americans. I know that's what you prefer to be called."

"Who told you that?" He eyed her over the rim of the cup, then sipped the hot coffee.

"I think I read that the preferred term is currently—" She looked at him across the narrow distance between them. There was something steamy about his very presence. She had read that Indians considered it rude to look directly into a person's face, but he was frankly assessing hers. His amusement lingered as a bright sheen in his dark eyes. "I seem to be saying the wrong things again," she said quietly. "What do you prefer to be called?"

"Sage."

He drew a smile from her as he handed her the cup. "It's a very unusual name," she said.

"Lots of Parkers around, but you won't run across too many Sages." He lifted one shoulder. "We've got some Native Americans at Pine Ridge. And we've got some Indians who aren't up on the current term. Columbus called us Indians, but he'd pretty much lost his marbles, too—or his compass, or some damn thing. And America was named for some Italian guy."

"How about Sioux, then?"

"That's the French version of what the Chippewa called us, and it was sort of like being called a snake in the grass. The old ones say we're Lakota, which has nothing to do with being from a certain place or being there first. It means 'allies.'" He raised an eyebrow. "You seem to want to be an ally of the allies."

"I certainly don't want to be an enemy." After swallowing a sip of coffee she added, "I want to be fair."

"And if the Office of Equal Opportunity Employment sends anyone out from Washington, you want them to see minorities working on this project." He laughed. "Hell, they'll see *you*. A woman at the helm oughta be worth at least half a dozen Indians working as flagmen, don't you think?''

"Indians?"

"Or maybe three Native Americans on 'dozers."

"Sage—"

"Or one damn-near civilized Sioux carrying a clipboard and driving a highway department pickup. That could be very impressive."

She passed him the coffee as she held up her other hand in surrender. "Truce, Sage. Please. It isn't just a matter of being in compliance with OEO regulations. I'm really trying to be fair. I know there's very little employment on the reservation, and I'll call you whatever you suggest if you'll just tell me what I can do to persuade Jackie and Gary to stick with us and get to work on time every day."

Sage turned, resting the cup of coffee on his knee, which was bent toward her. He looked at her for a moment, considering the sincerity he saw in her eyes. "What do you want to be called?" She tipped her head to one side, and her eyebrows puckered just slightly. "Like you, I'm kind of at a loss. What do you suggest I call you? Boss lady or Miss McBride?"

"Megan," she said.

"That's simple enough. Okay, Megan, here's the deal. If Taylor tries to make this a racial thing, he'll get trouble. I'll report it. If a guy's not getting to work, you deal with *him*, and you don't generalize the issue to include the rest of us. That's just good supervision."

"I think Taylor has it in for the Indians on the crew."

"You may be right." He offered the cup again. "Want another hit?" She shook her head, so he drained it himself. "*I* think he's got it in for you," he added, gesturing with the empty cup.

"I can handle that."

"And I can handle the other if it comes my way, believe me." The cup clattered against the top of the Thermos as he replaced it, screwing it down tight. "Look, Megan, you've got good instincts, but they're misdirected. Jackie has some growing up to do, and he's determined to do it the hard way. Gary—" He gave a careless shrug. "He'll hold up his end pretty well and cover for himself when he doesn't. You're giving them equal opportunity. You don't have to wipe their noses and pack their lunches for them."

"That isn't what I had in mind. I'm just trying to be—"

"Fair. I know. If the guys from OEO come around, I'll be sure and tell them how you went out of your way to be fair." Not much out of her way, he thought as he studied her face. She didn't have to. With very little makeup her face *was* fair, with smooth, dewy-looking skin and a bow-shaped lower lip that was naturally pink and pouty. He had to keep reminding himself that he was working for her.

"You were dead right about digging this stuff out," he told her. "It's a real deep pocket of pure moon...slime."

She smiled, wondering whether he had chosen his words carefully in deference to her gender or her position. She decided it didn't matter. It was a sign of respect either way. "I *am* good at what I do. And so are you."

"This is what I do to pay the bills," he told her as he slid the Thermos bottle back under the seat. "What I really do is ranch, and I can be good at that, too, when I put my heart into it."

"Are you...do you have a family?"

"Yeah." He sat up slowly, challenging himself to look her straight in the eye and answer this question as easily as he would any other. "I've got two kids. They live with my... They live with their mother in Omaha. We're divorced." There was a womanly softness in her eyes, and he knew he could play on her sympathy if he kept talking about himself. But he'd broken himself of that habit. "What about you? Ever been married?"

She gave her head a quick shake. "No."

"Close?"

"Once. Sort of." Squaring her shoulders, she glanced away. "I've worked hard to get where I am. I haven't had time for much else."

"You know what?" She looked back at him, and he smiled. A fine mist of perspiration gave his face a vigorous luster. "This conversation is getting pretty damn personal. We're fogging up the windows here."

They were surrounded by a silver-gray curtain and vapor-locked together in the cab of his pickup. It gave her a warm, cozy feeling.

"Warm enough yet?"

She looked at him, surprised, wondering whether he'd read her mind. "Oh, yes, and I do need to get going."

He turned off the ignition and pulled the keys. "You never did dry your socks out."

She laughed easily. "I think I can live with wet feet."

"Maybe I can help you out." He unlocked the glove compartment and produced a pair of white tube socks, neatly folded into a military roll. Turning to hand them to her, he caught her puzzled look. He glanced back into the open compartment. She'd seen the small bottle he kept for the more difficult calls he sometimes had to make. "I don't drink on the job, if that's what you're thinking." Closing the compartment, he turned his head and gave her a hard look. It wasn't necessary to tell her anything else, he reminded himself. "I don't drink at all...anymore."

"Why do you have that in there?"

It was none of her business. "For medicinal purposes, believe it or not."

"Cough medicine?"

He didn't laugh. Something in the tone of her voice said she'd heard that excuse before. "It isn't for me." He reached for her hand. Shock flashed in her eyes when he touched her, and he knew it had to do with the bottle and the fact that she didn't quite believe him. Still, she didn't pull away. He laid the roll of socks in her hand and closed her fingers around them. "I want you to keep your feet warm, Megan. My job may depend on your continued good health."

"What about you?"

"I'll be slogging through this mud until Randy comes on at two o'clock. What good will one pair of socks do me?"

She hardly knew the man. The fact that she was stuffing his socks in her pocket seemed an absolute absurdity. "Thank you."

"Now—" He handed her the top slicker, then picked up his own. "Since I can't see out this window, I'd better go check on the pumps."

"Thank you for the coffee, too." She drew the plastic raincoat around her shoulders, crunching it into the small space between herself and the door. "This conversation has really been helpful."

"Uh-uh, Megan. Watch the sarcasm."

"I mean it," she protested. "You've given me a lot to think about."

He gave her a sidelong glance as he snapped his slicker up the front. The lock of black hair that fell across his forehead made her think of a movie idol striking a sultry pose. "Then let me add one more thought for the day," he said.

"What's that?"

"Projects don't suffer from bigotry. People do." He pushed back the errant lock of hair and settled the bright orange construction worker's hat on his head, offering her a forgiving smile as he explained further. "The Indians aren't yours to lose. And we aren't yours to save, either."

"Did I sound that pompous?" she asked as she retrieved her hat from the floor.

"Yeah. You did." He grinned and jerked his chin toward the door behind her. "After you, Megan. This baby's only got one exit."

Sage shut the compressor off and waded through six inches of water toward a pump that wasn't functioning properly. Water filled his boots and crept up the legs of his jeans. Muttering a curse at the machine, he lifted his head and watched the highway department pickup barrel down the gravel road. He wondered why she was headed east. There was just a little one-horse town between here and Pine Ridge, and surely she didn't have business to do there. As he hauled the pump out of the water he asked himself a more pressing question. Why in the hell had he given that woman his extra pair of socks?

As long as they'd had to shut down for the day, Megan had decided to visit the town of Pine Ridge. In the rain it looked more bedraggled than she'd anticipated. Rows of tract houses, nearly identical except for the assortment of bland pastel colors, stood in various states of disrepair. Funding from the Department of Housing and Urban Development must be harder to come by these days, she thought. In her search for the Bureau of Indian Affairs office building, Megan passed the Indian Health Service Clinic and the tribal offices.

Her front tire hit a pothole and splashed a cascade of water on the words "THORPES NO. 1," which were spray painted in red on the sidewalk. Megan knew the high school athletic teams were named for Jim Thorpe, the versatile Native American Olympic athlete who'd been stripped of his medals because he'd earned a few dollars playing semi-professional baseball prior to the games. She remembered seeing a film about him. In later years he'd been plagued by alcoholism.

She had also seen a film about Ira Hayes, the Pima Indian hero from World War II who'd helped raise the flag at Iwo Jima. He, too, had struggled with alcoholism. After the war he had been wined and dined by a country basking in victory and anxious to honor its heroes. But the country had not been anxious to honor its debts to the Pima, for whom reservation life meant poverty and poor health. Megan remembered the scene in which a drunken Hayes had blacked out and drowned tragically in two inches of drainage ditch water.

She needed to assume some of the responsibility for all this. She wasn't out to save anyone, but there had been so much unfairness in the past. In her position, she needed to go out of her way to be fair. Sage was right. She was certainly naive in these matters, and she wanted to learn.

She'd taken some engineering classes from Pete Petersen, who was in charge of the BIA Roads Department at Pine Ridge. He recognized her immediately when she walked into his office, and he offered her more coffee and all the time she wanted.

"I hear you've got Sage Parker on your project," Pete said after the initial amenities and personal news had been exchanged. "He's spent a few seasons working for me. Good man. Damn good man, long as he stays sober. He's not one of the ones you're concerned about, is he?"

Megan flexed her foot and glanced past her crossed knees at the toe of her work boot as she paused to appreciate the fact that she was wearing dry socks. "Not at all," she reported. "I don't think there's a piece of equipment on the site he can't handle, and he's there every day, just like clockwork."

"He was a heavy equipment operator when he was in the Army years back. Kind of a local hero in his day, too. Hell of a bull rider. Had a pretty little wife. 'Course, everybody around here wants to ranch, and he did that, too. Sage had it all." The springs in Pete's desk chair squeaked as he leaned back and folded his hands over his droopy paunch. "Guess every one of us has at least one lesson to learn the hard way."

"What happened?" Megan asked.

"Sage always was a hard worker. Used to be a hard drinker and a hard swinger, too." Pete shook his head slowly as he tapped his thumbs together. "When the bubble burst, Sage came down harder than most. He had a lot to lose, and he lost it all. First time he went up to Fort Meade for treatment for alcoholism, they had to drag him kicking and screaming. They say he checked himself into a different program the second time around."

"I understand he's running a recovery program of his own now."

"Kind of a post-treatment program, I guess. They talk about traditional values and reviving the community. He calls it the Medicine Wheel." Pete sat up quickly. The springy chair swatted him in the back as he planted his elbows on the desk. "Yep," he drawled. "Some people around here think ol' Sage walks on water. Others want to see his program slide right down the tubes."

"Why?"

His humorless smile gave his answer a chilling edge. "Business. You got your liquor sales, your pawn brokers, your loan sharking. Those people are making money."

"Off other people's misery," Megan reflected.

"That's right. That's the way of the world, I'm afraid. One man gets well, and he goes out tilting at windmills. The blood-suckers start gunning for him." Pete slapped his palm against the desktop and smiled. "Damn, I hope he knocks a few of them flat on their butts. They've got a hearing going on in the tribal office at four o'clock." He checked his watch. "If they're running on Indian time, it should be getting started about now. It's four-thirty. Sage and some of the others want to see the council deny liquor license renewals on the reservation. You oughta take a walk over there—give a listen. Might be an eye-opener for you, Megan."

Chapter 3

Pete Petersen accompanied Megan to the tribal office building, where the meeting was in progress. They shook the water from their raincoats and made their way toward the double doors. Pete shouldered a path through the lingerers, and Megan followed closely behind him.

A man standing near the door directed them to two folding chairs. Megan noticed that people preferred to stand against the walls and gather near the door rather than fill the seats that had been provided for spectators. She was happy to take a seat, where she could keep a low profile. She'd felt people's curiosity as scores of dark eyes followed her from the door to the chair. Glancing around her at the sea of brown faces, Megan realized that this was the first time she'd been the racial minority in a crowd of people. She pushed her damp hair back behind her ears and slouched self-consciously, wondering whether her presence was viewed as an intrusion.

Her interest soon supplanted her discomfort. Pete tipped his balding head toward her and pointed out the tribal chairman, who sat on the dais with two other officers, and the councilmen, whose tables formed two sides of a square flanking the dais. The witness' table and the rows of spectators' chairs behind it completed the square. A young woman was speaking into the witness' microphone, and a child continually reached for her from the lap of a man who sat close by. Megan leaned sideways for a better view and discovered that the man was Sage Parker.

He shifted the toddler from one knee to the other and bounced him occasionally. The youngster attempted a quick slide over Sage's thigh, but a protective arm brought him up short and settled him back in place. Megan caught a glimpse of the little boy's black-eyed scowl as Sage pulled the small blue and white striped T-shirt down over his round little belly. Sage, too, appeared to listen with one ear, and he handled the baby as naturally as he did a jackhammer.

Megan leaned in Pete's direction and whispered, "Who's the speaker?"

"That's Jackie Flying Elk's wife, Regina. She's a beauty, isn't she?"

For some reason, she hadn't imagined Jackie with a beautiful wife. With the number of heads in her way, Megan couldn't see much besides the woman's long, satiny fall of black hair, and that was enough to trigger a pang of envy. Megan kept her own hair short. It was comfortable, practical, easy to care for and perfectly suited to her line of work. Secretly, though, she coveted long hair, and Regina's was worth coveting. The child on Sage's lap thought so, too, and he nearly managed to snatch a handful of it before Sage caught him. He brought the little hand to his mouth and playfully nipped the child's fat fingers. It was a side of the man Megan had not imagined, and it gave her a warm feeling just to watch. Mingled with the warmth was something else—something strangely akin to that envy of a woman who had something Megan might want.

"Is that her child?" Megan whispered.

"Which one?" Pete craned his neck for a glimpse past a dozen rows of intervening heads. He smiled. "Oh, yeah, there's Sage. Figured he'd be here." Then, in answer to the question, he shrugged. "Probably Regina's. Sage's kids are older. Besides, the wife took them somewhere out of state. From what I hear, she won't let him near them."

The boy on Sage's lap wasn't the only young child in the room. The voices of several others, along with the continual shuffle of people moving in and out of the room, caused an undercurrent that seemed to disturb no one but Megan. She was annoyed with herself when she realized that Regina had concluded her remarks, and Megan had heard little of what she'd said. She listened to Regina's response to a question from one of the councilmen. Yes, Regina was aware that revoking the license in question would not force the closing of all the bars on the reservation, but she hoped it would be a start.

"That's the guy they're trying to close down." Pete's nod directed Megan's attention to a brawny white man who was sitting near the exit at the front of the room. His ruddy complexion contrasted strikingly with hair and eyebrows the color of wheat. "Floyd Taylor owns one of two bars and the only grocery store in Red Calf, a little town about thirty miles north of here. If you didn't blink as you passed, you might have noticed it off to the east."

"I saw the sign," Megan whispered. "He's not related to Karl Taylor, is he?"

"Floyd's his younger brother. They've got three more built just like them."

If Floyd's personality was anything like Karl's, Megan already knew where her sympathies lay in this issue. She'd never joined the crew at the Red Rooster, their favorite happy hour spot, because she had no interest in finding out what kind of conversation Karl Taylor might make after a few beers.

Floyd Taylor raised his hand like a schoolboy as he came to his feet. "Mr. Chairman? I'd like to ask Mrs. Flying Elk a question, if I could." No one objected as the big blond barkeeper turned toward the witness table. "I'd just like to know if I'm to blame for the way your husband drinks, Mrs. Flying Elk. Are you saying it's my fault he ended up back in detox again?"

Regina's voice was strong and clear. "No, Mr. Taylor. I'm not saying it's your fault."

"It just seems to me that's what this is all about, this hearing. I'm a businessman. I abide by the laws, both tribal and state, and I do business with whoever comes in the door, unless he's under age." Taylor waved a hand about the room. "I see a lot of familiar faces in this room, and, hell, you all know me. Old Uncle Floyd. You come to me when you need gas money, when you've got a sick kid, or when you just run a little short at the end of the month, and I don't turn you down." His open-handed gesture was directed at Regina. "Everybody's welcome at Floyd's, but I never twisted anybody's arm, Mrs. Flying Elk. Your husband's a big boy, and he makes his own decisions."

"I know that," Regina said. "My husband is not the issue."

"Then what is?"

"Didn't you hear one word of what I said, Mr. Taylor?"

"Mrs. Flying Elk," the chairman said through his microphone, "is there anything you want to add to your statement at this time?"

"I've said all I have to say." She pushed her chair back and leaned forward to add, "Anyone who has no ears won't hear me anyway. Thank you, Mr. Chairman."

Regina moved to the chair next to Sage's and took the child from his lap. Two more speakers took the chair behind the witness table and offered prepared statements, but impromptu testimony from the floor was permitted, as well. Characteristic of each speech were the final words, "That's all I have to say." Much of the testimony gave personal witness to the far-reaching effects of alcohol within the community and ended with a plea for the people, as a whole, to reject its use. Megan heard the courage in each speaker's voice as heart-rending stories were offered publicly, but she knew that none of this would convict Floyd Taylor of anything in a court of law.

On the other side, people claimed that they should all have the right to choose for themselves. "If they're gonna drink, they're gonna drink," one man said. "We've got enough bootleggers around here now, selling to minors. It'll be worse if we close the bars down."

Finally, Sage came to the microphone. The room grew quieter, and there was a sense of expectation as he arranged several manila folders on the table. Megan wondered how he'd managed to work until two, stop to change into his red Western shirt and a pair of jeans that were certainly newer and drier than the ones he'd been wearing earlier, and get here for this meeting. He'd obviously defied all speed limits.

His introductory remarks reviewed his reasons for filing with the tribal court for an injunction against the renewal of Floyd Taylor's liquor license. From a file of police reports he cited numerous complaints against Taylor for disturbing the peace, serving liquor to customers who were clearly intoxicated and serving minors. In some cases Taylor had paid a nominal fine. In others no one would testify against him, or the testimony of a few had been refuted by a greater number, and the issue had died quietly.

"Mr. Taylor is not responsible for one man's relapse," Sage argued, "but he is responsible to this community to uphold its laws. Even when he gets off on a technicality, we all know what he's doing. We all know that 'Uncle Floyd' doesn't give a damn about our sick kids, or about the kids that this complaint alleges were sitting out in the car in front of the bar until two o'clock in the morning—" he waved a paper in Taylor's direction "—keeping nearby residents awake with their crying."

"Those kids aren't my responsibility," Taylor injected.

"When you continue to serve their parents long after neither one can stand up, whose responsibility are they, Taylor? Why didn't you call the police?"

"What difference does it make?" Floyd slouched back in his chair and waved the matter away with one hand. "Somebody called the police, and the whole thing was taken care of without any trouble. You know I don't let kids in at Floyd's."

"Not unless they've got the price of a drink," Sage grumbled.

"Hey, look, I do my best. I can't always be sure how old they are." A slow grin crossed Floyd's face. "You know damn well you got by a time or two, Sage. 'Course, that was when my dad was running the place, and the law wasn't as tough then. Speaking of which . . ." The smug-faced man braced his hands on his knees and leaned forward. "I can think of a few times when it was *your* kids out in the car."

There was a moment of heavy silence before Sage's voice came over the microphone again. "I'm paying the price for that, Taylor. My children are no longer living with me."

Megan felt a tightness in her chest as she drew her next breath. A shared sense of despair pervaded the room. Those with children drew them closer, and most of the others hung their heads.

"Mr. Chairman." Attention turned to the councilman who had broken the silence. "I move we table this matter. We need time to look over the reports Mr. Parker has gathered."

The motion was passed, and the meeting was quickly adjourned. Sage put the papers back in their folders and took them to the chairman. As he walked back from the dais, he saw Megan. He hesitated as though he'd lost his bearings for a moment. She smiled and waited near her chair, thinking he would come over and speak to her. Instead he acknowledged her with a nod, then turned his attention to the people who had been sitting near him.

Ignoring a quick surge of disappointment, she took her raincoat from the back of the chair and offered Pete a handshake. "Thanks for your time, Pete. This was interesting. How long do you think the debate will continue?"

"I don't know. Taylor wants it settled. That injunction keeps him from doing business."

"It sounds as though he shouldn't *be* in business," she said as she and Pete moved with the crowd toward the door.

"There are a lot of sides to this issue. Some people would accuse Sage's group of angling toward a return to Prohibition."

"I didn't get that impression." When they reached the lobby, Megan put on her raincoat. "I hope this lets up soon," she said, nodding toward the rain streaming down outside the doors. "I'm battling ground water as well as rain."

"Project's getting interesting, huh?" Pete pulled a floppy canvas hat down over his brow. "You were the first woman ever enrolled in any of my classes. Not that I've done that much teaching, but you did come as a surprise." He offered a warm smile, full of a teacher's pride in a student-made-good. "You'll do fine."

Megan dashed down the sidewalk and hopped across the rivulet of water that washed past the curb. Within the shelter of her pickup, she shucked her raincoat and stuffed it under the front seat. She was combing her fingers through her damp hair when the door on the passenger side swung open and Sage slid into the seat. Water dripped from the brim of his straw cowboy hat, and the shoulders of his denim jacket were wet. He tossed the hat on the seat between them and angled his body toward her.

"You drove a long way to satisfy your curiosity."

The guarded look in his eyes was unsettling. She found herself searching for excuses. "Pete Petersen was a teacher of mine. I came to ask for some advice. I didn't know about the hearing, but when he suggested...I thought I could learn more about..."

"And did you?"

"Yes, I did. I learned a great deal."

He seemed to stare right through her, and she imagined that her forehead had become a message display board betraying her every reaction to what she had just observed. She fussed with her hair again and wished he would stop looking at her that way. Finally he turned his attention to the dollops of rainwater that splashed on the windshield from an overhanging cottonwood tree.

"Even if we lose this one in the end, it's worth the effort," he said. Megan wondered whether he was confiding in her or simply coming to terms with something he'd decided was likely to occur. "It's a chance to bring things out in the open and make people take a look."

"With all those complaints, it's really shocking that they haven't closed Floyd Taylor down before this."

"Shocking?" He watched a small, waferlike cottonwood seed slide down the glass. "Was that the only thing you heard in there that shocked you?"

"I wasn't really shocked," she confessed quietly. "I don't live in a vacuum. I don't want to, anyway. That's why I came."

"To take a firsthand look at how the other half lives?'

"To *learn*, Sage. It's important to be sensitive to the fact that an employee is a human being and to deal with him as a person rather than a machine." She knew she sounded like something out of a book, but she couldn't seem to stop herself. "In order to do that, I have to—"

"Sensitive." He smiled at the windshield. "I like that." After a moment he turned his head, and his eyes became mellow as he looked at her. "Do you realize how soft that makes you sound?"

"A man like Karl Taylor might mistake sensitivity for weakness." Her eyes narrowed. "I didn't think you would."

"I didn't say weak. I said soft." He propped his elbow on the back of the seat and rested his temple against his prominent knuckles. "A lot of people are willing to drive extra miles to avoid passing through a reservation. They're sure we lie in wait to slash their tires and siphon their gas." He raised one dark eyebrow. "Since you're here, I guess I can't call you weak."

"I'm not soft, either." She folded her arms to cover her breasts.

There was little cheer in the smile he gave her. "And these aren't your tires. So what do you think all this sensitivity leads to?"

"Fairness," she said.

"Oh, yeah." He snapped his fingers. "I remember now. You're the one who's determined to be fair."

"I want to deal fairly with everyone, and I don't think that necessarily means dealing with all people in exactly the same way. I'm here to learn more about—"

"You being the dealer makes it pretty nice. You get to deal out second chances whenever you're feeling particularly sensitive." He eyed her with a challenge. "Do I get one?"

"I don't know," she answered quietly. She'd seen him expose himself before the crowd. He hadn't asked for sympathy then. What was he asking for now? "I think you're asking the wrong person."

She'd struck the right chord. He closed his eyes and used his fingertips to smooth the creases from his brow. "Sometimes I think I owe the whole world an apology, and I don't like the feeling." He lowered his hand and offered a tentative smile, made genuine this time by the soft luster in his eyes. "I was just taking a guilt trip and looking for a traveling companion."

"I'm sorry about your children, Sage."

"Uh-uh." He jabbed his chest with his thumb. "I'm the one who's sorry. What Taylor said about my neglect—that part was true." His sigh was a long, hollow sound. He settled back against the seat and watched two drenched figures hurry past the hood of the pickup. "I can go to these meetings and say all the things that need to be said, and they can say, 'Who the hell do you think you are? We all know you.' And they tell me who I am. They remind me. Every damn time."

"Two people so far have told me who you are," Megan said. Her heart had ballooned with sympathy at the sound of his sigh, but she was determined to deflate the feeling to a size and shape that might be more acceptable to him. "Bob Krueger and Pete Petersen both said you were the best man on my crew. They said—"

"They said I'm a hell of a good worker when I'm sober, and they'd heard I've really straightened out."

"They *knew* you've straightened out. It's been several years, hasn't it?"

"Four. I've got an anniversary coming up." He chuckled. "I never remembered my wedding anniversary, but I remember the day I quit drinking. I remember the hour."

"I understand you've started a recovery group," she said. "Is it like Alcoholics Anonymous?"

"Yeah, pretty much." He realized that he'd already entrusted her with a great deal more about himself than he'd intended, but Medicine Wheel was something beyond himself. He offered his customarily vague explanation. "It's a group effort."

"Nobody approved of the tactics Taylor used," Megan assured him.

Sage lifted one shoulder in a shrug. "The man's fighting for his livelihood. He'll use all the ammunition that's available to him, and I spent a lot of years building that munitions dump." He turned to her again and saw the look of expectation in her eyes. He was confiding in her, and she liked that. She was an outside pair of ears, and he wanted to talk. "Some of these people remember Prohibition, and they think we're trying to bring it back."

"That was a long time ago."

"Not for us," he said. "It wasn't until the 1950s that the laws began to permit the selling of liquor to reservation Indians. The people went to bootleggers instead of bars. Then they sat in their cars or went out behind the privy and slugged it down. That's the way we drink—like we're afraid a hand's going to reach out of the dark and take it away from us. We haven't cultivated any social drinking skills."

"You're certainly not alone in that."

"Maybe not, but I sure wish the old whiskey drummers and the bootleggers had brought along those classy traditions. You know, the etiquette—the towel over the arm and checking out the cork." He smiled, and his brown eyes brightened. "Aren't you impressed by a guy who knows how to order wine?"

"I haven't given it much thought."

"I have. Just lately, since I started trying to put the pieces together. I want to know, 'Why us?'" He braced his hand against the dashboard. "We have beautiful, old traditions, but not one of them has anything to do with having a drink before dinner. Hell, Muscatel comes with a screw cap, and who can tell anything about its 'bouquet' when you're passing the bottle with a bunch of guys behind the outhouse?"

Her laughter sputtered in her throat, and it was useless to try to hold it in. This wasn't something she wanted to laugh about, but the image he'd conjured up was wonderfully absurd. The heavy weight of her sympathy was lifted by the fact that they laughed together.

"Does Muscatel have a bouquet?" she managed.

"They used to call it 'Mustn't Tell.' I suppose 'Mustn't Smell' fits, too."

"Oh, Sage." Her laughter wound down, and she shook her head. "This isn't something we should laugh about."

"Why shouldn't we? Don't you know how much Indian people like to laugh? Through it all, we have to be able to laugh."

The notion seemed strange to her. Serious matters were to be met with complete gravity, and, she had to admit, she didn't know how much Indian people liked to laugh. "What's the difference between Prohibition and what you're trying to do?"

He ticked the points off without a moment's hesitation, because he knew them well. "I don't want *them* to tell *us* we can't drink. I want *us* to decide we won't. I want us to say *no*, individually and collectively. I want Taylor and his kind to be out of business simply because we don't want what he's got to sell. Every one of us suffers from it."

"Obviously not everyone agrees."

"Not yet, but we're growing in number." His conviction brightened his dark eyes. "Even if we lose, we've got people talking about it. Traditionally our decisions were made by consensus, which is hard to get. You have to keep talking, keep reminding people."

"Your meetings seem to offer everyone a chance to say his piece."

"That's right," he said with a quick nod. He lifted one finger to punctuate his promise. "You get a circle of Indian people together, and you'll hear some speeches. We love to make speeches, and we have a style all our own."

"Was it an intrusion?" she asked, suddenly worried. "My being there today, I mean."

"No, it wasn't. I guess I got a little defensive." His eyes were bright, and his smile spread slowly. The damp hair that fell across his forehead gave him an unexpectedly boyish look. "I wasn't expecting the 'boss lady' to be part of the audience."

"And I didn't come to spy on you." She returned his smile. "I wouldn't do that to someone who loaned me dry socks."

Sage knew he had to be crazy. For the second time in one day he was sitting in a pickup with this too-cute lady from Pierre while a curtain of rain dropped around them, interfering with his fragile connection with reality. And he was grinning about it.

Two weeks later Megan recalled every word that had passed between them in that pickup as she considered her problem with Karl Taylor. Sage hadn't said that she *was* soft. He'd said that the importance she placed on sensitivity made her *sound* soft. She hadn't been offended, because he hadn't been offensive. Taylor *had*—once too often. Bob Krueger had agreed to take him off the project.

Megan slid her report into a manila envelope and sealed it carefully. Her complaint would become part of Taylor's personnel file, and he would be reprimanded. Off the record, there would be those who would reiterate the notion that this was a man's job, and any woman who demanded the right to be out here with a road crew might expect an occasional sexual hassle. That notion had become obsolete, Megan reminded herself as she peered through her office window in time to watch Bob Krueger pull up in a highway department car. Bob wasn't there to give Taylor the news. Megan had done that herself, and since he hadn't shown up for work that morning, she assumed he'd gone to the State Highway Department office in Pierre. Bob was there to pick up her written complaint and to discuss replacing Taylor.

Bob listened to her tell her story exactly as she had told it over the phone. She needed to repeat it, and he saw her frustration in the way she waved her arms about, heard it in the way her voice kept climbing as she spoke. She wouldn't be bullied or manhandled, but she was still trying to convince herself that she'd been absolutely fair.

"So there were no witnesses," he concluded as he leaned across her desk and stubbed his cigarette out in the jar lid she'd put there for him.

Megan stood beside the window and watched an earth mover crawl up a hill. "There was no one else around," she confirmed.

"And this was the first time Taylor tried anything like this?"

Megan sighed. "It was the first clearly overt gesture. A couple of times he made a point to cut off my space—make me walk around him. He made a stupid remark once, and I told him he was way out of line."

"But this time he actually cornered you."

She nodded toward the metal cabinets and patiently repeated, "Against the files."

"And told you..."

"That my skin looked so soft it made his palms itch. It's in the report, word for word."

"And you told him..."

"To get the hell out of my way."

"Which he did." Bob leaned back in his chair. "I'm not defending these guys, Megan, but this kind of thing has happened before. By my count this is the third time."

She folded her arms tightly as she turned from the window. "It may not be the last. It's not a man's world anymore, Bob. I don't come equipped with a black belt in karate. I don't have to. I know the law."

"Taylor does, too. I knew you weren't a good match, but I wanted his experience." Bob dismissed his mistake with a wave of the hand. It was time to move on. "We've got so damn many projects going this summer. I've got everybody working. You said you've got a replacement in mind?"

Megan nodded. "Parker."

"That's what I thought. He's the logical choice." Bob shook his head slowly. "He won't do it, Megan. I've offered it to him before."

"*This* job?"

"Not this project, but others." With a smile, Bob remembered, "He doesn't want to give orders, he says. He just wants to work."

Megan turned toward the window again. Sage was the right man for the job, she told herself. The fact that she liked him wasn't a crime. The crew liked him, too. He was *likable*, for heaven's sake. He was also capable, which was why she had chosen him. "I'm going to offer him the position anyway," she said firmly. "With his experience and his skills, *he* knows he's the logical choice. It would be unfair not to offer it to him."

When Sage saw the dark green car parked next to the office, he knew his lunch break was shot. Megan had sent for him, Krueger was there, and he'd heard about Taylor. It wasn't hard to put one and one and one together and foresee the "great opportunity" on the horizon. As he mounted the wobbly metal steps to the trailer, he slapped some of the dust off the seat of his jeans and buttoned a couple of shirt buttons, leaving two still open. Hell, it was too hot to dress for the occasion.

"You wanted to see me?" Sage glanced from the man seated near the desk to the woman standing behind it. He wasn't sure whose idea this was, but he figured he could handle both of them if it became a joint effort.

"We've had to pull Taylor off this project," Bob announced. "You probably heard."

"Sure, I heard." He'd been hearing it all morning from the guys who'd been with Taylor at the Red Rooster the night before. And all morning long he'd resisted the temptation to storm the office and demand to know what that jerk had said to her, what he'd *really* done. Sage had had to remind himself that he wasn't her champion; he was part of her construction crew. She'd obviously taken care of the situation quite efficiently. It was none of Sage's business what Taylor had said or done, but when he looked at Megan this time, he knew damn well that his eyes conveyed his concern.

"I want you to take over as construction supervisor," she said simply.

"I don't want the job."

The offer obviously came as no surprise to him. Megan moved to the front of the desk and stood as rigidly as he did. "You should have had it to begin with. With all your skills, it's time you moved ahead in this business."

"Who says I want to move ahead?" He spoke to her as though explaining a new concept. "I need a job, Miss McBride. I need to put food on my table, gas in my bulk tank, and pay my child support. I don't need a foreman's headaches."

"Some foremen *cause* headaches," Megan pointed out. "Properly handled, this job—"

"Sage." Bob came to his feet slowly. "I know you've turned us down before. I also know you're trying to rebuild that ranch of yours." He adjusted his pants, rested his hands at his hips and smiled. "You'll damn near double your pay with this job, son. *Double* it. You'll be that much closer to getting that place back on its feet."

Sage had anticipated this argument, too. It was the one point the idea had in its favor. He'd never gotten along very well with money, but it was hard to get along without it. And it was impossible to build much of a cattle operation without it. He turned away and shoved his hands in his back pockets. "A foreman doesn't make an engineer's decisions," he reflected. "And an engineer lets the foreman handle the crew." He turned and gave Megan a pointed look. "You don't seem to want to work it that way, though."

"Taylor was letting his racial and sexual prejudices influence his decisions. Nothing works very well *that* way."

"What makes you think it'll work my way? You and I might be worse news yet."

Megan smiled as she held out the ring of keys Taylor had relinquished when he left the site. "I think it's worth a try."

Chapter 4

They'd stopped asking him to join them at the Rooster after work, but Sage always knew which of the crew had been there when he saw them the next morning. With Scott it meant sunglasses, and Randy drank a lot of coffee, no matter how hot the weather was. Gary wasn't talking to anyone this morning. And Jackie wasn't there.

Sage squinted into the sun as he approached the trio. Randy drained his Thermos cup while Gary leaned on a shovel handle and scowled at the approach of authority. "You guys taking another break?" Sage asked.

"It's hot," Scott grumbled. "We're thirsty."

Sage nodded. "Rough night, huh?" Gary propped his foot on the shoulder of the shovel blade. "You can either give me the time back at noon or after five," Sage said quietly. "You guys haven't done a damn thing all morning."

"This job's going to your head, Sage." Randy's affable smile enabled him to say almost anything without causing offense. "You know, Taylor had a mean mouth on him, but, times like this, he'd usually cut us some slack."

"You're not working for Taylor anymore." Sage looked at Gary, who appeared to be ignoring the conversation. "Did you see Jackie last night?" Gary lifted his shoulder and wiped his face against his sleeve, but he gave no answer. Sage glanced back at Randy, then at Scott. "Listen, I don't give a damn what you guys do on your own time, but when you come to work, you be ready to put in an eight-hour day."

Sage watched the three men in his rear-view mirror as he pulled away slowly in his pickup. They'd gone grudgingly back to the chore of laying gravel and clay as a base for the blacktop that was to come. Gary was mad because he'd been taken off the gravel truck. Randy was mad because Sage hadn't smiled back and told him everything was okay, and Scott was mad because his head hurt. Sage knew how that went, and, at the moment, he didn't much like his three-week-old job. A cloud of dust veiled the reflections in the mirror as Sage pressed the accelerator to the floor.

One truth he'd discovered about himself was that he didn't much like being disliked. In his drinking days he'd been in his glory when people were cheering for him, or slapping him on the back and calling him "friend." In his drinking days he would have told those three to take it easy today, and he would have relished the acceptance he would have gotten in return. He told himself that he didn't need that anymore. That was yesterday. Today he had a job to do, and if he did it well, he could get some satisfaction out of it. He didn't have to please the crew, and they didn't have to like him. They had to respect him. So he had to give them something worth respecting.

Jackie's car was parked near the office. Sage muttered a curse as he gripped his own steering wheel and arced it to park the pickup alongside the car. Jackie was asleep with his mouth open and his neck arched over the top of the seat. When Sage tapped on the roof to wake him, Jackie jerked his head up and looked around.

"Hey, Sage." He squeezed one eye shut and squinted through the other. "Sorry I'm late. Thought I'd check the office first, then follow your tracks."

Sage squatted next to the car door to put his eyes on a level with Jackie's. "You been home yet?" *Don't lie to me, Jackie,* he pleaded silently.

"Sure." Jackie grinned. "Sure, I been home. I'm okay, Sage. The alarm clock didn't work is all."

Jackie's breath smelled like sewer water. "Guess you forgot to brush your teeth, huh?" *It's too late, Jackie. Spare yourself the indignity of lying to me.*

"Yeah. I was in a hurry." The smile faded, and Jackie played his trump—the one reference that might gain him sympathy. "The ol' lady'll throw me out if I lose this job. She's countin' on fixing an old house up into a store. Smart woman." He grinned again. "So whatcha got for me today? Gravel or oil?"

"Your last paycheck. I'm sorry, Jackie." Sage straightened slowly and patted the roof of the car a couple of times the way he would the man's shoulder if it had been handier. "Go on back to sleep. I don't want you on the road again till you've slept it off." He turned and headed for the office, where he saw movement in the window.

"Hey, Sage, I'm okay. I swear it!"

Sage stopped and turned back toward the car. "Let me know when you're ready for treatment, Jackie. I'll drive you to Fort Meade myself."

Megan was waiting for him. He avoided her eyes as he reached for the clipboard on his desk.

"Are you sure he's been drinking?"

He looked up. His eyes hardened when he saw that innocent expression. She wanted him to be prosecutor, judge and jury while she played the bleeding-heart advocate. "Did you talk to him?"

"Yes, I did. He came to the office first."

He turned to the list on his clipboard and added some figures. She wasn't stupid. She was as sure as he was.

"You fired him."

Was that an accusation or an observation? "I read the policy. I intend to follow it."

"I think if you gave him something—the promise of a job, maybe—he might opt for treatment. There's a provision for that in the policy, you know."

The clipboard clattered when he tossed it on the desk. "I know about the provision." His eyes glittered with resentment, not at her, but at what he'd had to do. "Jackie knows about it, too, and he knows how to ask. He's been there before."

"Maybe he can't ask."

"Then maybe he's not ready."

"He needs help, Sage."

They heard the roar of an engine, and they both turned toward the window. Sage took two steps closer in time to watch Jackie pull away in a hail of gravel. "Damn. I told him to wait."

"For what?" Megan asked.

"I told him to go back to sleep for a while."

She folded her arms and injected a note of sarcasm into her voice. "You fired him, and then you expected him to curl up and go to sleep on our doorstep?"

"*Our* doorstep?" He whirled from the window and jabbed a finger into the air. "This is *your* doorstep. Mine's thirty-five miles east of here." And if Jackie showed up on *his* doorstep, Sage would give him his bed and make his own in the cab of his pickup. But he wouldn't tell Megan that.

She pointed toward the window. "You can't fire a man and not expect him to go off hurt and angry like that."

"How many men have you fired?" He shouted the question and allowed two seconds for an answer. Her blue eyes flashed her message of defiance. "That's what I thought. Look, if you're out to save drunks, you oughta get yourself into another line of work." He jerked his head in the direction she'd indicated. "Go after him. Go on! Coax him. Persuade him to get treatment again."

"What would be wrong with that?" She clenched her fists in the shelter of her armpits and loosed the stinging dart. "How many times have *you* needed treatment, Mr. Parker?"

His voice was steely and cold. "None of your damn business."

She wanted to bite her tongue. "You're right. That wasn't—"

"First you hired me to blast rock and dig out a road, and all I had to worry about was moving dirt. Now you've got me moving people. I don't enjoy moving people, Miss McBride." Anger dissolved as the realization dawned in his brain. "But I can do it. And since the job's mine, I *will* do it."

He moved toward the door and turned with one quiet comment. "You can't save drunks, Megan. It can't be done that way. But you come to a Medicine Wheel meeting sometime, and you can watch how they save themselves."

He climbed into his truck and headed downhill from the office toward the site where more earth work had been started. Halfway down the hill, the pickup lunged toward the shoulder, and Sage fought with the shuddering steering wheel with one hand while he downshifted with the other. The pickup lurched, listed to the right, and stopped. Sage glanced at the hood ornament and the empty air beyond, where the gravel gave way to a fifty-foot drop-off. His left hand was cramped from the strain of holding the wheel, and his right trembled. He pushed the door open and stumbled out.

"What happened?"

Sage looked up as he stepped back from the pickup. Megan was running toward him, and the words "to the rescue" flitted across his mind as he turned back to survey the crippled vehicle. "What happened?" he muttered as he hitched his hands on his hips. "The damn wheel fell off, obviously."

"I know," she panted. With a wave of her hand, she told him, "It's back there. I mean, what *happened*? How did it just—"

"How the hell do I know?" He stalked off, climbing the gravel hill well ahead of her. He hoped she hadn't noticed the way he was shaking. Maybe it didn't show on the outside.

"Good Lord, you almost went off the—"

"I know!"

The hubcap lay twenty feet from the tire, but he didn't see any lug nuts anywhere. A piece of paper was stuffed into the rim, and the rim itself wasn't even bent. The whole damn thing had just flown off! Not without help, he decided as he jammed the paper into his pocket before Megan reached him with her next question.

"What was that?"

He came to his feet and glanced away as she stepped up to him. "Nothing. Just a piece of... trash."

"Trash?"

"Trash. Road trash." Mentally he measured the distance he'd driven before the tire fell off as he viewed the top of the hill. It wasn't much. "You wanna help me find those lug nuts?"

"Lug nuts?"

"Is there something wrong with the way I pronounce these words? Trash," he said with exaggerated care. "And lug nuts." He started up the hill.

"I don't understand why you're picking up trash at a time like this." She scowled as she followed, scouring the road.

"Seems as good a time as any. Litter just brings tears to my eyes."

She ignored the sarcasm. "Sage, I think someone might have tampered with your pickup."

"Really." He knelt to retrieve one of the nuts he was looking for.

"You don't think it could have been... Jackie?" She angled to the left. "Here's another one."

"He didn't have time."

"Did you see anyone else around?"

"I was too busy arguing with you. How many have you got?"

"Two."

"One more."

"You know, you're entitled to the use of a department vehicle now."

"I'd rather drive my own." He spied another glint of silver in the dirt and picked up his pace.

"Why?"

"It's got character." And it didn't have South Dakota Highway Department emblazoned on the side. Randy's suggestion that the job had gone to his head had hit a nerve. He didn't want to wear any badges. He didn't even like having a desk. All he'd need was a sign on his pickup and they'd all hate him.

"You don't think it was someone who resented your getting this job, do you?"

"Hell, I don't know!" He rose from the ground with the last of the lug nuts. He looked up, saw her standing there, saw the concern in her eyes and felt like a piece of road trash himself. "Look, I'm sorry." With a nod of his chin he indicated the pickup. From the higher vantage point they could see just how close he'd come to careening over the edge. "That scared the hell out of me," he confessed.

"Me, too."

He gave a nervous laugh. Her, too? Why not? he asked himself. Who'd want to see somebody drive his pickup off a cliff? It didn't have to mean anything *personal*.

She lifted her arm slowly and opened her hand. His fingertips dragged lightly over the center of her palm as he claimed first one lug nut, then the other. She started to speak, but her voice failed her on the first try. "It...it must've been a prank. They probably thought it would just fall right off."

"Probably." He looked into her eyes, then lowered his gaze to her lips. They were full and naturally pink, and he had the worst urge to touch them with the same two fingers that had flirted with her palm.

"I don't think anyone wanted to hurt you." He was looking at her differently now. The heat from his eyes made her mouth go dry, and she had to keep talking. "I think it was just a prank. Don't you?"

"Please don't ask me questions when you know I don't have any answers," he said quietly. "I hate that." He hated the fact that he was clenching his fists against the urge to touch her. The lug nuts cut into his hand.

"I think it was just a prank," she said again.

"I think I'd better see if I can get the damn tire back on the pickup." Before you read my mind, he thought. He figured his close brush with death must have triggered this suddenly urgent lust for . . . life.

"Do you have enough tools?" she called after him as he ambled back down the hill.

He laughed as he stood the tire on edge and started rolling it. "I sure have," he sang out. "All I'll ever need."

Once Sage had the pickup on the road again, he pulled the crumpled paper from his pocket and smoothed it out in the center of the steering wheel. "Accidents happen," the penciled note warned. "Don't interfere with free enterprise, Parker. It's the American way."

Red Calf, South Dakota, was a hole in the Badlands' wall. Megan drove past Floyd's Tavern, allowing herself a quick glance at the single car parked in front to assure herself that there were no crying children inside. She told herself that she wouldn't trust any meat that came from Floyd's Foods, the clapboard building that stood next door. The windows on both structures were covered with bars. She wondered who was being locked out. The town looked pretty dead.

A phone call to Pete Petersen and a little research on Pete's part had turned up the information she'd needed to

attend a Medicine Wheel meeting. Sage had invited her, and
something in the back of her mind wouldn't let the idea fade
away. There was nothing wrong with caring, she told herself. But she wanted to care from an enlightened point of
view. She'd come here to be enlightened.

The size of the Red Calf Community Center said something about the size of the community. A hundred people
might have been able to crowd inside—if most of them were
small. The sign taped to the door announced that the Medicine Wheel meeting was in progress and that anyone was
welcome to attend. According to the sign, Megan was half
an hour late, but Pete had said 8:00 p.m. She dreaded
walking in late, but she opened the door and stepped inside.

A single bright, bare bulb in the ceiling illuminated a
small circle of people, who turned in their folding chairs at
the sound of the door. Megan searched for a familiar face
and felt a rush of relief when she found one.

"Join us, Megan." Sage got up and offered his seat. "I'll
get another chair."

"I'm sorry to interrupt," she began as she took a tentative step toward the chair. "I thought...I was told the
meeting started at eight."

Sage flipped another chair open and pushed it into the
circle, telling her again with a glance at the chair he'd vacated that she should sit down. "You must have seen one of
the posters. We're starting earlier now."

She'd changed clothes since he'd seen her at work. He
watched her smooth her pale blue skirt along the backs of
her thighs as she sat down. A wide leather belt the color of
her skirt made her look wasp-waisted, and he noticed for the
first time that her ears were pierced. When she turned to
look up at him, he saw the flash of blue stones. She'd done
something extra to her hair, and he noted signs of makeup.
Then he remembered that he was still standing, and he
joined the circle.

"We're all here because we want to make our lives over without alcohol or drugs," Sage explained. "You don't have to tell us anything. You've joined us. You're part of the circle. As the night passes, you're welcome to share what you will."

"Would I be breaking a confidence if I explained our—" Her hand fluttered between them. "How I know you?" From the flat look in his eyes, she could tell that she'd already said the wrong thing.

"Not at all." Let's get our disclaimers out first, he thought.

"I'm a highway engineer," Megan offered to the group. "We're working on a project just west of here. Sage—" She smiled, first at him and then at them. "Sage has just been promoted to construction supervisor." No one smiled back, and she realized that she had yet to tell them anything they didn't know, and, so far, they weren't impressed.

"I don't have a problem, really," she went on hesitantly. "Not a *personal* problem, anyway."

"How very fortunate for you."

She looked quickly at Sage and saw that he was amused. "I mean I don't drink—much." He knew damn well what she meant!

"Neither do I." One corner of his mouth hinted at a smile.

"I know that. I understand that." She looked at the ceiling, casting about for help. "I'm going about this all wrong."

"You don't have to protect yourself here, Megan. That's the beauty of the circle. Just tell us what's bothering you."

"Nothing," Megan said quickly. "I just want to learn. I want to know what kinds of things bother you . . . people." She looked around her and counted thirteen expressionless faces. Not a lucky number, she thought.

"I'll tell you something that bothers me," an older woman said. "Tourists. People who want to drive around in our backyards and then drive off to tell their friends about what it's like in Red Calf."

The woman's tone suggested no more emotion than her wrinkled brown face betrayed. Megan wanted to run. She glanced at Sage, but he was staring at the floor. "I'm not here because of curiosity," she said quietly. "A couple of the men on the crew ... our—" Again she gestured to indicate that she and Sage were in this together. "*Our* crew. Members of your community, I believe—well, they have a problem with drinking. That is, they *seem* to have a problem with drinking."

"A problem that interferes with their work?" Sage asked without looking up.

"Yes." She looked around the room again as her fear began to take a backseat to her cause. "We had to fire one of the men, and I hated to see that happen. He was a good worker before he started drinking again, and I'm sure he needed his job."

"Anybody else here need his job?" Sage asked, and there was a round of chuckling. "Most of these people don't have jobs, Megan. There aren't too many around."

"I know. That's why I'm concerned when I have to fire someone." She looked around quickly again. No one was looking at her. No one seemed to be listening, and she felt driven to regain their attention. "It seems like such a waste when a man is good at his job, and then, just because of alcohol, he's—"

"You're talking about my husband."

Megan turned toward the voice and recognized the woman with the beautiful black hair. "I'm sorry," Megan said. "I didn't mean—"

"Sage fired him, not you."

Megan's back stiffened. "Sage has his job to do, too."

"Jackie stopped coming to Medicine Wheel," Regina said. "He stopped going to work every day, and he deserved to be fired. Now he's stopped coming home at night."

"I'm sorry," Megan said again.

"Being sorry for him only makes him worse," Regina said. "Don't be sorry for him. He can get drunk on pity the same as he gets drunk on wine."

"But if he had his job, surely—"

"What we're telling you, Megan, is that the job was a small part of Jackie's loss," Sage told her. "He has to get his soul back before he can work again."

He looked at her now, and in his eyes she saw his acceptance of her presence, of her concern, of her fumbling attempt to understand. "Is there anything I can do?" she asked.

"You can pray," said the older woman who had spoken before. "For yourself, and for the rest of us, to whatever god you believe in."

That wasn't what Megan had had in mind. She looked to Sage for a better answer. "I think awareness is important," she explained. "For an employer, a supervisor. There must be something we can do to make it easier to... to adjust."

She didn't understand old Bessie's answer because she didn't understand Medicine Wheel, Sage thought as he nodded patiently. "Awareness is a good thing," he said. "So be aware that you can make it easy for a drunk to go on doing what he's doing. You can never make it easy for him to change."

"If somebody goes in for treatment, try to hold his job for him," said one man. "When I got out, I didn't have much to go back to. But I had this group." His mouth opened in a gap-toothed grin. "I'll have a job when Regina and Tootsie open their store."

"We've bought a house for it now," Regina announced. There was a low murmur of approval. "The White Shields' house. They're moving to Pine Ridge."

Conversation turned to plans for bringing grocery prices down in Red Calf. Floyd's was the only store, and, because the town was so isolated, he charged outrageously for food.

"Jackie borrowed money from Uncle Floyd again, and Floyd tried to get me to pay it," Regina complained. "You should see the interest he's got tacked on!"

"That's Jackie's debt," Sage reminded her. "You worry about opening up that store."

"I'll help you paint it."

"We'll need to knock out some walls."

"You guys can live upstairs."

"I know where you can get one of those big freezers for next to nothing."

The meeting had gone well. Sage lay across his bed from corner to corner and stared at the ceiling that curved three feet above his head as he played the meeting over in his mind. Jackie's relapse was a loss, but these things happened. The group members put it in perspective as they planned their course. Close down the bar and build a new store. Individual recovery would lead to community recovery. Ollie Walks Long had gone to Fort Meade. The group would have his house fixed up for him when he got back. They would clean it up and paint it, put new screens on the windows. It was important to have a decent place to live. Not fancy, but decent. You had to start someplace, and that was a good place to start. Jackie would come back, Sage decided, and they would help him start again, too.

Sage reached across the bed and groped for the switch on the little oscillating fan that whirred in the darkness next to him. He turned it up as high as it would go and promised himself that one day he would sleep in an air-conditioned bedroom again. He propped his head on his elbow and turned his face toward the hot breeze. Hell, just a bedroom would be nice. The back end of a fifteen-foot trailer could hardly be called a bedroom. He'd had a bedroom once, with an air conditioner in the window, but there had been too many times when that room had heated up even with the air on full blast. God, how the two of them had argued.

He remembered how pretty she'd been when she was seventeen. Riva Maxon. All he remembered about her from those days was that she had long blond hair, and she could do one hell of a spread-eagle at the end of a cheer. He'd gone to an Indian boarding school in Nebraska, and she'd gone to public school. She hadn't cheered for his team, but he'd soon had her cheering for him. She'd planned to go to college, but he'd changed her plans. He rodeoed in the summer, and she'd followed the circuit and learned all about cowboys. She'd had quite a teacher.

He was driven then, and he'd pushed hard—for thrills, for quick intensity, for sex on demand. To this day he didn't know what devil it was that had eaten at him so voraciously from the inside out. He had never been able to get enough of anything. He'd always wanted more. Drinking made him powerful and glib, made the women fun and easy, made the risks and the close calls seem like the best part of living. For a time he'd led a charmed life. He'd gotten by. He'd smashed the front fender, but he hadn't wrecked the car. He'd caught hell for flirting, but he hadn't gotten caught cheating. He'd paid most of his bills. But he hadn't catapulted himself high enough. Each time he'd come down, he seemed to find himself one rung lower, and he'd needed a closer call, a greater thrill, a bigger bottle, to get himself back up there again.

Just the memory made him sweat with fear. He edged closer to the fan and tried to replace those dark images with something else. Something that made him feel good. Megan. Clean, fresh hair that left the soft down on the back of her neck exposed. Clear-eyed innocence and courage. It had taken courage to do what she'd done tonight. At one point he'd thought she was going to bolt, but she'd stayed. She was a bona fide caretaker, sure as hell, but there was hope for her. She'd been willing to listen. And when she'd sat down in that chair and turned her face up to him, she'd looked so pretty that she'd made his insides turn to slush.

He commended himself for remembering that look on her face above all else. He'd spent hours wondering about her legs, and he'd finally gotten a look at them. They were nice, but it was her face that stuck fast in his thoughts. He couldn't remember when he'd given a woman's face such a big piece of his mind.

Yes he did. He remembered Riva's face when it wasn't pretty anymore. He remembered how she'd looked with her eyes narrowed and her lips thin and white as she spat obscenities at him. He wondered how he'd looked as he matched her curse for curse. Had he ever loved her? Was he capable of giving love? If he'd ever loved anyone, he didn't remember what it felt like. No, that wasn't true. He'd loved his children. God, he wanted to believe he'd always loved his two children. But he'd hurt them. He'd catered to himself and his addiction at their expense.

Sage rolled onto his back and studied the metal seams in the ceiling again. He didn't want to hurt anyone else. He didn't want to turn anyone else ugly. His pain was his, and he didn't anesthetize himself anymore. Losing his children would always hurt, but he didn't bottle it up anymore. He admitted it. He'd hurt them, and he lived with that pain. He would do what he could for the others who lived with the same kind of pain, and he would do his damnedest not to cause any more.

Brenda and Tommy. She was twelve now, and he was nine. It had been six years since Riva had left him and taken the kids. She'd remarried, and she wanted him to pay his child support and stay out of their lives. His letters were usually returned unopened, but not all of them. Some must have slipped through. He just wanted the kids to know that he cared. That was all. He didn't want to screw anything up for them, but it didn't hurt to care. Smiling to himself, he wiped the sweat off his chest with the corner of the sheet. It didn't hurt to care. That sounded like something Megan might say. He believed she did care about Jackie and Gary—

maybe even himself. Well, if she let herself get too deeply involved, she would soon find out how much it hurt to care.

Damn, he wished they would answer his letters. With a groan, he turned his face toward the wall. If they would just send him a picture....

Chapter 5

Terry Haynes wasn't satisfied with his assignment. Out of
the corner of his eye Sage had watched Haynes use his boot
heel to dig a hole in the soft ridge of clay base that the blade
had left along the edge of the new road. Sage flipped the
metal cover over his clipboard and waited while the rest of
the crew headed for the equipment. He figured he and
Haynes were about due.

"I want the overtime on the oiler," Haynes announced,
his colorless eyes aglow with the bravado he'd been working himself up to during Sage's brief talk with the crew.

"You worked overtime last week," Sage reminded him
quietly. There wasn't much Sage liked about Haynes. He
was sloppy, both in his personal habits and his work. Sage
didn't like the tobacco stains on the wiry young man's
scraggly blond mustache, nor the little bits of tobacco between his teeth, nor his off-color sense of humor. More-
over, he didn't like the way the man handled the oiler. Sage
had suggested, instructed and reprimanded, but Haynes

knew it all. "I'm turning the oiler over to Archambault and putting you on the ground for a while."

Haynes shoved his hands in his back pockets and spat brown juice into the grass. "I'm going to file a complaint."

"That's your right." Sage turned to walk away.

"I don't much care for the way you take care of your Indian friends first, Parker."

Sage mentally counted through the single digits as he turned back slowly. "I don't much care for the way you run the oiler. I told you how I wanted it done, and you chose not to listen."

"I don't know who the hell you think you are, Parker." Haynes shifted his weight from one foot to the other and stuck out his chin, adding emphasis to the obscene bulge beneath his lower lip. "You go from labor to foreman overnight. What do you know about oiling? How many jobs you been on? They got some kinda Indian preference with state jobs now?"

In his head, Sage saw his fist connect with Haynes's mouth, splattering blood and brown slime all over that seedy mustache. He gripped the clipboard tightly in his right hand. "You're on the ground, or you're on your way back to wherever you come from, Haynes."

"You got an in with Krueger. Everybody knows that. And McBride—"

"File your complaint." Sage turned on his heel, his gut churning as he headed toward a big yellow steamroller, the only piece of equipment that wasn't moving at the moment. The roar of powerful diesel engines filled his ears, and he fastened his mind on the noise. He associated the sound with ripping out and packing down, and he needed to get his hands on the controls. He needed to substitute the work for ripping Haynes's teeth out of his mouth and packing them down his throat.

Megan had spent the first part of the week in Pierre at the highway department office. It had been good to get back to her apartment for a few days. Staying in a Hot Springs motel for the better part of the summer was part of the highway engineer's territory, and she didn't mind it. She wasn't a homebody. Sometimes she wondered why she even needed her own apartment, but the answer to that question came quickly. The other choice was having a home base with her parents.

It was late afternoon when she climbed the steps to the office. She'd toured the site, and she planned to pick up some charts and head for Hot Springs. The project was going well. Krueger was pleased with the progress they were making, and he was especially pleased with her positive report on Sage's job performance. He'd long believed in Sage's potential, and he liked being right about people.

Sage pulled up in front of the office soon after she did. She smiled when she heard the old blue pickup's engine refuse to die even after he'd shut it off. She wondered if he did his own tune-ups, and if he did, when he would ever find the time. She knew he was burning the candle at both ends these days.

Black dirt ringed his eyes where his sunglasses had been, and Megan was reminded of a raccoon. Sage tossed the glasses on the desk and pulled the blue bandanna off his head. It left a marked crease in his hair, which he ruffled with impatient hands.

"How's life in the big city?" he asked in lieu of greeting her with a hello.

"Not as exciting as it is out here," she said, smiling. "It looks good."

"What looks good? Your road?"

"My road." She liked the idea, and she gave a quick laugh. "It's taking shape. This time next year, there'll be traffic on it."

Sage unrolled the bandanna and wiped his face with it. He'd spent the day fuming over Haynes. Ordinarily he might have been able to let the incident go, but he was tired.

He was just too damned tired to reason with himself. He knew his limits.

"Look, Megan—" He stuffed the bandanna in his back pocket and sat on the edge of his desk. "I want out of this job. I want my old job back."

Megan's face dropped. "Why?"

"This isn't my kind of thing. I'm a rancher who works construction to make ends meet. I don't like ordering people around."

Megan pushed the charts aside and sat on her desk, facing him. "There's always an adjustment period, Sage. The crew is coming around. They're beginning to see you as their supervisor instead of one of them." You can't make the changes any easier, he'd told her. But she still believed there was a way to help with the adjustment. "You're doing a wonderful job. Bob says—"

"I don't care what Bob says." He worked to control his tone, to keep it even. He wanted her to listen to *him* now, not to Bob. He had something to tell her. "I can't do this anymore. I don't *want* to do this anymore."

"Why not?"

He gauged the look in her eyes and decided she might be listening. "I've got a temper," he confessed quietly. "When somebody mouths off to me, I get knots in my gut. I don't want to lose it, Megan." He met her gaze, and it made his eyes sting. He glanced away. "I've got my temper under control now, and I don't want to lose it."

"Did something happen today?"

"Yeah." He hadn't talked to anybody since the incident. She was right; the crew members no longer regarded him as one of them. He couldn't talk to Randy or Gary or any of the rest of them about one of their own. She was all he had, and he wanted to tell somebody, just to get it out. "I took Haynes off the oiler, and he didn't take it too well."

"How did you handle it?" she asked.

"I handled it okay." He frowned a bit as he reconsidered. "I handled it better than okay, but that isn't the point. I don't want to handle stuff like that at all."

"Nobody does. But you did it because that's what you're getting paid to do." She felt compelled to move closer. She stopped only a foot from his desk. "Don't quit, Sage," she implored. "Show them what you can do."

He saw the fire in her eyes, and he tipped his head back and gave a short bark of mirthless laughter. "Show who?" he demanded. "The crew? The highway department? Who?" He came to his feet, and she followed him with her eyes, lifting her chin as he rose above her. "I'm not out to prove what a 'good Indian' I can be. I'm not out to be a 'super success story.'"

"That isn't what I meant," she said evenly.

"You know, you have a lot of trouble with saying things you don't mean. Who am I supposed to make this big effort for? You?"

"Yourself. Your... your..." She gestured helplessly.

"Don't say 'my people,' or you'll blow what's left of my patience all to hell." She looked at him through widening eyes as she closed her mouth. "Wise move," he told her, then turned toward the window. He needed space. "I know I help fill a minority quota. I can live with that, because I also know I can move as much damn dirt as any man. Beyond that, I don't have any point to prove."

"I'm filling a quota, too," Megan told him quietly. "I was given this project because the department had been accused of sex discrimination."

He turned just enough so that he could see her face. "Who made the accusation?"

"I did. When I asked for this project, Bob Krueger went out on a limb for me."

"So we're both tokens." With a nod he turned to the window again. "And that scrawny little buzzard is up there leaping from one limb to the next. I supposed you're anxious for me to pan out as foreman for his sake."

"Bob took a stand. I don't see how we can allow ourselves to fail him."

"Fail *him*?" Sage faced her and shook his head. "Uh-uh, lady, don't lay that one on me. You wanted to prove a point, and you did it. You gained some ground for women. That's fine. If you're looking to move from sexism to racism now, you're gonna have a little trouble. You're white."

"That's not fair!" Megan took a step closer as her pulse shifted into higher gear. "I've seen what you can do, Sage, and I'm only suggesting that you take the bull by the horns and do it."

"Have you ever taken a bull by the horns?" The wide-legged stance she took as she folded her arms and glared in response to his question made him laugh again. "Not literally, right? I have, and let me tell you, it gives you a rush of power. Just like the one *you* get from trying to fix things for people."

"What are you talking about? I'm not trying to fix anything. I recommended you for this job because ... because, like it or not, you were right for it."

"Did you go up to Pierre and let them all know what a great choice you'd made?"

"No."

"How the Indian boy you hand-picked was making good?"

"You're hardly a boy."

"Yeah, but I was hand-picked to carry your banner, wasn't I?" She stood her ground as he edged closer, the volume of his voice on the rise. "Wasn't I, Megan? How many causes can one little wisp of a woman push for, anyway?"

They stared at one another for a moment, both wondering how much of what they'd hurled at one another was truth and how much was pure frustration. Finally, Megan turned and walked away.

"I'd rather you wouldn't quit," she said. "But if you're determined to do it, do it in writing."

At her back, she heard the door close quietly.

* * *

If the tire was going to go or the pickup was destined to overheat, Sage figured this was the time for it to happen. Careening down the gravel hill, he took pleasure in plowing up a billowing wake of dust. He felt as though the top of his head was about to blow. The lady was using him, sure as hell. He'd tried to level with her, and she'd given him some guidance counselor's pep talk. She'd sooner talk than hear something that didn't fit into her master plan.

He felt cut off. He wasn't part of the family. He wasn't part of the crowd. He wasn't even part of the crew anymore. The one person on the job that he should have been able to talk to had told him everything was really terrific. This was the way it was supposed to be, according to her. He would get used to it, just the way he'd gotten used to the other ties that had been cut. Used to it, hell! Adjust? He would have liked nothing better than to adjust her high and mighty little nose a few pegs lower.

He was pushing too hard. The pickup fishtailed, and he caught himself enjoying the moment of peril before he managed to align the front end with the back again. No, he was *being* pushed, he told himself, and he needed to push back. Purely on impulse, he reached for the glove compartment. His hand froze when he felt the heat of the metal button under his finger. The glove compartment was locked, and the keys were in the ignition. He kept that little bottle sealed and locked up tight.

God help him, he was reaching for an anesthetic on an impulse from the past. That's all over, he reminded himself. Four years past. He felt clammy, nearly sick. Staring hard at the road, he passed his fingers over his forehead, and they came away wet.

Slow down, he told himself. Breathe deeply, slow down, keep driving, and let these minutes tick by one at a time.

Chapter 6

He had the weekend to cool off. Sage put road construction on the back burner that Saturday morning and busied his hands and his heart with other labor. It might have been *her* road, but this house was his. He'd resisted shortcuts and detours, and he was doing it right this time. The only parts he hadn't been able to handle himself so far were drawing the blueprints, pouring the basement and raising the roof beams. Though the design was his, he'd paid an acquaintance to do the prints. He'd hired a cement contractor, and Medicine Wheel members had helped him raise the wall frames and the heavy ceiling beams that would be exposed when the house was finished.

He'd chosen the site carefully. The cabin that had been here once was where the seeds of his life had been planted. His taproot was there. Taproots grew deep in prairie sod. In times of drought, they grew even deeper and clung tenaciously to the heart of the earth. Sage knew his was there, in this spot where his family's cabin had stood. The structures they'd built in the interim had been without foundation, and they'd disappeared. Though the cabin was gone, too, it had left him with good memories. He was determined to reconnect himself with that taproot. Without it, he'd withered pathetically during life's inevitable periods of drought.

Sage surveyed his work as he organized his tools. The studs and rafters cast long shadows in the slanted rays of the morning sun. It was beginning to look a lot like a real house. He'd given himself good-sized rooms because he was tired of being cramped, and there were two extra bedrooms. There would come a day when his letters would be answered, and Brenda and Tommy would each have a room when they came to visit after school got out for the summer. It was a dream he'd come to cherish. He wondered whether Brenda still loved horses as much as she had when she was a little girl, and whether Tommy ever sucked his thumb anymore. Every time his mother had plucked it out of his mouth, the dark-eyed little boy had waited until she'd turned her back, and then he'd shoved it right back in.

Sage tied his carpenter's apron over the wide leather belt that rode low on his hips and admonished himself to get to work. A man could drive himself crazy wondering about some things. He climbed the ladder to the roof. He had a subfloor, and all the wall frames and partitions were in place. Once he finished this part, he could say he had a roof over his head. By winter he hoped to have the shell finished and the shingling done. If he could afford to put in a woodstove, he could work inside during the winter. He was collecting a paycheck now that might cover those things—but only if he continued as foreman.

From the top of his roof he could see the edge of the world. To the north the rows of cottonwoods, silver-leafed Russian olives and thick wild plum bushes provided shelter from the winter wind. The great plains rolled to the south like a dun-colored blanket, with green and yellow beadwork applied deep within the nap. Flat-topped buttes ringed the horizon, and the sky was gloriously high, wide and blue.

Sage hummed to himself as he worked. The resounding, rhythmic tap of his hammer was his accompaniment, and the song was one he'd learned recently from a medicine man. It was a song to sweat by, the old man had told him, and Sage was doing just that. His body was purging itself. Yesterday's anger was dissipating, and he gave voice to the sense of relief that brought him as he basked bare-chested in the morning sun.

A bright yellow highway department pickup slowed at the approach to his rutted, gravel driveway. Sage willed the quick tie-up in the pit of his stomach to go away as he braced himself on one knee and stretched his torso. He watched the vehicle draw near. What was she doing there?

Megan stepped around a stack of plywood and squinted at a rafter that pointed the way to the sun. "Sage? Are you up there?"

The head that rose over the ridge of the roof caused an eclipse. His face was shadowed, and the sun's rays seemed to crown him. "Morning," he greeted her. "Taking the scenic tour?"

"Not exactly." She stepped closer to the ladder. "I came to see you. Could you use a short break?"

"I was just on my way down."

She watched him negotiate the ladder. He wore vintage high-top basketball shoes and well-worn jeans, and his hair gleamed blue-black in the sun. "I won't keep you long," she promised.

"That's too bad." He skipped the last three rungs and hopped to the ground. "I'd just about decided I wanted to be kept." He wiped the sweat from his brow with the back of his wrist and gave her a slow smile. "On the job."

"Really?" It was the one piece of news she hadn't anticipated. "I guess I can put away my speech, then."

"You came prepared with a speech?" Still smiling, he hooked his thumbs in his belt. "I've gotta hear this."

"I'll just skip to the last line. I'm sorry for anything I said yesterday that sounded patronizing."

"Patronizing?" He considered it and nodded. "Yeah, that's a good word for it."

"The truth is that I need a good foreman on this project, and you're good. You've let the crew know what's expected of them, and you don't let anyone slide by. They all respect you, Sage, including Haynes. They've all seen you work. They know you're not asking them to do anything you haven't done yourself. That's why you're right for this job. No other reason."

"All that was part of the last line?"

She smiled. "So I backtracked a little. The apology seemed a little naked."

"I'm sorry I flew off the handle. The truth is, I was mad." He shrugged. "I got over it."

"Haynes is a hothead," Megan assured him. "He's probably over it by now, too."

Sage laughed. "I've been called a hothead myself."

"But you've got it under control now," she reminded him.

"I'm working on it." He untied his carpenter's apron and laid it on top of his tool box. "How about some coffee?"

"I really don't mean to keep you from your work." She looked up at the skeletal structure. "And this looks like quite a project. You're building this all by yourself?"

"I've had a little help on occasion." He moved to the stack of plywood sheets. "Just let me rack up another load of lumber, and then I'll show you around."

The plywood rack leaning against the roof looked like another ladder, but it had two wedges nailed halfway up, which held a supply of plywood and put it within reach of a man on the roof. "That's ingenious," Megan said as she watched him lift a sheet into place.

"It's an extra pair of hands." When he'd filled the rack, he motioned for her to follow him through the opening that would become the front door. "Give me a woman's opinion of the floor plan."

Megan stepped across the threshold. "I'm better equipped to give you an opinion on the design of your driveway."

"You wanna help me rearrange the ruts?"

"There's one place that angles a little too far to the left." She indicated a sharp curve with her hand as she passed under the header of the doorway between the living room and the kitchen. Her pink sleeveless top and blue jeans skimmed her body as though they were all of a piece. The thick rubber soles of her running shoes emphasized the smallness of her feet. He stood in the middle of a rough lumber kitchen and saw nothing but delicacy as he watched her come toward him.

"It lacks good engineering," he said absently.

"So what's this?" She waved a hand at the rafters. "The gym?"

"The kitchen. Dining area over here. Nice view of the road, so you can see who's coming and throw on some coffee. Exposed beams. Patio door. The deck comes later." He drew pictures in the air. Everything but the view and the beams would come later. He hadn't bought any glass yet.

She imagined a redwood deck where he indicated that it would be on the tree-lined side of the house. "When did you start?"

"Three years ago." He laughed at her look of surprise. "It may be a lifelong project. I don't have any credit."

"You mean you're doing this without a loan?"

"I've had loans. I got behind on my payments, and the creditors sold everything on the place that was portable, even the house. It didn't cover what I owed, but they divvied up the money and went away satisfied." He leaned on a future windowsill and watched as the breeze made the tall grass ripple. "My land—the part that I actually own—was in trust, so they didn't try to mess with it."

"You mean because your ranch is part of the reservation?" she asked.

He nodded. "It's my land, but the trustee relationship between the federal government and the tribe makes it pretty complicated to use Indian land as collateral. So—" He sat against the windowsill and faced her with a smile that surprised her. "I lost the leased land, too, but I've got most of that back now. I lost everything but the land I actually had title to."

"It was precious to you," she concluded solemnly. "Part of your heritage."

He told her what she wanted to hear. "We call the earth Grandmother." She nodded as though she understood thoroughly, and he wanted to burst out laughing because her gullibility delighted him, but he knew she would misunderstand. He held it down to a twitching grin. "There was a time when I would have sold Grandmother in her wheelchair for another ticket on the merry-go-round. But there were federal restrictions that wouldn't let me go quite that far."

It was hard to imagine the man in front of her being the man he'd described. He was exaggerating. He was being dramatic, she decided, even though he showed no sign of self-pity. "If you weren't close to the land, then why all this?" Her gesture encompassed the house and all that surrounded it. "You're obviously sinking every penny you make back into this place."

"Almost," he agreed. "I'm a rancher. Rebuilding my life means rebuilding this place. When I was drinking, booze was the buffer between me and everything I cared about, so I wasn't really close to anything. Of the things that I cared about, the land is what I have left. It's where I have to start." He chuckled. "Everything else had legs."

He moved away from the windowsill and jerked his chin toward the rest of the house. "C'mon. We haven't finished the tour. Bedroom...bathroom...bedroom...*my* bedroom. Get this!" He walked through a wall and gestured with a flourish. "Room for a king-size bed." She looked a little startled, and he laughed as he pointed between the wall studs at the tiny trailer on the other side of the driveway. "That's what I'm sleeping in now."

"Looks pretty small." She leaned her shoulder against the door frame and folded her arms. "What about stock? You can't buy cattle without credit."

"Who says?" Pride glistened in his eyes as he rested his hands on his hips. "I've got fourteen stock cows and five horses now. And they're mine, free and clear. I'll sell the calves in the fall and buy bred heifers." She looked skeptical. "Hey, I've got plenty of time. I'm only thirty-four. When I was twenty-four, I thought time was running out on me. Now I've got all the time in the world. By next spring I might have twenty cows and all the outside walls up, but if I only have eighteen cows and a roof—" he shrugged "—I'll still be doing what I want to do. You like horses?"

"Yes, very much." He gave the familiar chin-jerk toward the corral. Then he stepped between two wall studs and hopped to the ground. When Megan got to the edge of the subfloor he was waiting to help her down.

He could see that there was an automatic protest on the tip of her tongue. His assistance wasn't necessary. Their eyes met, and she read the message. The offer of his hand was a chance to touch, just briefly. The choice was hers. He reached for her, and she put her hands in his. It was like thrusting them quickly in front of a fire. The rest of her body was suddenly flushed with envy as she indulged only her hands. When her feet were firmly planted on the ground, she tipped her chin up, and they made a silent pact to linger over the indulgence a moment longer.

A stout sorrel gelding stood in one corner of the corral, with a brown and white pinto mare and her colt in another. The colt stole the show. His springy white mane and sassy flag of a tail were set off by well-defined patches of dark brown. He pranced circles around his mother as Sage stepped onto one rail, swung his leg over the top of the fence and sat down. Megan clambered up one rail at a time.

"I was stretching it a little," he said, grinning down at her. "I've got four horses and a colt, but he's one hell of a colt."

"He's beautiful," she agreed. "I think he counts as a horse."

"The first thing I did was repair the corrals and put up the pole barn. I had a prefab metal barn that was auctioned off. I used wood this time, because it's warmer in the winter and cooler in the summer." She seemed interested, so he continued. "Maybe it's a little like building a road. I need to see it take shape. I'm watching it rise from the dust, kind of like me—my own resurrection. I'd been sober for about a year when I came back out here and dug the first post hole. I'd been avoiding the place for three years, but I learned something that day about making a start." He remembered the day, and the tears he'd shed as he'd rammed the post hole digger into the ground, making a mark. Taking a step. His eyes searched the east end of the corral and found that benchmark. "One post. I came back the next day, and it was still there, so I knew I'd actually done it. I'd taken that first step."

"I admire your courage."

He looked at her and found that the complete sincerity in her eyes embarrassed him. "Courage, hell," he tossed off as he jumped down from the corral. "No more than it takes anybody else to put one foot in front of the other. I only had one direction left to go, and that was up." He cocked his head to one side as he looked up at her. "I promised coffee, didn't I? How about some lunch?"

In three steps, Megan was down on the ground beside him. "I really didn't mean to keep you from your work."

"I have to eat sometime." He made a point of surveying her slim figure. "You do, too, and the eating establishments around here are few and far between. You can have a sandwich with me, or drive into Red Calf for frozen pizza at Floyd's Tavern."

"Which is closed."

"Damn, that's right!" Grinning broadly, he snapped his fingers. "A bunch of troublemakers shut him down. Guess it's sandwiches or starvation."

She returned his smile. "Sandwiches, then."

Her reply gave him a momentary feeling of buoyancy, and then he realized that he was taking her into the trailer. He hesitated at the foot of the small set of wooden steps. "There's not much room," he said. "And not much ventilation. It gets pretty hot and, uh, pretty cramped."

"I don't have much of a home, Sage. An apartment, just big enough to store some personal things." It was her turn to reach out to him. She laid a hand on his arm, then looked up at him. "I'm not even much of a cook, but I can spread mayonnaise."

"Should we eat in the dining room?" He nodded toward the new house, and his eyes twinkled in anticipation.

"Oh, yes, let's."

The trailer was, as promised, hot and cramped. Sage set the sandwich makings on the counter, and Megan put them together while he found canned soft drinks and potato chips to go with their meal. It felt good to get back outside, where the air was moving and space was unlimited. They sat crosslegged on the plywood subfloor, ate sandwiches and talked about the house. Sage explained his "master plan," and Megan complimented his design. "Three bedrooms is a lot for one person. Is there a chance that your family might come back to you?"

He shook his head. "My family belongs to somebody else now. My wife remarried, and she doesn't want any interference from me."

"If you're paying child support, you could probably insist on some—"

He shook his head and waved the suggestion away. "I'm not going to insist on anything. I'm hoping they'll give me a chance to redeem myself, but they have some pretty bad memories, and I can understand..."

"Were you ... physically abusive?"

"No. I don't think so." He took a drink from the can he held in his hand, then gave her an unguarded look. His dark eyes became haunted. "I started having blackouts. I'd wake up with a godawful hangover and realize I'd lost a day somewhere. I had no idea where I'd been, or what I'd done."

"That's scary."

"Damn right it's scary. You have to try to get people to tell you what you did without letting them know you don't remember. I had a black eye once, and I never found out who gave it to me." He chuckled. "I think it was my brother." His smile faded as he continued to recall the bad times. He drew a deep breath and glanced toward the highway. "Once I found that I'd driven my daughter to school, and I didn't remember doing it." He looked at Megan. "I was dead drunk, and I was out on the road with that kid in the car."

It was her turn to glance away. She thought of the way Sage had held Regina's little boy, and she remembered her relationship with her own father—or lack of it. "My father drinks too much, too." The words were out before she'd thought about saying them.

He saw the startled look in her eyes and knew her betrayal of "the family secret" surprised her more than it did him. "Maybe that's why you have this concern for—"

"He's not an alcoholic," she hastened to add. "I guess I would say he's more a . . . a problem drinker."

"A problem drinker? What's that?"

"Well, he's never lost his job over it or anything. He doesn't fight, and he doesn't . . . you know . . . do anything really *bad* . . . ." She stared at the hole in the top of her soft drink can as she lifted her shoulders in a helpless shrug. "He just drinks too much sometimes. . . . *Most* of the time."

Sage knew he was watching her become, for the moment, the little girl she'd once been—the one who'd been told not to talk about her father's drinking. "It bothers you to see him drink?" he asked gently.

She smiled quickly and swept her hair back from her forehead as she squared her shoulders. She was a woman again. "I don't have to be around it anymore. I do think my mother should do something about him, though. He's getting too old to behave so foolishly."

"I wish my wife had done something about me, too." He chuckled, shaking his head at the beauty of the notion. "It would have been a hell of a lot less work for me if she'd just taken the bull by the horns—" he gave Megan a lopsided grin along with the expression "—and made me quit drinking. Maybe she could have sewn my mouth shut or something."

"Well, it's just...it's just so..." It just wasn't funny, and she refused to laugh about it. Instead she crushed the empty pop can with the heels of her hands. "It's good that you've done it for yourself. I admire you for it. You've started the recovery group, and you're building this place from scratch." She lifted her hands to indicate the work that surrounded them. "I just think it's wonderful."

She sounded a little like that school counselor giving him a pep talk again, but he knew that was to be expected. She'd put all her eggs into her professional basket. There she was sure, astute, determined to achieve. In her personal life, she wore blinders.

"What do you hear about Karl Taylor?" he asked as he lifted his soda can and judged he had about two more swallows left.

"I saw him when I was in Pierre," she told him. "I ran into him in the parking lot at the highway department."

"Did he say anything to you?"

"Some dumb comment about equal opportunity." Taylor had actually wondered whether Megan was giving Sage equal opportunity at the trap Taylor had accused her of baiting first for him. She'd ignored him. The idea that she would actually flirt with Taylor was ludicrous.

"You know that Floyd is Karl's brother," Sage said, and she nodded. "I think one of them might have had something to do with setting my tire up to fall off."

Her eyes widened. "Really?"

"Really," he echoed with a nod. "And if I'm right, then I think you need to be careful, too."

"Karl's been with the department for twenty years, at least. He's not going to jeopardize his job by trying to get back at me."

"No?" Sage lifted one eyebrow doubtfully. "I wouldn't bet on it, Megan. I'd stay clear of him."

"I'm sure Karl Taylor and I will be happy to stay clear of each other." She smiled. "I'm glad you've decided to stay on as foreman, Sage. You've made my job so much easier."

"Oh yeah?" She nodded. "Well, how about you making *my* job a little easier?" He stood up, and she followed suit, looking at him curiously. "Can you handle a hammer?" he asked as he headed for the tool box.

"Of course."

"How about heights?"

"No problem."

"Then if you're going to hang around here on my day off—" He tossed a hammer in the air, caught it by the head and offered her the handle. "—I'm gonna put you to work."

She smiled as she took the tool in her hand. "You mean I get to be on the crew?"

"You get to be the *whole* crew, since I seem to be stuck with the foreman's job."

"We'll see if I can stand working for you. Lead the way."

"You've gotta wear one of these." He handed her a canvas carpenter's apron that advertised Schultz Lumber, then reached for his leather one.

"An apron!" She laughed. "For this I spent four years in college?"

"And we'll be using these," he told her as he dipped into a box of eight-penny nails and added some to his own apron. "So fill up your pockets. This project is on a tight budget, so if you bend too many nails—" She dropped a couple from the handful she was loading into her apron, and she glanced up quickly. He gave her a teasing grin. "I'll keep you after five and make you straighten them out."

"Tyrant." She knelt to pick up the lost nails.

"You bet. That's why I'm so perfect for my job." He gestured toward the ladder. "You go up first, and I'll hold the ladder steady."

He watched her step carefully from the ladder to the plywood sheathing that was already nailed in place. She turned, established her balance on the pitched roof and looked out over the prairie. "You sure you're okay up there?" he asked.

"I'm fine." She shaded her face with her hand. "What a gorgeous view!"

The breeze lifted her honey-colored hair back from her face, and she reminded him of a fine-carved figure on the bow of a sailing vessel. "I'll say."

Chapter 7

"I guess Regina finally reported Jackie missing."

Sage pushed the button under his thumb, but he hesitated in opening the pickup door as he turned a puzzled look toward Gary Little Bird. "I thought he'd run off to North Dakota."

"That's what Regina thought. He's got relatives up there, and that's where he always goes. But she got hold of them, and they said he never showed up there."

Sage left the door ajar as he turned around. It was quitting time, and crew members were heading for their vehicles. Out of the corner of his eye he noted that Gary's news had caught Megan's attention. She, too, had paused on her way to her pickup.

"It's been at least a week since he's been home," Sage reflected. "Nobody's seen him?"

"Well, the cops did some checking, and I guess Roger Makes War and Henry Beaver finally admitted they were with him Monday night."

Sage braced his hand on the top of the cab and peered at Gary with concern. "That's four days. Nobody's seen him since?"

Gary shook his head. "First they said they'd taken him home after a party and let him off near his house. Now they admit they're not exactly sure where they put him out of the car. He said something about going to work and told them to let him off." Gary shrugged. "They pulled over, and he got out. That was the last they saw of him."

"What time was that?"

Gary offered a feeble laugh. "Hell, Sage, they don't know. They were all pretty wasted. They figure sometime after midnight."

"And he said he was coming to work?" Megan asked as she joined the two men. "Poor Jackie."

Sage directed a sigh skyward. "Yeah," he said disgustedly. "Poor Jackie."

"Well, listen, I'd better be taking off." Gary shoved his hands in his pockets and took a couple of steps backward. "I'll let you know if I hear anything else." There was a note of pride in his voice as he explained to Megan, "My brother's a dispatcher at the police station, so I get all the news."

"Coming to work in the middle of the night," Megan mused as Gary walked away. "I wonder how far—"

"Oh, God, no." Sage closed his eyes as an olfactory recollection burst forth in his brain. Muttering a curse, he jerked on the pickup door and hopped in.

"Sage, what is it?"

Megan fastened both hands on the door handle, and he gave her a hard look through the half-open window. "Stay here. I'll be right back, so just stay here."

It had been somewhere between the construction site and the little town of Buffalo Gap. The pickup plowed furrows into the gravel as Sage pushed the pedal to the floor and tried to remember where he'd stopped to fix that flat on his way to work—when? Had it been Wednesday morning? How far down? The memory of the odor became sharper, and he began to feel queasy all over again. It wasn't only the smell. It was the strange feeling he'd had that the odor was beckoning him somehow. He'd ignored all but the fact that the stench was sickening, and he'd hurried to change the tire and move on.

He braked suddenly. There was nothing notable about the spot—no landmark to distinguish it from the rest of the four-strand barbed wire that separated miles of grassy prairie from miles of gravel road. But something appealed to him to stop there, and he knew instinctively what it was. He was attuned to it again. Wiser men than he would have cautioned him to resist this kind of eerie summons, but resisting wasn't possible this time. He left the pickup door standing open and cleared the roadside ditch with one long leap.

He ignored the approach of another vehicle as he negotiated the barbed wire, stretching two strands above his head and holding two down under his boot. The stench was still in the air. Putrefying flesh. It should have been an animal, the carcass of something meant to live and die out there in the middle of nowhere. Sage knew it wasn't. He dreaded what he would find, but he ran unerringly toward it. Two ravens sprang from the grass, black wings aflutter as they pumped hard to gain height quickly.

Sage slowed down as he approached. A snatch of blue lay in the grass ahead. The thudding of his own heartbeat was the single encroachment on the vast quiet. His boots trampled the grass that had served as a shroud, and Sage stood before the gaping face of death and heard its bleak cry echo in his head.

"Christ," he whispered. He tipped his head back, repeating the petition as he watched the white wisp of a cloud slip by.

Megan gripped the steering wheel as she watched Sage make his discovery. She knew what it was, but her heart said no, it couldn't be. It couldn't happen, not like this. She eased herself from the pickup and approached the fence.

Neither her hands nor her brain was functioning properly, and she tore the shoulder of her jumpsuit as she struggled to get through the fence. From a distance she saw Sage pass his hand over his face and take a step back, and her stomach twisted painfully. She began to run.

He turned when he heard the swishing grass, and when he saw her, he panicked. There were no conscious thoughts now—only an instinctive need to spare her. He ran like a man possessed and caught her, trapping her arms between them. She looked up at him, her eyes cold with fear.

"It's Jackie," he said. She saw that much of the color had drained from his face, and his eyes looked haunted and hollow. Whatever he had seen had done this to him. It made no sense, but she tried to pull away. "No," Sage barked. "You can't go over there."

"But—" Her face crumpled. "You mean he's been there...all this time?" He nodded solemnly, and she had no words. There were only the small sounds. "Oh...oh..."

Sage put his arm around her, and they started walking. He wouldn't allow her to see what he had seen. He was there to protect her...and Jackie. The living could share their grief, but the dead had a right to some privacy. Sage would shield Jackie's torn and bloated remains from the final indignity of being viewed.

Like a pair of automatons, they put one foot in front of the other. "How did you know?" she asked.

"I had a flat tire the other morning. I could smell... something dead. I assumed it was an animal."

"But then today..."

"Today I knew." *Today I heard him call me.*

"How could it have happened?" Megan asked as she put her arm around Sage's waist, hoping to return some measure of comfort.

"He must have passed out and died of exposure."

"But it's summer," she protested. "It hasn't rained this week, and it's not that cold at night."

"It can still happen," he said. "Any number of things could have happened. Something inside, like heart failure or alcohol poisoning. He could have gone into shock. He could have choked on his own vomit."

"Oh, Sage . . ."

"He's dead. That's all that matters."

"But what about those two men who left him out here in the middle of nowhere?"

"I don't know." He shook his head and sighed heavily. "I don't know. All I know is that Jackie found the other way to get off the merry-go-round."

"The other way?"

"You either quit drinking or let it kill you."

Megan leaned against his side as they walked back to the road, and Sage adjusted his arm as they drew closer. "Did you tear this on the barbed wire?" She lifted her face with a blank stare. "Your shoulder's bleeding."

She turned her head to examine the shoulder he held close to his chest. His long fingers pulled the torn edges of fabric apart to expose the bleeding patch of skin. "It's nothing," she said. "Just a scratch."

"You'll need a tetanus shot. That stuff's probably rusty."

She lifted her gaze from the scratch to his eyes. She wondered how a slight injury like hers could mean anything in the face of what he'd just witnessed. The light in his eyes told her that it did. Blood meant life, and Jackie had bled the last of his. "I'll be all right," she promised as she tightened her grip on his waist.

It seemed fitting, if tragic, that another liquor license hearing would be held two days after Jackie's body had been discovered. Megan went to the council chambers on her own this time, and when she saw that the chair next to Sage was empty, she went to it and sat down. He looked up, and his face betrayed no surprise at seeing her there.

"Hi," he said simply.

"Hi." She tried to assess the activity in the room. The councilmen were getting coffee and shuffling through papers, and there were people milling around the room, moving chairs and talking. "Have they started yet?"

"Sort of. We're between issues at the moment."

"Will you be speaking?" He nodded as he watched the chairman, who was examining some papers. Megan noticed that Jackie's wife was sitting only a few chairs away. "How's Regina doing?" she asked quietly.

"Okay." Sage leaned forward and rested his elbows on his knees, a manila folder dangling from his hand.

Megan realized that Sage had his upcoming presentation on his mind, and she settled back to wait with him. There was a good deal of conversation going on around her, much of it concerning Jackie's death.

"They said the autopsy was inconclusive," a man behind her reported. "They said it was like examining two-week-old hamburger."

"No ears, that Jackie," a woman's voice said. "Last time he was in detox, the doctor told him his liver was gonna get him sooner or later."

"Rotten hamburger, rotten liver—what's the difference? When your time comes, what's left is just coyote bait anyway."

"Eeez, what a thing to say. He was only thirty-five."

"I'm out of cigarettes." The complaint was punctuated with a smoker's cough. "Ask Boo Boo if he's got any."

"We'll be eating potato salad over you pretty soon if you don't quit that smoking. Listen to you."

The woman leaned past Megan and tapped someone who was sitting just down from Sage. Megan glanced up, curious to see who Boo Boo was, and realized that Sage was watching her eavesdrop. She felt her face grow warm.

"They always have a lot of potato salad at the wakes around here," he explained. Then he laid a hand on her arm and inclined his chin toward the side door. Megan followed the direction of his gaze.

Floyd Taylor had slipped into the room, accompanied by his brother, Karl. Side by side, the two reminded Megan of a pair of bulldog bookends that had always sat on her father's desk and defied anyone to tamper with his papers. Karl took a careful survey of the room, and Megan felt his cold stare the moment he picked her out of the crowd.

As the meeting progressed the chairman expressed his condolences to Regina and invited her to be first to speak on the issue at hand. Regina's voice cracked as she read the statement she'd prepared. She said that it was too late for Jackie, but she didn't want alcoholism to kill his children. For that reason, she wanted tighter control over the sale of alcohol.

When Sage came to the microphone, he asked whether the councilmen had had time to study the information he'd presented to them at the last hearing. There were a few nods and several voices indicating the affirmative.

"Once again I've come before this council to remind you of your duty to look out for the welfare of the people you represent. If you've read those reports, then you know in your gut that Floyd Taylor's business and the way he conducts it are a hazard to our health."

Floyd came to his feet. "I object to that kind of talk, Mr. Chairman!" He pointed a beefy finger at Sage. "And I could get you for slander, Parker. You've got no business accusing me!" He addressed the chair again. "I sell a product. I don't tell people how to use it. Why don't you prohibit the sale of vanilla extract and varnish, too? And how about cough medicine? If people want to get drunk—"

"Sit down, Mr. Taylor," the chairman ordered in a calm voice. "Mr. Parker has the floor."

"We're going to bury a man tomorrow," Sage continued without sparing Taylor so much as a glance. "Jackie Flying Elk tried to quit. We all watched him. Some of us encouraged him, and some of us laughed and told him he'd never make it. He didn't. So when we put him in the ground tomorrow, we can think to ourselves that this is the way it is, and nothing's ever going to change. Or, like Regina, we can tell ourselves that this is not what we want for our children. We can make this decision for ourselves." He lowered his voice and stirred the silence. "We can say *no more* to Mr. Taylor's...product."

After the applause the discussion continued, but it was largely redundant and uninspiring after the impact of Sage's presentation. Once again the issue was tabled.

"Tabled!" Megan snapped as they stood to leave. "What kind of a decision is that?"

"It's a reprieve," Sage said quietly. "We don't have enough votes, but we're being given a little more time, thanks to Jackie."

"I want to speak to his wife." Megan searched the crowd and spotted the beautiful fall of black hair. She made her way to Regina's side and offered her hand as she'd seen the others do. It was not so much a handshake as a pressing of one palm against another. Megan expressed her sorrow, and Regina nodded with sad dignity.

"Have they brought him home yet?" Sage asked.

"They're taking him to the church basement," she said. "He should be there soon."

"I'll drive you over." He turned to Megan. "The funeral's tomorrow morning. I won't get to work until about one."

She nodded and pulled back from the conversation, watching the crowd split and move past them on either side. She knew she'd done what she could; she'd given moral support at the meeting, and she'd expressed condolences to Jackie's widow. It was time she left Sage to share Regina's grief. Her peripheral vision blurred as she fastened her attention on them.

When they moved toward the door, she followed, giving them space. She was an outsider, but somehow she couldn't bring herself to make a graceful exit. She had known Jackie, too, and she'd been concerned about him. She had been there when Sage had discovered his body. She felt that she had a part in this, although she wasn't sure what her part was. She was an outsider, she reminded herself, but she cared about what was going on here. Couldn't they see that?

Mentally she chided herself for her selfishness. Regina had lost her husband, and Sage had lost a friend. Megan shared no real part in their grief. They hardly noticed when she moved away and headed toward her pickup.

At the last moment Sage turned, smiled and said, "Thanks for coming."

Responding to her own needs, Megan found it impossible not to return the following morning. The small white frame church was packed with mourners. A man offered her one of the folding chairs that had been arranged behind the pews, and she was handed a hymnal. She opened the book and found that the hymns were in Lakota.

Sage was one of the six solemn-faced pall bearers. They were all dressed differently, none in the traditional dark suit. One wore a plaid Western shirt buttoned tightly around his neck and adorned with a beaded bolo tie. Another wore a white shirt with a leather vest, and a third was dressed in a dated beige suit. This was the first time Megan had seen Sage dressed up, and, although his light blue sport jacket and tan slacks might not have been deemed appropriate for the occasion in other circles, she saw that fashion was not the measure of anything here. One dressed in his best, whatever it might be, and came to mourn.

As she watched Sage perform his duties and then take a seat in the front row, Megan was struck unexpectedly by the sheer beauty of the man. It wasn't just the rich contrast between his white shirt and his brown skin, or the shiny fullness of his black hair, but it was the way he moved, the way he carried himself smoothly, without any ado. He did nothing to call attention to himself, yet he commanded it. There was a kind of serenity in his face that inspired serenity in the heart of one who watched him. There was solace in knowing that he had survived so much suffering, yet the serenity was still there.

The service alternated English with Lakota, and it spoke of Jackie's death as part of life. Megan recognized the tunes of familiar hymns, but it was as though each note were being pulled through a sieve by mournful voices in a language that tore at the soul without any translation. By the time she pulled her pickup into line at the end of the cortege, she felt that her heart had been wrenched beyond repair, but she was drawn up the hill for the finish, even so.

There was no hearse. The casket, draped in a red, white and blue star quilt, was unloaded from the back of a pickup. The six men carried it through a gate that was marked by two tall, white poles. Megan waited inside her pickup, watching the crowd file along the perimeter of the woven wire fence. Old women wore dark sweaters and tri-cornered scarves to keep the warm wind off their gray heads. Children let the tips of their fingers bounce along the woven wire squares as they followed along to the gravesite.

Megan climbed down from the pickup and brushed at the wrinkles in her navy blue skirt. Overhead the clouds were thick and gray and rushing quickly across the sky. She took her place at the end of the line and followed unobtrusively. She walked past graves that were simply marked, some with wooden crosses, some with small white frames of wood. There were a few headstones and a few faded plastic floral tributes. For the most part, this was prairie. It was buffalo grass, prickly pear cactus and purple South Dakota coneflowers. And it was dust.

There were no blankets of fake grass to profane the earth that would receive Jackie's body. The casket was lowered by hand, and the ends of the ropes were dropped on top of it. As the mourners sang another hymn, Sage left the graveside and came to stand beside Megan. He saw the tears welling in her eyes, and he took her hand. Gratefully she hung on tight, for life was as dear at that moment as it had ever been.

When the last note of the hymn had drifted out over the grass, another sound took its place. It was Re-gina's keening—the high-pitched song of grief that only a woman's voice could carry and only a woman's heartbreak could produce. Her sorrow echoed in the hills while Sage and the other pall bearers filled the grave with earth.

"Why did you come?" Sage asked Megan in a hushed tone as he sat beside her in her pickup and watched the others drive away.

"I was with you when you found him." She glanced over her shoulder at the fresh mound of earth behind the fence. "I wanted to see him put to rest."

"Grief is one thing. Pity's another." She turned back to him, and he saw a glint of pain in her ice-blue eyes. He told himself to handle her carefully. "You know that, don't you?"

"I've never witnessed the kind of grief I heard today. I'd thought maybe..." She glanced away again. "Maybe people were disgusted with him...because of the way he died."

"Were you disgusted with him?"

She shook her head quickly and looked down at her hands. Tears burned in her throat again. "It must have been a terrible way to die. Alone like that."

"What makes you think anyone else would come to this hill today with feelings of disgust?"

She heard no malice in his voice and saw none in his eyes, but his question sounded accusing. She wanted to accuse him in return. "It just seemed that the man was floundering so pathetically, and no one wanted to...to..."

"To take care of him?"

His voice was soft, but she saw the challenge in his eyes. She sought the words to meet it. "Some people need to be taken care of...sometimes."

"Children do," he told her. "But if you treat a man like a child, he's tempted to behave like a child. We've been treated like children for a hundred years, Megan. It's damn tough to break the habit.''

"You've been treated shamefully," she agreed. "I know that. I don't want to be part of that. I want to be open-minded and fair, and I want to try to…to make things right in whatever small way—"

"Make things right?" He chuckled. "How is one little white lady going to make things right?"

"In my own small way," she repeated, emphasizing each word. "I cared about Jackie."

"Do you care about the rest of the crew the same way?"

"Yes," she said firmly, and then, "I think so. They haven't put me to the test. He didn't want to miss work, Sage. He didn't *want* to be late. He would apologize and explain, and all the while you knew he'd embarrassed himself again, dug a deeper hole for himself. And when he was doing well, he was such a good worker, and so willing—"

"Megan." He touched her shoulder and waited until she looked into his eyes. "A man can drown in pity, and you're pouring it out by the bucketful."

She stared for a moment. "Is that what it is? Pity?"

"It sure sounds like it. Can you tell me you respected Jackie? One rational, independent adult to another—did you think of him that way?" She looked down at her hands and gave her head a quick shake. "You felt sorry for him."

She lifted her eyes to his, and they were swimming. "I didn't mean to drown anyone. I got close enough to see his boot, lying there in the grass." She closed her eyes, and her throat grew painfully raspy. "The color of his shirt—I saw that, too. I feel bad about Jackie's death, Sage. I really do."

"Grief is okay," he said gently, and he slid his arm behind her neck and squeezed her shoulder. She tipped her head to the side, resting her forehead on his arm. "It's honest and natural. And what I see in you now…is grief."

Chapter 8

"This is where we've got problems." Sage pointed to the
map on Megan's desk. "This is pretty soft stuff."

"The old roadbed has a quarter mile of washboard
there," Megan said as she looked down his arm at the spot
he was indicating. "The culvert should go in here."

"Yeah, but the hill's there. I'm working down here, and
that clay just doesn't quit."

"Maybe one culvert won't do it," she decided as she
opened a plastic sandwich bag. "How far down are you?"

"I've scraped off a couple of feet. You're going to end up
with a real dip if you don't make some adjustments there."

"I need to get down there this afternoon. Now . . ." She
examined the sandwich, wondering what chance there was
that her cooler had transformed it into something interesting since she'd put it together that morning. "I'll trade you
half a tuna sandwich for almost anything else."

He pushed the map aside and leaned his hip against the
desk. "How about canned chopped meat?" he offered. She
looked doubtful. "Liverwurst? What about tongue?" Even

as his eyes danced, he wondered what he thought he was doing, teasing her. He knew he'd allowed too much friendliness to seep into this relationship, but he couldn't seem to resist.

"Which is it?" she asked, her eyes warming to his.

"Which would you like?"

They let the question stand between them for a moment before he reached across the desk and dragged his black lunchbox closer. He produced a plastic-wrapped sandwich and handed it to her. "Corned beef on rye. Be my guest."

"Just half." She tried to exchange half of hers for it, but he shook his head.

"I hate tuna."

"I can't let you go hungry." She pushed his sandwich back at him.

He edged away as it occurred to him that there were all kinds of hunger. "I've got another one." He proved it to her, then nodded at her cooler. "If you've got anything cold to drink in there, I'll trade for a share of that. All I've got is hot coffee."

"On a day like this?" She hiked herself up to sit on the desk, flipped back the lid of her cooler and brought out a bottle of lemon-flavored mineral water. "I've got another one."

Sage watched her unscrew the cap on the bottle before she handed it to him. They'd just discussed a hitch in the project like two professional equals, and now she was opening a bottle of water for him and worrying about whether he was going to get enough to eat. In recent weeks he'd become comfortable with their working relationship. If the crew had been taking bets on anything when he went into the office the way they had when Taylor had been working with her, Sage figured they'd given it up. Heads no longer turned at the sight of the two of them together, and he believed they were now seen as a team. Engineer and construction foreman. But when they took a break, he wanted to tease her about little things like sandwiches, and he wanted to smile at her in a way that had nothing to do with the project they shared. He took the bottle from her hand, and his fingers brushed over hers. His eyes met hers, and he saw a woman.

The flavored water slid over his tongue like fire-fighter's foam. Thanks, he thought. I needed that. When he lowered the bottle and looked at her again, he trusted the tart bubbles to eradicate any longing his eyes might betray. He scowled at the bottle. "You actually *pay* for this stuff?"

"The first taste is always the worst," she assured him. "Once you get used to it, it's sort of like the champagne of bottled water."

"Champagne?" He studied the label before he tried it again. Swallowing, he nodded. "You'd have to acquire the taste for it, I guess."

She uncapped another bottle. "I especially enjoy this when the weather's hot. It quenches your thirst better than sweet, sticky pop."

He admired the delicate curve of her neck as she lifted her chin and tipped the bottle to her lips. There was no denying the heat. It might reach a hundred degrees before the day was out, he thought, but Megan wouldn't wilt. She would probably bloom, in fact, if the color in her cheeks was any indication. Her face glowed with a soft sheen. Nothing sticky, he thought, but maybe sweet. He imagined touching his lips to her forehead, then licking them. She wouldn't be salty. She would be smooth and sweet.

"I can't resist sweets," he said. She lowered the bottle and blotted her upper lip with the back of her hand. He smiled. "I'm worse than a kid."

"Mmm, but when it's this hot—" She took the sandwich he'd given her in both hands and studied it. "A cold beer would be good with this."

"Sure would." She gave him the surprised look of someone who'd just stepped on his toe. He laughed. "You'll get no argument from me on that point. I've always been a great fan of cold beer on hot days."

"A fan," she said quickly. "That's what we need in here. Better yet, a bathtub. I'd spend my lunch hour in it."

"Really? We'd have a hell of a time keeping the maps dry." He bit into his sandwich and decided that the drink was more appealing than the food was at this point. "Ever tried a sweat bath?"

"You mean, like a sauna?"

"Sort of." The sauna lacked the spiritual quality of a sweat bath, but he doubted her interest in that aspect. "It's better than an ordinary bath. You sweat. You get rid of all the excesses and the need to indulge in excesses. You cleanse yourself from the inside out, and *then* you take a cool bath."

"Is this something *you* do? Like a religious thing?"

"Like a religious thing." It was probably her use of the word *thing* that made him hold back. He found himself teasing rather than sharing. "A tribute to Grandmother, sort of like buying her flowers or something."

"How often do you do this?"

"As often as I need to." He lifted an eyebrow. "How often do you bathe?"

She ignored the question, suddenly intrigued. "Do you do this as a group?"

"Not usually. Not unless—"

"I mean as part of the Medicine Wheel program." She'd conjured up a picture of him and Regina, and the jealousy was back. He studied her for a moment, taking the time to make her uncomfortable. Damn him—he was reading her mind!

"Men and women don't sweat together. At least, not in the sweat lodge."

She squirmed on the desktop. "You just..." She drew the idea of separation in the air. "The men in one, and the women..."

"I usually do it on my own or with a medicine man. It's a personal experience, not a party." She didn't understand, but something in the way she looked at him told him that she wanted to. "It isn't like a health club, Megan. It's more like—"

"Like going to church?"

"Well, no, not exactly." It occurred to him that it wasn't like anything else, which was probably why he did it.

"More like yoga?" she persisted.

"I don't know what yoga's like." He laughed. "It's like a sweat bath. Maybe sometime you'll, uh . . ."

"I'd like to." It seemed incredible, but she was suddenly anxious to experience heat even more intense than that inside the trailer. "How hot does it get? You don't think I'd faint, do you?"

"Not you. I think you'd come through with flying colors once you understood what it was all about."

"I'll have to read up on it. You know, you've given me lots of food for thought, Sage. Things I want to know more about."

He laughed. "I'm not even going to ask what."

"Well, things." She worked on her sandwich for a moment before she added, "I like to read up on topics that catch my interest. I've got a lot of time at night for reading. Not much to do in Hot Springs."

"There's that big natural springs swimming pool," he suggested, suddenly feeling uncomfortable.

She shrugged. "Yeah, that's kinda fun." She followed the sandwich with an apple, which she offered to share, but Sage declined with a shake of his head. "I've read a lot about Native American history, but not much on religion. What would you recommend?"

In addition to a reading list, he could have suggested a movie. He could have suggested they see it together. He climbed into the seat of the big yellow earth mover and brought it to life with the flick of a key. The thought had crossed his mind many times, but he'd dismissed it as a crazy notion. He didn't know how to socialize.

IT'S FUN! IT'S FREE!
AND IT COULD MAKE YOU A
MILLIONAIRE

If you've ever played scratch-off lottery tickets, you should be familiar with how our games work. On each of the first four tickets (numbered 1 to 4 in the upper right) there are Pink Strips to scratch off.

Using a coin, do just that—carefully scratch the PINK strips to reveal how much each ticket could be worth if it is a winning ticket. Tickets could be worth from $100.00 to $1,000,000.00 in lifetime money ($33,333.33 each year for 30 years).

Note, also, that each of your 4 tickets has a unique sweepstakes Lucky Number . . . and that's 4 chances for a **BIG WIN!**

FREE BOOKS!

At the same time you play your tickets to qualify for big prizes, you are invited to play ticket #5 to get brand-new Silhouette Intimate Moments® novels. These books have a cover price of $3.99 each, but they are yours to keep absolutely free.

There's no catch. You're under no obligation to buy anything. You don't have to make any minimum number of purchases — not even one!

The fact is thousands of readers enjoy receiving books by mail from the Silhouette Reader Service™. They like the convenience of home delivery . . . they like getting the best new novels months before they're available in bookstores . . . and they love our discount prices!

We hope that after receiving your free books you'll want to remain a subscriber. But the choice is yours—to continue or cancel, anytime at all! So why not take us up on our invitation, with no risk of any kind. You'll be glad you did!

PLUS A FREE GIFT!

One more thing, when you accept the free books on ticket #5, you are also entitled to play ticket #6, which is GOOD FOR A GREAT GIFT! Like the books, this gift is totally free and yours to keep as thanks for giving our Reader Service a try!

So scratch off the PINK STRIPS on all your BIG WIN tickets and send for everything today! You've got nothing to lose and everything to gain!

Here are your BIG WIN Game Tickets potentially worth from $100.00 to $1,000,000.00 each. Scratch off the PINK STRIP on each of your Sweepstakes tickets to see what you could win and mail your entry right away. (SEE BACK OF BOOK FOR DETAILS!)

This could be your lucky day - GOOD LUCK!

FOLD AND DETACH ALONG THIS DOTTED LINE—RETURN ALL GAME TICKETS INTACT.

TICKET 1
Scratch PINK STRIP to reveal potential value of cash prize if the sweepstakes number on this ticket is a winning number. Return all game tickets intact.

LUCKY NUMBER

4I 719559

TICKET 2
Scratch PINK STRIP to reveal potential value of cash prize if the sweepstakes number on this ticket is a winning number. Return all game tickets intact.

LUCKY NUMBER

2S 610877

TICKET 3
Scratch PINK STRIP to reveal potential value of cash prize if the sweepstakes number on this ticket is a winning number. Return all game tickets intact.

LUCKY NUMBER

9R 734933

TICKET 4
Scratch PINK STRIP to reveal potential value of cash prize if the sweepstakes number on this ticket is a winning number. Return all game tickets intact.

LUCKY NUMBER

7L 594882

FREE BOOKS

TICKET 5
Scratch PINK STRIP to reveal number of books you will receive. These books, part of a sampling program to introduce romance readers to the benefits of the Reader Service, are free.

AUTHORIZATION CODE

130107-742

FREE GIFT

TICKET 6
All gifts are free. No purchase required. Scratch PINK STRIP to reveal free gift, our thanks to readers for trying our books.

AUTHORIZATION CODE

130107-742

YES! Enter my Lucky Numbers in The Million Dollar Sweepstakes (III) and when winners are selected, tell me if I've won any prize. If the PINK STRIP is scratched off on ticket #5, I will also receive four FREE Silhouette Intimate Moments® novels along with the FREE GIFT on ticket #6, as explained on the back and on the opposite page. 345 CIS AQYP (C-SIL-BR-10/94)

NAME _____

ADDRESS _____ APT. _____

CITY _____ PROVINCE _____ POSTAL CODE _____

THE SILHOUETTE READER SERVICE™: HERE'S HOW IT WORKS

Accepting free books places you under no obligation to buy anything. You may keep the books and gift and return the shipping statement marked "cancel". If you do not cancel, about a month later we will send you 6 additional novels, and bill you just $3.21 each plus 25¢ delivery and GST*. That's the complete price, and—compared to cover prices of $3.99 each—quite a bargain! You may cancel at any time, but if you choose to continue, every month we'll send you 6 more books, which you may either purchase at the discount price...or return at our expense and cancel your subscription.

*Terms and prices subject to change without notice. Canadian residents will be charged applicable provincial taxes and GST.

019561919-L2A5X3-BR01

SILHOUETTE READER SERVICE
PO BOX 609
FORT ERIE, ONT.
L2A 9Z9

MAIL▷POSTE

Canada Post Corporation / Société canadienne des postes

Postage paid   Port payé
if mailed in Canada   si posté au Canada

Business   Réponse
Reply   d'affaires

0195619199   01

His wife had wanted what her people called a "social life," and he'd never really understood what that was. Whatever it was, it always involved drinking, and when he got drunk, she always accused him of ruining their social life. He'd thought he'd been doing what he was supposed to do. Hell, he'd always been the life of the party. Nobody ever made much of an impression on him when they were "socializing," at least not that he remembered. The people and their relationships and his relationship to them all ran together in a hazy blur.

Now he went to Medicine Wheel, and he worked. He had friends in both places. Relationships were clear to him. On the job there were fellow workers. In Medicine Wheel there were people who cared about his recovery as much as he cared about theirs. But this idea of a social life was still vague. He wondered if there was a sober way to manage it. What would it be like to be with a woman and be stone cold sober? Why did the words "stone" and "cold" seem to slip in front of "sober" so automatically? The cold part scared him. He'd given it a try a couple of times when he'd first sobered up, and cold was the only way he could describe it.

Megan was different. He thought about her in a way he remembered thinking of no one else. It wasn't in terms of his own needs. He liked to remember the talks they had about roadbeds and ranching, about solving problems with ground water and saving the bald eagle. He was haunted by the trickle of perspiration he'd seen slip down her temple, and he imagined brushing it away. Nothing more. Just to be granted the privilege of touching her face without asking, without explaining.

He wanted to be close to her, and the thought was frightening. She kept coming into his life through different doors, and he knew now that he wanted her to keep coming back. He wanted her to open his private doors, but he wanted her to understand what she was getting into. He wanted her to put away her blinders and still be able to accept him. Hell, he wanted her to be able to *like* him. That, in a nutshell, was his fear. Maybe without all the bravado, there was really nothing about him for a woman to like.

Her pickup was still parked beside the trailer. She'd spent part of the afternoon looking over the portion of the road-bed about which Sage had expressed concern, and he'd half hoped she would have left for the day. They'd been back to being engineer and foreman, and there hadn't been any problems. A problem with the contour of the grade, maybe, but no problem with the engineer and the foreman. After she'd left the site, he'd started working himself into a lather about talking to her again, this time about Megan and Sage. The notion wouldn't go away, so he decided to drive back to the office and satisfy himself that she was no longer there. So much for being taken off the hook.

"Hey, you're still here?" He pulled the door shut with a sweaty palm.

Megan looked up from her calculations and smiled—casually, she hoped. She'd seen him drive up. She'd put the pencil down then, but she was holding it again for effect. "I'm just about finished. I'm surprised *you're* still here."

He sat on the edge of the desk and twisted his head to get a look at her figures. They all ran together. His mouth was dry. "You got it all solved now?"

"I think so. I think we pretty much worked it out this afternoon. A little more elevation and another culvert." He nodded, and she tossed her pencil on top of her figures. "Is the roof finished yet?"

"The roof?" She disappeared behind the desk and came back up with her lunch cooler. "Uh, well, the sheathing, yeah. That's done." He checked his watch. "I'm on my own time now, right?"

She moved around the desk, feeling the heat from his eyes. She smiled. "If you say so. You're the foreman."

"Yeah, well... what I want to bring up is strictly personal business, so, uh, just so you know..."

"Nothing you say at this point will be used against you." She braced both hands on top of her cooler and leaned toward him. "What's on your mind?"

"Tell you the truth, it's you."

"Me?" she asked innocently.

"Yeah, you." He sprang away from the desk and shoved his hands into his pockets. "Don't act like you're surprised, Megan. You've been on my mind a lot lately."

"We've been around each other a lot lately."

"Yeah, I know. You have a way of appearing out of the woodwork." He lowered his voice and admitted, "Even when you're not really there."

"Am I giving you nightmares?"

He turned and caught her whimsical smile. "I might as well tell you that you'd be crazy to go out with me."

"Would I?"

"Yeah, you would. I don't know the first thing about dating." He turned to the window and stared at the tool box in the back of his pickup. "It seems like I went from pulling girls' braids in school to pulling them down on the backseat of a car after a rodeo and a six pack. There weren't any dates."

"Then how did you get to know your wife?"

"I didn't. And I never let her get to know me." He faced her and leaned back against the windowsill. "Somewhere along the line I just laid claim to her, I guess. I used to rodeo a lot, and she'd come along. When she got pregnant, we figured it might be nice to get married." He gave a mirthless chuckle as he shook his head. "It wasn't nice. Neither one of us was any good at it. After a while it seemed like all I did was argue with her or screw her." He saw her eyes widen, and he felt a little sick. He glanced away. "There's no other word for it," he said quietly. "That's all it was."

"I don't understand why you're telling me all this."

He sighed heavily. "Because at this point in my life, I'm about as backward as they come. I ought to be telling you that I've just had bad luck with women, because I know that would stir up those caretaking instincts of yours right now. But the truth is, women haven't had much luck with *me*."

"Your life has changed a great deal since...since you were married."

"Yeah, I know." He studied the toe of his boot. "That's why I was thinking...maybe if I went slow..."

She waited. The seconds ticked by, and she held her breath. When he looked up at her, she saw the hope in his eyes. "Are you asking me out, Sage?"

He gave a crooked smile. "Trying to."

She smiled back. "Then you really shouldn't tell me all your faults first."

"You mean I'm not going about this right?"

It was something she knew she said often. Laughing, she shook her head sympathetically. "About as backward as they come."

"That's the way I felt when we had lunch together today." He straightened away from the window and approached her slowly. "I figured we had a nice friendship going, and it was probably all wrong for us to start sweating over each other's hungry looks." He saw the color rise in her cheeks, but she didn't back away. He took another step. "I don't wanna mess things up between us, Megan."

"Then let's keep it simple," she suggested. "How about a movie?"

He smiled at the idea of keeping it simple. That had been a survival tactic of his for the last four years. "You said you like horses," he reminded her. "I'd like to take you for a ride up in the Badlands, out by my place."

"I'd like that, too," she told him.

Chapter 9

It had been agreed that Megan would pack a picnic lunch and Sage would provide the beverages and transportation to the Badlands. She wasn't one to fuss over food, especially in her little motel kitchenette, but she took extra care with this meal. She knew they were both tired of sandwiches.

Sage had been waiting for her. He hailed her from the corral when she slowed her pickup near the trailer. When she pulled up near the barn, he hopped down from the railing and walked over to the truck, shutting the door for her after she'd emerged with her cooler.

"Ready to ride?" he asked as he made an obvious point of appraising her attire. She wore a yellow knit tank top, jeans and a pair of cowboy boots that had been sitting in her closet for years. "You'll be getting a good dose of sun today," he warned.

"That's exactly what I want." He looked good in his straw cowboy hat. The wheat color contrasted sharply with his black hair and brown skin, and the loose weave of the brim created a pattern of sunlight and shadow over his face.

He wore a blue chambray shirt with the sleeves rolled nearly to his elbows, and his jeans fitted his long legs and slim hips as though they'd been tailored for him.

He ushered her through the narrow corral gate. "When you said you liked horses, I guess I assumed you had some experience with them."

"I do, but I haven't done any riding since I was in college."

"I'm going to put you on the sorrel so you won't have to contend with mama's baby." He nodded toward the colt. "If she thinks he's having trouble keeping up, she might get broncky."

"Broncky?"

"She'll start balking. She might even offer to crow-hop a little, like a bronc. That sorrel is a nice trail horse, though. I use him all the time. I've also got two young mares out in the pasture." He gestured toward the hills. "They're only green broke."

Megan saw that the horses were saddled. She held the cooler up for Sage's consideration. "What'll we do with this?"

"Transfer it to the saddlebags." He took the cooler over to the sorrel's side and began arranging its contents in one of the pouches of a set of canvas saddlebags, which was already strapped behind the cantle of the saddle. "You've got plenty of plastic ice in here. I'll put some on the other side, with the drinks."

"I hope you like fried chicken." She examined the construction of the bag while he added ice on the other side. "Do you think it'll be okay in here?"

"If you fried it, I think it's past complaining." She saw his grin above the horse's rump. "I'm not going to let it sit in there too long. It smells great. Need any help getting up?"

"Oh, no, thanks. I'm a cowboy, too." But she found that the stirrups had already been shortened for her, and the sorrel stood taller than she'd realized. She soon had her leg twisted up like one of the chicken wings she'd fried, with only the tip of her toe in the stirrup. She was grasping for any leather within reach when she heard him move in close behind her, chuckling.

"A short one," he allowed as he put his hands at her waist. "And quite a contortionist. Just let me give you a little boost, cowboy."

His strength took her by surprise. She was high in the air before she knew it. Reaching for the saddle horn became an afterthought as she swung her leg over the horse's back. "Thank you," she managed as she straightened in the saddle.

"Anytime." He led the mare through the gate. The colt pranced behind, apparently anxious for an outing. Sage closed the gate behind Megan, and she watched the fluid ease with which he swung himself into the saddle.

"It's only because your legs are longer," she muttered.

He flashed her a smile. "Eat your corn flakes, cowboy. You might stretch a little."

They rode through three quarter sections of pasture that were dotted with cows and calves before Megan turned in the saddle to tell him, "I've seen more than fourteen cows out here."

"Really?" He scanned the grassy flat. "They must be reproducing faster than I thought. How many do you think are out here?"

"Well, I'd say at least—" She frowned and peered past her shoulder at his deadpan expression. "I'd say you know exactly."

"Exactly a hundred and ninety-four," he told her with a smile. "I'm pasturing cattle for another rancher. Pays my lease and some of my other expenses."

"I thought this was your land."

"Not all of it," he told her. "Some of it belongs to other members of the family, and I lease it from them through the BIA. I also have a grazing permit for some park land."

"Why doesn't the other rancher just lease the land himself?"

"This is one of the few instances in which there's a legal advantage to being an Indian. White ranchers can only get the lease if no Indian wants it. I've got the lease, and he pays me to pasture his stock."

She peered ahead at the wall of wind- and water-worn rock that stretched across the horizon like an ancient, craggy ruin. The sheer rock face appeared to provide nothing that could sustain any life. "I don't see how you could keep any cattle up there," she said. "You don't, do you? Nothing could live up there."

"Wait till we get closer," he suggested. "The only way to see the Badlands is to ride through them."

"I've only driven *past* them," she said.

"Then you're in for an experience." He grinned at her. "You seem to have an interest in things that might be just a little on the bad side."

They rode into the Badlands. Once they passed the first grassy steps and their eroded risers, Megan felt as though she were being enveloped by draws lined with strange, striated tan and gray walls. Some of the eroded uprights supported grass-topped tables. Others were barren, carved by the wind to resemble the turrets and spires of gray and sandy-walled castles. Many of the walls were pockmarked with holes, as though they had been sprayed by a giant's machine gun. Sage explained that these were the burrows of a kind of bee, the solitary bee, whose larvae were hunted by pecking birds. Other rocky faces were visited by cliff swallows, who darted in and out of the clay blisters they'd fashioned on the sheer rock and tended their nests within.

"Some things live here." Sage pointed to the gray-green vegetation that dotted the landscape.

"Yucca," she acknowledged. "And lots of sage."

"Tough stuff."

They followed the lazy curve of a mud flat, which seemed a poor excuse for a creek bank, but then, the narrow stream of water seemed a poor excuse for a creek. The animals that had been there earlier in the morning obviously found cause to disagree. Sage pointed to crisscrossing lines of tracks, clearly embedded in the mud. "Coyote," he said. "Rabbit. Couple of pronghorns." He pointed at the ground ahead and said in the same even tone, "Sasquatch."

Megan twisted in her saddle, studying the tracks as she passed. "Sasquatch? You mean . . . ? Those look more like a horse's tracks."

"Sasquatch's horse. His big feet are killing him."

Once again she scowled at him. "Sasquatch my foot."

"Yours are too small." He scowled back, then broke into another of his engaging grins.

"You're an awful tease, Parker."

"You're an easy mark, McBride." He reined his horse toward the hill. "Come on. There's a spot up here I want to show you."

They picked their way among the huge mushrooms of clay, undercut by the rushing water of spring storms, and climbed the puckers of rainwash toward a grassy upper level. They rode to the edge of the table, where Sage dismounted with the announcement, "Let's eat."

He helped her down and handed her the saddlebags before picketing the horses several yards away from one another to avoid any contentious kicking while they nibbled at the plentiful grass. The colt was free to romp, but like the toddler he was, he never strayed far from his mother. Megan was sorry she hadn't packed some sort of blanket, but Sage didn't seem to notice that anything was missing as he settled on the natural cushion of curly buffalo grass and broke out a bottle of mineral water and one of orange soda. She smiled when he offered her the lemon water, and his eyes danced back with the obvious satisfaction of having remembered her favorite flavor.

The wind exercised unusual restraint for this barren part of the world, giving them only a pleasant midday breeze. Content with one another's company, they shared the food without much conversation. When they were down to the last of their drinks, Sage pointed across the chasm toward a higher wall and a higher grassy table. "That's where my grandfather's scaffold stood. That's the spot I wanted to show you."

"I thought scaffold burials were illegal," Megan said as she gazed at the high flat that seemed to have a special place in the sun.

"They are. But my grandfather said that beyond death the law meant nothing. He told my mother that his spirit wouldn't rest unless his body went to the scaffold in the old way. She chose to defy the law rather than her father's dying wish."

"How old was he when he died?"

"Ninety-four. He died in the cabin—the one I was born in." He plucked a single blade of grass and stuck the end in his mouth as he watched the grass across the way ripple in the sunshine. He imagined the scaffold standing above it. "I was only about six, but I remember hearing the death rattle in his throat. He crooned for days before he finally went. He spoke no English on his deathbed."

"Ninety-four! That's amazing."

Sage nodded, still gazing at the spot that brought back these memories. "He outlived his sons and all but his youngest daughter—my mother. He said it was because he shunned the 'white sins'—flour, sugar, salt and alcohol. My older brothers and sisters remember him better than I do, but I remember his death very well."

"It must have been terrible for you to watch him die."

"No, it wasn't. It was peaceful. He wasn't shut up in some antiseptic hospital with tubes stuck in his nose. Life went on as usual around him, and he was at peace when he slipped away from us." He leaned on one elbow and stretched his long legs out in the grass. "Then they prepared to raise him toward the sun. There was a lot of whispering and scurrying around to get it done quickly. I knew everyone was afraid the scaffold would be found, and I felt as though I had been entrusted with an important secret."

"Did the talk of restless spirits scare you?"

"Of course." He looked at her solemnly. "It's supposed to. People around here have a healthy respect for spirits. Most of my grandfather's personal possessions were buried with his bones after they were picked clean. The rest were given away."

Megan drew her knees up to her chin and wrapped her arms around them. "But surely you wanted to keep some things as remembrances."

"It might be safe to keep some things—things that weren't very personal."

"Safe?"

He looked into her eyes and tried to assess the degree to which she might have opened her mind during the time they'd spent together. Her gaze was clear and bright. Curious, yes, but her eyes didn't ridicule him as he had, at times, ridiculed himself for the old beliefs. He'd found that he could mock them, call them superstitions, brush them away with an impudent gesture and call himself a modern man, but the instinctive acceptance of them wouldn't leave him.

"They're called *wanagi*," he explained. "Spirits of the departed ones. I've told myself that when you live out here on the prairie, the night sounds alone are bound to make you believe in ghosts. When it comes right down to it, I can't explain them away to my own satisfaction. When I go hunting, I still leave a piece of my kill for the *wanagi*."

"Have you ever seen or heard anything yourself that convinced you of the presence of the spirits?" she asked. The mere idea was interesting, but the underlying thrill of fear was irresistible. Megan hugged her legs tighter.

He sat up and tossed aside the stem of grass he'd been chewing. "There was Jackie," he said quietly, feeling the risk in the pit of his stomach each time he said the dead man's name aloud.

"You mean, Jackie's ghost?"

"Something called me that day, Megan. I knew he was there, and I knew he'd been trying to tell me he was there."

He watched her take the information and turn it over carefully in her mind. "Do you believe me?"

"Of course I believe you. I was there."

"Did you feel it, too? That weird tugging, that—"

"No. I just felt scared watching you. I knew it was going to be something terrible."

He leaned closer. "Do you believe it was Jackie's ghost?"

"I don't know." She glanced across the chasm again. "I guess I believe there are some things that aren't easy to explain. Maybe they don't have to be explained. Maybe they just *are*."

He smiled, satisfied. Just that much margin in her thinking was enough. He got to his feet, offering her a hand. "Let me take you to another place where things 'just are'. Might save you a trip to the library."

They rode through an eroded gully whose history was recorded in dark and light striations, which seemed to change color as her viewing angle changed. A hawk glided above them on an invisible current of hot air, and on a nearby plateau a prairie dog barked a warning to its burrowing community.

"As beautiful as this land is, I can't imagine it's worth leasing for cattle," Megan said. "There isn't much grass."

"There's more than meets the eye. And there's good shelter in these breaks. It doesn't support too many head, but the lease is pretty reasonable. Besides, I like to come here. I don't have to try too hard to imagine what it was like here a hundred, two hundred, years ago. It was just like this."

She tried to imagine what he would have looked like a hundred years ago, without the hat, without the boots or Western saddle. It wasn't difficult. His hooded eyes were crinkled at the corners, and his cheekbones were chiseled and high. The whole effect was to protect the eyes of a man who faced limitless sky, sun and wind every day of his life. Sage belonged to these stony, wind-worn hills as surely as his grandfather had.

They came to another stream and followed its winding path through a valley. The water was clear and inviting, and the sun overhead seemed to grow hotter by contrast. Megan saw the willow skeleton of a small dome off in the distance and felt her blood course a little faster as they approached it. He was about to show her something special. He was about to confide in her again.

They watered the horses before tethering them to either end of a fallen, sun-bleached cottonwood. Sage led Megan to the small willow dome. "This is covered with hides and blankets to make the sweat lodge," he explained. He walked around it, indicating the steps with his hands. "You build a fire and heat the rocks outside." She noted the supply of stones, waiting in a small mound. "You roll the hot rocks inside, pour water over them for steam and sweat like crazy. When you've had enough, you jump into the creek."

"What a shock that must be." She examined the way the slender, flexible willows were curved and lashed together. "You just sit there and sweat?" she asked.

"Well, you... pray." He remembered when prayer had been suggested to Megan at Medicine Wheel; he'd had the sense that she'd rejected the idea as ineffective. He remembered a time when it had been suggested to him and he'd laughed, too.

"What do you pray for?" When she heard the question, she glanced up quickly, recognizing her own audacity. "I mean, generally speaking. I don't mean to pry or anything. I just wondered if there was a sort of..."

"Liturgy?" He smiled and shook his head. "I don't know of any. When you do this with a medicine man, he sings in Lakota. Unfortunately, I don't speak much Lakota. So I just pray."

He ran his hand along the smooth curve of a willow rib. It occurred to him that this woman was important to him, and it made him a little nervous to speak of these things to her. It seemed more natural to tease her, to flash his smile and put them both at ease. But he wanted something else this time. It somehow seemed right to talk with her.

"I'm looking for healing, Megan. I'm trying to put the pieces back together, and I'm finding out that the pieces of me go way back. There's a spiritual connection that got severed somewhere along the way."

"But so much time has passed, and so much has changed."

"Some things have changed. I used to think they were major changes—the way we get our food and clothing, the kind of homes we have. But our basic needs haven't changed. We still eat. We still put clothes on our bodies and live together in some kind of shelter. The missionaries and the government denied us our ceremonies, and we've always been a very spiritual people. We tried to make do or do without. Everything got watered down and wrung out. Pretty soon we were left with the desiccated remains of what we'd once been. We imitated ourselves for tourists, and we looked for something to kill the pain, something to fill the void. Alcohol seemed to be a ready cure for all that ailed us."

He squatted beside the mound of stones, resting one knee on the cracked hardpan. "I pray for healing," he told her as he lifted a fist-size stone and weighed it in his hand. "I pray for the strength to put my self-indulgence aside so I can hold my head up in the community. I pray for wisdom. Generation after generation has been stripped layer by layer. Some things are gone for good. We need to replenish ourselves. I want to know how."

"You need jobs," Megan said as she stood close and watched him. "In this day and age, in order to get the food, the clothing and the shelter, you have to have a job."

"Sure." He looked up, smiled and got to his feet, bouncing the rock in his palm. "We need to support ourselves. The government payoffs can't begin to redeem us. We need to look within ourselves, which is a tough place to start.

Most of us are scared to death we'll find there's nothing there."

"Nothing there! That's ridiculous, Sage. Look how far you've come."

He stared at her for a moment, giving her a sense, as he had at other times, that he was looking through her at the workings of her brain. He turned from her suddenly and mounted an assault on a sloping embankment.

"Sage?" She hurried after him to the top of the slope, which was lush with needle-and-thread grass. "What did I say? How can you feel—"

He spun on his heel. "I can feel whatever I feel. Don't tell me to deny it. If I level with you about a real, deep and abiding fear, don't tell me it's ridiculous. Don't try to pat me on the head and say, 'You've come a long way, baby.' And, by God, don't you try to tell me you never in your life doubted yourself, Miss Megan, highway engineer."

"Well, of course, I've—"

"Of course! Of course! Is it really that black and white? Is everything really that clear to you? My God, you must sleep well at night."

She hated herself for lowering her gaze, but his emotion had filled his own eyes with such power that she couldn't bear the pressure any longer. "I only meant to say that *I* see a lot in you," she said quietly. "Talent, ambition, determination..."

"And I told you that I pray for healing, wisdom and the strength to face another day. What you see isn't enough. Don't belittle my needs or my fears.... Don't..." Her eyes were too round and blue and filled with regret. He lifted his hand and placed it gently along her jaw, tracing the sharp curve below her ear with his long middle finger. He knew he could drown in those eyes. He rubbed her chin with his thumb, and the order became a soft plea. "Don't."

She stood there looking up at him, her stomach fluttering. "Don't what?"

"Don't look at me like that."

"I'm confused, Sage. I seem to say all the wrong things, and I don't want to."

"I know." He wanted to kiss her. God, he wanted to kiss her!

"I only meant to say that I believe in you."

His smile was tentative. "I'm a poor excuse for something to believe in, Megan. I'm still trying to understand what *I* believe in." He slid his hand the length of her arm and took her by the hand. "You've heard of *hanble ceya*, the vision quest?"

She nodded as he pulled her down to sit with him on the ground. "Don't you see some kind of an animal or something after you starve yourself for several days?"

He looked at the clouds overhead as he chuckled. "Yeah, right. Fast for three days so you can hallucinate herds of buffalo and skies full of eagles."

"That's what happened in *A Man Called Horse*," she reminded him. What did she know other than what she'd read, or seen in the movies?

He tapped his forefinger on her knee. "A man called Sage is here to tell you that there's a lot more to it."

"You've done it?"

He nodded. "Lakota tradition teaches that there are several aspects of the human soul. There's the part that lives on in the afterlife. There's also the shade—you know, the ghosts we talked about that haunt the living if they're not respectful. There's the earthly soul. That's the best part of you—your talents, your life's purpose, your ability to be noble and give love. It's that part of the soul that the vision quest is directed to. *Hanble ceya* is crying for a vision of your world and your place in it."

"Did you have a vision?"

He thought for a moment as he looked down at the crusty mud of the creek bank and the frame of his sweat lodge. By the very act of bringing her to this place he had made a decision to share himself with her. It wasn't necessary that she believe as he did, only that she respect what he believed. If he answered her question, he knew he would have to take the risk of being scoffed at in the hope of securing acceptance.

"I went to the hill three times." He smiled and shook his head as he recalled three fasts, three sweats, three days alone in the vision pit on each of three occasions. "I must have been a really hard case for the spirits to crack. The third time they saw me coming, they took pity on me and gave me a vision."

It was a confidence. She knew she had no right to ask for more, but she seemed unable to contain her interest. "I don't suppose you can talk about... about your vision."

He raised his brow. "I'll tell you this much: it had me building a road. And there was a wheel." He leaned back to allow his hand access to his front pocket, from which he pulled a two-inch ring with four spokes all covered with red, white, yellow and black quillwork. He handed it to her, saying, "It's a medicine wheel. I took it as my symbol and wore it when I did the Sun Dance."

"The Sun Dance!" Her eyes widened. "With all that torture and suffering?" Maybe she was thinking Hollywood again. "Or is it more ritualistic nowadays?"

"You mean, is it all just a show?" She returned his medicine wheel, and he held it between his finger and thumb, considering. "Generally, outsiders aren't allowed to watch, but tradition says there must be witnesses, those who will care for the dancers, attest to the fact that the pain was endured and learn from what they see." He lifted his eyes to hers. "Wasn't it so with the crucifixion? Without witnesses, no one would know. It would be as though nothing happened."

He reached out to pluck a blade of grass as he continued. "We've crippled ourselves by perfecting this 'secret suffering,' this 'stiff upper lip.' I spent a lot of time trying to avoid pain, numb it, deny it altogether. Others may know about the pain because they've heard gossip, but they mind their own business, because they're embarrassed by it."

She remembered his admission of pain at the loss of his children before the Tribal Council. Yes, she'd been embarrassed by it. "I would be afraid to suffer like that in public," she confessed. "I'd make a fool of myself."

"We need to admit the pain before we start healing. Through the Sun Dance, I accepted pain as part of life, and I made it a spiritual offering." He leaned to one side and pocketed his amulet. "That was my way. It may not make sense to you."

"It does," she said quickly. "It makes a great deal of sense. It just seems like such a . . . drastic measure."

"It *is* a drastic measure," he explained. "It's often done when someone in the family is very ill, or, in the old days, when you'd had a close call in battle and you knew damn well it could have gone either way. You're still scared. I had a close call and—" He looked directly into her eyes, and his voice barely rose above the rustle of the wind in the tall grass "—sometimes I'm still scared."

"Like . . . when you saw Jackie?"

"Yeah." His eyes glazed with the memory. "When I saw my own face lying in the grass and felt a piece of him in me."

"Does it help?" she asked. "Are you stronger, having done the dance?"

"I believe I am."

"Were you pierced? Where . . ."

She watched with fascination as he began unbuttoning his shirt. When he reached his belt, he pulled the fabric free of his pants and flicked the last two buttons open. He drew his shirt back to expose the scars—two puckered marks over his pectoral muscles. She wondered why she hadn't noticed them before. Identical and evenly placed, they were scars made by design, not by accident. He had borne them willingly in the hope of transcending the pain they caused.

Megan rose up on her knees as she lifted her hands to his chest, placing her fingertips over the scars. His skin was hot, and the small cords of scar tissue felt hotter still. He covered her hands with his and flattened them hard against his skin. She heard the catch in the deep breath he drew as he hooked the heels of his hands beneath her chin and curved his long fingers around her head. She looked up and saw the heat of his kiss in his eyes before she lifted her chin and accepted the offering hungrily with her mouth. Their kiss came tentatively in a quick coupling of moist lips. It came again and lingered longer, mouths moving over one another, exploring possibilities. It came a third time with mutual insistence, hard pressure, a soft whimper, a needy groan. Sage slid his arms around Megan's shoulders and lay back in the grass, pulling her down with him.

His scars seared her palms. She caressed them with circular motions and kissed the lips that moved anxiously against hers. His belt buckle pressed against her stomach, and his manhood grew quickly between her thighs. The sudden intimacy at once frightened and thrilled her, swishing a peppery feeling up and down her thighs. Then he rolled with her, tucked her underneath him and invaded her mouth with his softly stroking tongue.

The heat of the sun diffused over his back and in his hair as he gloried in the way her hands felt against his skin. He made a conscious effort to transfer the sun's warmth into his kiss, to return the feeling of power she'd given him with just the touch of her hands. His body surged with it. His heart pounded with it. His soul was nourished with it.

"Megan, Megan, sweet Megan," he chanted near her ear. He pressed his cheek against her breast and hugged her close. "God, you make me feel good."

She smoothed the thick, damp hair over the back of his neck. "I don't think we need any hot rocks to work up a sweat, Sage."

He shook with silent laughter. "Out of the mouths of aroused women . . ." He lifted his head and offered one bitter-sweet kiss before sliding down to pull off her boot.

"Wha—"

He had them both off before she had time to protest further. "Socks, too," he ordered as he crooked his leg to work on his own boot.

She wasn't sure why she complied as he shed his shirt. When he grabbed her by the hand and pulled her to her feet, she caught the direction of his intentions. "No way!" Digging her heels in was difficult. Resisting his strength was impossible. "Sage!"

He spared her feet by sweeping her up in his arms and covering the ground easily; his own feet were accustomed to being bared on this creek bank. "It's mandatory, Megan."

"It is not! Not for me!" But she didn't fight him. She wouldn't mind wading in the little creek.

"After the sweat comes the—" Splash!

Megan bobbed to the surface and sputtered into his face. "What is this? The Indian Ocean?"

He laughed as he treaded water. "It cuts a deep channel here. You can swim, can't you?"

"You'd better hope I can!"

She could. After they'd traded splashes and displayed their best strokes, they emerged, laughing and dripping and shaking their fingers at one another in teasing admonition.

Megan pushed her short hair back from her face. "Now look!" she demanded, spreading her arms wide.

"I'm looking." He raised an appreciative eyebrow. "You sure are wet."

Her thin bra and summer top did little to hide the response of her nipples to the breeze's caress. She folded her arms across her chest. "At least you still have a dry shirt, Mr. Parker, and if you were any kind of gentleman, you wouldn't stand there drooling."

"I'm not drooling, I'm dripping, and you're the one who told me to look. I thought you were showing off." He grinned as he tossed his hair back. "I don't blame you, either. You look great." But he offered her his shirt, and when she reached for it, he openly admired the way her own shirt clung and her nipples beaded. "Who thought up the rules for being a gentleman, anyway?"

"Probably Queen Victoria." She made a spinning motion with her finger, and he turned away.

"No wonder I never made the grade."

While Megan peeled off all wet cloth above her waist and slipped into his shirt, Sage took a seat on the low bluff above the creek and hardly peeked. She tied the shirt under her bust to keep her jeans from getting it wet, then she joined him, letting her legs dangle over the edge of the grassy table, just as he did.

"I've never seen the Badlands the way you've shown them to me today," she told him. She gestured toward the striated sandstone wall across the creek. "It's like a huge sand paintng—the kind tourists buy in those plastic containers, all filled with layers of colored sand. One minute you think the wind and runoff have eroded all the life out of it." She leaned over to pluck a daisylike purple coneflower from a cluster rising in the tall grass. "The next, you come to a lovely spot like this."

"You would have ridden right by a spot like this," he said. "You have to get down and take a closer look. Here." He held up a sprig of white-striped greenery. "You know what this is?"

"Indian paintbrush."

"Shall I color you beautiful?" His eyes were made warm by his soft smile as he feathered the tuft over her cheek. "'Behold, my brothers, the spring has come. The earth has received the embraces of the sun, and we shall soon see the results of that love.'"

She felt dewy inside. "That's wonderful. Is it yours?"

"If I said it was, would you believe me?"

"Of course."

He shook his head, still smiling, and put the Indian paintbrush in her hand. "You're an easy mark, Megan McBride. That was Sitting Bull."

"It sounds like something from the Old Testament."

"Then why were you ready to believe it was mine?"

"Because..." She glanced back down at the bright water flowing past them. "Because when you talk about the things that matter to you—your beliefs, your grandfather, Medicine Wheel—everything you say sounds...profound to me." She turned to him earnestly. "I don't care what you say, Sage. I think it's amazing what you've done, first for yourself and then for the others."

He wanted to bask in her praise. It felt so good to hear her say such things that he was tempted to allow her to romanticize his recovery. Hell, he might like being somebody's hero for a change. He knew he'd had enough of being the villain.

He straightened the collar of his shirt and lingered to touch the soft down on the back of her neck. "I wanted to make love to you. You know that, don't you?"

She nodded. "Wanting is natural. You didn't push."

"I don't have much experience with getting to be friends first. I want your friendship. I want to give you mine, for whatever it's worth."

"It's worth—"

"Kissing for?" He hooked his elbow behind her neck and brought her close enough to make the discovery that their friendship was indeed worth kissing for.

Chapter 10

Sage chewed on a toothpick and counted the shades of brown in the speckled linoleum floor of the Red Calf Community Center. There were fifteen people in the circle, and they were enjoying a time of reflection. To an observer, it might have seemed like a time of silence, but it wasn't. The voices of four children, who were chasing one another from corner to corner on the far side of the room, filled the people's ears. The consideration of what had been said thus far during the meeting filled their minds. The scent of the burning sweet grass that had been carried around the perimeter of the circle at the beginning of the meeting tantalized their nostrils. A steady rain pattered on the roof. The people moved easily from talk to no-talk and back to talk again, but no one felt compelled to fill the air with chatter.

Sage's reflections turned often to Megan and the day they'd spent together in the Badlands. He had wondered whether their working relationship would become awkward once they'd shared kisses. It hadn't. Monday morning had brought business as usual. Megan had gone to Pierre on Tuesday, and had stayed there for three days. He'd found himself missing her.

Initially it had come as a surprise. He'd allowed himself to miss Brenda and Tommy, but otherwise he'd generalized his loneliness. He missed women, family, even old buddies, but no one in particular other than the children. He was learning about real friendship through Medicine Wheel. Still, he spent most of his hours alone. Women, family and old buddies were difficult to deal with, so he'd put them all on the back burner in his daily life. Now he faced a longing to be with one person, one particular woman, and it scared him. He wanted too much too suddenly. He'd made too many mistakes in the past, and he didn't want to repeat them.

He knew all the wrong ways to treat a relationship, and he wasn't at all sure about the right ones. If a man weren't possessive, would a woman stick with him of her own accord? If he weren't jealous, would she still be faithful to him? If he weren't demanding, would she be inclined to give? And if he weren't any of those things, what would he be? Would he appear weak? Unmanly? He knew how to attract her, but when she started admiring him, what he was inside, not what he looked like outside, he had the feeling he was on shaky ground. Beneath the surface was a man who was learning to walk all over again, taking one careful step at a time. His experience had taught him how to build up the "masculine" image and take refuge behind it. His newly developing inclinations told him to try a little trust.

"We can't trust Floyd Taylor."

Sage straightened in his chair as he folded his arms over his chest and tuned his thoughts to Regina. No one stared at the speaker, but the circle assumed an attitude of listening.

"He's saying he's willing to take a temporary license," Regina continued. "He says he wants a chance to prove himself. That's what he's saying to the council, anyway. Out of the other side of his mouth, he's calling in a lot of old debts. He's saying no more credit at the store. People are getting scared."

"It's crazy to borrow money from him," old Bessie War Shirt grumbled. "You never know how he figures the interest."

"Don't ask him to explain it, either," another woman advised. "All you'll get out of it is that you owe him more money than you've got."

"We got no bank." Marvin Bad Heart was a new member who wasn't convinced that conditions could change. His voice was as expressionless as his face. "If we put Taylor out of business, we got no money. We've always borrowed money from the storekeeper. That's the way it's always been."

"We're gonna try it a different way," Sage said. "We can't be any worse off than we are now."

"Maybe," Marvin allowed. "But at least now we know what we got. May not be much, but we know what it is."

"I got a little insurance money," Regina announced quietly. "I think he'd want me to use it to open a store. He told me I was crazy to try it, but I think now . . . he'd like it if he could help me get it going."

The group allowed another quiet time to pass. They knew that Regina was wise not to mention her dead husband's name, but they felt his presence. They had a sense that Jackie approved of Regina's plan. Before the group broke up, there was more talk of support for Regina's store. Members also offered to help her prepare during the coming year for the giveaway that would commemorate the first anniversary of Jackie's death. The gifts to be given to his friends, especially those who had helped with the funeral, would be gathered over the course of the year. Regina would need help, particularly with the quilting.

Sage stood in the doorway and watched the other vehicles pull away from the building one by one. The slanting rainfall glittered just beyond their headlights. He thought of the low spot in the roadbed that was undoubtedly filling up with water. He could haul a compressor down there, get a pump going and maybe save the project some time and money. The yard light illuminated the moat that was fast gathering around the community center. Poor drainage, Sage thought. In this country, there was never enough water except when there was too much.

He paid no attention to the water running behind his back until it stopped. "Need any help?" he asked without turning around.

"The coffee pot's clean, and the windows are all closed." Regina closed a cupboard door. "My sister is watching the kids. We have time to talk if you want."

He turned now, smiling. "Aren't you all talked out?"

"You're not. You hardly said anything tonight." She leaned against the counter and waited, but he stayed where he was. His thoughts had strayed out into the night, and she thought it was a bad sign.

"I need to get going," he told her. "You ready?" He knew she wouldn't press. Megan would, but Regina wouldn't. She would let him keep his thoughts, if that was what he chose to do. But as he watched her shoulder her bag, he knew she was about to give him one of her own thoughts, anyway.

"You think it's a good idea, getting mixed up with another white woman?" Regina asked.

"Mixed up?" It surprised him to hear her use a term that was so direct and, for reasons that might surprise her, so appropriate. It made him laugh. He was mixed up, all right, but all on his own.

"We're trying to learn not to repeat our mistakes," Regina reminded him as she crossed the floor.

He let his smile fade, because she refused to return it. "I think of you as a sister, Regina. You know that."

"And I just lost one husband. I'm not looking for another one." Her boot heel skidded over the linoleum as she stopped beside him in the open doorway. "You're too important to this group. I don't want to see you getting your head messed up again by a white woman.''

"My head was messed up before I ever met Riva. Our marriage was a disaster, but it wasn't because she was white.'

"She was no wife to you," Regina insisted.

"I was no husband to her." He dug his keys out of his pocket. "It was *my* head that was messed up." With the heel of his free hand he tapped his temple. "My *head*, not my heart. Somewhere along the line I must have put my heart in cold storage."

"No one in this group cares more than you do."

He lowered his hand slowly as he realized that he could think of no greater compliment. "I *have* changed, Regina." He looked at her hopefully. "I have, haven't I?"

His hard hat and slicker were no protection against the downpour. Once again he found himself kneeling in four inches of water and cussing at a pump. Nobody would have expected him to come back to the site after dark just to get a pump started. Rain was one of the inevitable impediments in road construction. If you dug a hole in a spot that held water and it rained, you lost time. Nobody came out in the middle of the night to rescue a roadbed.

But the changes Megan had made in her design had already increased costs. If this stretch washed out it would mean more time, which would mean more money. While Megan was in Pierre, this was Sage's baby. If the rain let up a little and the pump had a chance to catch up—hell, it was worth a try.

The rain and the compressor engine combined to drown out the sound of an approaching vehicle. Sage only knew it was there when he realized that another pair of headlights had joined his own. The extra light illuminated the problem—a tangled hose—and was welcome, at least on that score. But ever since someone had tampered with his pickup out here, Sage had been wary.

"Anything I can do to help?"

Megan's was the last voice he'd expected to hear. He squinted into the bright lights at the top of the rise. "You already did," he shouted. "I think we're all set. Got any coffee with you?"

"'Fraid not. I'll meet you back at the office."

The lights were burning in the trailer windows when he drove up. He leaped over the puddle at the foot of the steps and yanked the door open. He'd already abandoned his hat and slicker in the pickup, and he was drenched.

"Catch." A towel sailed across the room. Sage lifted his hand, and the towel flopped over this forearm like a horse-shoe ringer.

He ruffled his hair with the towel, draped it around his neck and began unbuttoning his wet shirt. "When did you get back?"

"I got back to the motel a couple of hours ago."

Her hair was damp, but he could tell she'd just combed it. She wore a pink, V-neck cotton sweater and designer jeans, and her lips matched the sweater. Her feet were bare.

"My shoes got wet."

He moved his gaze back up to her face and realized that she'd watched him take inventory. She smiled, and he responded with a quizzical look. "What are you doing out here on a night like this? Didn't you think I'd take care of things?"

"I wouldn't have blamed you if you hadn't," she told him. "It's a lot to expect."

He phrased the question again. "What are you doing here?"

The tone of his voice said that he knew. He knew how restless she'd been, how she'd been wondering where he might be and what he might have on his mind. There had been a good chance she would find him here. They shared this much—this river of gravel becoming blacktop. There had been a good chance of meeting him on this common ground.

His scowl made her back away from the truth as she headed for the file cabinets. "I needed some figures from the daily reports."

"The hell you did." He tossed his shirt over a chair and moved in close behind her. She pulled out a file drawer, and he reached past her to stop it in its tracks. "Tell my why, Megan. Didn't you trust me to do the job?"

Her voice was small. "I knew you'd be here."

She let him push the drawer closed. He turned her toward him with a gentle hand, but cruel words came unbidden to his tongue. "Is this how it was with Karl Taylor? He backed you up against the files, and you—"

Her anger flashed in her eyes, but he braced his hands against the file cabinet, trapping her. "How can you even say that?" she whispered.

His chest tightened, and his brain did battle with itself. "I said it because...it was the first damn thing that popped into my head. Walk away, Megan." He dropped his hands to his sides, and his plea became ragged. "Be smart. Walk away."

She stayed where she was, watching him struggle. "Do you believe I led Karl on?"

"No," he admitted.

"Then why did you say that?"

"Old habits are hard to break." He couldn't stop himself from touching her, from pulling her against him and making it impossible for her to do as he'd asked. "They're so damn hard to break." He lowered his face into her hair and smelled the rain there.

"Maybe I can help," she whispered as she reached around his back.

"Maybe I can make you miserable."

"Maybe," she whispered again. His smooth shoulder was there for her lips to touch. "If I'm willing to let myself be miserable." She tipped her head back. "Is that how you want it?"

He showed her how he wanted it. He pulled her tight against his wet jeans and gave her a hard-driving kiss that made her go all soft inside. One hand slid beneath her sweater and caressed her back, while the other laid claim to her buttocks. His kisses made more claims, and his tongue made promises. Megan spread her hands over the corded muscles in his back as her tongue welcomed his and her body strained with the need to know more of him. When he lifted his head, he realized she'd made claims, too. She'd taken his breath away.

"I'm not miserable yet," she managed.

"I will be if we don't—" He pushed his fingers through her hair and shut his eyes as he tipped his forehead against her cool skin. "—go somewhere."

"My room's closest."

"My pickup's even closer." He cursed himself under his breath. Dragging her down on the seat of a pickup had been his first suggestion even when he knew damn well that that kind of a scene would be bad for both of them. "But we'd better take your room," he amended quickly. "And your truck. I'll leave mine, and we'll come back early."

She retrieved her shoes from behind the desk. Her slicker had gotten damp inside, and she shivered when she slipped it on. Sage grabbed his shirt and watched Megan fight with her shoes. They were wet and muddy, and her hands were unsteady.

"Come on, I'll carry you."

He was standing near the door with his shirt slung over his shoulder. She offered a tentative smile. "Is there a river out there I might get dropped in?"

He stuck his head outside, then ducked back in, smiling. "Wide as the Missouri. Come on," he urged as he cocked his head toward the open door.

She carried her shoes, holding them clear of his back as she was lifted into his arms. Sage sprinted through the puddles, and they laughed like mischievous children setting out for an adventure on a stormy night. He opened the door on the driver's side and put her in ahead of him, then got in behind her. She'd slid all the way over to the far side of the seat, and he wanted her closer. She read his message and scooted back, and he reached for her. Once he had her in his arms again, he kissed every drop of water from her face.

"God, I'm thirsty," he whispered. "Got anything to drink at your place?"

"If it's still raining when we get there, there'll be more water where that came from." She gave him a saucy smile. "I might be out of glasses."

He smiled back. "Maybe you'd like to take a shower."

It was only a ten-mile drive, but it seemed to take forever. Sage thought the whacking of the windshield wipers would drive him crazy. Megan watched the rain slash across the beams of light ahead.

"It's this one," she said, as though she'd just come awake.

Blue and yellow neon tubes made the words "Arrowhead Motel" jump out from the roadside. Then the U-shaped motor court came into view, with its zigzag of neon trim along the overhang.

The overdose of neon had never bothered Megan before. This was just a place to stay. But then, she'd never brought a man to her room before, and she suddenly wished the neon would evaporate. She wished her apartment weren't so far away. Sage had taken her to places that were part of him, and she was taking him to the Arrowhead Motel.

"Uh, Megan, do you think Kessler's would be open?"

They passed the motel, and she turned to him and stared. The drugstore?

Sage was suddenly aware of everything about himself that must have looked ridiculous. His pants were wet, his shirt was lying on the seat between them, he probably needed a haircut, since he could see a bunch of it hanging above his right eyebrow, and he had about thirteen dollars in his wallet and nothing else. *Nothing else.* It all came together in such an absurd package that he laughed aloud.

When had he last needed anything else? Thank God he had the thirteen dollars. It would have been embarrassing as hell to have to borrow money from her. It was going to be bad enough when he walked up to the cash register, looking like he'd just been let out of some cage, with that single purchase in his hand. If anyone tried to peek outside to get a look at who was with him, he would break their neck.

"What's so funny?" she asked.

He saw that she was just as uneasy as he was, and he tried to smooth things over with a smile. "I'm sorry. I know these things are supposed to be spontaneous." He lifted one shoulder to shrug away that expectation. "The guys with class are prepared to be spontaneous, right? The guys that order fancy wine and check out the cork." He saw the lights of Kessler's Drugstore. "I may be short on class, but I haven't run out of luck. It's still open. I need a candy bar or something. How about you?"

It felt good to laugh with him while he parked in a spot closer to the grocery store than the drugstore.

"Sage, it's raining. Look how far you have to walk."

She looked so damn cute, he had to kiss her. "Do I have to remind you that you've got your name emblazoned on the side of this pickup?"

"It says 'South Dakota Highway Department.'"

"Right." He planted another quick kiss on her mouth and grabbed his shirt. "Don't tell me what kind you like. Let me surprise you."

Megan slid down in the seat and grinned at the rain splattering the windshield. No one could accuse Sage Parker of being irresponsible. Megan McBride, maybe, but not Sage. Within minutes he was back with a small brown paper sack, from which he produced an almond-studded chocolate bar.

"Was I right?" He brushed the water off his forehead with his wet sleeve as he turned the pickup back onto the street.

"Excellent choice." She tore open the wrapper and took a bite. The creamy chocolate melted on her tongue. "Where's yours?"

He indicated the small bag next to his hip. "It's in there." He caught the movement of her hand. "Don't you dare," he warned. "Mine's for later."

"Have a bite of mine, then." She held it up to his mouth and heard him crunch into an almond.

Her room was neat. She could say that much for it. It held little more than a double bed and a bathroom. The kitchenette had a small stove and refrigerator, and the little Swedish modern table and two chairs did go with the blond headboard and the Eiffel Tower print that hung above it. Megan flicked the switch on a pole lamp that reached from floor to ceiling between the TV and a flat-cushioned arm chair.

"I don't know why they call this the 'Arrowhead Motel' when they have Paris on the wall." She kicked her shoes off quickly.

Sage heard the high note of nervousness in her voice. He closed the door behind him, then took off his muddy boots and set them near her shoes. The light was dim, but he stilled her hand before she turned another on. She glanced up at him, then at the room. "It's pretty dingy, isn't it?"

"You've seen where I live. At least you've got room to turn around."

"Your trailer is . . . quite masculine." He was still holding her hand, and it made her heart quicken.

He lifted one corner of his mouth in a half smile. "Is that a polite way of saying it's got no style?"

"No. It's a polite way of saying it's functional."

"So's this."

"But it's not pretty."

"You're pretty, Megan, and I swear to God, you're all I'm looking at right now." He hooked his arm behind her neck and leaned closer to whisper, "Are you scared?"

"I guess a little."

"We don't have to."

"I want to, Sage."

"Why?"

"Because I want to . . . share this with you."

He buried his lips in her hair, inhaled her scent and waited. She didn't turn his question back on him. What would he have said? Why did he want to do this? Because his blood coursed through him like river rapids, and if he didn't get inside her soon he was going to bust wide open? He wanted more reasons. Please make him capable of having one tender, unselfish reason somewhere in his mind. This woman was good to him, and he wanted to be good in return.

"I need a shower," he said hoarsely. "I've been down on my hands and knees in the mud, and that's not the way I want to come to you—not covered with mud."

"They have coin-operated machines here. I can wash your clothes for you while you—"

He shook his head. "I'll let you take care of me, just for tonight, but not that way."

"What way, then?"

"By sharing with me, just as you said." He tossed the bag on the bed and took her in his arms. "The best water I ever tasted came from your face, Megan." He dropped his voice close to her ear. "I need another drink."

"Sage . . ."

"Start by sharing a shower with me."

His kiss came hot and hard, but his clothes felt cold and soggy where he pressed himself against her. Her answer was to slide her hand between them and unbutton his shirt. She slipped her hand inside.

"You're cold," she whispered.

"Yeah." He nuzzled her neck. "Warm me."

She pushed his shirt off his shoulders, but she wouldn't let it go until it was draped over a chair. His wicked laughter sounded deep in his throat. "Megan, I don't care about my clothes. I care about yours." She stole a glance at him. "I want to undress you and touch every part of you while I do it. I want to do the things I never used to take the time for. And I'm not real sure..."

She laid her hands along his smooth cheeks. "We've waited a long time. Let's find out, Sage."

She raised her arms slowly, and he peeled the pink sweater away. He kissed her while he unfastened her jeans, slid his hand beneath the waistband and made the zipper crawl down tooth by tooth as he moved his hand over her firm belly. There was a band of lace and a triangle of cotton, but he felt the satin softness of skin kept covered, and his fingertips detected the intimate protection of springy hair. It was like plotting a course. He'd assured himself of his destination, but he didn't want to shorten the journey. He pushed her jeans over her hips, and she lifted one foot at a time so he could remove them.

She looked smaller now than he'd imagined. His hands could almost span her waist. He dropped one knee to the floor and tried it, and suddenly it wasn't important to her that her room lacked feminine frills. She had a female waist, female hips. He moved his hands over them and rested his forehead between the lacy cups of her bra.

"You're so small," he whispered.

"Is that bad?"

"It scares me. I've never... been with such a small woman."

"Small but strong. I build roads."

"*I* build roads. And I have a habit of blasting my way through."

She raked her fingers through his thick hair. "I'll show you where to set the charges."

He unfastened the clasp between her breasts and pushed one more bit of fabric away before he came to his feet to cover her breasts again, this time with his hands. He claimed her mouth with a caressing kiss, moving his lips over hers as he moved his thumbs over her skin, seeking her response. With her arms around his neck she filled her lungs with air, hoping to give him a little more of her to hold and touch.

The roughened pads of his thumbs found her nipples and whisked over them like pieces of corduroy polishing cloth, making them into small beads. She felt her nipples' new luster in the way they tingled, but the sudden shrinkage made her groan into his mouth.

"Don't ask me to set charges on such perfect little peaks," he whispered hotly. "I never knew a woman could be so—"

"Please don't say small."

"Delicate."

"I don't want to be delicate."

"What do you want to be?"

"Voluptuous."

He moved quickly, hiding his amusement by lifting her high off the floor. He had to find the bathroom by instinct, because his face was bracketed by her breasts.

"I want you to be wet, the way you were by the creek." He first turned the light on, then the shower. "I couldn't help wishing for *naked* and wet." He shed his jeans quickly, watching her all the while. Her eyes never left his face.

It was he who removed the last of her clothing, sliding his hands over her hips, and he who orchestrated the shower. The water was hot, and the soap made them slick, so that belly slid against belly, thigh against thigh. He moved his hands over her, making small swirls of suds and listening for the catch in her breath. She tried to do likewise, but he'd conveyed her to a higher plane, and her initiative waned as she gave in to her irresistible responses. When he slipped his hand between her thighs, she gasped and relied on his arm for support. He'd located the critical crevice, and he wondered how tenderly he could manage to set his charge there.

Steam filled the tiny room. Finally, Megan stepped out of the tub and into Sage's waiting arms. Using the tip of his tongue, he sipped water from her face and neck. She felt behind her back for the towel bar, but he reached past her, one arm on either side, and anchored the towel in place. At the same time he moved his mouth over her breasts, suckling each nipple in turn until she gave a sultry moan. Then he kissed his way downward.

She was slick, like a water slide, and he'd begun his descent. "So good," he whispered against her dewy skin. "Sweet and hot, like the perfect dessert."

She had no thought of stopping him, even when he reached the dense curls that shielded her femininity. She had no thoughts at all. There was only the spicy feeling rippling from the point of the contact to all the reaches of her body. She braced her hands on his shoulders and chanted his name as the pleasurable throbbing intensified. He rose through the mist and pinned her to the wall, sliding his body over hers.

"Was it enough?" he asked as his lips drifted through the damp sheen on her forehead.

She rolled her head back and forth against the wall. "I'm afraid your tongue's too small."

He lifted his head and saw the glaze in her eyes, the wistful smile on her kiss-reddened lips. His laughter started deep within his chest and emerged as a wicked sound. He took her hand and slid it down the front of his body. "You wanna try this on for size?"

"If we do it right here, you won't have to worry about opening up that pesky—"

He groaned, shutting her up and cutting off his own curse with a hungry kiss. Steam followed them into the bedroom. Sage lay down and pulled her into his arms, and he kept her mindless while he took his precautions. His body alone filled her senses—its hard planes and sleek skin, the heat of his breath and the pounding of his heart in time with her own. Finally he raised her knees to ease his entry and filled her so far beyond the physical bounds that she wept for his tenderness even as she arched her hips to help him make the explosion happen.

When it was done, he kissed away her tears. In the silence, he thought of all the things that might have brought them on. When he finally asked "Did I hurt you?" it came in a hoarse whisper that embarrassed him because it sounded so unmanly in his own ears.

"I can't imagine being hurt by you," she said. "I didn't know... anything like that was possible."

He allowed a slow smile. "It fit, then?"

"Like the key to a lock." She slid her hand along her side and cupped her own breast. "I know I'm small. I'd like to have long hair, like Regina's, and breasts like—"

"There's nothing wrong with delicate." He rolled to his back and gathered her in his arms. "I thought my heart would burst when I saw how small and pretty you were."

"I thought you were disappointed."

He kissed the top of her head. "Were you disappointed?"

"In you? Never. You're perfect."

"No, I'm not," he protested. "I'm far from perfect. You've got to know that, and it's got to be okay with you. I can't be perfect."

"Nearly perfect, then." She traced a line along his jaw. "You've come so far. I've watched how hard you work."

"I've got a long way to go, Megan." He looked down, searching for understanding in those tranquil blue eyes. He saw pure satisfaction. "I've never made love to a friend before," he confided. "Hell, I'm not sure I've ever made love before."

"What do you mean? You were mar—"

"I've had a lot of sex," he said quickly. "I've screwed a lot of women. I didn't do that to you. I made love to you."

She smiled. "I know."

He held her close and tucked her head under his chin. "I made love to someone I care about. God, it felt good." He swallowed hard, trying to soothe the burning in his throat. "Your tears scared the hell out of me. I thought I'd done something wrong."

"You were so gentle, Sage." She kissed the base of his throat. "You keep telling me how bad you've been, but all

I see is good. You've wrestled with the bad things, and you've won."

She made him feel so good that he couldn't argue with her. He couldn't bring himself to tell her just then how he struggled every day, and how he would go on struggling for the rest of his life. He wanted to be good to her always. That much he knew.

"I still want your friendship first," he told her. "Without that, we've got nothing."

"I know." She leaned back to look at him. His good looks always stunned her—his black hair, still damp from their shower, his dark, enigmatic eyes, and his deeply tanned face with its hard, angular features. She touched his lower lip with her forefinger. "So tell me things friends tell each other. From the very beginning."

"From the beginning, huh?" He nipped at her finger, then smiled. "Well...in the beginning, there was a harrowing buckboard ride. My mother was in labor, and my father was trying to get her to the clinic. She'd already delivered at home six times, and the doctor had warned her not to try it again. She was getting too old for that stuff."

"A buckboard ride?" she asked. "We're talking about your mother, now, not your grandmother."

"A buckboard ride," he confirmed. "We were, uh, between cars. About the time I started school, my dad had a Model A."

"A Model A!"

He reached for the chenille spread that had managed to work its way to the foot of the bed, and he tossed it over them. "You don't believe me? I'm telling you, a buckboard and a Model A. Now, this is the true story of my birth, so show some respect."

She made herself comfortable, pillowing her head on his shoulder and wondering whether she was really in for a tall tale. "Okay. Your father was driving the buckboard."

"And she kept yelling at him to go faster, and he kept saying they should have stayed home." He used his free hand to follow the motion of the story in the air above their heads. "So, they're bumping along, and the back wheel falls off the axle." The heel of his hand skidded to a stop in the middle of his chest.

"Are you sure you're not confusing this with the pickup?"

"Of course I'm sure. I've heard the damn story a hundred times. Between contractions my mom had to get down from the buckboard and shove the wheel back on while my dad held the axle up. 'Course, he couldn't drive it 'cause the burr was busted. He set the brake, unhitched the team and got back up there in time to catch me coming out of the chute."

Megan laughed so hard that the words, "You're making . . . all this . . . up," were barely intelligible.

"Hell, I could never invent anything this good," he assured her. "So my mom says to my dad, 'Husband, I have given you another son.'"

"Oh, come on."

"Well, words to that effect." His shoulders shook with silent laughter. "By the time the whole scene was edited for the retelling, that was her line. She never thought the story was too funny until it came to that line."

"I can imagine."

"So then he says, 'What name have you chosen for this lusty, strapping man-child?'"

"Give me a break," Megan groaned.

"So that's when she always turned to me with the real solemn look and said, 'I had your name all picked out, son. It was going to be Sampson. But you didn't lift a finger to help me with that wheel. I looked around me—nothing but jackrabbits and sage as far as the eye could see—and I looked down at you, and I knew who you were.'"

She shifted toward him, laid her arm over his chest and savored the sound of his name. "Sage."

"Uh-uh." He put his lips close to her ear and whispered, "Jackrabbit."

"Oh, you!" She pinched his side and discovered that he was ticklish. "A-ha! Now I know your weak spot."

He held her hand still and flashed his wicked grin. "Use it against me and I'll find every one of yours."

"How come you weren't this funny when we first met?"

"How come you weren't this friendly when we first met?"

The softness they saw in one another's eyes only hinted at the answers each chose to keep for now.

I would have been, if I had trusted you as I do now.

I would have been, if I had loved you as I do now.

Megan snuggled against him again. "How much of that story is true?"

"Nearly every word. It was my mother's favorite kid story."

"Is she dead now?"

"Mmm-hmm. So's my dad."

"It's a beautiful name," she said quietly. "It's a wonderful story."

"You know what I just discovered?" He turned the thought over in his mind for a moment just to be sure of it. "I can tell that story just as well sober as I can half-crocked."

"Better, maybe."

"Better, maybe," he agreed. He turned his head and kissed the top of hers. "You're the best damn audience a guy could ask for, Megan McBride."

"Most gullible?"

"Most eager," he told her. She lifted her head to see whether he was laughing at her and found only the softness in his eyes. "You're the first woman I've told that story to." He combed his fingers through her damp hair. "I really like this."

"What?"

"Lying here with you. Holding each other and just talking...touching."

"But you've been..."

"No." He laid a finger over her lips and shook his head. "No. This is new for me, Megan. I'm not half-shot and cocky as hell, and I wasn't looking for somebody to get off with." He slid his hand over her shoulder and down the length of her back. "I can't believe how good this feels."

"You were afraid to tell me what you were looking for."

"I was afraid it didn't exist. At least, not for me. I was afraid I didn't have . . . what you said . . . something to share with someone like you."

"I wish I had met you first," she said, and she kissed his shoulder. It was hers to kiss, she thought recklessly, and it should never have been anyone else's. "Before your wife. Before the other women."

"We couldn't have had what we've had tonight. If I'd had you then, you wouldn't be here now."

"Things might have been different."

"You couldn't have changed me, Megan. I had to do that for myself." He lifted his head to look at her face. Her pretty face. She was so confident in her ability to make things right. "I'm glad you came along when you did. I think I was ready for you."

"Well, almost." She propped her chin on his shoulder and hiked a teasing eyebrow. "You were after you stopped at Kessler's."

With a chuckle he dropped his head back on the pillow. "I'm doing good." Rolling his head to the side allowed him to see her face again. "See? That's a prime example. Years ago, I would have knocked you up without thinking twice."

"Sage! I . . . I wouldn't have let you."

He frowned. "You're not on the pill, are you?"

"N-no. I . . . had no reason to be."

"You got something else stashed around here?" She shook her head. "It was my idea, then, wasn't it?" She nodded, feeling foolish. "See? I really am doing good." He touched her cheek and whispered, "I hate the thought of hurting you."

She closed her eyes and laid her cheek against his shoulder again. "I didn't think. I just wanted us to make love."

He hugged her close, grateful for her trust and pleased with himself for proving worthy, at least tonight. "Tell me your story, Megan."

"Mine isn't as good as yours."

"It must be. Megan sounds like somebody they should write a song about."

"It's my grandmother's name," she said matter-of-factly. "My sister got my other grandmother's name. My parents live in Pierre, but I don't see much of them anymore."

"Why not?" He figured he knew why, but he wanted her to tell him.

"I wish my father could go to a Medicine Wheel meeting," she said quietly. "If he would just stop drinking once and for all—"

"There is no 'once and for all,' Megan. There's no 'happily ever after.' There's just one day at a time."

She smoothed her hand over his chest. "Four years is a lot of one days."

"Sometimes a day is too much. Sometimes, when it's really bad, when all you can think about is where the nearest bottle is—sometimes you tell yourself to hold on for another minute. And then you figure maybe you can go one more."

"Do you have days like that?"

"Not as often as I used to, but, yeah. Some."

"What do you do?"

"I go to a meeting. I find someone to talk to—someone like me. I try to sweat it out in the lodge. I pray."

"Could you ever... come to me?"

"Uh-uh." He felt her disappointment, and he rubbed her back, hoping the disappointment would melt away. He needed her acceptance. "You're not an alcoholic, Megan. You can't take care of us. But you can care. Don't cut yourself off from your father. There are no perfect people.

We're all struggling. Tell him that you want him to get help."

"He won't listen."

"Maybe not, but it's all you can do."

"Look at all *you* do." She rose up as though she were going to accuse him of something. "You're trying to get a whole bar closed down. Aren't you looking out for other people?"

"I'm hoping we'll start looking out for ourselves as a community. When I came back from treatment with the idea for Medicine Wheel, I felt like one hand clapping. Pretty soon we had a little group. We're growing, and we're getting healthy enough to try to make our community healthy."

"When's the next hearing?" she asked. "I want to be there."

He pulled her toward him, and she lay back down in his arms. "I don't think that's a good idea anymore, Megan."

"Why not? Just standing by you isn't caretaking, is it?"

"There have been . . . threats. Taylor stands to lose one business, maybe two, if Regina gets the store going. I don't want him to try to get to me by . . . maybe trying to hurt you."

"He threatened you?"

"It's just something you need to be aware of." He cupped her breast with a protective hand. "This kind of sharing is nice, but I don't want to share my enemies with you."

"I'm going to that hearing," she insisted.

"Whatever you say." Turning on his side, he adjusted her in his arms. "It's stopped raining," he told her. "If we went to sleep right now, we might get in four hours before daybreak, which is when we'd better get out to the site."

She nuzzled his neck. "I could make do with three and a half. I've been going to bed early all my life."

"What for?"

"Resting up for tonight."

He rolled on top of her and hooked his leg over hers. He was more than ready. "If you were so damn sure of yourself, why didn't you stop at the drugstore before you came to get me?"

"Came to get—"

Megan's protest was lost in Sage's kiss.

Chapter 11

Sage's cryptic comments about the threats against him worried Megan, but he showed no concern for himself. His only fear seemed to be for her. She decided to pay Pete Petersen a visit. He seemed to understand local politics, and she thought he was probably within earshot of most of the local rumors, as well.

Pete still hadn't oiled the springs in his desk chair. They creaked as he leaned back, linking his fingers over his stomach. "Sounds to me like you've developed more than a professional interest in Sage Parker."

"We've been working together all summer," she reminded him as she uncrossed her legs and resettled herself in her chair. "It can't be too surprising that we've become friends." She recrossed her legs from the other side.

"Not surprising at all," Pete returned with a smile.

"Besides that, Sage's pickup was sabotaged on the site." His eyebrows shot up, his interest piqued. "Sabotaged?"

"The lug nuts were loosened on one of the tires. The whole wheel fell off."

"Anybody hurt?" Pete asked as he leaned forward in concern.

"Sage might have been. He nearly went over an embankment. Frankly, I think he knows more about it than he's told me."

Pete picked up a pencil and tapped the eraser against his desk pad. "Well, you asked me if I thought somebody might be out to get him on this liquor license thing, and I guess you've answered your own question. Sounds like somebody is."

"Taylor?"

"Could be." Pete tossed the pencil aside in disgust. "Taylor's an opportunist. A taker, like so many of the people who've beaten a path to the reservations to make a buck. They've cheated these people out of land, food, program money, lease checks—you name it. It's been going on for over a hundred years. And they always seem to be taking with one hand and peddling whiskey with the other."

"If someone stands up to them, is he likely to be ... punished somehow?"

"Your friend might be found dead alongside the road." He punctuated the news with a clucking sound. "I've been here almost twenty years. I remember one guy who tried to blow the whistle on a fishy cattle-buying deal. Government program, tribe was buying cattle, some of the records didn't jibe. After this guy got shot at on the highway a few times, he decided he'd forgotten how to add. And the tribe figured if they didn't take what they got, they wouldn't get anything. That's the history of this place. That's why people tend to just let things go."

Megan tightened her grip on the arms of her chair. "Do you hear anything about ... how much support Sage has?"

"Oh, yeah, Sage is the talk of the town. He's either a saint or a sinner, depending on who you talk to. Some people are standing neutral on the issue itself, but there's no neutral ground where Sage is concerned."

"He, um, he thinks I might be threatened, too."

"Why? Because you've gone to a couple of council sessions? A Medicine Wheel meeting or two?" Megan shot him a scowl. "I'm the one who gave you the information, remember? I haven't heard too much talk about you, but everybody knows who you are. Around here, people see a man and a woman together more than once, they draw conclusions."

Good, she thought. Let them. If they want to shoot at him, they can shoot at me, too. She caught Pete's intuitive smile, and she returned it with pride.

"He's no saint, Megan, but he's a damn good man. He's been working at it for a good long time now, and he's doing fine." He bobbed his head as he repeated the conviction. "He's doing just fine."

"He's helping people. I saw that at the meeting."

Pete leaned back in his chair and clasped his hands behind his head. "Do you think you might be interested in a civil service job with the BIA? I've got a guy transferring out in September, and I'm looking at retirement soon myself. Be a good future in it for you."

Megan raised a speculative eyebrow. "I guess it wouldn't hurt to fill out an application."

Pete took her to the local café for hamburgers. It was after seven when she unlocked the door to her pickup. As she opened it, she caught a glimpse of a stern face in the side mirror. The unfriendly look in the dark eyes was chilling. Megan turned slowly, her mind spinning with possibilities that she didn't much like.

"Hello, Regina."

"I'm looking for Sage."

Megan's eyes narrowed as she frowned. "He isn't with me."

"I thought you might be with him," Regina said flatly. "We have a meeting scheduled for seven-thirty tonight. We're helping them start a group here like the one we've got going in Red Calf."

"Then I'm sure he'll be here. I left the site early. Sage did say he had a meeting tonight, but he didn't mention where."

The look on Regina's face betrayed her doubt. Let her think what she wanted, Megan decided. She wasn't following Sage. If she had known Sage planned to be in Pine Ridge, she would have planned her visit for another day. He might ask questions about her reason for visiting Pete, and her answer might be construed as "caretaking." Megan was tired of trying to figure out what the word really meant.

"He's always early," Regina said. "He always makes sure there's coffee, and we set up the chairs."

Megan laughed. "You could float a battleship in the coffee that man consumes." She touched Regina's arm, hoping the gesture would be taken as friendly. "I'm sure he stopped off to change his clothes, and he probably had a couple of chores to do or something. He's bound to be along soon."

Regina seemed to be intimidated by Megan's hand. She lowered her eyes and stood quite still. "I just thought you might have come together."

Megan dropped her hand, but she felt something more genuine reaching toward the woman from within herself. "We didn't. Medicine Wheel is something I . . . would never interfere with, Regina. Never. Sage asked me to go to a meeting and see how it worked. I'm glad I did. I understand why it's so important to him."

"It's his lifeline," Regina said. "It can't be replaced by a woman."

Megan felt a tightening in her throat. "I know that."

"Good."

Regina turned to walk away, but Megan spoke her name, and she turned back. "How are you doing?" Megan asked gently.

Regina nodded, and the tension dropped from her shoulders as she sighed. "Okay. It's hard," she admitted. "With the children. My two older ones took it hard." Her eyes grew cloudy with emotion. "I'm doing okay."

"Your husband was a good worker," Megan offered, choosing not to mention any exceptions. "I enjoyed having him on the crew." With another nod, Regina accepted the bid for a truce.

Megan backed her pickup away from the curb, but before she had it in gear, she heard someone call her name. Pete left his car idling on the opposite side of the street with the door standing open. His awkward attempt at a jog would have seemed funny if he hadn't had such a grave expression on his face.

He braced himself in her open window and struggled to catch his breath. "I just heard some bad news...about Sage."

The smell of it was the worst part now. Flesh on fire. It was more pungent than the acrid smell of wood smoke or burning hay. Sage's eyes stung, and his gut roiled. The air around him was heavy with that smell. He dropped his forehead against his fingertips and rubbed his eyes with the heels of his hands, hoping to find enough moisture in them to relieve the stinging. The heat had left them dry.

With his eyes closed there was only the swirl of sounds—the crackle and hiss, the call for water, the shifting of timber. And the smell. He saw Jackie's rotting flesh behind his eyelids and imagined the wild-eyed colt with its spotted hide ablaze. He tasted the bile rising in the back of his throat, and he wished his stomach would settle down. He would have been grateful just for that.

Another beam gave way behind him. He turned to watch the charred bones of his dream clatter one against the another, and, like dominoes, they finally knocked each other down. Within moments the subfloor gave way, and the smoking rubble collapsed into its own cement grave.

Sage watched the rural volunteer fire department reorganize its efforts to attack the barn from a different angle. There was little left to save. They'd kept the fire from spreading across the prairie, which was a commendable feat.

The house had gone quickly, but bright orange flames from the barn still licked the evening sky. Twilight had given the horizon a shrinking red rim, and the first few stars had claimed their places in the heavens.

Sage wondered where his place was since heaven had no use for him. He'd tried to change, and there were places in him that were still raw from the effort. But he'd made the effort. He'd shivered and sweated with it. He'd stumbled and dragged himself on his belly until he found his legs could hold him again. It must have been an unforgivably disgusting sight. Why else would God have turned His head while some son of a bitch set a torch to the only real dream he'd ever had?

He lay back on the hood of his pickup, where somebody had insisted he sit and rest for a while. He'd seen the smoke on his way home, and he'd had a sinking feeling well before he saw the blaze. Several neighbors and one of the fire pickups were already on the scene. Despair had turned to rage, and he'd been a madman for a while there. He'd probably scared the hell out of them at first, when he'd tried to get into the barn. Then he'd settled down and helped with the hoses and the buckets until the nausea had overwhelmed him.

What had he done? There was supposed to be forgiveness up there, wasn't there? A single star winked at him. It was all a terrific joke, wasn't it? It was the ultimate tease. Destiny enjoyed letting you think you had a say. He'd had the audacity to believe things could change. If people wanted to drink, they'd drink. Hell, he knew that.

And he knew better than to think a good woman could love Sage Parker. He'd had his chance, and he wasn't supposed to get another one. He'd been puffed up with pride again just because he'd nailed a few boards together and bought a few cows. And then he'd taken a woman. He wasn't supposed to have a woman. He wasn't good enough for any woman. Women meant family, and he wasn't supposed to have that, either.

The smell was proof. He was fond of saying he'd been to hell and back. Now he knew different. Hell was the end of the line.

"How're you doing, Sage?"

He sat up. It took him a moment to think of his neighbor's name. Old Bernie Richards. He'd known the man since he was a kid. Bernie's gray hair was covered with soot; maybe that was why Sage hadn't recognized him. And he hadn't really heard the question.

"You okay, Sage?" Bernie laid a hand on Sage's shoulder in an attempt to cut through the blank stare. "This is a hell of a thing. I think you oughta stay with somebody for a while, son." Bernie waited for a reaction, but got none. "How 'bout your brother George? He still around?"

Sage shook his head. "Moved to Montana." He covered the old man's hand with his own. "I'm okay, Bernie. I appreciate your help."

"You can sure stay with us," Bernie offered.

"I've still got the trailer." His stony gaze strayed to the barn again. "I'll be fine."

"Well, I just wanted to warn you. A couple of young fellas got a bottle going around over there." He nodded at a trio taking a break near the corral. "You keep your head on straight, son. You hear?"

Sage stared at the small party that was being held in honor of his barn-burning.

"You got any insurance, son?"

His gaze was riveted on the three men. "No. No insurance."

"That's the hell of it. Who can pay for it nowadays?" Bernie patted Sage's shoulder. "Not much more I can do tonight, Sage. This is gonna burn itself out now. Lucky it didn't spread."

"Yeah. Lucky."

"Anything you need—"

"Thanks, Bernie."

He had no idea what they were drinking, but he could taste it. His throat was raw from the smoke, and his mouth was dry. He turned his head quickly and tried to fix his mind on something else. There was the trailer. One of his saddles was in the bedroom. Most of his tools were in the back of the pickup. He still had a job. He needed Medicine Wheel. Now. There was a meeting going on right now, and he needed . . .

"I'll bet you could use a drink right about now."

It cut deep, like an electrical shock. Sage pressed his lips together and turned slowly, trying to remember how to refuse. He wasn't even sure who this man was, but he knew one of the guys he was drinking with. Lonnie Crow. Sage remembered drinking with Lonnie, too.

"You've had a tough night. One drink won't hurt."

Sage tried to ignore the bottle. "Did you come with the fire fighters?"

The man stuck out his hand. "Gordon Brown. I came with Lonnie. He's a friend of Chet's, and Chet's a volunteer."

Sage caught himself watching the man take a long pull on the bottle. In the dark it was hard to tell much about him. He wore a cowboy hat and sounded pretty South Dakota. Sage could feel the potent liquid roll down the man's throat as he watched him swallow.

Gordon wiped his mouth on his sleeve and leaned on the hood of the pickup, setting the bottle in front of him. "This is a damn shame, Sage. Lonnie said you did most of the work here yourself."

Sage took a deep breath and held it. Whiskey. He could smell it. It smelled a hell of a lot better than burning horseflesh. He watched his hand close over the neck of the bottle.

The first taste singed his tongue and burned going down. He filled his mouth with it again and made his peace with it. He'd screwed up somehow, and he was being punished. He thought he'd changed, but his insides were still filled with scum. Something that tasted like lye might clean that out for him.

It was hard to see the extent of the damage in the dark, but the barn was obviously a complete loss. As Megan's pickup neared the trailer, she could see that the basement of the house had become a firepit, and she felt physically sick. She remembered Sage's imposing figure on the roof top and the halo effect the sun had given him. With two separate fires there was no pretense of an accident. She left her pickup near the trailer and went searching for him.

He saw her coming. His first instinct was to hide the bottle. His brain buzzed from the effects of the whiskey, but he hadn't reached the stage of not caring about anything. He wouldn't enjoy having her see him this way. It would be like getting beaten up right in front of her. But his instincts were overruled by a greater need to be honest with her—to let her see the truth.

When she saw him sitting there, she mouthed his name and hurried toward him. Her look of distress was fixed on his face, and she saw nothing else. Waves of regret washed over him. He would have given anything at that moment to be the man she thought she was running to. Then he remembered he had nothing to offer up in trade.

He slid down from the pickup hood, leaving the open fifth standing at his back in plain view. Still she saw nothing but him as she slipped her arms around him and laid her ahead against his chest. She asked no questions, gave him no words of sympathy. She simply held him.

Tradition said there should have been an argument right at the outset. The sooner he could get angry at her, the sooner he could stop feeling like a piece of trash. If he worked it right, he could convince her that his failure was hers, too, and he could add her contempt to his list of reasons to finish the bottle. But she was ignorant of the tradition. In her mind she was still holding the man she'd said goodbye to earlier in the day.

There was no place to put his arms but around her shoulders. He felt her shudder against him and hoped to God she wasn't crying. He had no comfort to offer. He wanted to crawl inside her and shut the rest of the world away. Maybe he could walk away from the bottle. Maybe Megan would forgive him this one trespass and take his pain away by that very act.

His shirt reeked of smoke, but she buried her face against it anyway. If she'd been there sooner, she could have helped him fight the fire, and then the smoke from his home would have permeated her clothing, as well. She imagined him battling the blaze and finally had the presence of mind to ask, "Are you hurt?"

"Hurt?" he repeated, confused. Shouldn't that have been, Are you drunk?

She looked up at his soot-smeared face and saw the glazed expression in his eyes. She ran her hands along his arms, and he winced when she came to his hands. They examined them together, finding scrapes and blisters. "You're burned," she said as evenly as she could manage. "We need to get you to a doctor."

He found it strange that he hadn't noticed his hands, when just looking at them now seemed to make them hurt. "Must've happened when I tried to get the barn door open. Tried to get the horses . . ." He lowered his hands as the account became a sickened groan.

"Horses," Megan whispered.

"I always leave that side door open during the day so they can go in for shade. There's a latch that holds it open—I *always . . .*" He tipped his head back and searched the sky for help, but none was there. Blinking hard, he swallowed the sting in his throat and told himself to hang on to what was left of his dignity. Finally he risked looking down at her face. "The mare and her colt were in the barn, Megan. That door had been bolted shut."

"Oh, my God," came her thin whisper.

"I know I didn't shut that door." He'd gone over it in his mind a dozen times, retracing his steps, but this was the first time he'd said it aloud. "I filled the water tank this morning. I fed them, locked up the storage closet and secured that latch." He'd broken a sweat just talking about it. In an impatient gesture he wiped his brow with his sleeve. "You could smell the kerosene. Hell, I don't even keep any kerosene out there."

"Sage, it was set. We'll tell the authorities. They'll find out who did this." She had both his shoulders in her grip when she noticed the bitter-sweet scent. Her eyes widened as she stiffened. "Sage?"

He reached behind him and slid the dark bottle to his side, watching her all the while. She blanched. He was sure of it. There in the darkness she lost all color in her face. Some sinister need to shock her overcame him, and he tipped the bottle to his mouth and sucked the stuff down greedily.

"Sage, what are you doing!"

He set the bottle down, wiped his mouth on the back of his hand and gave her a cold smile. "I'm getting drunk."

"You can't do that," she said, trying to keep the sound of panic from laying claim to her voice.

"It's been a while, but I think I remember how it's done."

He started to raise the bottle again, and she grabbed his arm. "You don't need that, Sage. You're through with that. You've beaten it!"

He transferred the whiskey into his other hand and took another drink. Pressing his lips together, he stared her down. "Don't ever try to separate a drunk from his bottle, Megan. You can get hurt that way."

"You'd never hurt me."

"You can't be sure of that," he warned. "You can't be sure of anything in this life."

"And you're *not* a drunk anymore, so stop calling yourself that."

"Oh yeah?" His laughter sounded cruel. "That's where you're wrong, baby. You're in way over your head, and there's a hell of a storm brewing." He latched on to her upper arm, and the pain that flashed in his eyes had origins far deeper than his blistered skin. "I know you can swim, Megan," he said, desperately struggling with the gravel in his throat. "Remember? Head for higher ground. There's nothing left here."

"You're here," she whispered in a voice full of tears.

He touched her cheek with raw fingers. "I'm going under."

"You've got a lot of friends, Sage." They both turned toward the voice of reason, which came from Pete Petersen. "They're not going to let you down. This doesn't end here."

Sage looked back at Megan, his eyes suddenly cold again. "What? You brought reinforcements?"

"Pete was the one who told me—"

Another car arrived, and two doors slammed shut. Sage peered over Megan's head. "Damn," Sage muttered between clenched teeth. "What's next? The Seventh Cavalry?" He dropped his hands and sidled away from her, glaring. "Where's your bugle, baby? Let's have the whole show."

The approaching feet swished in the grass. Megan turned to find that Regina had brought another group member. Lonnie, Gordon and Chet were converging from another direction.

"Sage, let's get your hands taken care of," Megan urged. There was no disguising her anxiety anymore. It rolled down her cheeks in glittering tears.

"Yeah, let's." In defiance he splashed whiskey over the worst of his burns. He sucked his breath between clenched teeth and took masochistic pleasure in the wild stinging. "There. All taken care of."

"Hey, don't waste it," Gordon called as he sauntered through the tall grass. "That's good stuff."

"Give it back to them, Sage," Regina said quietly. "Talk to us. Let's have the circle right out here."

Sage glanced from one face to another, then past them to the handful of firemen still soaking the smouldering timbers of his barn. He felt like an animal caught in a trap. They all wanted pieces of him, and if he stood there much longer, they would get their wish. He'd shatter.

"We're gonna take off, Sage." Sage swung his head toward Lonnie. *Take off* reverberated in his brain. "Thought we'd hit some spots. It's been a hell of a thirsty night."

"We got room for you, if you wanna come along." Gordon's offer rolled off his tongue like a bolt of silk.

Sage made his move.

"Please don't go, Sage."

The voice was small and pretty and wet with womanly tears. He got behind the wheel of his pickup and kept his eyes on the remains of the barn as he shut the door.

The little group huddled together and watched the lights of one pickup trail the other.

"He's in no condition to drive," Megan said. "He won't be hard to find. There aren't that many bars—"

"Don't do it, Megan," Pete warned. "He's on his own now."

"But he'll get into trouble."

"You can't prevent that," Pete told her.

"He's in trouble now." Regina's resignation was chilling.

"We can't just stand here and watch him do this to himself," Megan insisted.

"The best thing you can do is call the police." Megan looked horrified, but Pete continued. "They'll stop him from hurting himself, or someone else."

"I . . . couldn't do that to him," she said.

"Then you haven't learned anything." Disgusted by the white woman's weakness, Regina headed back to her car.

Megan felt lost. "Pete, I can't sit idly by—"

He laid a hand on her shoulder. "Go home. Get some sleep. I'll take care of the call. And if he comes to you, don't try to talk to him when he's drunk. You won't get any-where."

Feeling shell-shocked, Megan allowed herself to be es-corted to her pickup.

The face in the mirror was ghastly. A night of little sleep had left its shadows beside traces of soot. Cavernous eyes seemed to lack a human soul. A puffiness reminiscent of death made Sage turn his eyes downward toward the sink It was a sight that would drive young children to hide be-hind their mothers' legs. His own often had. Taking both sides of the sink gingerly in his hands, he lowered his entire face into the basin of icy water. Much to his dismay, he hadn't drowned during the night. He had half a mind to correct fate's error there in the sink.

On his way back up he bumped his head on the faucet. He muttered a curse. The bump was only a small insult to add to the injury he'd already heaped on his own head. His hair was plastered around his face, and the water rushed to form a single stream over his square chin. He looked down and considered his hands, which reminded him of rashers of bacon. The aching intensified as he eased them, palms up, into the water. His fingers trembled, and he saw the bacon curling, bubbling up in a cast-iron skillet. The mere image of cooking produced an imaginary odor that turned his stomach.

Minutes passed, and the cold water dulled the pain in his hands as he listened to Elmer Fudd harangue the "cwazy wabbit." Hell, he must have left the TV on all night. He pulled the black rubber stopper up by its chain and leaned his forearms on the edge of the sink as he watched the wa-ter eddy toward the drain. Then the pint bottle on the back of the commode caught his eye.

It was in his hand before he thought about reaching. Funny he hadn't drained the bottle the night before. Ap-parently it hadn't taken as much as it used to to make him pass out. He studied the label. Maybe he didn't know anything about wine, but he had good taste in whiskey. But the taste in his mouth wasn't good. He was afraid that if he opened it in front of the mirror, he would find a coating of mold. Whiskey killed bacteria, he told himself as his mouth yearned toward the bottle. Whiskey...

He struck the bottle against the side of the sink and watched the brown liquid slide over the shattered glass and down the drain. Whiskey would kill him, and he didn't want to die. The realization made him quiver. He wanted life. Despite all the losses he'd sustained in one chaotic night, he would live. He *would* live.

Picking up the pieces might be almost as tricky as cleaning up the mess he'd just made. He sliced his hand with the first shard of glass, and he saw that he was bound to bleed a little. What did he expect? Bleeding occasionally was part of life. Besides, he was a little short on dexterity just now. It might be a week or so before he could manage a hammer again.

The knock at the door echoed the clatter of glass as he tossed it in the waste basket. He jerked his head around and took a quick survey. Hot Springs. Easy Rider Motel. It was definitely a step down from the Arrowhead. Bugs Bunny was in black and white, and the picture was rolling. A lot like his gut.

After the second knock he yelled, "Yeah, I'm coming." He was going to add "Keep your shirt on," but he realized he was missing his. He'd slept in sooty jeans, and the bedding showed it. He flipped the bedspread over the sheets and picked his shirt up off the floor. No doubt the manager had come to give him hell over the TV, which he switched off on his way to the door.

It was Megan. He stared at her dumbly, unable to draw breath. She looked tired, but her eyes were clear; her face looked fresh, and everything about her struck him as immaculate. The Easy Rider Motel was not her turf.

"You look like hell," she told him.

"Thanks." He wanted to laugh, but he hadn't rallied that far yet. Getting enough air into his lungs for a one word response he'd been a major accomplishment. "Come on in."

The room was small, dark and oppressive. Faded flowered wallpaper was peeling above the bed, and the sculpturing in the green carpet had worn to fuzz. The pronounced smell of whiskey prepared Megan for signs of an all-night party, but she saw none.

"How did you find me?"

"Your pickup is one of a kind. I wasn't looking. I was just on my way to work. Frankly, I'm surprised you're not in jail."

He saw the judgment in her eyes, saw how the sight of him sickened her. He felt cold. His shame had left him naked, and her eyes chilled him. He groped for a comeback. "Just lucky, I guess."

"Pete said we should call the police just to get you off the road."

"He was right. You should have."

"I thought he was going to."

"He probably called the Indian police. They don't have any jurisdiction off the reservation." He raised his hand to offer her a chair, and blood dripped on the carpet.

"Oh my God, what have you done?" Her hands shot out reflexively, and she grabbed his arm.

"I cut myself on a bottle." Her eyes flew up to his as she took charge of his hand, cradling it in both of hers. "Not intentionally," he added quickly. "If I wanted to do myself in, I'd cut off my aching head."

"Sage, your hands need attention. Have you washed them?"

"Yeah, sort of." He let her lead him back to the sink because it was her attention he craved. Even if she cared only for his hands, it was an acknowledgment of his humanity. The mirror had suggested to him that he might be something less.

"I have a first aid kit in the car. Let me get it."

By the time she returned, he'd washed his hands with soap and water, and they were dripping to form a puddle near his bare feet. She told him to sit on the bed, while she washed her own hands and then pulled up a chair, lining her knees up with his. After laying his hands palms-up on a towel in her lap, she blew his skin dry. When he told her how good it felt, she refused to look up and let him see any commiseration on her part. She wanted to be angry, not so much because he'd started drinking, but because he hadn't stopped when she'd asked him to.

She painstakingly dabbed antiseptic cream over his damaged skin and bandaged the cut at the base of his thumb. "This is the main reason I stopped when I saw your pickup."

By that time he felt up to a chuckle. "You wanted to make sure I washed my hands?"

"You should have seen a doctor," she insisted, still fussing over his injuries.

"It took a lot of guts for you to stop here. You didn't know how bad off I might have been...or whether you'd find someone else in this bed with me."

She glanced up at him. "I wasn't thinking that way."

"Neither was I. But you had no way of knowing, did you?"

She lowered her eyes and shook her head.

"After what we...after the other night, I can understand why you're here. But you can't be running after me when...if this happens. Before long you'll be as crazy as I am."

Megan took a deep breath as she covered his wrists with her cool hands. "This is something I can do, Sage. I can see the injury here, and I can tend to it. The other..." Her eyes betrayed her fear. "I want to help you, but I don't know how."

He lifted his hands, and she let hers slide away. "This much is fine. I would have had a hard time doing this on my own. Otherwise…" He shook his head. "You can't fix it for me, Megan, any more than you could for Jackie."

"You're not like Jackie," she insisted.

"I *am* like Jackie. Look!" He held his hands up in front of her face. "I'm flesh and blood, just like he was. I'm an alcoholic, just like he was. And if I choose to, I can lie down in the grass and die, just like he did." He laid his hands back on the towel in her lap, holding her attention with the passion in his eyes. "I can also choose to live. I have an incurable disease, but it doesn't have to be fatal."

She blinked back tears. "I was so scared…when you went off with those other men."

"I didn't stay with them long. I bought my own bottle, brought it here and drank until I couldn't smell burning horseflesh anymore."

"Oh, Sage…"

"It's good that you saw…how it is with me. I can't be the perfect recovered alcoholic for you, Megan. There is no *recovered*. I'm recovering. I'm not the perfect anything." He offered a tentative smile. "Just like the highway system in the summer, some part of me will always be under construction."

"But four years is such a long time, and now—"

"It's still four years of sobriety. I didn't just erase them."

"Why didn't you do something else?" she asked urgently, as though what had happened could still be reversed if he were penitent enough. "You said that when you still felt that—that need once in a while, you always went to a meeting or talked to someone."

"I was busy watching everything I'd worked for burn to the ground," he reminded her dryly.

"Or you said you…prayed sometimes."

"Yeah." He straightened his back and sighed. "But you can't ask God to give you strength at the same time you're cussing Him out for turning His back on you."

"So you believe in God."

"Didn't I tell you I did?" He looked at her as though he couldn't believe she'd forgotten something that important. "I told you what I practice. There has to be a power stronger than mine. My ancestors used other words, but I'm comfortable with the word *God*. I sat up in that vision pit for days on end seeking His will for me. That's what a vision quest is. My own will is completely self-serving, and I'm powerless when it comes to alcohol."

"Powerless?"

"That's right." He watched her digest that bombshell. Her hero had toppled. He couldn't help feeling a pang of regret.

She pushed back the chair and rose to her feet abruptly. "I can't think of you as being absolutely powerless over anything. Especially something you can choose not to consume."

"And that's what I have to do. But last night—"

"Last night was heartbreaking. I don't think last night counts. It would have taken a superhuman effort—what's so funny?"

"You are." He flopped back on the bed and rolled his head from side to side, chuckling. "You're so beautiful, it's funny. And what makes it even funnier is the fact that you're absolutely serious. God, how I'd love to let you make excuses for me, Megan, but I'm afraid last night *does* count." He lifted his head and caught her eye. "Unless you know of some way to rewind our lives back to yesterday and edit last night out."

"What happened yesterday can't be changed. What happened last night—"

He jackknifed into a sitting position again. "Is an old story. The Indian gets screwed, so he goes out and gets drunk. Which doesn't change the fact that he got screwed, and it limits his chances of making a comeback. So last night counts. If I don't deal with it, I'll be back where I was four years ago."

He stood up, facing her with more conviction than he'd had when she'd arrived. "I've decided I don't like getting screwed. I'm not letting them have the final say. It wasn't the barn they wanted, or the house. It was my sobriety." He turned a hard glance on the waste basket in the bathroom. "And they damn near got it, because I damn near started in again this morning."

She followed his glance, then reached for his arm. "Sage—"

He backed away. "I'm not done, Megan. There's something else I don't like. I don't like it when you look at me like I'm some orphan kid who just got off the boat. What do you get out of that? Does that boost you up above the masses? Do you look at your dad that way, too?"

"My father?" She stiffened, tilting her chin up as she informed him brusquely, "My father has nothing to do with this. My father is not an alcoholic."

"He's not? Then why do you want him to quit drinking?"

"I just think he drinks too much, that's all. I just…" She crossed her arms over her chest, as was her custom. "I don't feel sorry for you, Sage. I'm sorry about the fire, but I don't feel sorry for you. Okay?"

"Okay." They stared at one another through several silent moments. Finally he asked, "So, without your sympathy, do I still have a job?"

"If you don't show up for work today, you get a warning," she told him. "That's policy. If you have a medical excuse, of course, that's different, and you should have a doctor look at those hands."

"And you should stop telling me what I *should* do. I'll be a little late, but I'll be there."

"You can't come to work with hands that are all blistered like that."

"Or a face that looks like hell?" He snatched his shirt off the bed. "Calling in sick is less embarrassing than walking in with an obvious hangover, right? If we cover it up carefully enough, maybe we can convince ourselves that I really didn't get drunk last night. Maybe we *can* edit it out."

She took a step closer to him. "Maybe we can stand around in this dump and argue about it all morning."

He moved closer, putting them almost nose to nose. "Maybe you can get out of here so I can get myself together and get to work."

"Fine." They watched each other ease off slowly. He took a step back and let her walk past him. She turned at the door, unable to resist trying for the last word. "I don't care what you do to your hands. And you're going to be late anyway." In a huff, she jerked at the door.

"I've got news for you, lady." She hesitated, and it amused him that she had to hear *his* parting shot. "So are you."

Chapter 12

Sage faced a steep uphill climb, and he found his first handhold in his job. He made it through the first day on a box of gauze bandaging and a tin of aspirin. That evening he saw a doctor, who told him not to use his hands for a couple of days. Since following such a suggestion would have meant certain insanity, Sage stocked up on gauze and antiseptic and decreed that his hands should not be idle except during sleep. And he worked. After work, with some help from friends and neighbors, he hauled rubble from the ruins of his buildings. After dark he met with the members of the Medicine Wheel. No matter how small the circle, he needed to be there, and the others knew it, so they came.

Megan's attitude toward him was guarded. She seemed to be afraid to laugh around him, as though there had been a death in his family and his feelings might be fragile, like eggshells. They had always worked well together, and that hadn't changed. They let the road be their focus, the visible thread that bound them together. They discussed layers of compaction with such studied interest that their concern for the levels of their relationship wasn't apparent. When Sage felt her eyes on him, he held his breath and allowed the moment to pass. He was glad when his hands started healing. Once she'd discovered him washing them after they'd cracked open and begun to bleed, and he'd waited for her motherly comment. It hadn't come.

It seemed, then, that she was recovering, just as he was. Her recovery from her close call with a risky relationship would be healthy for both of them, he decided. It was good to see her, good to be near her so much of the time. By the time the job was over, maybe he would be content with a friendly parting, a congenial acknowledgment that working together had been a pleasure. By that time he hoped the need to touch her would have dulled and the exquisite memory of love's pleasures would actually feel like part of the past.

It bothered him to have to take time off from work to attend another liquor license hearing. This thing had gone on long enough, had played enough havoc in his life. It bothered him most of all because it meant bringing the issue up with Megan. She knew immediately why he needed an afternoon off. This time, when her blue eyes glistened with the soft light that said she was looking at Sage, the man, rather than Sage, the co-worker, he held her gaze. Despite the knot in his stomach, he knew it was time to talk.

"Pete tells me they've arrested someone in connection with the fire."

He laid his clipboard aside and leaned against the desk, resting his thigh along the edge. Megan took the cue and the space he'd left on the desk. "A guy named Gordon Brown. He was the guy who decided the barn burning was bring-your-own-bottle."

Megan shook her head slowly. "I thought for sure it was Floyd Taylor."

"I'm sure it was, but it looks like he used Brown. And so far Brown's not talking."

"And you didn't know this Gordon Brown?"

Sage turned his mouth down as he shook his head. "Never saw him before. Somebody who hired on for the summer with one of the local ranchers. I knew one of the guys he was with—good-time Lonnie. I don't think Lonnie knows anything."

"I wish they could get Taylor."

He chuckled. "A woman after my own heart." She glanced at him quickly, surprised, and he looked away. They endured an awkward moment of silence.

"How are you, Sage? I mean—" He turned his palms up to show her the healing. "I mean, how are you do-ing...otherwise."

He lifted his eyes slowly and let her see inside himself, if she cared to look. "Otherwise, I'm doing okay. I went back on Antabuse." Her puzzled look led him to explain. "It's a drug I took for about a year after I got out of treatment. If you drink any alcohol at all while you're taking it, you puke your guts out."

She winced. "That oughta cure you."

"Careful how you throw that word 'cure' around." Smiling, he lifted a forefinger. "Remember what I told you, there is no 'recovered,' only—"

"Only recovering. I know. And you are. I'm glad."

Her smiled warmed him inside. "I've started over be-fore. It wasn't as tough this time. I had Medicine Wheel."

You had me, too, she thought. Only you didn't seem to notice. "What made you decide to quit the first time?" she asked. "Was it losing your wife?"

"The divorce was a long time coming. It was a relief to have it over—for both of us. But I wanted to be able to see the kids. I told her I'd fight for that much, at least. I told her—" He studied his hand and the healing that had al-ready taken place, and he asked himself why it took so long to heal up inside.

"My daughter, Brenda...she was just six years old, but they grow up fast, you know? Anyway, the judge asked her how she'd feel about living with her dad. She told him she wanted to go with her mother." His voice became gruff, and he grimaced as he spoke. "She said she loved her dad, but she didn't want to be around him anymore because he was always drunk." His eyes were dewy with his pain, and the story seemed to echo, as though he'd forced it from the bottom of a well. "That didn't leave me with any delusions about fighting for my kids. Kids don't like watching their parents get drunk."

Megan's eyes widened as she wondered at the possibility. "So you made the decision to stop drinking for your daughter's sake."

"Hell, no." His chuckle was self-derisive. "I made the decision right then and there to drown the memory of that little face in a quart bottle. I ended up in treatment when one of my sisters committed me because I wasn't paying my lease."

"Oh," she managed quietly as she glanced away.

"Hey." He caught her chin with two gentle fingers and turned her face back to him. "If it's any consolation, you can't drown out the memory of disappointing someone you care about. It's still there when you sober up."

"So you start in again?"

He drew his hand back reluctantly. The contact, however small, had felt good to him. "That's the way an addiction works. Something has to break the cycle, and it's usually not the addict. In my case it was the wrath of a sister who wanted her lease check."

She caught his hand, touched her fingers to his palm and moved them slowly to the tips of his fingers. "Through it all, you worked so hard, even though your hands... When I saw how sore they were that time, I wanted to—"

"I know," he said in a raspy voice. "I know what you wanted to do."

"But you're healing yourself."

He shook his head. "I'm letting the healing take place." He sought understanding in her eyes. "So are you, Megan.

By letting go. By not trying to claim that you have the power to *make* me get well."

"It's hard to believe that doing nothing is ... is all I can do to help."

"You were pulling for me, weren't you?" His dark eyes glittered with his smile. "In your heart you were saying, 'God, I hope he makes it.'" She nodded and returned his smile. "See how that works? I need a lot of that."

Sage hoped a few of the people in the crowded council chambers were pulling for him as he took the witness' chair and adjusted the microphone. A clerk was distributing papers to the council members, and a man was offering coffee refills. Sage found that he'd missed a snap on his cuff, and he pressed it together. He'd hurriedly unrolled his shirt sleeves moments before, and now he wished he'd thought to wear a sport jacket. His tarnished image needed some polish.

He glanced over his shoulder to reassure himself that Regina and Bessie were still there. They were, but the fact barely registered as his eyes met Megan's. Why had she come? This was not to be his finest moment. He'd come forth with all the mortification of the prodigal son, and many of those present would take satisfaction in that. Why the hell did she have to be there? He took a deep breath and turned back to the microphone. The chairman gave him the signal to speak his piece.

"Mr. Chairman, I'm not going to repeat my position on this matter. You've heard it twice now. Mr. Taylor is asking for a temporary license, and I'm opposed to issuing him any license at all. Now, Mr. Taylor has already testified that denying his license would not prevent anyone from getting drunk, and he made a point to look at me when he said it." The room grew very still as Sage scanned the faces of the councilmen. "I had a relapse. It was nobody's responsibility but mine. The last time I sat in this chair, I was able to say it had been four years since I'd had a drink. Today I can only tell you it's been fourteen days. But those fourteen days were just as hard-won as the four years, and they tell me Medicine Wheel works if I work.

"So I'm working. I'm learning. I'm finding out that what tradition tells us about ourselves is true. We're a community. We're a circle of people whose lives are interwoven. The circle can be a source of strength for us. It can also be a weakness. When alcohol eats away at the fabric of our circle, our interdependency becomes a weakness. That's why I'm asking us to reject this application. I believe that as a people we need to say no to the way this man, Taylor, operates. Alcohol is taking too high a toll of us, and we need to get it out of our lives. For whatever reason, we're too susceptible. It destroys us.

"It was brought here and given to us a long time ago, and we had no more resistance to it than we had to measles. Then, later, they said, 'No, you guys better not drink that stuff. It's bad for you.' But by that time we were saying, 'Who the hell do you think you are? We'll drink it if we want to.' So we did. And we're suffering for it. And now it's time to say, 'We don't want to.'"

Megan listened to Sage's voice as it came through the microphone, filling the room with a rich, deep rumble. He slipped one hand beneath the table and wiped his palm on his thigh, and she rubbed her own together. They were sweating, too. No longer her image of an iron-willed hero, here was a man who was even more dear because he struggled with his imperfections and more courageous because he was not without fear.

"I know I said I didn't want to," Sage continued. "I said it loud and clear, and then I weakened. I know you won't forget that—I don't ask you to. I only ask you to accept me the way I am today—sober, and sincere in what I'm saying. Whatever you decide today, I'm going to keep saying it." He directed his gaze at Floyd Taylor and fought to control the anger he felt at the sight of the man. "I'm going to keep urging you to turn people like Floyd Taylor away. I've started rebuilding my barn. If it burns down again, I'll build it again. You can't stop me, Taylor. There's only one person who can destroy me, and that's *me*."

Taylor nearly tripped over himself trying to get to his feet. "If you're accusing me of anything, Parker, you damn well better have proof!"

"That's all I have to say, Mr. Chairman."

There was more testimony. Taylor had hired a glib attorney, and the proprietors of other liquor establishments objected to the precedent that might be set by turning one license down. In the end, a temporary license was granted, and Taylor was admonished to clean up his act. Megan stood aside as Medicine Wheel sympathizers gathered outside the front doors of the tribal office building, some shaking Sage's hand, some shaking their heads.

When Floyd Taylor and his associates appeared, heads turned and heated looks were exchanged. Taylor postured as he walked past Sage, throwing his shoulders back and looking around to be sure this was, indeed, the proper moment for a parting shot.

"You haven't changed, Parker. You come on down to Floyd's tonight. Your first one's on the hou—"

Sage's left fist hit Taylor's gut like a cannon ball. Over the man's breathless grunt, Sage muttered, "I *want* to change, Taylor." As Taylor's chin dipped, Sage caught it with a cracking right. "I've been working... damn hard at it." Taylor's big frame toppled into his friends' arms, while Sage's companions moved to restrain him, and to protect him from reprisal. He grinned broadly as he shook the cramp out of his right hand. "Guess I've still got a pretty bad temper."

Megan's heart pounded as she watched his friends spirit Sage away. She pressed her own right fist into her left hand and gave a secret smile.

After a solitary supper at the local café, she left town. The sun was August-evening gold hanging low in the western sky. She came to a junction and told herself that if she took

the west fork, she would be squinting into the sun most of
the way. The north fork would take her the long way around
with less eye strain. She dismissed the added fact that she
would pass Sage's place as she drove north.

His pickup was parked near the trailer. She surveyed the
fire's aftermath as she negotiated the turn. The places where
the house and barn had stood just weeks ago had been
razed. Part of the corral had been saved, and the enclosure
had been repaired with new lumber.

He stood on the small wooden platform that served as his
front step. His white T-shirt was a beacon in the waning
light.

"Checking up on me?" he asked quietly as she approached the steps. The pointed end of a wooden toothpick
peeked out of the corner of his mouth.

Megan rejected "just passing by" as quickly as it came to
mind and instead confessed, "I was hoping you'd be
home."

"I haven't been here long." With a sweeping gesture he
offered the wooden step. "Have a seat. It's cooler out here."

"You've done a lot of work already."

"I've about had my fill of the smell of charcoal." He sat
beside her on the step and stretched his legs so that his boot
heels rested on the ground. "I saw your pickup at the café.
I thought about stopping, but decided I'd better get out of
town before sunset." With a dry chuckle he leaned back on
his arms and tipped his chin up. "I really blew it, didn't I?"

"Not at all," she protested. "You were eloquent."

"Eloquent?" He shifted the toothpick from one side of
his mouth to the other as he raised a teasing eyebrow. "I
never heard of an eloquent gut-buster before."

"Oh, that." She laughed and hugged her knees. "That
part was magnificent."

"The lady's got a real mean streak."

"Only when somebody's got it coming, and I can't think
of anyone who deserves it more than Floyd Taylor."

"That's probably the extent of the satisfaction I'm likely to get." He sat up and looked across the yard at the little corral as he draped his forearm over one bent knee. "Gordon Brown's white, so they can't try him in tribal court."

"It's a federal charge, isn't it?"

"Yeah."

"Isn't that better?"

"We'll see. Better than county court, I guess. Taylor's got too much local influence." He shrugged. "I'm not the court system's biggest fan." As he stared at the empty space where a barn would one day be resurrected, a slow, sinister smile spread across his face. "In this case, I'd be in favor of trial by fire. I've got plenty of charcoal. Turn them both on a spit, and if they get crisp, we pronounce them guilty as hell."

"Sage!"

"No, I was thinking salt, maybe Tabasco sauce." He watched her eyes brighten with laughter and considered how pretty she looked in pink. "Why did you come to the hearing today?" he asked quietly.

The laughter died, and she looked at him solemnly. "Not out of curiosity," she assured him. "I'm allowed to pull for you, right? That's all I was doing. Didn't you tell me there had to be witnesses? Somehow I think today's ordeal was more difficult than the Sun Dance must have been."

"Megan..." He sighed heavily, glanced away and then looked back at her. "The night of the fire, when I saw you drive up, I wanted to crawl into a hole. Not just because I was ashamed of the drinking, but I was...I was..." He groped for the words. Defeated? Beaten? He didn't like any of the words that came to mind. "A man feels...totally emasculated when a woman sees him pinned to the ground like that." God! That sounded worse than any of them.

"They've never pinned you to the ground." She put her hand on his shoulder. The warmth of his flesh under the soft cotton T-shirt stirred a matching warmth in her. "They take clumsy pot shots at you. As long as you keep coming back, they can't touch the man you are."

She could, he thought. She could touch the man he was, and he would never stop coming back. But she had to change, too. "Why did you come here tonight?"

She stiffened and drew her hand away. "Just to see you."

"To see if I was still sober?"

"I didn't think you'd..."

"I was disappointed over the decision, but I'm not going to get drunk over it. There are other ways." He leaned back on his elbow and admired the way the rosy sky behind her turned her into a softly shaded silhouette. "Regina's going to be able to open her store soon. If people are as tired of being jacked around by Taylor as they say they are, they'll take their business to Regina. If not—" He took the toothpick from the corner of his mouth and tossed it into the night. "If not, the hell with them."

"Really?"

"Really. You've gotta learn to recognize when enough's enough."

"You?" she asked. "Or the others?"

"Both." He offered a quick smile. "I'm not much of a host, am I? Would you like coffee?"

"If I can help you make it."

He laughed as he got to his feet. "Will you let *me* take care of *you* for once? Besides, it's made."

She took the hand he offered and followed him inside. "I'm not sure I understand this 'caretaker' thing. I'm far from a domestic, but I can make coffee." She closed the screen door behind her. "It just seemed polite to offer to help."

"It was." He pointed to a small overhead cupboard. "Get the cups. I hope you like it black, because I don't have anything to lighten it."

"Black is fine," she said. She set the cups down, and he poured from an aluminum percolator, which he'd left sitting over a low gas flame.

"Tell me about your dad," Sage suggested almost offhandedly. "Does he handle the checkbook, pay the bills?"

"Oh, no, he's no good with money. My mother takes care of that."

"Because she wants to?"

"She hates it." He nodded toward the door, and she swung the screen open again, assuming it bothered him to be cooped up inside. "He'd have it all messed up inside a week, that's all. I think if she could get him to stop..."

The conversation stalled as they settled on the steps again. Sage watched Megan hide her face behind her coffee cup. "Stop what?" he finally prodded.

She flashed wide, wary eyes. "I wasn't going to say 'drinking.'"

His patient smile was lopsided. "What else weren't you going to say?"

"I wasn't going to say that I don't ever have any thought of taking care of you...because...that wouldn't be entirely true."

"Fight the urge, Megan. It's destructive." The light from the kitchen illuminated the doubt in her eyes. He set his cup down and leaned closer, boring at her with his eyes. "It'll make you crazy," he told her. "It'll make you just as sick as I was when you saw me the morning after the fire. Sure, I needed a friend, but I didn't need a crutch. My disease is my problem, and if I do end up needing a crutch, it's got to be a wooden one, *not* a human one." He made an effort to inject a note of tenderness into his tone as he added, "It sounds to me like that's what your mother is, Megan. A human crutch."

Megan lowered her cup to the step slowly as her back stiffened. "That's not true, Sage. That's not even fair."

"It's not? Why not?"

"Because you don't even know them," she accused huskily.

"I know you." His voice was smooth, his tone sure, and that irritated her. "Alcoholism is a family disease, and I know one member of the family quite well. I see the symptoms."

"You're taking what I've confided in you, and you're blowing it out of—"

"You call him a 'problem drinker.' Why can't you call him an alcoholic?" He struggled to control the accusing edge in his voice, but it was there because of the way she sat up in front of him, so prim and perfect. "Why should your family be granted immunity? Huh? What other diseases *can't* you get? It's killing my people, and if you've got a vaccination against it, you damn well better—"

"I don't need any more of this." Megan pushed herself to her feet, tottering a bit as she reached her full height. "I have never said anything... unkind or..."

Sage set his cup down. "I'm not being unkind," he said evenly. "I just want to understand the real meaning behind the terms you use. Here we've got drunks. Winos. Off the reservation we've got 'problem drinkers.' I guess that sounds better. Does it look prettier? I mean, you haven't seen me when I'm really wasted, so it's probably hard to compare—"

She'd begun to tremble inside, and she wasn't sure why. She opened her mouth for a crisp goodbye, and it didn't come. Her throat burned, and she couldn't catch her breath. When he stood up gradually, she had the terrible feeling that he might hit her over the head, not with his hand, but with something worse—something that would hurt far more. She searched for some defense, and it came in a high-pitched retort.

"I've seen you with a hangover, and it looks the same on you as it does on anyone else. An old man's face, and sick to your stomach like a child!"

For a moment his boots were nailed to the step. He'd had no right, he told himself as he watched her turn and run. He'd pushed her too far. When he could move, he vaulted over the side of the step and caught up to her just as she reached her pickup.

"Megan!" He reached for her, but she jerked her arm away. "Look, I'm sorry. You're right, I don't know—"

"You know all about it, Sage. You're an expert!" The last word was nearly lost in her wild-eyed frenzy to get into the truck.

He felt as though, in one word, she'd thrown everything he'd confided in her back in his face. An expert! He grabbed the door. She tried to pull it shut, but her strength was no match for his. They eyed one another through the open window, black irises glittering, blue glinting back. Megan's chest heaved with each shallow breath as she waited for him to relinquish his hold.

"You can become an expert, too, Megan. You might as well. You're up to your eyebrows in it." His voice was soft and smoother than he'd thought he could manage. "Come to Medicine Wheel. They've listened to me for two solid weeks, and they're ready for somebody else. Or find a group that meets your needs. All you have to do is own up to the problem."

With that he shut the door and backed away. He watched her fumble with her keys, then go through the steps of putting the pickup in motion as though it were a new skill. She ground the forward gears, turned the headlights on as an afterthought and put thirty yards between them. The red brake lights came on. Sage gave her a few seconds, and when he was certain she was going no farther, he followed, stretching his long legs to cover the distance quickly. He found her slumped over the wheel, her shoulders shaking.

"Slide over," he said as he pulled the door open. She fought with the gear shift on the steering column until the pickup surrendered, choking out. Sage wanted to laugh at the muttered obscenity that sounded so unnatural on Megan's tongue, but he knew better. "It's okay," he said quietly. "Just let it go."

Let it go. He meant the pickup, but she heard more. The words were inviting, the concept incredible. It was a relief to let him take over, and when he took her in his arms, there was deliverance. She gave herself over to the tears and the awful quaking, trusting him to shield her while she did, indeed, let go. The solid flesh beneath his soft shirt offered support, and she leaned all her cares against it as she wept.

"He's not a bad man, Sage," she whispered. Whispering was all she could manage. Such a thing, even in the form of a denial, could not be said aloud.

"Am I a bad man?" he asked gently.

"No. Oh, no."

"I've done some bad things," he confessed. "I've had to recognize that and try to do something about it."

"He's my father." Her voice tripped over tears as the words tumbled out. "I can't not like...not love..."

"I know," he whispered. "It's okay, Megan."

"I can't help loving him," she choked. "I *do* love him, and it hurts because..."

"Because..."

"Because I love you too and I don't know what's wrong with me!" she shouted in a breathless rush.

"Nothing." His heart soared. He held her tighter and cherished the warmth of her tears against his neck. "There's nothing wrong with you, Megan."

"But I should know better!"

"Who says?" He coaxed her with kisses at her temple and in her hair. "It's okay to love me." He'd never been able to convince himself completely of that notion, but he wanted her to believe it. "I'm not a bad man." He poured small kisses over her face, praying she'd believe it, and she responded, straining to touch her lips to his face because it didn't matter whether she knew better. She loved him because she loved him because she loved him....

His mouth was close to her ear, and his heart wedged itself in his throat. "Is it okay that I love you, too?"

"Yes."

"Will you stay with me tonight?"

"Yes."

"Sleep where I sleep?"

"Yes."

"Make me believe that I deserve to be loved?"

"If my love can do that for you."

He took her face in his hands and kissed the salty corners of her smile. "I believe it can."

He took her to the trailer, and for the first time since he'd lived there, he delighted in the walls' closeness. The little fan whirred in the dark as they undressed one another, maneuvering in a small warm space that reminded him of the sweat lodge. The earth's womb. Small and feminine, like the breasts he covered with his hands. Persistent, like the nipples that formed hard pebbles to tickle his palms. Round and smooth, like the hips that housed the hearth of his heart's choosing.

The walls kept him close, as snug as a cocoon his body had nearly outgrown. She slid her skin against his, and he couldn't move away; it was as if some wariness had grown in his mind.

The scent of musk filled her head and drove her to touch him with boldly seeking hands. He was moist satin skin over hard muscle everywhere she touched, and he would fill her with power before they were through. The thrill of anticipation rippled along the insides of her thighs in a trail his fingertips blazed. She spread her hands over his chest and made his nipples tighten with her thumbs as she pressed him back upon the bed.

"You deserve to be loved," she swore hotly.

Her hands worked magic.

"Oh, Megan..."

Her lips drove him mad.

"You're beautiful and caring, and I love you. All of you."

Her tongue laved him to rigid readiness.

"You're too good," he said. "I want... too much of you."

She took the device he clutched tightly in his hand and slipped it over him with painstaking care, caring for herself and for him and for the time they would need to devote to one another. Then she sheathed him within her body, letting him fill her, letting him know her, crying out when the joy could not be contained.

And Sage's tears touched her shoulder with the gentle beauty of a warm rain on rich earth, newly turned and springtime fertile.

Chapter 13

Megan's road lay like a shiny licorice whip over the small stretch of South Dakota prairie to which she would always lay some sentimental claim. It was mid-October, and though the evenings had grown cold, Indian Summer warmed the tawny hills through the waning afternoon hours. Megan's own little white Honda chased the broken yellow line from hollow to crest as she pushed past the speed limit to keep her date. She'd been invited to a picnic.

Sage was driving nails in his new subfloor when the white car turned into his long driveway. He'd been waiting for her, checking his watch every few minutes and keeping his hands busy with the hammer. The floor was nearly finished, as was the new pole barn. He hopped down from the plywood deck, untied the leather apron and stashed it with his hammer in his tool box just as Megan pulled up beside the pickup.

"Is this one of those working dates you're so famous for?" She smiled as he took her in his arms, but he kissed the smile away. She wound her arms around his neck and said hello his way.

"If I'm famous for them," he muttered between nibbles, "it's because you've been bragging them up."

"I can't help it," she murmured into his mouth. "I love to be envied."

"Me too. One of these days you can get dressed up, and I'll take you out to some big event. Make every guy in the place jealous of me." He lifted one corner of his mouth in a teasing smile. "Soon as the high school basketball season starts."

"Promises, promises."

"Aren't you going to say anything about the barn?"

He took her hand from the back of his neck and held it in his as she turned around. Her face lit up. "It's finished!"

"Almost. I've still got to get shingles and doors."

"But how did you . . . I mean, the last time I saw it, there were just . . ."

"Just a few poles. I know. A couple of the women from Medicine Wheel employed a time-honored Indian custom." He grinned, and golden sunlight glinted in the warmth of his autumn brown eyes. "They raffled off a couple of star quilts. Then they rounded up a bunch of people, and we had most of it done inside a day."

"That's wonderful, Sage." She slipped her arm around his waist and gave him a squeeze. "I think we should celebrate."

"I think so, too. I hope you didn't bring a bunch of food, like you usually do."

"Why not?"

"Because I told you I'd cook. Don't you trust me?"

The aroma of the freshly deep-fried bread she'd come to love in recent months filled the little trailer. It had been served at every function she'd attended on the Pine Ridge Reservation, and she'd attended quite a few. "I don't believe you actually made frybread," she said as he opened the door for her. His proud smile said that he'd just opened a package full of surprises. "Did you really?"

"You think I can't make anything but cold meat sandwiches? I learned a secret." He tossed her a conspiratorial wink. "Frozen bread dough."

"It works?"

"Pretty well." He handed her a stack of paper plates and a roll of paper towels. "You take the china." Then he reached for a cardboard box. "I'll take the picnic basket. Everything else is over there. You gonna be warm enough?" She glanced down at her fisherman knit sweater and nodded. "I'll take an extra blanket anyway. When that sun goes down, you really know it's fall."

He'd spread a star quilt over the grass amid the rows of cottonwoods. Its burst of orange, yellow and red gave the scattering of withered cottonwood leaves a taste of what autumn color should be. Megan giggled when she noted the plastic ice-cream pail at the corner of the quilt. Two green bottles of Perrier were planted in ice.

"I spared no expense for this occasion," he told her as he set the box next to the blanket.

"I did bring a little dessert."

"Did you, now." After taking the plates from her first, he pulled her down beside him and cupped his hands over her breasts. "A little dessert? I always love your *little* desserts."

"You may not get any if you say 'little' one more time," she said imperiously, but she gave him a small kiss, which held out some promise.

"Keep that up and we'll have cold frybread."

She settled on the blanket and watched him open the first bottle. "Frybread and Perrier make a very interesting combination."

"Oh, it gets better," he promised as he poured a small amount of the sparkling water into a plastic glass. "How do Indian tacos and Perrier strike you?"

"Sounds heavenly. I won't have to worry about being little much longer with this kind of feasting." She lifted the plastic glass toward the setting sun and smiled as the tiny bubbles became glinting jewels. "Excellent clarity."

"Well, hell, it's French. What can I say?"

She swirled, sniffed and sipped. "Tangy. It has a life of its own. I believe you can actually taste the granite from the spring."

Sage poured himself some and tossed it down. "Not much kick to it," he judged. "Let's try the tacos."

The flat pieces of frybread were piled high with hot, spicy hamburger and fresh salad. Megan held the plate just inches from her mouth, which she stretched wide to accommodate the layers of food. The taste of chili and Cheddar cheese complemented the warm, chewy bread. Spicy red juice dribbled down her chin, and Sage tossed her the roll of paper towels. When the same thing happened to him, she tossed it back. The messiness of the concoction was part of its appeal.

It was impossible to talk with their mouths full of shredded lettuce and heavy bread, but when they were down to the Perrier and the prospect of dessert, Sage announced that he'd sold his calves and gotten a good price. He'd bought seven bred heifers, which brought his herd up to twenty-one.

"I kept one steer calf," he told her. "I'll feed him over the winter and donate him for the dinner when Regina has her giveaway next summer."

"How's her store doing?"

"She's taking a big cut out of Taylor's business, *and*—" He raised one eyebrow in delight. "Old Floyd isn't selling as much booze these days as he'd like to."

It had been slow in coming, but Sage's victory was beginning to taste sweet. Gordon Brown had been indicted on charges of arson, and he was awaiting trial in federal court. There was still hope that he might implicate Taylor.

"The Medicine Wheel program is growing, isn't it?"

"They've got a strong group in Pine Ridge, and we're running a meeting just about every night now in Red Calf."

She held her cup out for more water. "Do you think I'd be welcome, sort of... on a regular basis?"

He gave her a puzzled look. "Sure, you're always welcome, but that's a long way to drive from Pierre. I thought you'd found a group there that you liked."

"I did." She studied her glass. She hadn't told him, because she didn't know how he'd react. She suspected the distance between them was a kind of safety valve for him. "I'm moving," she announced finally.

"Moving," he repeated slowly. "Moving... here?"

"I'm going to work for Pete Petersen at the roads department in Pine Ridge."

"You didn't tell me you were applying for a BIA job."

She made herself look up. "I applied last summer. I didn't know whether I'd get it, and when it was offered, I didn't know whether to take it. I talked to Pete and Bob Krueger, and then I gave it a lot of thought." The look in his eyes didn't change. He was disturbed. "It's a good opportunity for me. Pete'll retire in a couple of years, and if I like the job and I'm what they need, I might..."

"I don't understand why you didn't tell me."

She sighed. "I didn't tell you because...I needed to look at the job...apart from us. It had to be good for me, for my career."

"It does bring you... more within reach, though."

"It does," she said quietly.

"I don't know about you, but I like that idea." A broad smile slid across his face and touched his eyes. He lifted his glass. "In fact, I'll drink to it."

When the glasses were drained, he pulled a letter from his shirt pocket. "Here's something else I've got to celebrate. It's from Brenda."

"Your daughter? She finally answered your letters?"

He nodded as he pulled the lined notebook paper from its envelope. "You can read it. It's not like she's dying to see me or anything, but she remembers me, and her mom said it was okay to write to me if she wanted to." His eyes glistened as he handed Megan the letter. "She wanted to."

Two small school pictures slipped out when she unfolded the paper. There was a dark-haired boy whose new permanent teeth were still too large for his little-boy face and a dark-eyed girl who, in a few short years, would be a lovely young woman. Megan knew how much older they must have looked to Sage, and her chest grew tight at the thought of all he'd missed.

"They look so much like you," she said.

"You think so? I ... I kinda thought so, too."

Megan unfolded the letter and read the message written in the carefully rounded hand of a twelve-year-old. "She says she remembers riding double with you, and she remembers how you used to call her 'Shorty.' And—" She looked up as she folded the letter and tucked it back in the envelope. His eyes were filled with a bitter-sweet mixture of emotion. "She's so glad you've stopped drinking."

"I told her I was working hard at it. I didn't tell her—"

"You told her the truth, Sage." She reached for him, putting her arms around his neck. "I need to hold you," she whispered, pressing her palm over his soft sweatshirt.

"I need to hold you, too." He pulled her into his lap and crushed her to him. Their needs had nothing to do with pity. There was pain to be acknowledged and joy to be shared, but there was no bid for sympathy and no caretaking.

"I went to see my father," she told him.

"How did it go?"

"I just told him that I was participating in a group for adult children of alcoholics."

"What did he say?"

She leaned back, holding his head in her hands. "He said he'd never heard of such a thing, and my mother said that groups were the in thing these days. I think he was hurt. I think she was a little angry."

"You're not doing it for him," he reminded her.

"I'm doing it for me."

She was learning. He grinned as he sneaked his hands beneath her sweater. "That's right. Now, how about doing something for me?"

"I suppose you want dessert."

"Right again." He lowered her back against the cotton quilt, and she heard the crackle of the bed of leaves beneath it.

"I really did bring some, you know."

He pushed her sweater out of the way and nuzzled the ivory satin that covered her ivory skin. Both soft. Both powder scented. "I know you did." He nudged at the satin with his nose. "Little tart."

"I warned you about—"

"Mmm, two little tarts." He sucked at her through the satin.

She took a deep breath. "That word *little*."

"Two for me," he muttered as he moved to taste the second one. "And none for you."

"I brought..." He released the clasp between her breasts, and she sighed. "...something...that probably isn't very..."

"I'm stealing these tarts," he whispered, "with these sweet little round..."

He unbuttoned her jeans and inched the zipper down while he feasted. "...very good..." Megan breathed. She buried her fingers in his thick hair for support as her thighs went slack. "Oh, Sage, that feels...very, very...good."

"You like that?"

"Mmmm."

"You hungry?"

"Mmmmmmmm."

"How about an éclair?"

Her hand crept under his sweatshirt and over his belly, and he sucked his breath in when it reached the waistband of his jeans. "Do you have one for me?" she whispered hotly.

"Mmm-hmmm. Somewhere."

"Let me find it."

* * * *

The sky ran riot with bright white stars, and a pumpkin-colored harvest moon hung low above the jagged horizon. Wrapped together in a blanket and in one another's arms, they shared dreams and intimate touches and listened to the last of summer's leaves answer the night breeze with a dry rustle.

"Do you think we'll ever build another road together?" Megan asked.

"I think I'm supposed to build roads," he said absently, enjoying the feel of the soft down on the back of her neck as he stroked her. "All kinds of roads."

"If I did a vision quest, do you think I'd find out what I'm supposed to do?"

He dipped his chin and feathered his lips across her forehead, wondering what she dreamed about now when she closed her eyes. "What if you did one and it told you to go back to Pierre and find some guy who's already got his act together? Then what?"

"How many times did you say you went back to the vision pit?"

"Three."

"Then I'd try again." She levered herself up on one arm and traced the lines across his brow with her thumb. "I've learned a lesson from you, Sage Parker." Care lines, she thought. She cherished each one. "You're only beaten when you stop trying."

"I love you."

"And I love you."

* * * * *

If you enjoyed this book, look for SOMEDAY SOON, Kathleen Eagle's first Silhouette Special Edition, available again this November—only from Silhouette Classics.

Author's Note

The town of Red Calf and the Medicine Wheel program are fictitious. The concept for Medicine Wheel, however, was inspired by the story of Alkalai Lake, a community of the Shuswap people in British Columbia. There the courageous decision of one woman led to recovery for herself, her husband and, eventually, almost the entire community. Native American people in a number of North and South Dakota communities are designing their own recovery programs, revitalizing an ancient heritage of spirituality as they attack the problem of alcoholism with new self-confidence and a tradition of wisdom as old as the rolling hills of the Dakotas.

A Note from Heather Graham Pozzessere

I'm delighted to see this book included in
Brave Hearts. It takes place in the Everglades, near
my own home in South Florida. It's an area I've always
loved—having a mystery and beauty that's unique,
dangerous and very special. It's also the home of very
special people, the Seminole and the Miccosukee,
who made their stand here and never surrendered to
government forces. To this day, like so many other
Native Americans, they still battle for their place in the
American dream.

In Eric Hawk, I've tried to embody the pride,
intelligence and spirit of the Native American in
today's world. I hope you enjoy his story.

Heather Graham Pozzessere

BORROWED ANGEL

Heather Graham Pozzessere

Chapter 1

"There's nothing a woman needs. . . . Nothing . . . but the primitive earth . . . and her Tyler jewels. Nothing, nothing at all. . . ."

Stretched atop a fake boulder in the midst of wild orchids and lush foliage, the woman whispered the words softly and sensually for the camera. She was leaning on an elbow, her knees slightly bent, her mane of red hair curling over her shoulders. She wore a strapless tiger-striped bikini. Her lipstick was a fiery orange-red, and her green eye shadow brought out the highlights in her eyes. She wasn't just beautiful; she was as erotic and sensual and arrestingly pagan as any man could imagine. Perhaps it was the abundance of her fire-colored hair. Perhaps it was her eyes, or the curve of her body, or maybe just the pulse of life that seemed to exude from her—seething, simmering, exciting. And dangerous, perhaps, but so vital that the sight of her, the sound of her whisper, seemed to dip into the very heart of every man's fantasy and every woman's dream of what she should be.

Around her throat she wore an emerald pendant. Emeralds dangled from her earlobes, and she wore one emerald ring and one emerald bracelet. Against the light tan of her flesh, the jewelry was striking. The emeralds matched her eyes. Eric Hawk was convinced that no woman could wear them more beguilingly.

He shifted suddenly, feeling uncomfortable. She was seducing him. She was making his heart beat too quickly, his breath come too hard, too fast. His muscles felt tightly wired. She seemed to be calling to every part of his body.

"Good!" someone called to the model.

She sighed, about to move from her perch. "Wait! Let's go again!" the director of the commercial shouted.

The redhead gritted her teeth and glared at the man. She quickly covered the emotion, though, and waved to the young couple standing behind him.

She settled back down on the boulder. "There's nothing a woman needs.... Nothing...but the primitive earth and her Tyler jewels. Nothing...nothing at all...."

She seemed to purr. Fascinating sensuality gleamed from her eyes. She was feline and graceful and striking.

Watching her, Eric Hawk had little notion that he was striking also. He was a tall man, nearly six-three. His hair was not just dark but the blue-black color of a raven's wing. He wore his hair layered and slightly long. It fell over the edge of his collar and sometimes tumbled over his forehead and into his eyes. From the ancestors who had given him the color of his hair, he had inherited an arresting face. His cheekbones were high and and broad, his chin decidedly square, his nose long, and his eyes large and set wide apart. His brows matched his hair, and he was highly bronzed from constant exposure to the sun. Eric was an integral part of the wild and savage land where the company had come to film. He could move in absolute silence over the grasses and swamp and hummock alike, and he did so not with conscious thought, but by nature. He was as lean and sleek as the endangered panther that wandered the land; he could strike as swiftly as the snake.

From a different set of ancestors he had acquired one of his most striking features—his eyes. They were not the emerald shade of the model's, but they, too, were green. And bright, penetrating, startling against the dark bronze color of his face. People looked his way and were caught by those eyes.

"One more time."

"All right, all right!" the beautiful redhead called out. "One more time." She paused, looking up at the sky.

The sun was leaving them. It was only early afternoon, but clouds were rolling in. Eric looked at the sky, too. There was a big storm brewing over Cuba and South Florida was on hurricane watch. The storm had barely gathered hurricane force during the last weather report Eric had seen, but he knew that storms picked up strength over the open water. Besides, here in the swamp, even a minor storm could be serious and even deadly. These people needed to finish—and get out.

He turned around and walked over to the handsome young couple who stood some distance from the director.

Rafe Tyler, tall and with a commanding presence, flashed him a friendly smile. "Mr. Hawk." He extended a hand. "Nice to see you. We didn't hear you'd come."

His wife, Tara, a beautiful blonde with wide blue eyes, an enchanting smile and belly swollen with child, spoke softly. "Thank you for coming! And thank you again for the use of the property. I think it's wonderful."

"The ad was Tara's conception," Rafe explained.

Eric nodded, smiling at the couple. He had been startled by his liking the Tylers. Eric had read somewhere that Rafe was one of the hundred richest men in the world. He hadn't expected a lot from the man, bu⁺ curious about Rafe's proposition, Eric had agreed to see him. He had been impressed with the man's energy, but Eric had explained that he didn't feel right about letting his land be used for a commercial and receiving a fee. Rafe had convinced him with a deal—Eric wouldn't be paid; instead Rafe would make a large contribution toward building a vocational school for which Eric had been working long and hard. In the end, the contribution had doubled, because Rafe had liked the children and seen the need.

"Mrs. Tyler—" Eric began.

"Tara, please."

"Tara, I think that it was a wonderful idea."

"Thank you, Mr. Hawk."

"Eric," he said grinning.

She laughed easily. "Eric. Anyway, I'm very pleased. We thank you sincerely."

"Thank you," Eric said. He looked at the sky again. "I was just thinking that you should wrap up here soon. I could be wrong, but I think that the storm is coming this way."

"We'll leave soon," Tara promised him. "I just want to say goodbye to Ashley."

Rafe handed Eric a card. "If you're ever in New York, or if I can ever do anything for you, please don't hesitate to call."

Tara touched his hand. "Please do come see us!" she urged.

He nodded. "Sure. I'll come sometime," he told her. "I'm going to go and see that my family is all battened down. Don't take too long, now. A storm here is nothing to take a chance with."

Rafe's arm tightened protectively around his wife. "I promise you that we'll be out quickly."

Eric nodded to them, smiled again and headed for his airboat. His sister-in-law Wendy's house wasn't far, just right across the canal, and he wondered if he shouldn't go back and bring the Tylers to Wendy's. Then he shrugged, deciding that he should check on his own family first and return to see if the Tylers had made it out. With that plan in mind, Eric hastened on his way.

On her rock, Ashley Dane repeated her lines again. For the fifth "one more time."

She knew that Harrison Mosby, the director, was giving her a hard time on purpose. He was talented, young, handsome—and up-and-coming. She couldn't stand him, and she was tired of the way he treated her, touching her, taunting her with off-color remarks. She had almost protested to Tara and Rafe about his being there, but she knew that Rafe thought Harrison was a good director. Rafe didn't know him as a man. Ashley had decided to endure.

"That's great, Ashley!" Tara called to her, smiling happily from behind the cameraman. Ashley grimaced. Tara would have said that she had done great even if she had looked and sounded like the Incredible Hulk. Tara had talked her into the assignment.

"Thanks."

"Ashley, super!" Rafe proclaimed. He was the owner of the illustrious Tyler Jewels and Tara's husband and Ashley's good friend. "Let's get one more, though, okay? We don't want to have to come all the way back here to film again." He looked at Harrison. "Just one more, Harrison. We have to get out of here. The storm is going to break."

"The storm?" Harrison asked.

"The storm," Rafe said firmly. Harrison shook his blond head, but he didn't dare argue.

"Is one more okay, Ashley?" Tara questioned worriedly.

"Sure!" Ashley agreed. She looked Tara straight in the eye and shivered. Tara laughed. "Come on, Ashley, it's not that bad!"

"You come over here and stare at this giant, man-eating reptile for a while!" Ashley said indignantly, indicating the live creature leashed not twenty-five feet away from her.

The reptile wasn't all that big by alligator standards, Ashley had been assured. The gator's name was Henry and he was only four feet long, but two feet of that seemed to be his mouth alone. Besides Henry, who had been hired and whose trainer would be well paid, there might be dozens of other creatures just hanging around for whatever—and whoever!

Ashley and Tara had come to the Florida Everglades years ago when they had both modeled for the world-famous Galliard. A cloud of scandal and danger had hung over Tara's life at that time. It had been solved in Caracas only two years ago when she had met Rafe and they had discovered that the danger had been caused not only by an ex-flame, but by Galliard himself. Wealthy, charming Rafe had fallen in love with Tara, and she and Ashley had gone into fashion design for themselves.

When Ashley had first heard the setting for the commercial that would kick off the massive new ad campaign for Tyler Jewels, she had protested. "I don't think that it's right for me. I just don't care for things that crawl."

"Oh, Ashley!" Tara had laughed. "Rafe will be there and I'll be there, and nothing will crawl over you, I promise. This is a big deal for us. We're putting months of planning into it!"

"There are snakes and alligators and who knows what else out there in the Florida Everglades."

"But we'll be fine!"

"You do it! You're a model."

"I can't do it!"

"Why not?"

"We're going to have a baby!"

Ashley had stopped protesting then, because she had been so happy for Tara. Tara explained that they were planning the shoot earlier than Rafe really wanted just so she could be there.

Still, Ashley had never liked the idea of coming out to the swamp. She simply didn't like things that buzzed and flew and crawled and slithered. Not insects, not snakes and certainly not the disgusting alligators that opened their mouths that were filled with endless rows of teeth and made noises that sounded remarkably like the grunts of pigs.

"Harrison," Ashley said impatiently, wondering what he was waiting for.

"Makeup!" Harrison shouted. "Come on, people, get with it! She has a sheen like a neon light on her face. Let's move, people, let's move."

Mitchell Newman, the makeup artist, quickly approached Ashley and powdered her face. Grace Neeley, his assistant, rushed up behind him to redo Ashley's hair. Ashley closed her eyes and waited patiently. She gave Mitchell an encouraging smile; Harrison had been on his case all day, too.

To her horror, Ashley blew her lines on the next take.

"Ashley, how could you!" Harrison groaned.

"What's the matter with the first takes?" she demanded.

"Take five!" Harrison snapped.

Gritting her teeth, Ashley jumped off the rock. She'd been afraid to leap to the ground in her bare feet, but she had been watching Tara, and thought that her friend looked very tired.

She smiled at Norm Dillon, Gene Hack and Tory Robinson, the three cameramen. Susie Weylon, the representative from Tyler Jewels, looked as if she were about to have apoplexy. "Ashley! The jewels!"

"I'm walking ten feet to see Tara, that's it!" Ashley promised.

Susie stood back, looking disgruntled. "Be careful!" she warned.

"Of course!" Ashley said. She watched where she was walking and hurried to Tara and Rafe. Rafe smiled and kissed her on the cheek. "Perfect, Ashley."

"Thanks." She grinned, then laughed. "I feel ridiculous. As long as I've been a model, this is absolutely the least that I have ever had on. I wouldn't do this for just anyone, you know. I feel as if I'm half naked."

"You are half naked. And you're a sweetie," Tara said. She grinned broadly. "But honestly, you look great. Doesn't she, Rafe?"

"Now, am I damned if I do and damned if I don't answer that?" Rafe asked her, his eyes ablaze with tenderness.

"You're to answer honestly."

"You look great half naked, Ashley. And you, darling, look stunning pregnant."

Tara laughed delightedly. "I look like a house, but I don't mind it a bit." The wind lifted her blond locks.

Ashley looked up at the sky. The storm was supposedly going in another direction, but now Ashley felt nervous. "Rafe, take her out of here."

"We'll wait for you," he said, glancing at his watch with a shrug. "It shouldn't be much longer."

"No, please."

"Ashley," Tara said, "I know how you feel about Harrison—"

"I can handle Harrison. I'll get a ride with Grace. I'll be fine, I promise. Please, Tara, you're making me so very nervous. I don't like you out here with this storm."

"Okay, okay. We'll leave right now, and we'll see you back at the hotel."

"Okay! Now go!"

She kissed them both quickly. Rafe cast Harrison a warning look. He seemed about to say something, then seeing Ashley's imploring eyes, clamped his mouth shut. "All right. Take care. And you're perfect."

Ashley watched them head through the dense foliage. It was difficult to believe that a major road lay just beyond. Well, not a major road. Alligator Alley was growing—or so Ashley had been told—but it seemed to her that there were still endless stretches of absolutely nothing but saw grass and swamp and canals and the occasional crane or egret standing one-legged in the water.

Ashley shivered and stepped back, looking up at the trees. There were snakes here, which could drop from the branches. She rather liked her boulder, come to think of it.

Nothing was really close to her when she was on top of it. The mosquitoes didn't even bother her.

"Ashley, let's go," Harrison called to her.

"I'm ready when you are."

"Norm, get some extra shots of that gator," Harrison commanded the cameraman. Norm nodded in silence. Ashley climbed back up on her rock. Harrison called for hair and makeup and she was primped and powdered again.

Ashley gritted her teeth. She wouldn't be here if it weren't for her friendship with Tara and Rafe. She had started to grow weary with modeling when she was still with Galliard. Then, she and Tara had gone into fashion design. They did well. Ashley made enough money to support herself comfortably, and that was all that she needed. Rafe was paying her an absurd amount for this assignment, but she hadn't done it for the money. She had done it for him and Tara— because it had been Tara's concept and because the jewelry was Rafe's.

She sighed. Not much longer. She could survive it.

One more time...

She said the lines without a hitch. She offered, very sweetly, to do it again. Harrison smiled at her. She hated his smiles; they were purely lascivious. "Right, sweetie, you do it one more time. For me, especially, hmm?"

He wouldn't have dared sound that way had Rafe stayed, Ashley thought. But she didn't want Rafe fighting her battles. She could handle herself. She had lived in New York City alone for years, and she knew how to handle the Harrison Mosbys of the world. She had met enough of them.

"Let's just do this and go home, huh?" she said sweetly. She looked up. The sky was growing black. There was going to be a storm—one heck of a storm.

"Ready? Let's go. Roll 'em," Harrison said.

Finally the last take was in. Ashley sighed and watched idly as the cameramen packed their gear. She hesitated to ask Grace for a ride, seeing that Grace was still busy. She started when Harrison touched her back.

"I want to talk to you, Ashley."

The first time that she had met him, she had thought he was handsome, talented and witty. She had gone out with him once. He had drunk too much at dinner and bragged about himself all through it. He had forced his way into her apartment, and he had nearly forced himself on her. But she hadn't been afraid to scream like a banshee and he had left her, swearing that she would never work in a commercial again. She had laughed at the threat; she hated commercials. It hadn't been so long ago.

"I don't want to talk to you, Harrison."

"Come on."

"No!"

He grabbed hold of her wrist, dragging her from the rock. Norm looked up. Ashley saw confusion and worry cross his features. He didn't know what do do. He needed to keep working, and he didn't want Harrison Mosby blackballing him back in New York City. On the other hand, Norm was a gentleman, married to a lovely woman, the father of three beautiful daughters. He couldn't watch ill come to Ashley without taking some step. He would try to help her—and wind up jobless himself.

"He'll be sorry if he interferes," Harrison muttered.

Ashley smiled at Norm and waved, assuring him that she was all right. She could handle Harrison herself. He was just an obnoxious braggart. Harrison wrenched her wrist again, pulling her barefoot into the swamp.

"I hope a rattler gets you, Harrison," she said sweetly.

"The coral snakes are the deadly ones, I hear," he replied. He glanced back at her and smiled, showing gleaming white teeth. "They're small snakes and bite between the fingers—or the toes of barefoot people."

"I think that the snake might well worry about chomping into you," she said pleasantly. She was starting to tremble. She should have let Norm help her, and let Rafe help Norm.

They were moving deeper into the savage swamp. Trees and roots grew thicker, with vines tangled in the branches. Muck and mud were beginning to show in potholes. An occasional wild orchid dangled from the treetops. The earth seemed dangerously silent as the sky turned black overhead.

Harrison stopped very suddenly and Ashley crashed into his back. He swung around, taking her into his arms, bringing his lips down hard upon hers. She struggled against him and found he was surprisingly strong for his lean appearance. His hands might have belonged to an octopus; they were everywhere. He was tugging at her bikini top, and she was afraid that she was going to lose it at any second.

She managed to jerk her head aside. "Harrison, stop it!"

"Quit playing hard to get. I saw you looking at me when you were whispering. I saw your eyes. You want it, Ashley, and I'm going to see that you get it."

"You're sick."

"I can't stand it any more. I can't leave you again."

"Let me go, and I mean it."

He just wasn't listening. His arms held her tighter, bringing her flat against his health-spa toned chest. She gritted her teeth and looked up. "Let me go."

"Feel it, Ashley. Feel the storm in the air, feel the storm inside me. Feel the pagan earth beneath our feet. We were meant to be. We were meant to be—right now."

"We've been through this before! Now let me go!"

He didn't let her go. He tried to drag her down.

Ashley was growing desperate. She kicked him as hard as she could.

He groaned. His hold on her slackened, and she shoved him with all her might. He staggered, bending over, still moaning. Then suddenly he reached into his pocket and pulled out a pocketknife. He flicked it open and pointed the blade at her.

"Don't be a fool!" Ashley gasped, feeling stunned. Don't panic, she warned herself. She'd been in tough situations before. She'd been kidnapped and held at gunpoint once, when Tine Elliott had used her as a bargaining point to get his hands on Tara and Rafe. She hadn't panicked then and had come out of it okay.

"Harrison, if you stop this right now, I won't say anything, and nothing bad will happen. If you come near me one more time, I will accuse you of battery and rape. Do you understand me?"

"Get over here, Ashley." He was straightening up, his teeth clenched against the pain.

She felt the hair rise at her nape and goose pimples appear on her arms. "Harrison—"

"I can do things for you that you wouldn't begin to believe."

"Harrison—"

He took a step toward her. She didn't give a damn about being barefoot. She spun around fast.

But not fast enough. He caught her arm, wrenching her around. He forced her back against a tree, placing the blade on her throat, then lowering it to the valley between her breasts. He made a quick movement, slashing the bikini top. It fell to the ground. She kept staring at him, hating him. "I will prosecute you to the full extent of the law, Harrison Mosby."

"You do what you think you can. Not a man alive who saw you on that rock would call another guilty on a sexual charge."

"Rafe Tyler—"

"To hell with Rafe Tyler. Toss his name up to me again and you'll really be sorry."

He pressed the cool blade against her left breast and smiled. "Now, come on, Ashley, cool down. I know that you liked me when we met. I've thought of no one else since. You're a tigress, honey."

"Let me go."

"Not on your life."

"Someone will come looking for us soon."

He shook his head. "No, they won't. I told Gracie that you and I were going to dinner. No one will come, and no one will wait. And honey, if you want to get away from the snakes and other creepy things, you'll just have to lean on me."

"You're the creepiest living thing in this swamp, Harrison, and I'd walk the entire distance out of here on my own."

He was going to touch her, and she didn't think that she could bear it. She couldn't believe that she had sent Rafe and Tara away, and that this was happening to her. She had managed to survive in New York, and thus she had gained a false confidence. But now she was in a swamp with a treacherous storm brewing overhead.

"Ashley..."

His free hand closed over her bare midriff and inched toward her breast. There was a knife against her flesh, but she lost all sense of reason. She brought her hands up against his chest, shoving him and screaming.

He fell backward, flat upon his rear.

He stared at her with pure, murderous rage. Ashley didn't take long to think about it. She turned to run as fast as she could. Thunder cracked in the air and the clouds roiled dark and threatening.

"Ashley!" Harrison screamed.

She needed to get back to the clearing, to the crew. She had to reach them before they left her here with a storm and Harrison Mosby.

Suddenly the rain was falling. It didn't begin gently, with a soft pattering. It poured with a driving, blinding force.

Ashley tried to trace her footsteps back to the clearing. She pushed past trees and when something brushed against her, she shrieked, certain that a snake had found her.

She must have taken a wrong turn; she couldn't find the clearing.

She heard a loud sound. A loud snorting sound. Her heart thundered in a sudden panic. She knew the sound. It was the sound Henry had made.

There were alligators nearby.

She paused, fighting for reason. She pushed the wet hair from her face and blinked against the onslaught of rain. Blackness had descended. She could barely make out the trees before her.

"Help me!" she screamed.

Had the makeup and camera crews managed to pack up so quickly?

No. She could see people up ahead in the darkness. She heard a heavy splashing sound.

"Help me!"

She staggered forward. She wrapped her arms around her naked breasts and fell against a tree. She saw that there were three people in rain slickers standing near one of the deep canals. She couldn't tell if they were men or women.

She opened her mouth to call out again, but no sound came out.

One of the figures reached for another, dragged it to its chest, and produced a huge knife. She could see the blade through the darkness and the rain. But she couldn't see faces—their backs were to her. She just saw the slicker-clad forms and the blade.

One figure drew the blade against the other's throat. The body collapsed, just like a deflated blow-up doll. And the murderer very calmly tossed the body into the water of the canal.

A scream tore from her.

Suddenly the two remaining figures turned her way and stared straight at her.

The cold of the rain sliced through to Ashley's bones. Then thoughts rushed in her mind. She had just witnessed a murder. She could recognize none of the persons, but they could see her standing there, bedraggled and dressed only in the tiger-striped bikini bottoms and her Tyler jewels. She was nearly naked and dripping with emeralds. They would know her. . . .

One of them took a step toward her.

She roused from her shock and spun around. Gasping for breath, she turned to run again. The rain was beating on her so mercilessly.

She hated the swamp. And now she was racing through it, in a blind panic. She couldn't find her way. Her feet were sinking deeper and deeper into the mud, and the foliage seemed to reach out and grab her, trying to trap her. Sobs tore from her throat. She was growing hysterical.

She had to calm down. She had to think and reason, find the clearing, then the road leading away from the snakes and the alligators and the storm—and murderers who stalked their victims in the mud.

She fell against a tree, bowing her head against the rain, gasping for breath. She heard a snap behind her and pushed away from the tree. She started to run.

She suddenly found a trail beneath a row of pines. She tore down it, slipping, falling, rolling through the mud. She rose and ran again, keeping her eyes straight ahead.

But then she slipped again, crying out as she fell into the mud. She came up on her knees.

Then she saw the boots.

Someone was standing before her—someone wearing black, knee-high boots.

She allowed her gaze to rise to the thighs encased in tight denim, to the lean hips and a drenched colorful cotton shirt stretched across a broad chest. She looked up higher and brought her hand to her mouth, holding back a scream.

His hair was as dark as the night that had come with the storm. His features were hard, his jaw was set, but his mouth was full and sensual. He was a striking, powerful-looking man.

A man with piercing light eyes that stared down at her, offering no mercy. She stared back at him. She couldn't help but do so for his eyes held hers—and fascinated and haunted her. He was the most potentially dangerous man she had ever seen.

A murderer?

He reached down to her.

"No," she whispered. "Please!"

The rain fell on her, running over the curves of her bare breasts and down the line of her spine. The mud was rinsed off, and all that remained was a beauty. Like a supplicant, she remained kneeling before the tall dark man towering over her.

"No, please," she gasped.

Strong, dark arms closed around her bare flesh, lifting her from the mud. She wanted to scream, but her scream froze in her throat when she met his eyes. They were like the sea, startlingly alive during a tempest.

She started to struggle and realized she hadn't the strength.

"Stop!" he warned her.

She went still, aware that she could never break the steely band of his arms. She looked into his eyes, aware of their color, feeling the world swim around her.

"Don't... don't hurt me," she whispered.

"Hurt you? My God, woman, I'm trying to bring you in from the rain," he said irritably.

It was too much. Her eyes closed. The blackness of the storm consumed her, and she saw no more.

Chapter 2

Ashley felt as if she had come out of a thick fog only to be cast into a field whipped by wind and rain. She was running again, running for her life, down paths with tangled vines and roots. She tripped and fell and ran again. It didn't matter which path she chose; she always stumbled upon the same thing. Three figures, silent in the storm. And one figure produced a knife that flashed and glittered, and plunged it into the heart of another.

She ran. . . .

But she couldn't escape the vision.

Then she jerked up, a scream forming on her lips. She held it back just in time, realizing that she had awakened. There were no roots, no tangled vines around her, only muted shadows and darkness. The swamp was not real; she was dry, warm and wrapped in a cocoon of softness. Only the wind and rain were real, sounding as if all the demons of hell had been let loose.

The murderers were not real, not anymore. . . .

Ashley shuddered violently, then looked down. The softness she sat on was a queen-size bed covered with a luxurious deep-blue comforter and crisp white sheets. She was wearing a man's tailored shirt and underneath that . . .

Nothing, she discovered. Her sodden bikini bottoms were gone. The Tyler emerald pendant lay cold in the valley of her breasts, and she still wore the ring. But the bracelet and earrings were gone.

She turned, and in the dim light of the room, she saw the missing jewels. They flashed from a bedside table.

She swung her feet over the side of the bed and stood, glad to see that the tailored shirt fell well down her thighs. She looked around the room. There was a tall pine armoire and a handsome matching dresser with a brush, after-shave and other toiletries on it. Masculine toiletries.

Ashley drew in a sharp breath, remembering the man who had accosted her in the swamp. Accosted? No. He had helped her, hadn't he? He had brought her here, out of the swamp, out of the rain. A peculiar warmth snaked along her spine. This was his room, whoever he was.

She started to shiver. She'd never seen anyone like him, not with such ebony hair and striking green eyes. She'd never seen features like his—hard, proud, rigid, ruggedly masculine. They were also cold, betraying no emotion.

Were they the features of a killer?

"Oh," she murmured, shivering again. Where was he? Her tongue went dry. She had to get out of there, back to the city.

What light there was in the room filtered in through a partially opened door. There was another door, partially opened, too. Ashley tiptoed to the first doorway and saw that it led out to a hall—and to the rest of the house, Ashley imagined. He would probably be out that way. Perhaps the second door led to a back exit?

She tiptoed toward it, pushed it open, and discovered a modern bathroom. It was so dark that she could see little, but she could make out a huge whirlpool tub in front of a glass window. Some sort of shutters had been pulled down over the window outside. She moved closer, trying to see if there was any opening. She bumped her head on a towel rack and swore softly. This was not a way out.

Her heart started to hammer hard as she wondered anew about the figures in the swamp. She tried to assure herself that the man who had picked her up could not be one of them. Why carry her here? It would have been easier to murder her on the spot. Slit her throat clean through—

"Stop that!" she whispered to herself. She needed to slip out of the room, find a phone and call a cab. Or she could call the police. Maybe she could sneak by him. Maybe he wasn't even here. Maybe—

Stop with the maybes! she chastised herself firmly. She turned around, on her tiptoes again, and came out of the bathroom. She started across the room for the other door, then stopped, a scream in her throat.

He was there—leaning against the doorframe, arms crossed over his chest, watching her. He had been there for some time, she decided. She hadn't heard him at all.

She tried to swallow her scream, but it came out anyway—as a little squeak.

In the dim light, she thought that she saw him smile. He was dry now, too, in jeans and a long-sleeved denim shirt. His dark hair fell in layers that just brushed over his collar.

"How—how long have I been out?" Ashley asked.

"A while."

"Where . . . am I?"

"My house. Were you looking for something special?" he inquired politely. His eyes didn't leave hers. They didn't flicker over the length of her once. She had the feeling that he didn't need to look at her—he already had. And he hadn't been very impressed with what he had seen.

"A—a phone," she said.

"In the bathroom?"

"Er, lots of people have phones in their bathrooms," she said defensively.

He shrugged. Dark lashes fell over his flashing eyes. "Not in these parts, they don't, Miss . . . ?"

"Dane. Ashley Dane." She gave him her name hurriedly, then she quickly fell silent. What if he was the murderer? What if he just wanted her name so that he could go out and kill all of her friends, too?

That was insane! she told herself. She was letting her imagination run rampant, and if she wasn't careful, her imagination would be her downfall now.

"It doesn't matter," he said softly. "The phones are out."

"Out?" she repeated. She could be locked in with a murderer, and she couldn't even call for help.

"Out," he said, watching her curiously. His face was enigmatic. He was perfectly polite; his voice was low-key. She sensed that he didn't think very highly of her. "There's a storm out there, Miss Dane. A bad one. You shouldn't have been running around in it. Phones, electricity—everything goes off at a time like this."

With that he turned around and left her, walking down the hall. For several seconds she just stood there, frightened and confused. She shouldn't have been running around! Well, she hadn't been running around on purpose, what did he think? He hadn't even asked her what had happened! Could she have told him? He might very well be the murderer.

No. She determined that he couldn't be since he hadn't killed her, and he'd had ample opportunity. She ran after him, passing a few more doors along the hallway and then coming to a large room with stone walls, a fireplace, comfortable earth-colored sofas and carved wood side tables. A counter separated the huge living and dining area from the kitchen. Ashley knew that he had walked into the kitchen but she paused anyway, looking around.

Candles covered the tables and the counter, giving off a warm glow. She could hear the vicious cry of the wind and the slash of the rain. But here inside, she was safe. And the room, for all its size, was an inviting place. It was curiously decorated, however. There were western landscapes on the wall, and two striking sculptures made of etched buffalo skulls and feathers flanked the doorway. Little straw dolls adorned some of the tables, and a Navajo rug covered much of the hardwood floor. She turned around and nearly jumped, having discovered that he was leaning casually against the counter, and was watching her with his eerie silence once again.

She gasped, looking from the hard contours of his face to the decoration of the room. "You're an Indian!" she said, and then she wanted to bite her tongue because the words had sounded so bad when she hadn't meant them that way at all.

He didn't move, not really, but everything about him tightened—his jaw, especially—and his eyes seemed to take on an especially cold glitter. "Yes. How very observant you are, Miss Dane."

If he hadn't meant to kill her before, he probably wanted to do so now. She wanted to say something more, to explain, but he was already turning away from her with that disdain he had previously shown her. Undeserved disdain, she thought, and her temper soared. She was at his mercy, even if he wasn't the murderer, but she wasn't about to sit still for his attitude problems.

She strode to the kitchen and reached for his shoulder, spinning him around. She was glad to see the frown that furrowed his brow and the sharp narrowing of his eyes. She smiled sweetly. "You've a chip on your shoulder a mile wide, Mr.—sir. You've no need to take it out on me."

He picked up her hand from where it lay on his shoulder. Ashley knew he meant to drop it, but he didn't. His fingers curled over hers as he stared at her. She looked up into his eyes and a startling whisper of heat seemed to settle over her. She felt it first in her fingertips, felt it sweep through her limbs, then streak like laps of fire down the length of her spine. She should have pulled away from him. But she didn't.

There was very little space between them, and she felt that she really saw him for the first time. His skin was so bronzed it was nearly copper, and her own tan seemed pale next to his. His scent was clean and both rich and subtle, and so overwhelmingly masculine that she was aware of him as a man as she had never been aware of any other man before. She was fascinated by the square contour of his chin, the arch of his brows, and his eyes, so vividly green against his bronze skin. She was even aware of his breathing, faster now, like her own. She was aware of his heartbeat, aware of her own pulsing faster and faster with the sound of the wind and the rain, as if the earth itself had found a rhythm within her. Color mounted onto her cheeks.

They were alone. This man had carried her here. He had stripped away her sodden bikini bottom and he had dressed her in the shirt. He was a stranger who knew her intimately. He was a man who frightened and compelled her. She had felt his arms around her, and she had no doubt of his strength of muscle or strength of will. He confused her; he made her hot and breathless. She didn't know him at all!

Suddenly she jerked her fingers free, as if she had been burned. She pulled away, turning her back to him, staring over the candlelit counter. "I'm sorry. I'd just like to leave if I could, please."

"Leave?"

"Leave. If I can't call for a cab, I've some friends—"

"Phone for a cab!" he repeated incredulously. Ashley spun around indignantly. He was laughing at her, his perfect teeth flashing white in the candlelight. "Don't you understand yet? There's a killer—"

"A killer!"

"A killer storm out there, Miss Dane. Most of the people out here have moved into shelters. The phones are already out; the electricity is gone. The swamp is swollen, the canals are swollen, and I assure you, not even the gators are moving. There is no way out of here right now. No way at all."

"But—"

"Lady, this has become a full-fledged hurricane. Cara, that's her name, if you're interested."

"Cara," Ashley murmured. She couldn't stay here. Not with this man. Not after what she had seen. She needed to get to the police. She needed to get away from him. "But—"

"Can't you understand? There is a storm—"

"But it wasn't that bad when we came out."

"What it was before doesn't matter. If you'd had the sense to leave instead of running around—"

"Running around!" Ashley protested furiously.

He was reaching into his dark refrigerator, but he paused, turning to look her way with a brow arched in question.

"I was not running around in your stinking swamp!" she hissed.

He shrugged, pulled out a can of beer and hesitated. "Want one?" It almost sounded as if he begrudged her a drink! Ashley gritted her teeth and didn't answer him. She was starving; she was thirsty. She was miserable.

Damn him. Let him begrudge her to his heart's content!

She walked over to him and icily took the beer from his hand. "Thank you. Thank you so much for your charming warmth and hospitality. I'd like to thank you personally, but since you haven't bothered to introduce yourself, I can't quite do that."

He watched her. She thought that the hint of a smile tugged at his lips, but he didn't move, and he didn't speak right away. Then he reached for a second beer and popped the flip top. "It's Eric," he said.

"Eric?" She should have shut up while she was ahead, but his attitude had gotten to her. "Eric? It isn't Running Brave or Silver Arrow or—"

"Hawk," he interrupted her very softly. "Eric Hawk." He said it with tremendous menace.

Ashley went still, inhaling deeply. She walked back to the living room and sank down on the sofa. Her tailored shirt rose and she tugged the tails down. She swallowed several mouthfuls of the beer; her head started to swim instantly. She hadn't eaten for hours. She didn't even know if it was day or night. It had been such a long day. First she had been attacked by Harrison, then she witnessed the murder in the swamp. Then she had run into this brick wall of a man, and now she was stuck with him.

And he might be the murderer! He might be the very man she had been running from!

He was behind her again, she realized. She hadn't heard him move, she hadn't heard him come, but she knew that he was there. She swung around, her hair flying around her face and shoulders. She swept it back from her forehead, leaped nervously to her feet and stared at him. "What? What is it?"

He grinned at her. "Do you like your burgers rare or well-done, Miss Dane?"

"What?" she asked blankly.

"I have the sterno going for dinner. Hamburger it is, though, I'm afraid. How do you like yours?"

"Oh. Rare. Please."

He nodded and walked away. Ashley watched him go back into the kitchen. She hesitated a minute; then followed him. She didn't speak to him. She didn't offer to help, and he didn't ask for her assistance. She pulled up one of the bar stools and sat at the counter. The smell of the ground beef searing in a frying pan was irresistible.

"What time is it?" she asked him.

He shrugged. "Around midnight."

"Midnight!"

"Yes, around midnight," he repeated.

"Then—then I was really out a long time."

"Yes. I tried to find your friends, but they were gone. Some people do have the sense to get out of the rain."

Not all of them! Ashley almost said. But she couldn't mention the murder to him. Not when she still didn't know whether he was the murderer or not.

"My friends," she murmured. "So you knew about the shoot?" she asked him.

His gaze lifted from the frying pan to meet hers. "Yes. It was my land you were on."

"Oh." Absently she rubbed her earlobe.

"Your earrings are in the bedroom," he said sharply.

"I know."

"I thought you were imagining me a jewel thief."

"You do have a chip on your shoulder."

"Actually I haven't. I like everything that I am."

"Do you? I haven't known that many people who take pride in being hostile and rude."

He stiffened, and Ashley smiled sweetly. "I said rare, if you don't mind?"

He flicked the burgers out of the frying pan and onto a plate. His eyes were hidden in the shadows, so she couldn't tell if her remarks had angered him or not. She saw the bowl of salad greens on the counter, and he served that along with the hamburgers. Ashley kept her eyes lowered and thanked him.

"What were you doing running around in the swamp?" he asked her. "What were you running from?"

She glanced up. His eyes were so sharp, so piercing. She was tempted to reach out and touch him. She wanted to run her fingers over his cheeks and his jaw.

Except she was certain he didn't want to be touched. And she still didn't know anything about him. He had been in the swamp, too. He was probing her carefully. Maybe he just wanted to know what she had seen.

She answered with wide eyes and innocence. "You allowed Rafe to film on your property. You know what I was doing there—a commercial." To emphasize her words she reached into the V of her shirt and pulled out the emerald pendant. His eyes fell upon where it lay in the valley of her breasts.

He impatiently waved a hand in the air. "You know what I mean."

"Why should I? You're treating me like a featherbrain."

He hesitated, then bit into his hamburger and chewed. He was leaning over the counter. Too close to her, Ashley thought. Why was it that she became unnerved whenever he was near? He was rude and hostile.

He was also unlike any other man she had ever met. She liked his low voice. She even liked the way he moved in silence. She had liked the feel of his arms, muscles rippling, as he had picked her up in the swamp. He was tall and lean, but he was like steel. Yet he was warm to touch....

He was staring at her intently again. She swiftly reminded herself that killers were often very regular-looking people, even attractive.

"What were you doing in the swamp?" he repeated.

She sighed. "The director is not a friend of mine. He insisted on having a conversation. I didn't like the way the conversation was going. I ran."

His eyes flicked over her. She knew that he was remembering how she had looked when she had crashed into him. There was a certain amusement tinging his words when he spoke. "Maybe he didn't mean to... frighten you. Maybe he just got a little carried away himself. Maybe he believed that you needed 'nothing, nothing at all but the primitive earth and your Tyler jewels.'"

Ashley gasped and leaped to her feet. He had been there for the shoot, she realized. And he was assuming that because of it, Harrison had had a masculine right to attack her.

She tried to control her temper. But she had always thought—with remorse—that the saying about redheads having bad tempers was true. She just couldn't take the taunting remark.

She shoved her plate toward him with a vengeance. The china slammed into his and sent it sliding off the counter, right into his lap. Then it fell on the floor and broke.

Guilt struck her. She hadn't meant to cover him with his dinner. The plate had simply moved with great speed and violence.

He was looking down at the chopped beef and lettuce leaf that fell on his knees. Then his eyes came up to hers. Her throat went dry and her knees threatened to give. She fought for the return of some courage.

"I'm sorry. It's just that you have no right at all to make assumptions about me. You've been incredibly rude and hostile, and I don't deserve any of it!"

"I just said—"

"I know what you said! And I know what you've been thinking every step of the way!" Her temper was back.

She spun around, not sure of what she intended to do, but anxious to be away from him. She strode toward the living room, but she hadn't taken two steps before he was behind her and whipping her around by the shoulders to face him.

"*I'm* rude! You come crashing out of the bushes screaming for help and pass out in my arms. I bring you in out of the storm, dry you and dress you, feed you and offer you a safe harbor, and you call me rude!"

"Yes!" she flared, staring at him. "Yes! You just acted like . . . you acted like—oh, never mind! You wouldn't understand. You couldn't begin to understand. You don't have to offer me 'harbor'! I didn't come here to disturb you on purpose. And I have no desire to be here whatsoever!"

"You're acting like a featherbrain!" he told her furiously. "Don't you hear the wind and the rain?"

She could hear them raging and roaring. But she suddenly felt that the tempest outside was no greater than the one within her. She couldn't begin to understand the feelings that played havoc with her heart. One second she was shivering, wondering what manner of man he might be. The next second she was feeling warm, wondering what he would look like without his shirt, and what it would be like if he took her into his arms. She trembled, thinking that he would kiss a woman with fire and demand, that he would be fierce and tender, and that his touch would consume all thought and all reason.

She tried to jerk free from him. She could not. His powerful hands were fast upon her.

"I'm sorry," she said stiffly. "I really am. I just know that you don't want me here, and I'm trying to tell you that it isn't my fault at all."

He sighed deeply. "I know that it's not your fault. But there's nothing to be done about it, Miss Dane. Not now, not for quite some time."

Her teeth were chattering. "I'll stay away from you, all right? I'll just keep out of your way."

"Perhaps that would be best."

"Fine."

His hands dropped away from her, and he walked back toward the kitchen. Once he had turned, her courage came flooding back in a vehement stream. "Arrogant, red-skinned bastard!" she muttered beneath her breath.

He heard her.

He turned around very slowly and stared at her with a burning gaze. "Come here, Miss Dane. If you would be so kind."

She shook her head.

He arched a brow and spoke softly. "If you don't, you just might regret it all of your life."

Her pride somewhat salvaged her courage.

"Oh?" she said. "And just what will you do if I don't?" It was an outright challenge. She never should have issued it, not unless she was ready for the next battle, and she certainly wasn't.

His smiled deepened, his eyes narrowed. "Why, I'll scalp you, Miss Dane."

He took a step toward her. Panic surged through her, and she turned to run for the bedroom.

She realized that he was right behind her, running silently. Her pace quickened. She thought only of reaching the safety of his bedroom and slamming the door.

But the hallway was too short and he was too fast. She was just reaching the room, breathless and almost triumphant, when she was suddenly lifted off her feet. She landed flat on the floor with him on top of her. Her shirt rose high on her thighs and his denim jeans were rough against her bare flesh. She writhed and struck at him to free herself, but he caught her hands and leaned down close to her face.

"Get off me!" she charged.

His jaw twisted. "What the hell is the matter with you? I just wanted you to help me pick up the pieces!"

"What?" she gasped.

"I said—"

"But you came after me, as if you were assaulting me!"

He laughed suddenly. "The assault and battery was on my dishes. Did anyone ever tell you that you have a dangerous temper, Miss Dane?"

"You provoke it," she said quietly.

He started to smile, and she suddenly felt the anger and the fear within her drain away. His fingers were still wound around her wrists. He was straddling her, but he didn't hurt her—he held his own weight. She wished that they were still arguing. She was suddenly and keenly aware of her near nudity and his touch. She felt the heat and power of his thighs, and she felt the magic of his eyes.

Then he wasn't holding her at all anymore. His fingers threaded through her hair. He spread the thick, rich tresses out, his eyes a green fire of fascination as he watched his own handiwork. Ashley caught her breath, watching him in turn. She should protest but she couldn't. She was completely mesmerized by his hands upon her. She lay completely still, and again the desire to touch in return came to her. She wanted to stroke the hard and handsome planes of his face, to touch his ebony hair and feel the coarse strands against her fingers.

He moved his hand away suddenly, as if her hair really were fire and it had burned him. He straightened, and Ashley quickly pulled down the tails of the shirt.

He started down the hallway in silence.

She bit her lower lip in consternation, then got to her feet and followed him.

When she walked into the kitchen he was busy with a broom and a dustpan, picking up the mess.

"I'll do it," she said. "I caused it."

"It's already done."

"But I don't want to make you mad again. I, uh, I really don't want to lose my scalp."

He paused. He actually seemed to smile, his lashes falling over his eyes. Then he looked at her, and his smile deepened. "Miss Dane, that mass of red hair is glorious where it is. I wouldn't dream of denuding you of it." His gaze ran over her, from head to toe, lingering along the way.

Then he continued with his task. Ashley held still, startled by the compliment. She finally stepped forward and bent down to pick up the large pieces of plate. "Where's the garbage?" she asked him.

"In the closet."

She opened the closet door, found the trash can and pulled it out. He swept up the small pieces and dropped them into it. He turned away, walking toward the counter, and smothered the sterno.

Ashley stood still, watching him. Then she nearly panicked. Her breath caught in her throat; her heart beat like wildfire.

He turned toward her with a huge butcher knife. The razor-sharp blade glittered and shone in the candlelight. He took a step toward her.

He would never reach her. Her heart was beating so frantically that she thought she would simply drop dead, and he wouldn't have to kill her.

He took another step. Her scream rattled in her throat; it refused to burst from her lips.

"Could you hand me the dish detergent, please?"

"Wh-wh-what?" she gasped.

"The dish detergent." He tossed the knife into the sink and walked past her to the closet door. "I'll let this stuff soak in cold water," he murmured, picking up a plastic bottle of pink dish soap.

She was going to fall to the floor. She felt so relieved and so weak.

He set the soap on the counter and reached for her shoulders, holding her carefully. Concern narrowed his eyes.

"Are you all right?"

"I'm—" She paused, moistening her lips. "I'm fine. Just fine. Honestly."

"You look as if you've seen a ghost."

"No." She shook her head. "No ghost."

Her fear faded. His presence and his nearness were overwhelming. His hands fell from her shoulders, but he stayed there before her. They were very close again. He brushed her cheek with his knuckles. He reached out and picked up the emerald pendant that lay between her breasts. His fingers brushed her flesh, and sparks of fire and life seemed to leap in her. He studied the stone, and then his eyes rose to hers. "No insult intended, Miss Dane. You do wear emeralds—and the primitive earth—very, very well." His smile took away any edge to the words. He laid the stone against her, and again she felt the brush of his fingers, and a hunger, unlike anything she had ever known, swept mercilessly through her.

"I'm going to shower," he said huskily, turning away from her and picking up a candle.

"But you haven't any electricity. It'll be freezing," she murmured.

"I know," he replied pleasantly enough. "Excuse me. I don't wear hamburger meat and salad that well."

He disappeared down the hall. She realized that he was going to the room where she had awakened. It was his room. It was his shower.

She wandered into the living room and sat and realized that her teeth were chattering. She didn't know anything about him.

She wanted him.

She had never felt this way, so swiftly and so completely.

Ashley hugged her knees to her chest. For the life that she had led, she was innocent in many ways. She had always imagined that she would fall deeply in love, that she would marry, that she would have children. But she had always been careful, not stupid. She enjoyed the company of men, and she dated. But she hadn't become involved. She had been close to Tara, and she had seen the horror of her friend's involvement with Tine. Then she had been stunned to realize that her trusted employer would have gladly killed them all to better himself. Men were not proving to be very trustworthy, not in her world. If it hadn't been for Harrison Mosby, she wouldn't be here now.

She smiled. There was Rafe. She had liked him from the beginning, but she had known that Rafe had been for Tara and Tara had been for Rafe. They were both her very dear friends.

And it was thanks to them that she was stuck here in this storm with Eric Hawk.

She groaned and paced the floor. She had never been more miserable. She kept telling herself that Eric couldn't be a murderer—but she had seen a murder, hadn't she? Or had she gone absolutely insane out there?

Ashley suddenly stood dead still.

The rain had stopped. The wind had stopped.

It was over! she thought. The storm was over!

Ashley inhaled, thinking that she owed Eric some thanks and an explanation. But perhaps she owed herself more. She was in a situation that she couldn't control. She was terrified, and she was excited beyond belief. It was a dangerous brew, an explosive combination.

She wanted him.

She needed desperately to be away.

She didn't even have any clothing! she reminded herself.

That didn't matter. Surely he had a car or some other vehicle outside. She would borrow it. She would send him reimbursement later. And a thank-you note for carrying her out of the swamp.

But first she had to escape from him.

She started for the door and then remembered the earrings and bracelet. Rafe and Tara wouldn't blame her if they never got the jewels back. Rafe always cared for people more than he did for things, even if those things were priceless emeralds. But she was responsible for them. It would take her only two seconds to go back to the room and retrieve them.

Ashley ran along the hallway and entered the room. She could hear the shower going strong. She hurried over to the side table and picked up the bracelet, slipping it over her wrist. She put on the earrings, then paused.

There was a framed picture on the side table. She picked it up. Straining her eyes in the poor light, she saw there were four people in the picture, including a beautiful, petite blond woman who smiled broadly. She seemed to be in Eric's arms. Then Ashley realized that it wasn't Eric but a man who looked just like him. A brother or a cousin—they had to be related to look so much alike.

The other man in the picture was Eric. He was with a beautiful and exotic woman, with hair so dark it seemed to be a cobalt hue, so sleek that it was a satin blanket hanging over her shoulders. Her eyes were black too, and her features were striking. She was a full-blooded Indian, Ashley thought, and looked stunning with the pride in her eyes and a gentle, knowing curve to her smile. She was slim and elegant, full of laughter and full of love.

Ashley set the picture down suddenly as if it were hot. She felt she had intruded upon something. It wasn't the woman's smile that had gotten to her; it was Eric's.

He looked so different in the picture. No cynicism shadowed his eyes. He smiled with ease, with warmth, with an abundance of love, as the woman did.

Who was the woman? Ashley wondered. And why did the picture make her feel like crying? It was none of her concern.

She turned and fled from the room. It couldn't be any of her affair. She hated the swamp and the shoot was done. If the storm was truly over, she could fly home. At the moment, New York City, as crowded, dusty, dirty and crime-laden as it might be, seemed a haven of safety.

When she returned to the living room she glanced around for a set of keys but didn't see any. If he had a car, she reasoned, he probably left his keys in it. Who would come out here to steal a car?

The front door, however, was locked. There were two dead bolts on it, and both had been locked. She opened them and stepped outside, carefully closing the door behind her.

Everything was so deathly still.

She looked around, amazed at the destruction.

If Eric had a lawn or a car, she couldn't see it. Nor could she tell if there were canals nearby, or where there might be trees and where there might be saw grass. The whole panorama before her was green. Palm fronds and branches lay over everything and were ankle-deep on the porch where she stood several steps off the ground.

She wasn't going anywhere, she thought bleakly. Nowhere at all.

Suddenly she felt the breeze pick up. Her hair rose and curled around her face. She looked out at the horizon. A bolt of lightning suddenly zigzagged in a long and furious streak across the sky.

It was like a signal to the tempest. The wind rose in a shrill cry; the cold rain came back in an instant, beating upon her. Amazed, Ashley whirled around to go back into the house.

She didn't make it. The wind caught her at the midriff and pulled her down like icy hands. She screamed as she fell on top of the leaves and fronds at the base of the steps. She tried to rise, but the wind was too strong. It swept her around again, pulling her farther and farther from the house. She saw a tree and clung to it. The wind roared as if it had life, as if it had a murderous streak. Like an evil demon, it sought to tear her away from the tree and throw her out into the tempest.

She could scarcely hang on. Her fingers were frozen and almost numb. They would lose their grip any second, she thought. She couldn't hold on any longer.

She cast back her head and started to scream.

"Fool!"

Suddenly warmth surrounded her. Something hard and determined pressed against her back, and then strong arms were around her. She tried to turn, but she couldn't fight the force of the wind, or of the man.

"Come on!" His voice rose in command over the fury of the storm. "When I say move, move!"

She nodded, blinded by her sopping hair. His fingers curled over hers and he tugged her. "Now!"

She tried hard to follow him. But when she turned, her foot caught in a root, and she stumbled, falling with a scream. He caught her and lifted her into his arms. He braced himself and fought against the wind, step by step, heading back toward the house. They reached the porch. He staggered, then staggered up. He opened the door quickly, dropped her on the floor and caught the door before it could disappear into the grasping fingers of the wind. He slid both bolts. Then he fell down to the floor beside her, gasping for breath, soaked to the bone.

They both lay on their backs, panting. Only then did Ashley realize that he was wearing nothing but a big white towel wrapped around his hips. The wind had nearly managed to strip it away.

He turned to her. She saw the whole slick breadth of his chest, hairless and coppery and sinewed with muscle. She saw the furious set of his jaw and the cold green sizzle in his eyes. He reached out for her throat, and if she'd had the least bit of energy left she would have screamed.

"No!" she murmured. He meant to kill her, she was certain.

His fingers just lay against her flesh. "You *are* the worst featherbrain I have ever met in my entire life!" he thundered. His fingers crawled over her shoulder and he shook her with a vengeance. "Make a move toward that door again and I will scalp you! I'll skin you alive!"

He released her and stood with agility. He nearly lost the towel but it didn't disturb him. He wrenched it into place, then turned back to her, ready to yell again.

His words died on his lips.

Ashley realized that once again she was barely clad. Her shirt was soaked and torn open, revealing her breasts, and it had risen up to her hips.

She was clad in practically nothing at all....

Except for her Tyler jewels and the primitive earth.

Chapter 3

"I'll say one thing for you," Eric muttered darkly.

"What's that?" she murmured nervously, trying to pull down the tails of the sodden shirt.

His eyes fell upon her. "You're a beautiful featherbrain. Come on, let me help you." He reached down to her. She hesitated, then accepted his hand.

"I am not a featherbrain," she told him. "I have a college degree. I worked hard for it, too." What difference did it make? she wondered. She had tried to leave; she had failed. She was stuck in here with a man who might well be a killer.

"You could have fooled me. That was one of the most idiotic stunts I've ever seen."

"The storm had stopped."

"That was the eye! It hasn't stopped at all."

"Well, I know that now," she retorted.

He left her standing there, went down the hallway and returned with a handful of towels. He tossed her one, watching her with unabashed curiosity.

"Why?" he demanded.

"Why what?"

"Why would you be so desperate to get out of here that you would run barefoot and half naked right back into the storm?"

"I thought that the storm was over!" Ashley insisted, toweling her hair. He was walking around her in his soaked towel, heedless of the water that dripped to the floor. He circled her, like an inquisitor.

"But you were still willing to take off—barefoot—into the swamp," he said sharply.

Like a featherbrain, she thought resentfully. She didn't know if she wanted to hit him or run. She wasn't sure at all if the greatest danger lay in the storm—or in the man. "No," she said flatly. "I was planning—"

"Oh, wonderful!" he interrupted her, throwing his hands up in the air. "You wanted to steal my car."

Ashley looked at him, inhaling deeply for courage. Custer, she was certain, had not faced such a menace at the battle of Little Bighorn. This man was furious with her; he was like a keg of dynamite with a slow fuse. He crossed his arms over his chest. She inhaled again.

"I didn't mean to steal your car."

"Excuse me. You were going to take my car."

"I told you—"

"No, you haven't told me anything at all, have you?"

Her own temper soared and snapped, and no desperate reminder that he might be a murderer could do anything to control it. She exploded with a sound of fury, throwing her towel down on the ground and setting her hands on her hips. "I have to get out of here! Don't you understand that? You stop acting like a damned DA and leave me alone! Do you understand?"

"Do I understand." His black brows shot up in astonishment. "Listen, lady, I dragged you out of the swamp— twice. Now I want a few explanations."

He was walking toward her, and she found herself backing away, heading toward the kitchen. She turned suddenly and fled. When she reached the kitchen, she realized that he was behind her. She felt in the cold soapy water for the knife he had tossed there and faced him, braced against the sink, the knife raised high.

He had stopped short before her. He watched the knife not with fear, but with respect. He stared at her as if convinced that she was not a featherbrain but a complete maniac.

"What do you think you're doing?" he asked her calmly.

"Just stay away from me!" she insisted.

"You should never, never pull out a weapon unless you intend to use it," he warned her.

"Don't push me," she advised him.

"Put it down and tell me what the hell is going on."

"I—I can't."

He smiled and leaned back against the counter, watching her. "The storm could go on for another day. It could sit right on top of us and go on for two days, even three. The roads will be impassable for at least a week, I imagine. Even the canals will be clogged and swollen and dangerous. Can you hold that knife on me that long?"

No, of course she couldn't, and it had been foolish to dive for it, but he had scared her so thoroughly. She bit her lower lip, trying not to panic, trying to convince herself once again that he couldn't be the murderer.

She thought about it too long. One second he was as still as the calm of the storm, then the next second he was in motion, reaching for her wrist with the speed of lightning. She screamed as he caught hold of her, snapping her hand so that the knife went flying down to the floor where it clattered and glittered. She was pulled hard against him and her eyes widened and she gasped with shock—he had lost his towel in the maneuvering.

If he noticed, he gave his own state of undress no heed.

"Talk to me," he told her.

"I can't."

"You'd best!"

His breath warmed her cheek, and the heat and vibrant strength of the length of his body seemed to touch her with flames. She was terrified; she could barely stand, and she was painfully aware of every inch of him. His fingers were iron around her wrists. She even felt the pulse of his heart and had to wonder just where his beat began and her own ended. And most of all she felt his eyes on her.

"Talk to me! Now!" he insisted. She fell to her knees— and gasped. She found herself facing the very masculinity of him. Quickly he was down with her, still insistent. "Talk to me!"

She looked up at him. "Don't—don't kill me!" she whispered. And she was horrified by the other thoughts racing through her mind—that she wanted him to touch her.

"Don't kill you?" he asked incredulously.

"Please."

"Don't be absurd." A confused and rueful smile touched his lips. "I'm upset, but I'm not mad enough to kill. I was kidding, you know. I'm almost positive that the Seminoles haven't scalped a single soul since the last decade. And we were never known for skinning women alive. We were always much bigger on keeping our female prisoners captive than we were on murdering them."

She hadn't expected the light, easy tone from him, not after his fury.

Nor had she expected the soaring sensation of relief that filled her. It came to her so swiftly and completely that she lowered her head, and to her horror and absolute disgrace, she started to cry.

"Hey!" He took her into his arms, holding her so that she cried on his shoulder.

She was all too willing to bury her head against his neck, and he let her remain there for some time as she sobbed. Then she started to sniffle. He disengaged himself and without any awkwardness at all managed to rise smoothly, wrap his towel around him, then pull her to her feet.

Ashley, her pride shattered, wiped the tears from her cheeks. He helped her, finding a napkin to dab away the last of them. She caught his hand and the napkin. "I'm all right. Thanks."

He nodded. He didn't believe her. "Ready to talk yet?"

"I . . . never thought that you were going to scalp me or skin me alive," she told him.

"Well, that's a relief."

"I thought that you were going to stab me."

"Oh. Well, that's better, I suppose. Murder without tribal torture?"

His tone wasn't so light this time. She shook her head desperately. "I saw . . . I saw a murder."

He frowned and turned away from her. "Maybe we need a little stiff drink here," he murmured. He reached under the counter and came up with a bottle of Jack Daniel's Black. He drew two glasses from the cupboard, poured, and handed a glass to Ashley. She managed to smile. "Have you got any ginger ale?"

"Probably. And I'll bet I still have ice."

He fixed her drink, then sipped his own straight. He leaned against the counter, watching her. "Hang on," he told her. He set his drink down and walked off. A moment later he was back with a floor-length velour robe. He offered it to her. She started to slip it over her shoulders but he cleared his throat with a little smile. "You're soaked underneath, and that won't help. I hate to state the obvious, but I've already seen what there is to see, so you can ditch the shirt here. I'll even turn around like a perfect gentleman. We haven't been known for too much plunder or rape lately, either."

Ashley blushed furiously but he had already offered her his back. She knew that he meant what he had said and in that moment, she realized that she could trust him. She stripped away her shirt and wrapped the warm velour robe around her. It dragged on the floor and carried a pleasant scent—his soap or his after-shave, she wondered. She felt wonderfully comfortable and secure in it.

He turned around. He was still slightly amused, and it was the way she liked him best. She loved the gleam in his eyes and the very slight curl of his lip.

Except that it wasn't an amusing situation at all.

"I really did. I saw someone murdered."

"Who?" He picked up his drink and handed her the bourbon and ginger ale, then steered her toward the living room. He sat her down on the sofa and took a seat beside her.

"I don't know who," she told him earnestly.

"Then—"

"Honest to God, I'm not hysterical, and I'm telling the truth. I saw three people—"

"You don't know who any of them were?"

She shook her head. "They were in yellow slickers."

"How did you come about seeing them?"

She hesitated.

"Come on," he urged her. "Explain. Why weren't you with the Tylers?"

"Tara's baby. One more shot was needed, but Rafe and I didn't think Tara should stay any longer—"

"They're good friends of yours?"

"The best," Ashley said solemnly. "Why?"

He shook his head. "No reason." But there had been a reason, Ashley thought. "Come on. Tell me the rest," he said.

"There's very little to tell. I already told you about Harrison, and you already gave me your reaction."

He shrugged. "I said I understood how he might have gotten carried away. I'm not sure how many emeralds that ad will sell, but men across the country will be racing for cold showers."

"I wonder if that's an insult or a compliment, Mr. Hawk," Ashley said sweetly.

"It's a statement of fact, and that's all," he told her. "You were talking about a murder."

"Tara and Rafe left because of the storm and the baby. I stayed behind for the last take. Then Harrison said that he wanted to talk to me."

"So you just blithely went along."

"I didn't want to cause a scene. I had other friends there who might have tried to help me and Harrison could have hurt them."

"Hurt them. How?"

"In New York, when they wanted to work again."

"The almighty dollar, huh?"

"No. Survival, Mr. Hawk."

"You must really scrimp and save to survive."

"Cameramen do not make fortunes."

"Finish the story."

"I'm really trying. It's just that you really are capable of being one nasty—"

"Injun?"

"Mr. Hawk, I don't care if you're a spaceman!" Ashley straightened, putting all the distance she could between them. He could anger her so easily and so quickly. She didn't understand it. He came close, and then it was as if he wanted a wall between them, as if he purposely built barriers. "You've problems, sir."

"No, I don't," he murmured, his dark lashes covering his eyes, his head lowered as if he spoke to himself. "Except with . . . you."

He looked up quickly, as if he hadn't said the words. "All right, I'm sorry. What happened next?"

"Harrison got carried away in the bushes. I got away from him and started running. Then I saw them. There were three of them, all in slickers. Two of them were arguing with the one in the middle, I think. Anyway, the man to the left drew out a knife and stabbed the man in the middle. Then he threw him right into a canal."

"Then?"

She frowned, then shivered. "Then they looked at me."

"Who were they?"

"I—I don't know. The rain was coming down so hard. The victim's back was always to me, and I couldn't begin to see the killer's features. I ran. I ran and ran—and I ran into you."

"Why did it take you this long to tell me this?"

"Because . . ."

"Because I might have been one of them?"

"I have no way of knowing."

"Um."

Ashley swallowed some of her drink, deep in thought. She reached out suddenly to touch his arm, her face full of hope. "If I couldn't see them, then they couldn't see me, right?"

He hesitated. "If they were there, and you saw three figures, you can be sure that they saw you."

"How?"

"Unless they were completely blind, they would have seen a woman dressed only in a bikini bottom and those emeralds sparkling all over the place."

"Oh," she murmured, lowering her eyes. Then she stared at him sharply. "You said 'if'!" she accused him.

He shrugged. "Yeah. I said, 'if.'"

"You don't believe me!"

"There's a very bad storm out there, you know."

"So what?"

"So how can you be absolutely sure of what you saw?"

"Because I'm not blind! I'm telling you the truth, the absolute truth."

"I'm sorry, it just doesn't make sense. That's my property you were running around on. Most people would have been wary of the storm, and if they didn't have to be out in it, they wouldn't have been. Maybe—"

"There are no maybes," Ashley said stiffly. She grated her teeth. He didn't believe her, and that was that. She was a featherbrain to him. One who saw things.

"In the morning, things might look different."

"They aren't going to look any different, but you're not going to believe me no matter what I say." Ashley finished her drink and set the glass on the table. He was still watching her, still clad in his towel, still with the same dignity. "You've no right to judge me, you know."

"I'm not judging you. I just—"

"You've been judging me since you brought me here. No, you were judging me when you watched us shooting the commercial. I can wear a bikini and I happened to be modeling Rafe's emeralds, and so I'm a featherbrain."

"You're a featherbrain because you have a tendency to act like an idiot," he corrected her warily.

"I didn't know about the eye of the storm."

"You didn't know that this whole place could be dangerous, storm or no storm."

Ashley shook her head, and stared at him, her eyes as brilliant as the emeralds she wore. "No. None of that is true. You judged me from the very beginning. You assumed that I was a stupid, chattering fool because I was a model. And you assumed that I would be a prejudiced against you for being an Indian."

"I—"

"You did, deny what you like. Well, you're wrong. I come from New York City, and every kind of people live in New York. The United Nations meets there, you know."

"Does it really?" he inquired politely, settling back. "They haven't invited the tribe in yet, you see."

She smiled sweetly. "You, Mr. Hawk, are the bigot."

"The hell I—"

She didn't know what she was doing, but she reached across and caught his chin in her palm, squeezing his jaw. "Yes, Mr. Hawk, you, not I, are the prejudiced one. I didn't make a single judgment on you. Not a one—"

"Except that I might be a murderer," he said, freeing his jaw from her grasp. He held her hands tightly.

Ashley tossed back her hair. "That wasn't personal. You just happened to be in the swamp. While you—"

"Yes, do go on."

His eyes glittered, his tone was dangerous, and his fingers were warm and strong on hers. She didn't care. She lifted her chin. "You almost came right out and said that I deserved whatever I got from Harrison—because of a commercial! And, of course, I must be stupid. And I must be careless of others and crude because I have money, too. So before you ever got to know me, Mr. Hawk, you had me branded. I was a foolish, stupid, callous, rich girl. Right?"

He was smiling. There was a certain cynicism there, but still it was nice, and a warmth spread throughout her. She felt as if she had reached him—reached in and touched just a little bit of him.

"I made only one assumption," he told her.

"And what was that?"

Outside the wind raged and the rain poured down. But at that moment, she knew only the power of his eyes as he stared at her for a long time. Then he released her fingers and touched her cheek, and she didn't draw away. He smoothed back a tendril of flame-colored hair. "I just assumed that you were every bit as sexy and beautiful and sensual as the woman who was perched on that rock and totally destroyed my equilibrium."

Ashley smiled slowly. "Is that a compliment?" she whispered.

"The highest."

She thought that he was going to kiss her. That he would pull her against him, cradle her in his arms and kiss her.

And if he had, she wouldn't have protested. She wouldn't have been able to do so. She had studied the fullness of his mouth time and time again now, and she knew that his kiss would be instant wildfire.

And so little lay between them. If he kissed her, more could follow. She had ached too many times to stroke his shoulders. She had been fascinated by the ripple of his muscles, by his hard, lean belly, by the copper glow of his skin, so dark against her own. If he kissed her, more would follow, and she wouldn't protest. It wouldn't matter that she had spent all the adult years of her life taking the gravest care in every relationship, in learning to distrust, to search out the heart. None of that would matter, because it would be him. That she barely knew him wouldn't matter. She wanted him. She ached for him.

He did kiss her—but not as she had expected. He didn't draw her near. He sought out her eyes, then he leaned forward, and his lips just brushed hers.

Instant wildfire. The briefest caress, his lingering nearness, ignited deep yearnings within her. His fingers grazed her cheek and touched her jaw. They slipped around her neck, and he drew her close. His tongue traced the outline of her lips, then probed deeply into her mouth, and she was enveloped by the sweetness of the sensation. There was no hesitation about him. His fingers slid beneath the collar of the robe and over her shoulder, curling over the bare flesh of her breast, exploring the shape and weight and contour. His palm scorched her nipple, and she choked a cry of ecstasy.

He drew away abruptly. His touch ceased, his lips left hers. Startled, and suddenly ashamed, Ashley closed her eyes and leaned back.

She had known that he thought little enough of her already. She should never have allowed this.

Eric stood and looked down at the woman on the couch. A fierce shudder suddenly went through him. He'd never seen anyone more beautiful in his life, but it was more with Ashley Dane. He'd never seen anyone more sensual. The sound of her voice was in his head, in his soul and body.

Maybe it was her hair. As red as fire, long, thick, a fascinating and feminine cape about her shoulders and face. Maybe it was her eyes, so darkly lashed, so emerald. Her skin was fair and slightly tanned. She had no freckles, just a smooth, perfect complexion. All of her was smooth and perfect. Her breasts were full and firm, the flare of her hips was as evocative as the rounded firmness of her derriere. And her lips...

They were moist from his kiss. From the contact that had left him shattered and barely in control—and hating himself and hating her even more.

His wife had been dead for a long time now. Almost four years. And it wasn't as if there hadn't been other women since.

But he had never seen their faces. Never.

Certainly not as he saw Ashley Dane's. She drew out every primitive ache and longing inside him. She touched his senses and his soul. She was like a perfect angel cast down from the heavens.

Not an angel. A tormenting little witch. One covered in emeralds and dripping with wealth and savvy and he sure didn't need to be touching her. She needed to be back in New York City. She didn't belong here in the swamp. She didn't know the swamp, its people or wildlife, and she could never appreciate its beauty.

He shouldn't touch her. He would get burned.

"My room is yours," he told her curtly. "You may as well get some sleep. I'll be in the guest room if you need me, but I really can't see why you would."

He turned around and left her. He didn't see her eyes open wide with shock and hurt. He didn't see anything at all as he walked blindly into his office, slammed the door and cast himself down on the couch.

He didn't see....

But he still felt her. He stretched out his fingers, closed them and stretched them out again. And still, he felt her. He felt her breast, heavy in his hand, felt the pebble-hard peak of her nipple, the very softness of the silky skin surrounding it. He felt her cheek, her face, the slope of her shoulders, and whether he opened his eyes or closed them, memory taunted him.

She had been so cold when he had carried her here. He had tried to warm her. After he had assured himself that she breathed and that her heart beat, he had cleaned away the mud and stripped off the soaking bikini bottom. He hadn't meant to pause, but he had. She had looked very beautiful and perfect, and she had somehow seemed as pure and sweet as well.

Angelic . . .

An angel, yes, perfect and pure, and so enticing that the whisper of her breath haunted his soul mercilessly. She had lain upon his bed, and all of her had been more glorious than anything created on earth.

God had created that beauty, he had thought.

Maybe, just maybe, he had hoped that she would be vain and callous and shallow.

It might have been guilt. Because he really had thought that she was more beautiful than any other woman he had ever seen, including his wife. Maybe he had determined to dislike her from the very first.

He rolled over, groaning. She made him think, and he hated to think. He hated to remember love.

Eric lay there in the darkness and breathed softly for a long time. Then he rose and went out to the living room. He picked up a candle and carried it with him into the kitchen. He dug beneath the counter until he found the Jack Black. He reached for a glass, shrugged, then just swallowed a whole fiery gulp straight from the bottle.

It felt good going down. It warmed the part of him that had grown cold.

It eased the parts of him that had knotted with lust and desire and yearning.

He turned around at last and carried the bottle into his office. He closed the door, tightened the towel around his hips and lay back on the sofa. He stared into the darkness and frowned.

Her story couldn't be true. She believed it herself, but it just couldn't have happened. No one would have been out in the swamp in the storm.

Not an Indian, not a white man.

He sighed. It didn't matter; there was nothing he could do. It would still be some time before the downed wires were fixed, before the roads were cleared.

When the rains stopped, he would see what he could find.

In the meantime, it seemed to make some good sense to drink himself to sleep.

All through the night, the wind howled.

Ashley lay awake for a long while, listening. Sometimes it seemed that the wind and the rain would destroy the house, but the building always stood firm. Ashley reflected that Eric Hawk would not be here if his house hadn't been built strongly to weather the elements. Just as he would weather them himself.

She twisted, wishing that she could sleep, wishing that she had never allowed him to kiss her. She wasn't accustomed to feeling so miserable. Nor was she accustomed to being the one doing the wanting. She'd been hurt one time, but she had weathered it well. She knew how to take care of herself. Perhaps her life was easy now because Tara was her best friend and the shadow of Rafe's power fell her way. Life was charmed, but only to a certain extent. She was still independent, and she still had the Harrison Mosby types to deal with, and she still had attitudes like Eric Hawk's to deal with.

She gave up trying to sleep while listening to the fury of the wind. Swinging her feet over the side of the bed, she stood and walked back to the little table. She picked up the picture again and wondered about the woman with the long black hair. Who was she? His wife, his friend, his lover? All of the above?

The woman meant something to him. A chill passed over Ashley's heart, and she was suddenly convinced that the woman was dead. If not, she would be here in this room, not Ashley.

Curious, she picked up a candle and walked over to the armoire. She hesitated, then opened the pine door and looked in.

It was as she had expected. The closet was filled with a woman's clothes. Ashley gently touched the shirts, blouses and skirts. There was an array of styles. Denim jeans and T-shirts, attractive dresses and a beautiful sequined evening gown.

The colorful clothing of the Seminole nation was there, too. Beautiful beaded blouses and skirts, with bands of red and yellow and black—striking and typical.

In the rear of the armoire, Ashley found a gown in a clear wrapping. It was a wedding gown, an antique one, more cream than white from age. It combined the elegance of European fashion with Indian beadwork. It was one of the loveliest things Ashley had ever seen.

"What do you think you're doing?"

She almost dropped the candle as she spun around, so startled that she cried out softly.

He was there again, standing in the doorway, his hands on his hips.

He was wearing a pair of jeans now, but his feet and chest were still bare. She couldn't see his face, but she knew that it was filled with fury.

He strode into the room with such purpose that she cried out again, jumping out of his way. He didn't come near her, though. He slammed the armoire door shut.

"You've no rights here!" he lashed out suddenly.

Ashley sniffed the scent of Jack Black in the air. She backed away from him, wishing that she had never met him. "I didn't mean any harm."

"You're a snoop!"

"I wasn't snooping!"

"What were you doing?" he demanded.

"Looking! Just looking."

"What—"

"All right! I was trying to figure out why you act like such a complete bastard!"

"Why, you . . . !" he muttered. Then he added with a bitter growl, "You had no right to look in there."

"You have no right in here!"

"It's my room."

"I'm a guest," she declared.

"An uninvited guest."

"A guest, nevertheless. And you're drunk."

She still couldn't see his face. The candle was shaking in her hand, the shadows in the room were spinning crazily, and all the while, she could hear the wind increasing again. The storm was raging with an even greater force.

He was watching her tensely. "Didn't you know? That's a big problem out here. We have a lot of alcoholism."

"You're not an alcoholic," Ashley retorted. "You're just trying to ruffle me. You like to disturb and upset me, and I'm not at all sure what I did to you to deserve it." She was trembling, and she didn't know why. He hadn't even touched her. He stood his distance, but she was so acutely aware of him there that it hurt. She wanted him to leave.

And she wanted him to stay. She wanted to demand to know just what hold he had over her, and she wanted to tell him that she was sick of his temper and his attitude and that she didn't want anything to do with him. He was right—this was the swamp, and he was part of the wilderness, and she hated the wilderness.

"What you did to me?" he repeated. She thought that he smiled. She thought that there was a flash of green fire within his eyes. "What didn't *you* do to me?" he said.

"What?"

Suddenly the candle was snatched out of her hands. The holder rattled as he set it upon the table, and the soft glow fell upon him. His dark hair fell over his forehead. The hard planes of his face were filled with a fascinating tension and his lips were curled into a sardonic, haunting smile.

Then she saw his face no more.

He snuffed out the flame with his thumb and forefinger.

He reached for her, pulling her against him in the darkness. His voice was husky, his body seemed to be an inferno. "Come here, Miss Dane, Miss Ashley Dane. I'll show you exactly what you've done to me."

Chapter 4

His arms went around her. She felt his lips come down
hard on her own, felt the moist heat of his tongue as it
seared past the barrier of her teeth to delve deep within her
mouth, bringing into her the very soul of his passion and
longing.

The darkness was a sweet deliverance, allowing her to
yield to her own desires, to give to him in that first kiss all
that he demanded. Liquid heat invaded her and she trembled. It was only the strength of his arms and the power in
his lean body that kept her from falling.

The wind was with them once more. It lived inside her—
wild, tempestuous, heedless of the night. She felt its pulse
and its strength. She cried with the wind's abandon. She
didn't understand him, she didn't understand the night, but
she was glad and reckless.

She could no more deny what burned within her than she
could deny that the wind did swirl and rage. They were both
its captives perhaps.

His lips broke away and his eyes met hers, and she realized that the darkness was not so complete that she couldn't see something of the man. She saw the blaze in his eyes, and she realized that there was fury in them, that he didn't want to want her.

But she saw, too, the anguish and the hunger. She opened her mouth, wanting to protest. She never spoke, for his lips closed upon hers again, and it wasn't the anger she felt at all, but the force of a need beyond time and place.

She was in his arms, lifted high, then brought down on the bed where she had lain before, only now she was so much more aware. The sheets were fresh and cool...or else her body was hot. Her mouth had gone dry and her limbs felt weightless as she lay there waiting.

She heard the hiss of his jeans zipper, and she tried desperately to tell herself that now was the time to stop before it was too late. He barely liked her; no, he despised her, but he would leave now if she asked him to.

He didn't despise her. He waged war with some past devil, she thought, and it was because of her tonight that he had been waging his war with a bottle of Jack Black. She needed to reason.

He stood over her.

She wanted nothing of reason, not tonight. In the dim light she could see him—whipcord lean, coppery dark skin as smooth and sleek as metal. Muscle rippled in his shoulders, across his chest and his belly. Not a single hair marred the golden expanse of his chest, while below, at his groin, there was a thick ebony profusion of it, a nest for his maleness, pulsing now, aroused, raw and exciting. She felt her breath catch, and she looked at his eyes. But shadow covered him now, and she couldn't see his face.

There was still time to protest....

His hands fell on the robe's sash and she couldn't speak. Her lips were slightly parted, they went dry and she had to wet them with her tongue. She remained still, watching his long fingers as they untied her simple knot and moved aside the velour. He stared at her, then drew her against him, and she felt the raging fever of his body. She tried to hold him, but he was pulling off the robe with impatience. Then she was down again and he was straddling her. He was as magnificent naked as man could be. She knew that he watched the emeralds she still wore sizzle their green fire against her bare flesh.

A deep, harsh cry escaped him. It seemed to come from the very earth and was older and deeper than time. She knew at that moment that she would never deny him. She didn't understand him, but she could feel him and all of the things inside him.

She kept her eyes on his as he reached out and brushed his palm over her nipple. He enveloped her breast, then his fingers closed upon the peak. She caught her breath again, seeking not to cry out with the sensation. His left hand came upon her, too, and he covered both breasts and touched each hardened peak until she couldn't bear it any longer and a cry broke from her lips. Then he bent his head toward her. He caught the pendant between his teeth and tossed it aside. His tongue drew a burning path in the deep valley there and where his hands had lingered. Moisture formed around her breasts. His hand caressed their fullness, his lips and teeth and tongue closed around the buttoned peak, nipping, suckling. Ashley dug her fingers into his hair. Whispers tore from her, words that had no meaning.

Small, sweet fires broke loose inside her. Flames that teased and tormented and raced like the wind. Deep within, the flame took root. She arched against him, gasping. She felt the pulsing length of his maleness against her bare belly, and that made the fires race more fiercely. They reached the juncture of her thighs, the very core of her desire. She gasped softly. His hands roamed free, curving over her breasts, her hips. She, too, made an eager exploration. Sensation soared like lightning from her fingers as she stroked his flesh, marveling at the smoothness of his shoulders, the ripple of muscles on his chest and the strength of

his back. He swept his lips over her midriff and down below, taunting her belly. His hands, large, fascinating, exciting, moved up and down the length of her thighs, then
swiftly parted them.

His eyes were upon hers, but she couldn't meet them as he
rose over her again. Her lips went dry once more and she felt
that she ceased to breathe. He stroked the downy red triangle between her legs.

She felt his fingers deep inside her, exploring, demanding.... Her eyes flew to his and she saw the fascination
within them. Her lashes fell to shield her own secrets as a
moan of sheer ecstasy burst from her. She tried to rise but
he fell against her, holding her to his leisure and his exquisite play. His lips found hers. Then the fiery thrust of his
body replaced his taunting touch. She shuddered and cried
out again, stunned by the sheer impetus of him and quivering with sensation.

The wind had ceased, or so it seemed. The world had
ceased to revolve. There was only one thing of which she was
aware, and that was the power of this man, joined with her
in their intimate lock.

He held still, holding her lips to his, stroking her breasts,
grazing her throat with the tip of his tongue.

And then he moved.

The wind began to whip again beyond the harbor of their
bed, and then within it. The rain came down, slashing with
fury against the walls. Ashley didn't stroke his back or run
her fingers through the hair that had so fascinated her. She
clung to him. Each thrust touched her with a little lap of
fire. She trembled in his arms, and husky gasps escaped her,
until the gasps became cries, and she didn't recognize the
sounds as coming from her. She didn't realize that she
arched and writhed and twisted, finding him more necessary than the air she breathed. Without him, she thought,
she would die. The flames burned brighter between her legs.
Then they rose high, burst and cascaded down all around
her. She'd never thought that such sweet ecstasy really ex-

isted, that the body could reach such heights. She held him and felt him still. Eric groaned, going tense and rigid. Then he shuddered and fell beside her, groaning softly again. He pulled her against him, his fingers playing gently with her hair. They heard the wind again, and they were silent together. The silence stretched on.

Ashley closed her eyes and bit her lip. Her body grew cold, and she longed to cover herself, but she didn't dare move. There was so much to be said, and yet she couldn't say anything at all. She opened her mouth, but words wouldn't come, and so she kept still, all the while feeling colder.

How, she wondered, could anything so beautiful have become so horribly awkward?

The seconds ticked on. The wind continued to moan and howl. She tried to turn. Her hair was caught beneath him.

"Eric?" she murmured tentatively.

He didn't respond. Ashley carefully tugged her hair. She pushed up on an elbow, searching out his features.

His eyes were closed. He hadn't noticed that she had moved. She took the opportunity to study the man she barely knew, the man with whom she had just made love so intimately. She should be ashamed of herself, she thought. But she wasn't. Through all of her life she had been careful and distant, but something about Eric Hawk had enticed her beyond reason, and because of that, it had to be all right. Maybe she had known that making love wasn't necessarily like this; her previous experience had certainly left her untouched. Maybe that was why she had waited, and why everything now seemed like a touch of heaven.

She was tempted to reach out and touch him, but she didn't. She just looked at the way his black hair fell over his forehead, and she gazed at the high, broad planes of his cheekbones and the long, straight line of his nose. She liked his mouth—in repose, when he smiled, when he laughed, even when he was angry.

And she was fascinated by his body. She loved the sleek feel of his flesh, the hardness of him, the ripple of his muscle beneath her fingertips. She loved the leanness of his hip and the sinewed length of his legs, and she loved the very part of him that made him so intensely male, so demanding, so combustible. She probably shouldn't be studying him so. . . .

She glanced back to his eyes, and she saw in the dim light that they were open, that they glittered upon her. "Anything different?" he asked her with a long drawl.

She stiffened. He was going to ruin something that had been special and precious to her. She wouldn't let him. "Different from what?" she demanded.

"From the men you're accustomed to," he said huskily.

"What men am I accustomed to?"

"White men," he said flatly.

Ashley tossed her hair back and sat up, throwing her feet over the side of the bed. She spoke with her back to him. "Yes. You're incredibly insensitive and rude. Are those special traits?"

She started to rise. She gasped, startled, when his fingers caught her hair. He released her as quickly as she cried out, but she was already down on the bed once more and he was leaning over her. She expected some awful flare-up of his temper but that wasn't what she received at all. He studied her with his eyes and stroked her cheek.

"I'm sorry. I didn't mean to hurt you."

"Physically?" she asked softly. "Or with the barb of your words?"

"I didn't mean to hurt you," he repeated. "It's just that—"

She stared at him in the dim light, wishing that she could see more. But she knew that what she wanted to see lay inside of him, and no light would help her see that. Only he could allow her the vision she wanted, but he wasn't about to.

"Just what?" she whispered.

"You're different." The words were tender. "You're very different from what I'm accustomed to, and I'm not doing well, am I?"

He didn't wait for an answer; he didn't want an answer. He lay down, turning his back to her. Ashley listened to the wind and to the steady beat of the rain. The tempest was dying again. And she was colder than ever.

"Eric?" she murmured. She rose and looked at him, then sank back down, not sure whether to be furious or perplexed.

He was very definitely sleeping.

Ashley shoved him, grabbing the covers. She plumped up her pillow and in the darkness she wondered how on earth she had begun her day that she had wound up here tonight. She should get up and leave him and go elsewhere.

But she didn't seem to be able to do so. She hadn't the energy. She hadn't the will.

Then he moved. His hand landed on her stomach, then his fingers curled around her midriff and he pulled her against him. The soft rush of his breath moved over the top of her head, ruffling her hair. She lay still, feeling how his fingers fell just beneath her heart.

He slept on, and she gritted her teeth, innately aware that it was the woman in the picture he held so warmly and so gently. She definitely should move.

But he sighed then, deeply. His fingers moved gently upon her, and he drew her even closer.

"Eric," she whispered. Tears filled her eyes. She didn't want to be here. She was being used, she thought. She, Ashley Dane, who could turn any man down sweetly, coolly, determinedly, with great sophistication, whatever the occasion demanded. This man had used her—and used her still. She had to get away from him. It hurt.

But she didn't move. Something told her that maybe it was good for them both, and so she stayed. For a long time she remained awake, looking up at the darkness, seeing patterns on the ceiling. She refused to give up the taste of heaven. He couldn't hurt her, not unless she let him.

She shivered suddenly, listening to the rain. A man had been killed out there today. Or a woman. Eric hadn't believed her, but she knew what she had seen.

And the murderer had seen her, perhaps recognized her. She hadn't thought about it all. She had forgotten the events in the swamp when she had been in Eric's arms.

Then she knew why she didn't move away. She felt safe with him. Even if he had stripped away the rapture and the fantasy, she still felt safe.

The rain beat on. Ashley prayed that it would stop. Then, with tears scalding her lashes, she prayed that she would be able to go home, to escape the swamp and the fear and the man by the next day.

Especially the man. His effect on her was more disturbing than everything else.

Eventually light from outside began to seep in through the shutters into the room. Only then did Ashley sleep. It was morning. And with it would come freedom.

Eric awoke with a splitting headache. He knew that he opened his eyes in his own bed. His mouth tasted like turpentine; it was dry and sticky and awful, all at the same time. He thought that the wind was still swirling, then he realized that it was only in his head. Even the rain, it seemed, had stopped.

He tried to move—and groaned. He hated himself for the way he felt. He'd been no more than twenty the last time he had imbibed so freely. No, that wasn't true. After the shooting he had drunk himself clear into oblivion on a few occasions. But he had lived in a haze then, in the midst of a nightmare. Thanks to his family, and especially Wendy, he had survived. He'd learned to care again—about his writing, about his heritage. There had been very bad months when he'd lived in total reckless abandon, not caring if he died. But that had been over three years ago now. He knew that he mattered, that the things he had done mattered.

But last night . . .

He stiffened and realized that he was not alone in his bed. He turned around and found that she was still beside him. She slept sweetly, silently.

Her breath escaped from slightly parted lips. She lay with the covers just below her breasts, the curve of her body revealed beneath the white sheet. Her hair fanned out in a burst of flaming color. It curled over her breasts and framed the perfect shape of her face. Redheads were supposed to have freckles, he thought, but she had none. She did have green eyes. Enormous green eyes, dazzling green eyes. They were closed now, but he would never forget their brilliance. He would never forget anything about her.

Damn, he wanted to forget. . . .

But he never would.

From the moment he had first seen her, first heard the whisper of her voice, he had felt the overwhelming draw. He had trembled to touch her, and right or wrong, that touching had been inevitable. Now he was tempted to draw away the sheet, to reach out and feel the warmth of her breast, to savor the lushness of its feminine fullness. His body grew hot and tight, and he quickly looked away from her, wincing, willing his body to forget her.

Never.

What the hell was she doing in his life! he wondered furiously. He didn't want her. She was a contradiction in every move and word. Her sensuality was bedazzling; her honesty was a slap in the face. She had played no games with him; she had walked into his arms as sweetly as an angel. . . .

An angel from New York City, he reminded himself. A woman in business with one of the richest men in the world. A woman who had traveled the world, who could have anything at all. A woman entertained by him, he well imagined.

Never to be his. Not really.

His fingers clenched and unclenched. He didn't want her to be his. He had known once what it was like to love and hope and dream with a woman who loved him, who lived for the times they spent together, who dreamed with him of a better world and a better time in which to raise their children. He could never have her back again. With her gentle laughter and quick smile and earth-warm loving, she was gone. She would never come again.

Ashley Dane. Even the name sounded big city. Like a high-fashion model. Like someone with lots and lots of money, dripping in jewels ...

Dripping in emeralds. They sparkled now in the daylight. Green fire lay against her hair where it dangled from her ears. It shone from her wrist, from her fingers. It dazzled there against the rise of her breast, next to the rose-colored peak.

He didn't want to touch, but his fingers were already moving. He touched the cold stone, then the warmth of her body. Fire seemed to singe him, sizzling down the length of him. He wanted her more than he had ever wanted her before. Now he knew that she could be an angel, breathing life into him, crying out with surprise and pleasure, arching to his touch, writhing beneath the rhythm of his hips. Now he knew how her breasts could swell in his hands, how his touch could bring her hot and moist and make her want him in return....

He drew his hand away from her, gritting his teeth, swallowing hard, as if he could swallow down the rise in his anatomy. Damn her for stumbling half naked into his life, for tearing him to pieces with this desire. If he thought that he could wake her rudely and have his fill of her, he might have done it. But something warned him that that wouldn't be the end of it.

That would only make him want her more.

She was a sultry temptress and an angel all in one. Peaceful and pure in sleep, sensual in movement. And whenever her eyes looked at him, it was with a shimmering, dazzling light to vie with the sun.

A borrowed angel, at best, he reminded himself sourly. And he had already borrowed her. A shower was in order. He was not a slave to his wants and desires, and he would walk away without touching her again.

Cursing and furious with her and with himself, he got up.

He showered in the icy water for a long time, then dressed in jeans and a polo shirt. Coming back into the bedroom, he saw that she still slept. She had not moved. He tensed and his body went hot again. Swearing soundly beneath his breath, he turned around and strode out of the room.

He had to get rid of her.

He hurried to the front door and flung it open. The wind and rain had stopped. The sky, though, was gray. The destruction before him was complete. Each plant in his yard had been ripped from the ground and tossed everywhere.

He walked outside carefully. Storms could toss up some mean snakes, too. He stepped over the debris and looked out to the road and the canal. He couldn't even see the road, and the water had risen very high. If he was lucky, maybe he could make it as far as Wendy's house in a day or two.

No one was going anywhere that day.

He muttered an expletive and stomped back to the house. He had always loved the solitude he found there. Today, though, he despised it. Solitude was only good when he was alone. This wasn't solitude anymore.

He made coffee, almost cracking the pot as he set it over the sterno burner. He closed his eyes and started to breathe slowly. It's what his grandfather would have told him to do. Close your eyes and remember that for all men, there was a greater purpose. Peace did not come from without; it came from within.

He opened his eyes. At the moment he was convinced that his grandfather was full of rot. He had no peace inside himself whatsoever.

With a sigh, he poured himself a cup of coffee. The storm had moved on. Maybe it would return—hurricanes had been known to double back on places where they had already done destruction—but right now he desperately wanted some daylight.

He went to his office, opened the shutters and looked out the window. He had always loved it here. He loved the tall grasses and the cranes and egrets and great herons. He loved the sunsets that stretched on for eternity. The Everglades wasn't for everyone. It was a wild and lonely beauty. It was his heritage, and the swamp had shielded his people when nothing else could. Though peace had failed, though war had failed, the swamp had endured. The Indian had never been removed from the Everglades, and he still had his tenacious hold here on the land. In the nation of greatest plenty on earth where political refugees flocked, the Seminole still fought to be an ordinary citizen. Eric believed in the future. Change came slowly, but he believed it came. Wendy had taught them all that men and women were all alike. His white mother had fallen in love with his Indian father and they had combined their dreams of happiness. It was a good world, a good fight, and he loved it.

It was all that he had.

He sat down with his coffee, smoothed back his hair and picked up some of the research notes that Wendy had left him last week. His eyes strayed to the mantel and the pictures there. Wendy and Leif, hugging and laughing, in the airboat. Wendy and Leif, Eric and Elizabeth, together. Then there was the newest picture—Wendy and Brad and Josh. Brad the proud father, Josh a beautiful baby, and Wendy looking beautiful because she was always beautiful, inside and out. Eric smiled slowly, and his eyes touched upon Josh's face. He knew that he was as much an uncle to Brad's son as he would have been to his own brother's. Love was always the tie that bound men, not blood.

"May I have some coffee?"

The soft words startled him so badly that he rattled his cup against his desk.

She was dressed in his robe again. She'd been in the shower. Every trace of makeup had been washed away and her face was even more beautiful without it. Her hair was wet and slicked back and her ears were stripped of the emeralds.

Her eyes, though, still dazzled. Just like jewels.

Eric stretched out a hand, grudgingly indicating that she should take the swivel chair in front of his desk. "Yeah. Yeah, I'll get you some," he told her.

She sat, folding her hands in her lap. He walked into the kitchen and poured her coffee, then realized he hadn't asked her how she liked it. Black, he decided. If she wanted sugar and dry creamer, she could come back for them herself.

He walked back to his office with the coffee and handed it to her. She nodded without looking up at him, her fingers closing around the cup. Long, elegant fingers. Her nails were glossed with a fiery orange-red color that complemented her hair.

He remembered those nails, never hurting as they raked over his flesh, bring him alive. He remembered those elegant fingers stroking his shoulders, clinging to him....

"There's sugar in the kitchen," he said curtly, walking behind his desk. "Help yourself."

She didn't move. Her gaze rose to meet his at last. "The wind has stopped. Can I get out of here today?"

He shook his head. "No."

"Why not?"

"There's just no way. The roads are flooded. Power lines are down."

"Oh."

She stood and started to wander toward the open window. The V on the robe dipped low. It wasn't her fault. It was just that the garment had been made for a man, not a woman. She was tall, so it didn't hang ridiculously, but watching her move was still the most disturbing thing that he had ever seen.

"It's beautiful out there," she murmured.

"What?" he snapped. Sitting behind his desk, he swirled around. She had her hand on her throat and was staring out at the endless sea of grass. She didn't look his way, and he wondered at her words.

"I rather thought you hated the swamp."

She flashed him a quick smile. "Oh, I do. But seeing it from here, it's beautiful."

"Beautiful and deadly," he corrected. Just like you, angel, he thought, then he almost laughed aloud at himself. She wasn't deadly; it was his soul she was consuming alive. He started to stand but sat back down quickly because she was walking by him to the bookshelves. He loved to read and he had everything—research books by the scores, classics, ancient masterpieces and contemporary spy thrillers. She honed in on his research material, running her finger over the spine of a book entitled *Seminole*.

"It means runaway, right?" she asked.

He shrugged. "That's the general consensus."

"But you're not the only Indians down here. The Miccosukee live in the same area, too, right?"

His eyes narrowed sharply and Ashley was pleased. She knew something about the area, and a lot more than he would suspect about North American Indians.

"Yes," he replied.

Smiling very sweetly, Ashley continued, "Two separate and distinct tribes, although they weren't recognized as such by the American government until fairly recently. Two different languages, although both peoples practice some of the same feasts and rituals, such as the Green Corn Dance."

"How do you—" he began, but broke off quickly with a shrug. "What did you do? Go and watch the alligator wrestling? Take a stroll through the village?"

She ignored his question. "Why do you hate me so much?" she asked suddenly. "Someone in your family was obviously white. Hawk—that's your father's name, I assume. So your mother, maybe?''

"She was Norwegian," Eric admitted with irritation in his voice.

Her eyes widened tauntingly. "Well, that's certainly white," she muttered.

He didn't reply. His hands folded in his lap, and he stared at her. His life was none of her concern.

Ashley turned back to the books, wishing she could quit feeling like crying. He was acting as if nothing at all had happened between them. Well, two could play that game. She could play it very well.

She faced him. "When do you think that I'll be able to get out of here?"

He shrugged. "Tomorrow, the next day. It may take a whole week for the rescue people to get out here."

"A week!"

"Don't worry. As soon as the water in the canals is down a little, I'll get you over to Wendy's."

"Wendy's?"

"My sister-in-law's. I think you'll be happier there. Brad can take you into town as soon as possible."

"Your... brother?" Ashley said.

"My brother is dead. Brad is Wendy's husband. He's with the Drug Enforcement Agency in Fort Lauderdale."

She nodded and sat down. Silence fell between them. Ashley lifted her hands, then let them fall back to her lap. "Well, thank you."

He stood abruptly then, almost knocking over his coffee. "Wait a minute," he told her curtly.

He walked out of the room. Ashley leaned her head back. She was still exhausted even though she had awakened so late. She felt as if blood and life were drained from her.

He reappeared carrying a pair of jeans cutoffs and a short-sleeved tailored blouse. "Here. Try these."

The clothing fell on her lap. She looked up at him. "Your wife's?" Ashley asked.

He shook his head. "Wendy's. She's much shorter than you are, but I thought that they might do."

Ashley nodded slowly. "Fine. Thank you." He wasn't about to let her touch anything that had belonged to the woman with the raven hair and warm smile.

"Maybe you could read," he told her.

He wanted her out of his office. She smiled. "Sure." She walked over to the bookcase and purposely picked out *Seminole*. "Maybe I can find out what gave you your warm and witty personality."

Eric didn't respond. He watched her as she walked out of the room with the clothing and the book.

Ashley went into the bedroom and changed. The shorts were very short, but they fit. The blouse was a little better. She decided they were better than worrying about losing the robe at any minute.

Worrying...

How on earth was she going to endure the day? It was terrible just being near him. It was awkward and painful. She hadn't expected anything from him, not flowers, not avowals, not commitment, but neither had she expected the ice, the absolute coldness, his acting as if he really did hate her.

There was a knock on the door. Ashley hesitated, but he didn't wait. He pushed the door open and stepped through but kept his hand on the knob.

"I just—I just wanted to say that I was sorry."

"Oh?" she said. "About what?" Being rude. He knew that he had been rude.

"About last night."

Ashley gritted her teeth. "Last night? Just how do you mean that you're sorry, Mr. Hawk?"

"Too much Jack Black—"

"I see," Ashley broke in coldly.

"No, you don't!" he countered. "I'm trying—"

"I don't think that you've really tried to do anything in years!" she told him.

"Oh, really?" He paused, his jaw twisted, his fingers tightening on the doorknob. His eyes narrowed as he stared at her, his muscles constricting. "Just what do you know?"

"Enough," Ashley said defensively.

"You don't know anything."

"I know enough not to deny what I've done, or felt!" she cried.

He took a step toward her and she didn't know why but she panicked. She backed away to the bed, picked up a pillow and held it before her like a shield. He kept coming toward her. "You don't seem to know anything!" she told him. "Not about honesty or courtesy."

"I don't?" He was closer. But smiling, she realized. She smiled, too, as he snatched the pillow from her. She grabbed the second pillow.

"You don't remember how to laugh or how to have fun. Or how to apologize or—Wait!"

He was almost on top of her and not listening at all. She thrust the pillow against his chest to stop him, but he deflected her move with his own pillow and she staggered down to the bed. "Wait!" she cried, "you're not listening—"

She struck again.

He staggered back, his hair tumbling over his forehead and his eyes. He stopped in his tracks, staring at her. And then he started to laugh.

"Eric..."

Disheveled, striking, sexy, he leaped down beside her, still laughing. He caught both of their pillows and cast them aside, sweeping her into his arms. She shrieked in protest, trying to regain her pillow as a barrier against him, but she couldn't begin to counter the strength in his arms.

Her hands went still upon his upper arms and suddenly she was breathless. For a long moment, they just stared at each other. Her wet hair was in wild disarray and fell over his fingers. Her eyes were alive with laughter.

"I'm not half as bad as you say I am," he told her.

"No?" she asked, moistening her lips.

"I really am sorry," he said softly.

"Do me a favor?" she whispered.

"What?"

"Don't be. Sorry, I mean. I wasn't."

He shrugged. "All right. If it was nothing—"

"I didn't say that it was nothing. It was everything. Think what you like, I can't change you. But I don't do things like that. Ever. It meant everything."

When his smile faded, the laughter left her eyes. He pulled away from her. "Don't say that."

"Damn you, will you stop that! How can you so horribly ruin something that was decent and wonderful." He stared at her blankly. Ashley knew that he saw her as the sophisticate, the big-city girl with tons of experience. She knew then that he was just the opposite, that he might have been in love once, but that nothing had been special to him since. "Don't you—" she began, then broke off with a sigh. "Never mind. Just move, please!"

But he didn't move. He was staring down at her as if he hadn't even heard her. He smoothed a tangle of hair from her face, his green eyes intense and brilliant. Then he leaned back and gave himself a shake. "What?" she murmured.

He seemed to regretfully push away from her and stand. He took a step but then turned back. He reached out a hand to her, and a rueful smile touched his lips. "Once more, Miss Ashley Dane, I'm truly sorry that I'm such a rude bore. Try to forgive me?"

She hesitated.

His smile deepened. "Honest. I'm sorry—About being rude, crude and abrasive. And have it your way—I'm not sorry at all about last night. I enjoyed every second. Every touch, taste, scent and move."

That wasn't exactly what she had wanted. His words brought a deep flush to her cheeks, and more. They brought back memories. Of his hands, of his lips . . .

She lowered her head and accepted his outstretched hand quickly. He helped her up.

"Want more?" he asked softly.

"What?" she murmured, looking up and meeting his eyes in confusion.

"I could go on," he told her blandly. "About last night. About everything that I liked about last night. In detail."

"No! No, that's all right."

"All right," he said agreeably, then laughed at her perplexity. The sound was easy and good, and she was glad of it. His fingers curled warmly around hers, and she was glad of the touch, too. Their eyes met, and his gaze was warm.

But maybe that wasn't so good. Her breath quickened and her heart took flight, and she was left wishing desperately once again that she could leave him then. Right that very second.

There were murderers out in the swamp. Even if he didn't believe her, a murder had taken place. There might be extreme danger for her. But she could hardly think of it now that she was with him.

Because it wasn't her life that was in peril then, she knew; it was her heart.

Chapter 5

Warily, Ashley followed Eric into the kitchen. He went to the refrigerator and felt around inside. He seemed satisfied. "Still cold," he told her.

"Without the electricity?"

"I've got synthetic ice blocks in there," he said. "They're great. Well, what will you have?"

"What are my choices?"

"Oh, koonti bread, alligator tail. What's your preference?"

She didn't know if he was teasing her. With her nose imperiously high, she took a stool by the counter. "I've had alligator tail, Mr. Hawk."

"Have you?" He turned around with a wry smile. A little shiver shot along her spine. She wished he wasn't quite so attractive, not that he was attractive in any nice, civilized way. He called upon something primitive inside of her with the curve of his lip and the sure, casual sway of his walk. The way he stood now, black hair falling over his forehead, that smile in place, somehow suggested energy and passion and something wonderful and vital that was just barely leashed.

"Yes," she said with dignity and arrogance. Then she smiled, too. "They serve it at Disney World."

"Disney World!"

"In the Grand Floridian, at the restaurant out on the lake. They serve it as a steak, and they make the most wonderful bread spread out of it, too."

"Oh, do they?" His brow was arched high; he was still smiling.

"Yes."

"Damn. Then it will have to be koonti bread," he told her. "Or do they serve that at Disney World?"

Ashley laughed. "Who knows? Maybe they do, but I haven't tried it. What is koonti?"

"A root. We survived on it for years and years, and women like my grandmother still grind it the old-fashioned way and make bread from it. I think she's convinced that if I eat enough of it, I'll come to a good end after all."

"Oh? Are you heading toward a bad end?"

"A terrible one," he assured her. "Iced tea?"

"Umm. Love some."

He went back to the refrigerator for a pitcher and poured them each a glass of tea.

Ashley watched him. "Seriously, do you often eat alligator meat?"

"Only after the season."

"The season?"

He nodded. "Once, they were endangered. They've made a remarkable comeback, so now there's a yearly alligator season, and so many hunters are given licenses." He smiled. "That's when you really have to watch out in the swamp. Reporters follow the hunters and it's as if a pack of wild animals had been let loose!"

"You don't mean that," Ashley said with a laugh.

"I do. Have you ever met a newsman hungry for a good story?"

"Yes, as a matter of fact, I have," Ashley said. Media people had come after Tara like vultures at times. "Okay, so they can be bad. But not as bad as an alligator, I'm willing to bet."

He shrugged. "Alligators aren't my favorite creatures, but they're fascinating. As old as the dinosaurs, as simple in their being. There have been some horrible incidents with them lately. 'Nuisance' alligators, that's what they're called. Gators that get into canals and make it to the residential sections, things like that. There was a little girl killed just a few years ago. A beautiful, blond girl. An alligator took her right down. I hated the creatures like crazy when I read that. But I've seen the hunters out here, too. They kill the alligators using everything, and it can get quite gruesome. I doubt, though, that the alligator meat at Disney came from hunters. There are alligator farms all over the northern part of the state now. People breed them for their hides and their meat."

"And yours?"

"Brad bagged him. He'd taken to playing around too close to the house."

Ashley shivered violently. Eric grinned gently. "That's why you shouldn't just go running out of here," he said softly, then added, "but don't worry. They're usually very wary of humans and since they've been hunted again, they've grown shy." He returned to the refrigerator and rummaged around. "I've got it!" he cried.

"What?"

"Ham and cheese?"

Ashley started to laugh, and she was amazed because it was so easy. "Perfect. Want me to help?"

"No, I think that I can handle ham and cheese. Mustard or mayonnaise?"

"I like surprises," Ashley told him.

He smiled and turned to the task. A few minutes later, he tentatively set a plate before Ashley. "You're not going to throw it today, are you?"

"Not unless you're absolutely obnoxious," she told him sweetly.

"Maybe we'd better eat fast."

"Can't control that nasty streak, eh?" she teased. But then she wished that she hadn't spoken because something dark clouded his eyes. She thought that it was truth, that there was something in his behavior toward her that he couldn't quite control. She looked quickly at her plate. "Hmm. Looks wonderful."

"Thank God. I was worried. Not a drop of caviar or paté in the house."

She glanced up at him. "For your information, Mr. Hawk, peanut butter is one of my very favorites. I can't bear to eat anything at all that's green or greenish or mushy brown, such as paté. I never, never liked fish eggs."

"Excuse me," he told her lightly.

"I will try," she promised.

He chewed a bit of his sandwich, watching her. "I like you that way," he told her.

"What way?"

"Without the makeup."

Ashley shrugged, wondering if he meant it. She wished that he wouldn't look at her so. It made her feel as if her flesh came alive. She became achingly aware of herself all over. She let her lashes fall over her eyes. "Thanks."

"So tell me about New York."

She glanced at him again. He had about downed his sandwich and she was still picking at hers. "What's to tell? Have you ever been there?"

He nodded. "Interesting jungle."

She laughed. "Yes, it is."

"Do you live alone?" It was a pointedly personal question. Of course, Ashley thought quickly, they'd already been as personal as it was possible to be. But then he had been the one to start building the walls.

He had also been the one to call the truce.

"I live alone. I have an apartment on Columbus Avenue, not far from the Museum of Natural History."

"And what do you do when you're not wearing a bikini in the Everglades?"

"What do you when you're not rescuing women in bikinis in the Everglades?"

"Bikini bottoms," he reminded her.

He wanted to draw a reaction. She wasn't going to let him. "Bikini bottoms," she agreed sweetly.

"I asked first."

"But you should humor the weaker sex."

He offered her a very slow, amused and strikingly sensual smile. His words had a soft drawl when he spoke. "I'm not at all sure that there's anything weaker about you, Miss Dane."

"All right. I design clothing. With Tara Tyler. We both worked for a man name Galliard for years—"

"Galliard?" He frowned. Ashley was certain that he must have read something about it in the papers. Galliard had been a very well-known designer. When he had been arrested in Venezuela for murder, the news media had played up the story.

"Of course, Galliard," he said. "I remember reading something about it in the papers. I looked it all up again when Rafe Tyler reached me about using the property." His eyes were very sharp upon her. Wary even. "It must not have been a very good time for you," he said.

"Well, I don't think that I was ever more frightened in my life. Tara had been involved with a man named Tine Elliott. By accident she met Rafe's brother who was working for the authorities. Tine was trying to steal priceless artifacts, and Tara got involved in a shoot-out. They tried to accuse her of murder. Later, when we all came to Venezuela together, Tine kidnapped me to get to Tara." She shivered violently.

She saw his hand move on the counter, as if he would reach out to her. But he did not. Ashley frowned. "But I wasn't alone, you see. Rafe's brother was there, and Sam, an old friend and employee. And then finally Rafe and the authorities arrived, and everything was all right. But I'd never been so scared in my life, and never was again until..." Her voice trailed away. She flashed him a furious glance. "Until I saw that murder take place in the swamp."

He had been chewing. He stopped. "All right. So maybe I didn't believe you," he admitted.

"Do you believe me now?"

"I don't know. I believe that you think that you saw something take place."

"That isn't the same thing at all. I'm not given to hallucinations, and I'm not the delicate type to fly off the handle at anything."

"You've said that you hate the swamp. The rain was coming down in torrents, and you were frightened of everything already. Maybe you did—just this once—hallucinate a tiny bit."

"I did not!" Angry, Ashley stood. "I can't wait to get out of here!"

He stiffened like a poker, straight and hard, and something as cold as ice fell over his eyes. He stood, too. "Well, we'll get you out of here just as fast as we can, Miss Dane," he promised her. He came around the counter. "Excuse me, will you? I've got work to do."

He walked away down the hall. Ashley followed his departure, wishing her temper wasn't quite so explosive.

He opened the door to his office and disappeared into the room. The door closed with a slam. Ashley even heard the lock bolt home.

"So go sulk!" she whispered after him. But, she thought, he wasn't sulking. He was angry with her. And she would never change his mind about her.

"And why should I care?" she muttered. He was just a temperamental stranger who had dragged her out of the swamp. She couldn't wait to leave. She wanted to be with buildings, not saw grass. Her type of jungle was concrete, not this overwhelming swamp and muck and canal and wilderness. It was best if they kept their distance.

"Stay in there!" she told the empty hallway softly. "You just go ahead and stay in there!"

She felt like throwing a dish again, but that seemed to be what he expected of her. Instead she inhaled and exhaled slowly, picked up the few dishes and determined to wash them.

Despite the storm, his water was still running, and it seemed clean and fine. Ashley decided that he must have his own well on the property. She was glad of it. She not only washed the dishes but also scrubbed the sink and the counter, not that they were particularly dirty. Eric Hawk seemed to be neat and organized.

When she was done she sat in the living room for a moment, studying the buffalo skulls with their feathers and etching. They were wonderful art pieces, she decided, and she'd love to have them herself.

Then she noted that it was growing dark again. She rose and looked around the kitchen and dug through the drawers until she found candles. She walked around the living room picking up the holders and digging out the previous night's candles, then setting the new ones into them.

Eric still had not appeared.

With the candles lit, it seemed that night came on completely. Ashley had no idea of the time; she wasn't wearing a watch. The clock over Eric's mantel said that it was one, and she knew that that wasn't true. Her stomach was growling, though, so she dug through his refrigerator. When she opened the meat drawer, she found that his meat was neatly wrapped in white butcher paper and clearly labeled. She stared at the markings, annoyed that her fingers moved over the handwriting. She even liked his script. His letters were big and bold, well formed and slanted, and somehow, they endeared him to her even more.

She glanced down the hallway and her lip tightened. "Damn him!" she muttered. She almost shoved the package of meat back into the refrigerator and slammed the door. She held on instead and read the wrapper. A slow smile curved her lips. It was alligator tail.

Newly determined, she lit the sterno and found a covered frying pan. She dug around in his cupboards for seasonings.

A half hour later the kitchen smelled deliciously of garlic, butter, cayenne and black pepper. She'd cooked the meat along with some green peppers and onions and potatoes, and whether it was a recipe or not, it even looked really good, too.

She found a bottle of German Riesling, poured a glass and added a few of the remaining ice cubes. After preparing herself a plate, she sat down to eat. She tasted her creation and decided that it was really darn good. But Eric Hawk still hadn't appeared.

She sipped her wine and took her time. He still didn't come. Finally she gave up. She washed her plate and set out one for him. She poured herself a second glass of wine and went to knock on his door. He didn't answer. She didn't care. "There's dinner in the kitchen if you want. If you don't want, make sure you go blow out the sterno. I just put your stuff back on to warm."

She quickly went down the hall, balancing her wine and a candle.

In his room, she set down her candle and wine, plumped up the pillows and lay down, finding the book she had chosen earlier from his study. She opened the pages and looked at the door. She still hadn't heard a thing.

She wouldn't be able to concentrate, she thought. But she opened the book to a page past the introduction and started to read. Without realizing it, she quickly became absorbed.

The first chapter was on the advance of the Seminoles, an offshoot of the Georgia Creeks, into Florida during the beginning and middle of the eighteenth century. The next chapter focused on the First Seminole War, and Ashley found herself more engrossed. The narrative spoke about

Andrew Jackson's dead-set determination to eliminate the Indians, and it spoke, too, of the Indians' desperate struggle to survive. Their way of life had already changed. The "chickee," the thatched-roof house on stilts, had not always been their home. They had built houses of logs at one time, but these were burned time and time again, and so they adopted the cool shelter of the chickee.

The stilts protected them from creatures of the night, from the Florida alligator, from the snakes, from any other hungry creature. But nothing had protected them from man. Nothing but the swamp itself.

The telling was wonderful. It was not fraught with detail, and yet everything was there. Her heart was torn for a people trying desperately to survive, but there was an explanation about Jackson's hatred—he had lost kin to an Indian attack. If there was a message or a moral in the book, it was not that the white man was to be entirely mistrusted or abhorred, or even hated for the endless treachery practiced upon the Indians. Savagery created more savagery, and to this day, the United States and her native sons and daughters were working on coming to terms.

A slight sound finally caught her attention. She looked up. Eric Hawk had made his appearance at last. He was standing in the doorway, leaning there actually, watching her. She thought that he had probably been there some time. She didn't know why she was so certain, but she was.

"You shouldn't sneak up on people that way," she told him.

"I didn't sneak up on you. You just weren't paying attention."

"I was reading. Can I help you?" she asked sweetly.

A slow smile came to his lips. "I just came to say thanks."

"Oh?"

"That . . . that whatever it was, was delicious."

"Oh, the alligator tail."

"Umm. I enjoyed it thoroughly."

"Good."

He came into the room. She was looking right at him, and he was staring right at her, and she still had the sense of being stalked. He moved with such utter silence, with such smooth confidence. He was completely dressed, but she discovered herself imagining him naked again. He was so beautifully built, offering everything in a woman's fantasy, even when the woman didn't even know that she'd had fantasies.

His green eyes flashed when he came to the foot of the bed. He rested an elbow on the bed and grinned up at her. "Like the reading material?"

She flushed, then forgot his eyes with a rush of enthusiasm. "Yes! I love it. It's the most marvelous book. It's all history, it's factual, but it reads like a novel. It made me feel as if I knew them all—the Seminoles, the whites, all of them. I love it." She cast him a semisweet smile. "I'm going to finish it right now, even if I read all night, because of course I know you would never dream of lending it to me, and I want to get in every single word of it."

She thought that her sarcasm would irritate him. It didn't. "You're just saying that," he told her.

"I'm not."

"You are. To appease me."

Ashley sat up straight, tossing her brilliant red mane over her shoulder. "First off," she informed him, pointing a finger straight at his nose, "I wouldn't dream of appeasing you. Secondly, why on earth should I appease you by liking a book? Just because it's about the Seminole Nation?"

"Because I wrote it."

"What?" Ashley gasped, looking into his eyes. They still danced with humor, but there was a seriousness there, too. He was telling her the truth.

She looked at the book again. The title was in huge print. The author's name, down at the very bottom, was much smaller. But it was there, sure enough. Eric Hawk.

Startled, she stared at him again. "You did write it."

"Yes," he said softly. Then he crawled forward, very much like a circling cat, pulled the volume out of her hand, and let it drop to the floor. She stared after it. "Why—?" she began.

"Because," he interrupted her. He was beside her then, sitting cross-legged and facing her. Close. "You don't have to finish it now. And you don't have to borrow it. It's yours. Take it with you when you go."

"You don't have to—"

"Yeah, I do," he said. He reached out and stroked her cheek softly. That rough and tender touch evoked a whole new tempest of longing within her. His eyes continued to hold hers. His fingers moved, his knuckles brushing the length of her neck, then grazing down over her breast. He touched her lightly, and she realized that she ached to be held by him, ached to be bare and to feel his hands hot and demanding, upon her. But still she didn't move. She met his eyes because the things that couldn't be said out loud were spoken there. He had to want her without the bitterness, without the dreams of a past. And then she realized that he did. He still might not like her, and perhaps he even still judged her, but his wanting was for her. And at that moment, that was enough for her.

She cried out softly and threw her arms around him and he captured her within his own embrace. Their lips met and simmering passions exploded. He delved deeper and deeper into her mouth with his tongue, searching and hungry, as if he demanded the soul of her. Their lips parted and met again, and she sought the liquid thrust of his tongue with her own. Then she broke away from him, panting, yearning.

"I should stay away from you," he whispered.

"Why?" she demanded.

He sat back again, touching the ring on her finger. "Because you're like a Tyler emerald. Beautiful to look at...and far beyond bounds."

"I'm not a stone!" Ashley protested. "I'm not a thing, or an object, or an ice-cold piece of rock. I—"

"No, no, you're not rock!" he agreed heatedly, lacing his fingers through her hair, then catching hold of the buttons on her blouse. They opened easily beneath his practiced fingers and he held her bare breasts in his hands. Rising up on his knees and bringing her with him, he kissed her again. His lips trailed from her mouth to her earlobe. His thumbs found the peaks of her breasts and rubbed them, creating twin streaks of fire that shot through the length of her to the very center of her longing. His lips hovered above her again. "And you're not cold. There's nothing about you that's cold in the least. And there is everything, everything that's beautiful."

"Oh," she whispered softly, and her lips came against his throat as she held him tight. She thought of his bare chest, how the ripple of muscle fascinated and drew her, and she tugged on his buttons. She was not as deft and tore off a button.

She pulled away in horror, gasping out an apology, amazed that she could have wanted anyone with so great an abandon that she would have ripped clothing. She opened her mouth to speak, but she was quickly back in his arms. "It's the best button I've ever lost!" he assured her, laughing. But the laughter was tempered by fire. It was throaty and husky, and entered inside her just like his touch, making her hunger, making her yearn.

He pulled away from her for a second to strip away his own shirt. He crushed her back against him and just held her there. Together they knelt on the bed, and his passion took flight again. His hands scorched endless trails over her back, bringing them together hip to hip. Ashley bent her head, nipping his shoulders, trailing her tongue over the smoothness of his flesh. Her fingertips brushed and kneaded him, and her lips and teeth and tongue followed. She tentatively set her teeth over the hard brown knot of his nipple, moving her tongue around it. She grazed her fingers low over his belly and felt him shudder, heard his ardent groan.

He caught her hair and held her face away, searching out her eyes. "You are like an emerald. Sparkling, dazzling green fire. Hard to touch, hard to hold, tempting beyond all measure. God, what you do to me...."

He kissed her again. While their lips met he found her hand and brought it against him. She almost recoiled, startled by the fierce pulse of his arousal. Then everything about him came to her in a rush. She felt the tempest of his breath, so ragged, and she felt the ferocious thunder of his heart, the burning constriction of his body. His palms, calloused and hard and masculine, were demanding, yet so tender as they closed over the fullness of her breasts.

Suddenly he broke away from her lips with a cry that rocked the length of her, saturating her with a liquid shimmer of deep desire. He cradled her breast with his hand and took the hardened peak into his mouth, to lave it with his tongue, tease it with his teeth, to suckle it. She couldn't believe his touch on her upper body affected her whole length, and she tugged on his hair, hardly aware that what she begged him for was mercy. He released her at last, but only to caress and suckle and tease her other breast until she could kneel no more, until she fell against him, desperate for more of him, yet not at all sure that she could endure more of his fierce lovemaking.

She was not about to be denied. He laid her down upon the pillow and shed his jeans. Breathing hard, she watched him and tried to rise when he came to her. He wouldn't allow her to do so. He kissed her lips and then trailed his tongue down her body, between her breasts, over her ribs. He paused, twisting her, to kiss the length of her spine. She tried again to reach for him, to bring herself against him, but he held her still.

He found the snap on the cutoff jeans she wore and began to tug them down her hips. He put his lips on her waistline and belly, and when the cutoffs were finally off, he parted her thighs. The tip of his tongue teased her thighs until it came between them. Then he delved into her with leisure and determination, finding the tiny button that coursed out its hunger and ecstasy and need to all of her— to her blood, her limbs, her heart . . .

The world blackened around her. Life before this night faded, and all she knew was the sweet blinding urgency, and then the shattering, volatile storm of rapture that broke and cascaded throughout her. She screamed, shaking and trembling, and barely knew that she had done so. Blackness did come. She died, she came back to life, and then discovered the tension in his face and the sheer masculine pleasure and triumph in his eyes as he crawled over her. Embarrassment racked her and she stared at him in dismay, trying to lower her eyes as if she could hide. He laughed—deep, rich, throaty—and found her lips and kissed her hard. Slowly he laid the length of his body over hers. She felt his sex, huge and pulsing and unappeased, against her thighs, and then she felt his movement and she forgot to be embarrassed. She melted to his touch. He sank into her, slowly and completely, while looking into her eyes once again. When he was fully inside her, she felt a touch, as if it were deep down inside her womb, and it awoke every hunger within her again. She opened her mouth, but no sound came. She wetted her dry lips, and his came down upon them again and he locked his arms around her.

All hell broke loose within him.

She felt as if she rode a tempest, rode the wind, rode the wild splendor of the earth itself, and it was wonderful. He was fury itself, liquid motion. When she thought that she could take no more, he held himself away from her and moved slowly . . . until she became the tempest, arching against him, setting her own rhythm. Then he ceased to tease and caught hold of her desperate flight, smoothing it into a sensual, sweet rhythm once more. It went on and on until she reached the final peak and clasped it tightly. She closed her eyes, and the stars exploded before her. Emerald stars, dozens of them, dazzling in the darkness all around her, settling her down, within the damp enclosure of his arms.

They lay there in silence for a long while. The candle flickered against the walls, and its glow grew smaller and smaller. Ashley closed her eyes. She must have halfway dozed, for she didn't so much awaken but rather became aware of him again. His fingers moved up and down her back, along her spine. Then his hands slid over her buttocks and caught hold of her hips and pulled her taut against him. He slipped inside her. Her breath came hot against his earlobe, and his whisper encouraged her to take flight along with him again.

When it was over they didn't break apart. His arm remained around her and her back lay flush against his chest. He stroked her arm softly and she didn't sleep. She heard his whisper.

"You're addictive," he told her.

"Am I?" she whispered.

"Um. Like caviar. I like caviar. I like it a lot."

She laughed softly. "First I was like an emerald. Now I've been reduced to fish eggs."

He chuckled and pulled her around to face him. She buried her head against his chest, loving the smoothness of his flesh, the tautness of the muscles there. She suddenly wished that there was no world other than their own, that the storm had taken away all roads forever, and that she could stay just where she was for eternity.

With a man who barely liked her, she reminded herself. But that was hard to believe at the moment. His long fingers moved tenderly through her hair, and she couldn't accept the fact that he hadn't come to care for her if only a little bit. She blessed the storm that had brought them together.

"It's almost daylight," he said.

"Is it?"

"Umm. I should have taken the shutters up yesterday. There was no reason to leave them down." She felt him grimace. "They're automatic. A touch of a button and they slide up."

"Umm," she murmured, content to be where she was.

"Did you sleep at all?" he asked her.

"Very well, except someone woke me up."

"Sorry."

"Please, don't be. It's quite all right."

"Good, because I'm really not sorry, not in the least." He was silent for a moment, then he sighed. "I'll be able to get you out of here either today or tomorrow, I'm sure."

Ashley didn't say anything. Her heart seemed to slam painfully against her chest. She couldn't believe that she really didn't want to go. Going meant returning to everything that she loved. The Met and the theaters and the massive buildings and Central Park in autumn. Macy's chocolate chip cookies. Her and Tara's cozy offices by Rockefeller Plaza. Ice skating...

Staying meant this man, the strength and security of his arms.

Except, of course, that he didn't want her to stay. He wanted her out. He liked his privacy and his quiet world. She was an intruder, even if she could cook and be entertaining in bed.

She pulled away from him, biting her lower lip as she stared up at the ceiling. She felt him prop up an elbow to watch her, but she didn't look his way.

"What's wrong?" he asked her.

"Nothing," she said, shaking her head.

"You're anxious to leave, I take it."

"That's not what I was thinking. Not at all."

"Then what?"

"Then what?" she repeated, and hesitated. Then she rolled over to look at him. The candlelight was not quite gone. "I was just thinking how strange things are, the way that they happen."

"Meaning?"

"This. The storm. Everything that happened. Being here. No matter what, I'll never regret it." She didn't like the way that he was looking at her. She wondered what she had said wrong.

"You'll never regret *it*? *It* what? You, me, the two of us? Making love? What are you talking about?"

"Do you have to get so particular!" Ashley exploded. "I—I meant us. I meant you. Everything I've learned from you and about you. I love the book about the Seminoles. I love what it says about you as a man. And I'm talking about us, too. Making love, or having sex, whichever the hell it is with you!"

"Oh," he said coolly. "I passed muster then, I take it?"

"Stop it!" she lashed out. It was ridiculous. She was going to start crying any second. No, she would not. Never in front of him. "It was wonderful. You were wonderful—"

"Well, I'm so glad!" he muttered, shooting up from the bed with fury. He reached for his jeans, and stepped into them as he continued to speak with a controlled wrath. "Wonderful, huh? Maybe I should be really grateful for the description. Maybe I'll have a whole flock of little socialites down here to try out the goods, huh? What is it with you? Try out an Indian, ye old noble savage, then fly down to Tijuana and try out a Mexican?"

Furious, Ashley stared at him, speechless for a moment. Then she jumped up, screamed something completely savage and came tearing around the end of the bed. She did so with a vigor and vehemence that made him wary but she didn't pelt him. She stopped just a foot before him. "You bastard! You stupid, egotistical, self-centered, neurotic, lousy bastard! Noble savage! There isn't a single thing noble about you, savage or otherwise!" She slapped him across the face as hard as she could.

Then she nearly cringed. Anger unlike anything she had ever seen leaped into his eyes. They glittered like knives. She prayed that he wouldn't strike back. She was frightened and was sure that she would scream and cry and...and either run or beg for mercy. No! She couldn't, she couldn't.

But if he took one step toward her, she probably would.

He did not. He didn't touch her, and he didn't say a word. He stepped around her and left the room. She didn't hear his footsteps as he strode down the hall. She did hear the front door open and slam with a terrible vengeance.

Ashley sank on the bed. She could still feel her palm stinging from the slap. He was gone, and she allowed hot tears to well in her eyes.

Thank God she would be out of here soon.

Swiftly, almost desperately, she raced into the bathroom. There wasn't much light, or hot water, but she didn't care. She jerked on the shower and stood beneath the water, which felt no colder than her heart. She picked up the soap and scrubbed herself furiously, not so much to remove any traces of their lovemaking, but because it seemed that if she tried hard enough, she could scrub him out of her mind and from under her skin.

When she was finished and shivering, her teeth chattering, she toweled herself dry with great fury. She was still seething. No, she wasn't seething—she was miserable. If it were in her power, she would stomp out the front door alone and find whatever help she could.

If she wasn't able to leave soon, she would do just that. She would run out again, reckless and heedless, just to get away from him.

She came back into the bedroom and started to straighten the sheets and the bed with a vengeance. Then she paused.

There was someone or something behind her. She didn't know how she knew, whether she had heard something or just sensed something. But it was there, in the doorway.

Eric, she thought. He had come back. He was either going to say something curt or cruel, or he was going to break down and apologize. Grudgingly she admitted that he was capable of a very good apology. Maybe he thought that she was the one who should be apologizing. She had actually struck him, and he had leashed his temper fairly well. She didn't owe him an apology, not after the awful things that he had said.

No, he had come back to tell her that he was sorry. Well, she wasn't forgiving him. Not this time.

But he wouldn't say anything. He would stay there in perfect unnerving silence until she turned around and acknowledged him.

She dropped the pillow she had been holding and spun to face him, crossing her arms over her chest. "Don't ask me to be sorry, Hawk, because I'm not—"

Her eyes widened with horror. It wasn't Eric standing in the doorway. It wasn't even a man.

It was a cat. A huge cat. A huge, tawny cougar—a mountain lion. It looked at Ashley, then it opened its mouth and gave an awful screech, displaying enormous curved teeth.

She moistened her lips, opened her mouth and stood perfectly still. Don't move, stare the creature down! she thought. But it wasn't courage holding her still—she was simply paralyzed with fear.

Then the huge cat moved. A lot like Eric. Step by step, massive paw after massive paw, the cat began to move. Big eyes, seemingly rimmed in black, surveyed her.

As if she were prey.

The cat stepped toward her. And then began to run for the bed, leaping toward it.

At last Ashley's scream tore from her throat.

She screamed and screamed again.

Because the giant cat was coming straight for her.

Chapter 6

"Ashley!"

Eric burst into the room. For a second he stood in the doorway, searching out the danger. Then he made a flying leap, landed on the big cat and wrestled with it on the bed. Ashley, terrified and backed against the wall, closed her eyes. The big cat growled in fury. Eric yelled something, but she didn't understand his words. She remained flat against the wall, trembling.

Then she realized that the cat and man were off the bed and moving into the hallway. Eric slammed the bedroom door behind him, and after a while she heard the front door slam, too. She staggered over to the bed and sat down. She realized that he might get hurt. The great cat could scratch him or bite him or mangle his limbs. And there would be no way to reach help.

"Eric!" She leaped up and hurried to the door, flinging it open. He was already standing there. She threw herself into his arms with a tremendous burst of happiness and relief. "Oh, you're all right! I was so afraid of what that awful cougar—"

"Panther. It's a Florida panther. On the endangered species list," he said.

"Who cares!" she gasped. Her cheek lay against his shirt, her arms wound tightly around his waist. His hands fell on her shoulders slowly, then he pulled her close. "You could have been hurt! Oh, Eric, I was so desperate, and you came so quickly when I screamed, and you might have been torn to bits. Just torn to bits."

"Ashley, I was never in any danger—"

"Eric, thank you. Really."

"Ashley, honestly—" Eric broke off, mesmerized by the liquid green eyes that stared up into his. It was on the tip of his tongue to tell her the truth—that the cat's name was Baby, and that Baby was a pet. Wendy's, Brad's and his. Like any cat, Baby was independent. She was a bright creature, too, affectionate and very loving. She could be trusted with his cousins' little children. She was also a good ally. He and Brad had worked with Baby, and she could be commanded to attack, to run and leap on the enemy and hold him down. She could also be told to get away.

She hadn't threatened Ashley. Baby had just been curious. She wasn't accustomed to finding strangers in Eric's house.

He meant to say all of that to Ashley. He meant to explain. It was just that harsh words rose between them so easily. His fault, he thought. He didn't want to want her, but he did. He didn't want to care that she was a dazzling angel cast down from the heaven of the north, and that she would return to her glittering high palaces in no time at all. She was just a touch of green fire that lit up the dark swamp. Or maybe his soul, he didn't know. She was a red-haired angel, a borrowed angel.

He should really tell her the truth. He should explain....

It was just that she was shivering so violently in his arms. And she had that look in her eyes, as if she forgave him for all things. Then there was the feel of her skin as he held her, and the soft scent of soap emanating from her body mixed with everything so feminine and magical about her. Her hair fell against him, soft as a silken web, radiant as a blaze.

Words died on his lips. He had just left her. He had to be with her again. He lowered his mouth to hers and kissed her. Then he kissed away the dampness on her cheeks. His lips fell on her throat where it was arched to him. Her breasts were crushed against him and despite the clothing lying between them he could feel the hardness of her nipples and the fullness of her breasts. He groaned because he was lost.

He swept her up into his arms and brought her to the bed. He couldn't get enough of the touch of her, or of the beauty of her eyes. She was only borrowed, he reminded himself time and time again, but that made it harder for him, because he had to touch her more thoroughly to remember her. He had to lose himself within her completely, because the chance might not come again.

He groaned, and his arms came around her fiercely, and his mouth, teeth and tongue raked her endlessly. Nothing had ever touched him as she did; nothing had ever made him forget the pain.

In her arms, there was only the sheer fascination with every part of her—the satin feel of her flesh, the velvet texture of her hair sweeping over his shoulders and chest, teasing the length of him as she moved. She nuzzled his breast, nipped his flesh and moved down over him. There was the molten warmth of her mouth upon him, the stroke of her fingers. There was the feel of her knotting him into explosive ecstasy, making him soar over the world.

He allowed her to lead until he could take no more. He shuddered and cried out at her caress, and then he seized her and swept into her fiercely, hungrily. He thought that he branded something of himself upon her, and still he realized that her arms took more. Her soft and tender touch and her whispers took something of him. In her arms he was healed.

He was whole. His anger seeped from him just like his seed. She took from him gently, and when he lay back, soaked and shuddering and spent, he knew that his world had changed, and that she had changed it.

He let the air cool his body and curled his fingers around hers. "I have a confession to make," he told her.

"Oh? What's that?" she asked warily.

He turned around, propping up on an elbow, looking down into the emerald sea of her eyes. He wished that the moment could go on forever. Her hair was a spill of fire all around her. She was damp and beautiful and so natural at his side. She was naked, except for the emerald ring and pendant. Her lips were curled into a rueful, curious smile.

He touched her lower lip with his thumb. "She's a pet," he said.

She frowned, and her gaze fell on him, narrowed with suspicion. "She . . . ?"

He laughed. "No, there's no pleasure palace in the basement. I don't even have a basement. She, the cat. Her name is Baby. Wendy picked her up as a kitten, her mother was dead. She spends her time prowling around between the two houses and the village for handouts. She wouldn't have hurt you, not in a thousand years."

"She's a . . . pet?" Ashley repeated.

"Yes," he said, then hesitated. "Are you angry?"

"Hmm. I should be," she muttered, her lashes falling low over her eyes. But she stared at him with the familiar fire in her gaze. "I should be furious. You kissed me, and all—" she paused, then indicated the bed with a sweep of her hand "—all this, under false pretenses!"

"Well—"

"I should—" she interrupted "—slug you. Right in the jaw."

"But you already did that," he reminded her, and with a broad smile he crawled over her, straddling her hips and catching her wrists. He bent low over her. "You already did that."

"And I'm not sorry. You deserved it."

"Oh, yeah?"

"Yeah."

"Well, I didn't take kindly to it," he warned her. He loved holding her and feeling the length of her. And he loved the way her chin tilted up in defiance. He knew that she wasn't afraid of him in the least, and if she had been afraid, she'd still have fought. Their fingers were wound together and he felt the thrust of her breasts against him. His lips very nearly touched hers as he spoke. "I let you get away with that once, but not again."

"You let me get away with it because you knew you deserved it," she said sweetly.

"You're impertinent, did you know that?"

She shrugged. She seemed about to retort, but those words died. Instead she whispered, "You're the most fascinating person I've ever met. And I'm sorry if that offends you, but it's the truth."

He held still, then kissed the tip of her nose and her lips. He carefully rolled his weight away from her. He stood and looked toward the east, and a small part of him urged him toward the window. He found the switch for the shutters and pressed the button, and with no more sound than a slight jingle, the shutters began to roll into their casings. The day appeared before him, beautiful, with the sun bathing the landscape. It was a wilderness out there, complete, alien and harsh to those who did not know it.

She was a borrowed angel, he thought. Brought by the storm. Borrowed angels sprouted big silver wings, and then they flew *away*. Maybe it had been all right to touch her, even to lose himself within her, and maybe she had done more for him than anyone else. But the storm was over. Their time was over.

He turned around and came back beside her. He knew that she had been watching him and wondering at his thoughts, but she hadn't spoken. He touched her hair and kissed her. "And you're the most beautiful woman I've ever seen. On screen, in a picture, in the flesh, ever."

He left her again, going to his dresser to dig out some clothing. He turned around to tell her that he was heading for the shower, but his words faded away.

Her back was to him. She was propped up on an elbow. The sheet just fell over her hips, her hair cascaded from her shoulders to the bed, and the long line of her back was visible down to the rise of her buttocks. She was framed by the rays of the sun beating down upon the hummocks and trees and the river of grass. She looked so beautiful. He wished that he could hold that moment forever, too.

Except, he reminded himself, that things were hidden from him. He couldn't see her eyes. And he was certain that they stared out on the forbidding swampland with fear and loathing.

"I'll be in the shower," he said softly. She didn't acknowledge him; he wondered if she had even heard him. He walked into the bathroom and pushed the button for the shutters there, too. They rolled up, showing what lay behind the tub. There was a redwood privacy fence surrounding the windows, and within the fence grew philodendrons, vines, creepers and a few wild orchids. Soaking in the tub was almost like lying in a pool in the wilderness.

He needed to go out and kick the generator, he told himself. He could use some hot water right now.

He grabbed a towel and walked through the bedroom. Ashley seemed to be sleeping so he moved silently. Outside he unlocked the wooden shed and went in. He wished that the generator worked as easily as the shutters. He had to rev the engine again and again before he could get the generator to kick into action. Finally it began to hum. Eric looked around. The day was almost deathly still. It wasn't hot, though. The storm seemed to have swept away a lot of the late summer heat.

Where else could a man stand in nothing but a towel and fight with his generator? he asked himself. There was nothing around him. The road wasn't really far at all, and the canal by his property led north to the Big Cypress, or south toward the Tamiami trail. There were other homes like his. Not many, but there were some. And there were still the small villages, like the one where his grandfather chose to live. Grandfather preferred the company of his old friends. Eric understood. If there was one thing he cherished most about his family it was that they all sought to understand one another and to give each other room.

The generator was humming away. He looked at his airboat at the back of the shed and thought that it was time to take it out, too. If Baby had made it to his house, then there was surely a way to reach Wendy's by now.

A sharp pain suddenly ripped through his midsection and he almost bent over. He didn't want to let Ashley go.

All the more reason to get her away just as quickly as he could.

He gazed out over the expanse of his property and a little trickle of unease touched his spine. Maybe it was more important than he was imagining it to be to get her to Wendy's place right away.

He had thought that she was hysterical when she had told him about the murder. And even when he had convinced himself that she wasn't the hysterical type, he still thought that the storm had frightened her so badly that she had imagined things.

But why should she have? The swamp had long been a place where grievous sins could be hidden. Men had been lured to murder here time and time again. What better place to hide a body than this endless river of grass where little was seen by any eye?

Maybe she had seen something. And if she had, Brad would be the best one to deal with it.

Eric picked his way through the fallen shrubbery back toward the house. He should never have come out barefoot, he told himself. Storms threw up snakes. There had been a time when Indians very rarely died from snakebite, a time long before antisnakebite kits and antidotes. They lived with the snakes, they were bitten, and they gained immunity. From the rattlers, anyway. The coral snakes could be deadly, though, their venom was so powerful. To this day, any Indian child living in or near the Everglades knew a coral snake very well by sight and avoided it.

And anyone with half a brain wouldn't be walking over the fallen vegetation without shoes!

Cursing to himself, he went inside the house, still haunted by a feeling of unease. He locked the front door carefully, then came into his study. He opened his closet, took down his shotgun and loaded both barrels. He set the gun back on the high shelf. Then he went to his desk and dug in the bottom drawer for the ammunition box, assuring himself that he had plenty of bullets. He set the box back in the drawer and headed for his bedroom.

Ashley was still sleeping. He went into the bathroom and turned on the hot water. He had to let it run a while. When he noted the steam rising, he switched on the whirlpool jets and crawled in. It felt good. He'd taken so many cold showers lately that the hot bath was wonderful. He closed his eyes and leaned back.

He jolted up almost immediately, aware that the door had opened. It was Ashley.

"Hi there, fellow—" she started to tease, but then she saw the steam rising and the foliage outside the window. "Oh, how lovely! And hot water!"

"Want to join me?" He raised his eyebrows devilishly. She laughed, wound up her hair, then sank into the tub. She closed her eyes, sinking lower. Her toes met with his calves, and she smiled, allowing her feet to be bold and brazen. He caught her toes. He kneaded her feet and drew her closer, stroking the length of her calves. She smiled, but then her eyes shot open and she gripped the side of the tub, stiffening.

"Heat! Hot water! Then you've got electricity!"

"Yes."

"Then the phone must work!"

Something inside him seemed to die a little bit. He hadn't expected her to be so desperately eager to leave. His jaw clenched tightly. He shook his head. "The phone lines are still down. I've got a generator." He sat directly in front of one of the jets. The water shot against his lower back. It eased his tension, but he found new constrictions forming within him. He caught hold of her ankles and pulled her against him. She paid little heed.

"Oh," she said disappointedly. Her lashes fell, then they flew open again. "A generator! Then we could have had electricity this whole time!"

"If I had wanted to go out in the midst of the storm," he said dryly, "I suppose we could have."

"But yesterday—"

"I can live without it for a day or two."

"But—"

"Sorry. I didn't realize that electricity meant so much to you."

She shook her head impatiently. "It isn't that! It's—"

He didn't let her finish. He found her mouth and kissed her almost savagely. Maybe she wouldn't realize the awful tension inside him. Maybe she would think that the tempest was simply the swirling water, the steaming heat.

It wasn't. It lay within him. He just wanted to taste all of her one more time.

She tried to pull away from him once, then no more words escaped her. He made love to her with a fierce and vehement passion that was all encompassing and completely overwhelming. When it was over, she was as exhilarated and exhausted as she had never been before. She lay against his wet chest in the water and Eric idly stroked her hair. "I'm taking you out of here this afternoon," he told her.

Ashley stiffened, wondering at the coldness in his words when there had been such incredible heat in his arms. She opened her mouth to speak, but Eric went ramrod tight against her, his fingers winding like wire around her arms. He pushed her forward slightly to stand and grab a towel.

"What is it?" she asked.

"Nothing. Nothing," he told her. But there had been something. He wrapped the towel around his waist and pulled her out of the tub. He put a towel around her shoulders and took her into the bedroom. He pushed her down into a corner by the bed. "Stay there."

"But—"

"Stay there!" he commanded in a sharp whisper.

Not daring to take any more time, Eric hurried along the hallway to his office. When he was about to enter he ducked down low.

Someone in black was passing by his window.

Eric crawled to his desk and dug out the .38 Special. Then he stood, back against the wall, thinking. He'd heard someone come. There were a dozen good reasons why he shouldn't have expected anything other than a friend.

And yet he had known that this was no friend.

The figure was gone.

He hurried back into the hallway and looked down it. Walking silently, he came to the bedroom door and peered in. Ashley was there, in the corner, where he had left her.

He smiled at her.

Then suddenly, the day came alive. The window shattered into a thousand pieces, bursting in upon them like tiny diamonds. A bullet whizzed by and struck the wall.

Ashley screamed, covering her head. Eric screamed to her, "Down! Stay down!" He turned toward the window in a split second, aiming his gun quickly. He fired, then ducked as he saw the nose of a gun come around the corner of the window. A bullet soared past him. He fired in the direction of the shot. He heard a thumping on the porch and then a thrashing in the grass. He leaped for the broken window and used the butt of his gun to clear away the shards of glass, so he could jump out. He landed on the porch and searched the area. There were drops of blood leading into the brush. He followed the trail, but even as he rushed along, he heard the sound of a motor. Out in the canal, a boat was leaving. He would never catch up on foot.

Swearing, he turned back. He realized that he had cut his foot, and hobbled on through the grass. Then he sped up. He didn't want Ashley alone, not for a minute.

He leaped over the window ledge, intending to hurry to her where she sat in the corner. She pitched herself into his arms instead.

"I told you to stay still!" he yelled at her, catching her arms and shaking her.

"You shouldn't have gone after him!" she countered, meeting his gaze boldly. But she was trembling. He relented slightly, pulling her against the thunder of his heart.

"What in the hell is going on here?" he muttered.

"I told you. I saw a murder," she murmured softly, her voice quivering.

He pushed her away from him, slamming the button to lower the shutters again. They crunched over the broken glass but closed with resolve.

"Ashley, it's all right. It's over," he said.

"It isn't over. It's just beginning," she said dully. She slammed her fists against him. "You shouldn't have gone out there! You might have been killed!"

"Stop it. I know how to take care of myself, especially out here."

She sank down on the bed, believing him. Still clad in the towel, he paced the room. She noticed that his foot was bleeding and she pointed to it. "Your—your foot."

"What?" He glanced down. "Oh, yeah." He smiled. "Want to get me a Band-Aid?"

She hurried into the bathroom and searched through the medicine chest until she found the Band-Aids. Then she paused, feeling as if the big picture window that had delighted her so was now a giant eye. She stared at it uneasily, then realized that Eric was behind her, holding her shoulders. "It's all right, Ashley. He's definitely gone—for now, anyway." He released her and pushed the button to lower the shutters. "It's safe, see?"

She nodded. She did feel safe with him, but she began to tremble again. He might have gotten himself killed out there, and if he had, it would have been all her fault.

"I'm sorry that I involved you in this."

"You didn't involve me in anything," he told her harshly.

"But I did."

"Listen, I still don't know what I believe," he said sharply. "You saw a murder. Maybe. But tell me, how did the murderer follow you here? How did he—or she—find you here?"

"I—I don't know."

"So maybe you're not at fault at all. Maybe it's someone after me."

Ashley didn't believe it for a minute. But then again, how could the murderer have found Eric's house? She started to shiver. "Maybe he followed us here when you picked me up."

"No. Unless he's an incredible tracker. Unless he knows this area. Listen, I don't know what's going on."

"Who would be coming after you?"

"Who knows?"

Ashley turned away from him worriedly. She almost screamed when he touched her shoulders to turn her around.

"Ashley—"

"I'm still afraid that I've put you at terrible risk."

He hesitated a second. Then a smile curved his lips and he touched her chin and gave a wonderful Bogart imitation. "If you have, you've been worth the risks, kid. Here's looking at you."

She smiled, but then her smile faded. "What are we going to do?"

He shrugged. "We could stay here. With the shutters down, the house is like Fort Knox. I'd have the advantages . . ." His voice trailed away, and he shook his head. "No, because if I don't show up at Wendy's, she or Brad will come here, and they could be taken unaware. We should move. Get dressed," he told Ashley. "Get something from the armoire. Jeans, socks, boots and a long-sleeved shirt. There might be a lot of mosquitoes out."

Her eyes held his and she nodded, as if in a daze. He gave her a little shove out to the bedroom and picked up the clothes he had already chosen for himself off the bathroom floor. When he came back into the bedroom, he paused.

She was in jeans, just as he had suggested. And in a soft pink long-sleeved and tailored shirt with mother-of-pearl buttons. He hadn't seen the outfit worn in a long time. Not in over four years. He hurt for a second. And for another second, he wanted her to look horrible in it. Her hair should have clashed with the pink. Elizabeth's hair—black as ebony, straight, lush—had been beautiful over that pink.

But he couldn't remember his wife's face at that moment, not as he was looking at Ashley there. Her eyes emerald bright, she was pale but resolved, calm and almost stoic, awaiting his next words.

He glanced to the side table. The emerald earrings and bracelet were still there. He snatched them up and shoved them into his pocket.

Was someone after the Tyler jewels? Or were they after Ashley?

Or had someone come to settle an old score with him? He just didn't have the answers.

"Come on," he told her, reaching for her hand.

"Where are we going?"

"To Wendy's. I told you before, Brad is with the DEA. Maybe he'll have some idea what's going on."

"But what—what if someone's out there?" Ashley asked.

Eric shook his head. "Whoever it was is gone now, and it's going to be almost impossible to reach us if we're moving in the swamp. Here, take this."

He thrust the gun at her. He was afraid that she would jump back or refuse to take it, but she closed her fingers over the handle. "It's loaded."

"You just saw it fired," he said.

She nodded.

"Do you know how to shoot?" he asked her.

She nodded. "Yes. Not well, but I've been at a range a few times."

"That'll do," Eric told her. He gripped her free hand and drew her along the hallway with him. He paused in his office for the shotgun and to close the shutters. Ashley winced. He glanced at her with a frown.

"I'm afraid I've got longer feet than ... than your wife," she said softly.

He didn't reply but took her out the front door.

"Eric?" Ashley asked him quietly.

"What?"

"How did your wife die?"

She searched his features. No anger touched his eyes or tightened his face, but he didn't answer her, either.

"It's too long a story for now," he told her. "I want to get moving."

"But what if someone *is* out here?" she demanded.

"No one's here."

"But how—"

"I would know," he assured her. Looking at him, Ashley fell silent. She knew that he was telling her the truth.

He led her around the back to the large shed. He went in but left her standing outside. She heard the loud hum of the generator and saw him walk toward a large airboat.

Ashley determined to keep silent. It was hard. She was terrified.

Almost as frightened as she had been when she had watched the one figure plunge a knife into the chest of the other. What was happening? How had she been traced to Eric's? How could anyone find her here? They had seen her...and they had seen Eric, too. They had seen him sweep her up and take her away, and they had only waited for the storm to abate before coming for her.

She heard a startling clang. Eric had opened the back doors and pulled out a ramp, and the airboat was clattering its way down the ramp to the grass. He reached for her hand. She frowned. "Don't we need a canal?"

"That is the canal," he told her.

"Oh!"

Despite the danger, he smiled. And she smiled, too.

She was glad of the boots she wore, even if they were too small, because she sank ankle deep into muck as he led her to the airboat. She saw that he was right, that they were on a canal. But it was swollen with grass, and it was very hard to tell what was supposed to be water and what was supposed to be land.

"Have a seat," he murmured to her. "And keep that gun ready. Just in case we need it."

He turned to start the motor, but then he paused, looking toward the land. Ashley started to shiver, not knowing what he heard. Then she heard it, too. A certain rustling through the grass.

"Eric?" she whispered.

"It's all right," he told her.

"All right?"

"It's just Baby."

Ashley swallowed hard as she saw the big cat come bounding out after them. Neither muck nor grass nor water seemed to bother Baby. She headed toward the airboat full speed. Ashley felt her heart rise to her throat. The cat suddenly leaped off the ground, landing almost on top of Ashley.

She fought hard not to panic as she stared into the panther's huge tawny eyes. Baby stared at her, then shoved its silky soft head against her shoulder.

Ashley almost screamed. She gritted her teeth and looked up at Eric. "Nice kitty. Nice, nice kitty."

Eric grinned. "She likes you."

"Wow."

He laughed, then started the motor. He must have kept it in good repair, for it burst to life almost immediately.

Baby sat down at Ashley's feet.

Eric crawled up to the seat and took the wheel, steering the craft over the canal. Ashley leaned back, feeling the wind on her face. They went faster for a moment, but then Eric slowed down. Ashley looked around in dismay, feeling as if she had dropped off the face of the earth. She had never seen anything so forlorn. It seemed that destruction was everywhere. Branches and whole trees were in the water. The airboat could glide over the long grass easily enough, but she had a feeling that the endless tangle of fallen branches and shrubs was harder to negotiate.

She looked up to find him studying her. She tried to smile, but he didn't smile in return and only continued to watch her.

"How do you know where you're going?" she shouted against the roar of the motor.

"It's just like New York when you get used to it!" he said.

"How!"

"Well, we're on Fifth Avenue now. But we'll have to start taking the little side streets soon!"

She laughed and looked down at the cat. Tentatively she placed a hand on the panther's head. Baby closed her eyes, delighted as Ashley stroked her ears. A pet, huh? She'd heard of the "love me love my dog" type, but this . . .

This was more, she realized suddenly. To love Eric, a woman would need to love his world. It wasn't that he wouldn't accept another, it was just that he would always need to come back here. It wasn't simply the swamp, or his family, or even his people, it was the whole way of life. It was the choices he lived with, the solitude and the independence. Even if he said that he would give it up, he most probably could not. He wasn't a crusader, but he was a link between the old world and the new, between progress and heritage. He would never let one go for the other; he was always open to both.

She rested her chin on her hands and closed her eyes, and she wasn't afraid. No one could reach her as she was soaring across the swamp. She didn't need to be afraid.

It wasn't circumstance, though. It was Eric. No matter what he chose to do, she would feel safe with him. She would believe in him.

She swallowed hard and wondered what had happened to her in the past few days. She couldn't help but think what it would be like to stay. She found it hard to remember New York City, harder still to remember that her goals had centered on her business, and even harder still to think of dressing up in silk for drinks at the Plaza.

She'd always loved the city. It had its own magic, its own dangers, its own pulse and personality. But she didn't want to return. Instead she wanted to pretend that a bullet had never shattered her dream world and that she could go back into Eric's bedroom and lie with him....

With her Tyler jewels and his primitive earth.

The wind blew hard on her face again and she set the gun down to wind her hair into a knot. Baby settled her head on Ashley's lap. Then Eric lowered their speed once more. Ashley looked around her. A thick mass of wild orchids clogged the way before them. The water was strewn with logs. Then she realized that one of the logs came equipped with eyes. Beady, dark alligator eyes. They stared at her and she shivered as the alligator's nose moved into the water. Farther along the embankment she noticed a second alligator. Its mouth was wide open. The endless rows of teeth were fully visible, along with the creature's tongue and throat. It waited, Ashley realized. It waited dead still for its dinner to come along and walk right in.

She sensed he was looking at her again. Ashley looked up and grimaced. "Cute!"

He didn't reply, but his dark lashes fell over his eyes, and she thought that he hadn't been too disappointed in her response to the creatures. She hadn't gone completely with instinct. She hadn't screamed hysterically and begged him to get her far away.

She shivered, then set Baby's head on the deck. She stood, coming close to Eric. "They're horrible-looking things," she told him.

After a moment, he placed an arm around her shoulders. "But as you might have noticed, Miss Dane, the deadliest creature in any jungle is still man."

"I noticed," she said softly.

He pointed ahead. "There, up there. See the hummock?"

She didn't, at first. Then she did see the large island and the spot of color just beyond the trees. A house. A home. Life in the midst of wilderness.

"Your sister-in-law's?" she asked.

"Yes!"

Ashley tried to smooth back her hair, but the wind wouldn't allow her a pretense of tidiness. Even as they came around the last bend and Eric cut the motor completely, the breeze tossed around tendrils of her hair. The airboat slowly came toward something like a dock, heavily laden with bracken and brush, as everything else was. She could see the house then. It was neat and storybook perfect, and a lot like Eric's. The front door burst open and a small blond woman came running out. A tall, broad-shouldered and dark-haired man followed her more slowly, a grin on his face.

"Eric!" the woman called. He leaped from the airboat to the mucky shore, and she hugged him fiercely. "You're all right? Any damage? I thought that you were going to try to come back. But then everything picked up so suddenly, didn't it? I was anxious—"

"Wendy!" the man interrupted her softly. "He's not alone."

Eric turned around, reaching out a hand to help Ashley to the shore. "Ashley, Brad and Wendy McKenna. Brad, Wendy, this is Ashley Dane."

"But we know that already!" Wendy said, her voice soft and musical and touched with a pleasant laughter. "We've been waiting for you."

Shaking hands with the woman, Ashley frowned. "You've been waiting for me?"

She nodded, looking over her head at Eric. "Your friends are here. Didn't Eric tell you?"

Ashley looked back at Eric and smiled sweetly. He shrugged. "I didn't know if they were still here or not. You were going to try to get them into town, Brad."

"I couldn't get them into town. It was too late and too much was happening."

"What are you talking about?" Ashley asked.

Then the door slammed open again and she heard her own name called. "Ashley! Thank God you're all right!"

Tara came running out and threw her arms around Ashley. They almost fell. Ashley hugged Tara in return and realized that there was something very different about her friend.

"The baby!" she cried in alarm, stepping back.

"The baby is inside and just fine," Brad said. "And Wendy, don't you think that you should get your patient back inside?"

"Yes, we should all get inside," Eric said.

Ashley saw that Brad cast him a quick glance, and she knew that Eric had managed to convey a sense of their danger with those few words.

"We should all get inside," Brad agreed. He lifted a hand, indicating that the women should precede him. Anxious to see Tara's baby and Rafe, Ashley started walking. But then she paused.

She looked back at Eric. He stood some distance from her, but he was watching her.

She shivered suddenly, because his glance was cold. And he seemed very distant.

His lashes fell, and he shrugged at her questioning gaze. What had been between them was over, she thought desperately. He had delivered her here, and that was that to him.

"Shall we go in?" he persisted.

She turned around blindly to follow Tara, praying that she wouldn't cry, then determined that she would never do so.

Chapter 7

There were several moments of confusion after they entered the house, and Ashley didn't realize that Eric and Brad
had not followed them in. Rafe was there, sitting on a sofa
with a bright-eyed toddler on his lap, and watching the tiny
infant who slept in a crib created from a bureau drawer. He
stood quickly, throwing the little boy onto his hip. "Ashley, thank God!" He gave her a fierce hug, with the little boy
pressed between them looking on in wide-eyed wonder.

Wendy rescued her son, saying, "This is Josh. Josh, this
is Miss Dane. Get your sticky fingers out of her hair."

Ashley laughed and untangled her hair from the beautiful little boy's fingers. He couldn't have been two years old;
his coloring was his mother's, his handsome features were
his father's. He would grow up to be a heartbreaker, she
thought. "You can pull my hair whenever you like, Josh,"
she told him. "And you can call me Ashley."

He gave her an enchanting grin. "'lee!"

Wendy smiled, shrugging ruefully as Josh reached out

again for the bright hair. "It's the color, I think. Oh, that sounds so rude! But it's just beautiful—"

"Please, it *is* red!" Ashley laughed, bending down to study the baby clad in a long sack gown. "A girl or a boy?" she asked. The infant had a head full of dark hair. Rafe's hair, certainly not Tara's.

"Amy," Rafe told her proudly.

"Amy! Oh, she's just beautiful, too. But how? When? Shouldn't you be in a hospital, isn't—"

"Ashley, everything went beautifully!" Tara swept her arms around Ashley's shoulders and sank to the couch with her. "Wendy used to be a nurse. She was wonderful, I'll never be able to thank her enough." She flashed a grateful smile to Wendy, who flushed and shrugged.

"It was nothing, really."

"It was everything," Rafe said softly. The McKennas had a friend for life, Ashley thought.

"Wendy doesn't think that Amy is really premature. She thinks that I miscalculated, which is possible, I suppose. The sonogram readings always were a bit off."

"And I'm glad!" Wendy admitted. "We would have had to take some drastic measure to reach a hospital if the baby had needed an incubator. But—" she paused, grinning again "—by the meat scale in the kitchen, Amy Elizabeth Tyler was born at a good eight pounds, one ounce."

"Ready for the world," Rafe commented. "Although her mother deserves a good talking to."

"Rafe, I promise I'll never, never do anything like it again."

"You're right. When we have another child, I'll lock you up in a tower for the last two months."

Wendy laughed. "You're not supposed to talk about another child when your wife isn't even a week past her introduction to labor pains, Rafe Tyler. Ashley, how about a glass of wine?"

Ashley glanced at the door. Eric and Brad were still outside. Eric must be telling Brad about the shots, and surely

about the murder she had witnessed. She should feel relieved. The police would have to be notified. She was aware
that the DEA and the regular homicide department were not
the same thing, but she was also aware that drugs poured
into south Florida from South America, and so the murder
might be in Brad's jurisdiction after all. They would all believe her now. Eric's house had been shot up.

"Ashley?" Wendy said.

"Yes, I'd love some wine. Let me help."

"No. You sit and watch the baby. I think that Tara was
more worried about you than she was about her labor pains.
I told her that you'd be okay since we sent Eric back to make
sure that everyone had gotten out." She gave Ashley a dazzling smile, and Ashley smiled in return. "Brad can help
me." Then Wendy frowned. "Where is he? Out with Eric
still? What can they be doing?"

Ashley looked at the baby. Amy was so tiny and perfect,
and she slept so peacefully. Tara was radiant and everything seemed to have come out so very well.

Thanks to Eric.

Wendy, holding a bottle of white wine in one hand and
balancing Josh on her hip with the other, looked at Ashley
worriedly.

"I'll call in Eric and Brad—" Rafe began but broke off
when Ashley jumped to her feet.

"Eric is telling Brad . . . what happened."

"And what happened?" Rafe asked, frowning.

"We . . . were shot at. In his house. And I think it's because I saw a murder."

"A murder?" Rafe echoed.

Wendy was very still. Tara stiffened. For several seconds, they looked at one another, and then at Ashley. Rafe
walked over to her and took her gently by the shoulders. "A
murder? Where? When? What are you talking about? There
was the storm—"

"Rafe!" Ashley loved her best friend's husband, but at
the moment she didn't like the tone of his voice. "I'm tell-

ing you the truth and you know that I don't imagine things."

"But, Ashley—" Tara began.

"All right, tell us about it," Rafe said. "Wendy, let me help you with the wine. I'll have a scotch myself, if it's handy."

"Of course," Wendy murmured politely.

"Come on, Ashley, talk," Rafe reminded her gently.

She shook her head suddenly. "I shouldn't have come here! Tara is here with the baby, and Wendy has her little boy, and I shouldn't have—I shouldn't have taken any chances!"

"Tara and Amy are going to be fine," Rafe assured her.

"Ashley, will you tell us the story, please!" Wendy said, and she smiled with serene assurance. "Trust me. We can deal with it."

Ashley hesitated just a second, then started to tell her story. After she described everything that had happened, they all stared at her.

"Ashley, are you sure about what you saw?" Rafe demanded.

"Absolutely."

"But still—"

"Rafe, we were shot at today in Eric's house. He'll tell you that that's the truth."

Wendy moistened her lips and started to hand out the drinks. She smiled at Tara. "We do believe you. But it's going to be all right. You're safe here now. We're all with you."

"And in danger," Ashley added.

Rafe sat her down, taking her hands. "Brad is with the DEA and you've known me a long time, I can handle whatever comes up." He brushed her chin lightly with his knuckles.

"Ashley, whatever you're into, we're with you, and you know that!" Tara announced.

Wendy pressed a glass of white wine into Ashley's fingers. "You needn't worry about us. No one could have followed Eric here, not in an airboat. You can see for miles and miles."

"If he goes home," Ashley murmured miserably, "he'll still be in danger."

Wendy watched her with a curious smile, then shrugged. "He made it through three years in Vietnam and helped Brad and me once when we were involved with one of the most cold-blooded killers in history. And no one—no one— knows the swamp like he does. Trust me. Eric will be fine." She clinked her wineglass with Ashley's. "Cheers. Come on now, Ashley. Dinner is almost ready, and we'll get to the bottom of this. I promise."

Outside, Eric was telling Brad what he knew, from the time that he had found Ashley running through the swamp up to the shots that had been fired into his bedroom.

They sat together on the high slope of lawn leading to the house. Baby had crawled between, as she often did. Eric and Brad had been good friends since Wendy had first met Brad. Then Brad had been the one lost in the swamp, the victim of an undercover operation that had burst wide open.

It had been strange at first, seeing Brad in his brother's house with Wendy, his brother's wife. And despite the fact that Brad had brought danger down upon them all, he had liked Brad. He had probably tormented Wendy and Brad by trying to make them see that they could live without one another, but that it wouldn't really be living.

And he had become involved in the drug case that had brought Brad into the swamp. If he and Brad had not trusted each other instinctively and instantly, Wendy might have been lost to them all.

As it had happened, Eric had found himself the best man at Wendy's wedding, and his grandfather had given her away, just like a true daughter. And Brad McKenna had become his best friend.

"I didn't believe her at first," Eric told Brad as he chewed on a blade of grass. "I thought that she was hysterical. I mean, she came out of that swamp half naked, screaming wildly. And she hates the swamp. She hates it more than you did. I thought that maybe she'd seen a snake or a gator or something and gone a little berserk."

Brad shook his head worriedly. "But then you were shot at—in the house?"

"Yep. We sat out the storm. I even let a day go by after the storm before rolling up the shutters." He looked at Brad sharply. Brad's tawny eyes were clouded.

"There was a murder out here," he said slowly.

"What?" Eric demanded, half rising. "How do you know?"

"Billy Powell with the tribal police airboated his way here this morning. He had a few messages for me from the office, and he warned us about the body."

"The body?"

Brad nodded gravely. "They found a man in a yellow rain slicker in one of the canals. He had been stabbed to death."

"Then she was telling the truth," Eric said. "Obviously she was telling the truth. First the shots, and now the body. Those prove the whole thing."

"And that's why you brought her here?"

Eric shrugged, then grinned. "Where else would I bring my problems?" he asked.

Brad surveyed him for a long moment. "She's a very beautiful woman. Probably the most exotic I've ever seen."

"Careful," Eric warned. "You're married to my sister-in-law, remember?"

Brad laughed. "Sure, I remember. I was just commenting on your behalf. Just in case you hadn't noticed."

"I'll bet he has noticed," a voice said cheerfully behind them. Eric swung around. Wendy had come out. She fluffed her shoulder-length hair and slid down into her husband's arm. Looking at Eric, she said, "I think he's noticed, don't you, Brad?"

"Wendy-bird, you're trouble," Eric warned her, using the nickname he had given her when they had been very young.

It didn't bother her in the least. She stuck out her tongue at him and smiled up at Brad. "Uh-oh." Her eyes widened as she watched Eric's narrow, but her smile deepened. "I think he has even noticed that she isn't an ordinary woman in any shape or form. Look at him, Brad. He looks as if he wants to scalp me."

"She needs a good one on the rump, Brad," Eric said.

"Hey, I sympathize, but what can I tell you?" Brad replied.

"Brat," Eric commented.

"Hey, watch it, Tonto!" Wendy protested.

Brad looked at his wife sharply. Wendy was one of the few people who could get away with such things with Eric Hawk. And she was pushing it now. "Children, children! We've got a problem here."

"She told us all. I think that she's concerned about Rafe and Tara's baby more than anything else." Wendy smiled demurely. "I told her that we weren't the type to panic, that we'd weathered a few of our own storms. And I don't think that Rafe Tyler is the type to panic and run half-cocked, either, do you? Let's go in and have dinner."

"Dinner?" Eric murmured.

"Yes, it's a meal one eats at night," Wendy said sweetly.

"I think maybe I ought to head out. Talk to the police, see the family—"

"Dinner, I think is what Wendy suggested," Brad said flatly. Then he smiled, his eyes on Eric. "Runaway. That's what Seminole means, right? You're the one who taught me. You aren't thinking about trying to run away from a redhead, are you?"

Eric scowled fiercely. "I don't run from anything, and you know it."

Brad grinned. "This is fun. I never thought to see you behaving so strangely. It must have been one heckuva storm."

"You know that it was a bad storm. You weathered it here."

"No, no. I'm talking about the one that took place inside your house."

"I told you about shots being fired and that Ashley saw a murder take place and—"

"And I'm talking about your love life. Hmm, this is going to be fun. Remember how he tortured us as first, Wendy? He didn't want to leave you alone with me."

"For good reason," Eric retorted.

"Then he kept telling us all the reasons we shouldn't be together."

"So that you would see how stupid you were being," Eric told him with exasperation.

"This is going to be fun," Brad repeated to Wendy.

"It isn't going to be anything," Eric said softly. "The emerald lady is going to fly away. Back to New York, away from danger. And that's that."

"What did happen during that storm?" Wendy whispered softly to Brad.

"Shots were fired—" Eric began.

"But this is far more important in the long run," Wendy insisted, her silver eyes huge and taunting.

"There won't be any long run if this doesn't get settled," Eric said, standing. He stared at the swamp, pointedly ending the conversation.

"Let's have dinner," Brad said. "No one's going to bother anyone with Baby prowling around out here. And I haven't taken down many of the shutters. We'll be safe inside. I don't think that anyone could have followed you here anyway, not without your seeing them. You didn't see anything, did you?"

Eric shook his head slowly. No one had followed him here, he knew. He relaxed. "Dinner," he agreed, and they went in together.

Rafe was in the living room, and he was quick to demand to know Eric's version of everything that had happened. Then he thanked Eric for keeping Ashley safe.

"I don't need to be thanked," Eric told him.

"None of us would have made it without you," Rafe said. Eric noticed that Ashley, talking to Wendy across the room as she sipped a glass of wine, had looked up. His eyes met hers, and he quickly turned away with a shrug. He shouldn't have come here, except that he'd had to. But then he should have dropped Ashley off and run. Runaway. Just like Brad had said.

He turned back to Rafe, who was sipping a beer. "I'm just glad that Wendy knows her stuff." Tara appeared and kissed Eric's cheek, demanding he come to see the baby. Amy was in the guest bedroom now, in her little drawer, and sound asleep again. Something about the infant and her mother's sublime happiness touched him and he smiled, daring to caress the tiny cheek. "She's...beautiful," he told Tara.

Tara shivered. "And alive, and healthy, and so am I! We're so very grateful." She laughed softly. "Well, we might have survived without you. Rafe is resourceful, but he wasn't counting on my miscalculations. He didn't want me to be out there, but I had been so insistent, and well...never mind. I'm awfully glad that you found us and brought us here." A shadow passed over her eyes and she shivered. "And then there's Ashley. She's like a sister, and if she'd been left alone there with a murderer...I don't even dare think about it."

"I didn't do anything. She stumbled into me."

Searching out his eyes, Tara smiled suddenly. "Don't ever kid yourself, Mr. Hawk. Ashley is tough. She's made it through a number of very rough spots before, and she's never lacked courage."

"She did very well," he heard himself say.

"She's been shot at before."

"I heard about the trouble in Venezuela."

Tara blushed. "Yes. I guess it made a lot of the newspapers."

"I'm glad everything came out so well."

"Yes, so am I." She tucked a tiny blanket around her baby. "Thank goodness your sister-in-law has supplies for a baby!" She looked up at him. "The police have promised to get us a chopper tomorrow. I have to go to a hospital with the baby. I've never felt better in my entire life, but Wendy insists that I should go and Rafe agrees. I almost hate to leave, but I'll be glad to get Ashley away, after what has happened."

She was smiling and speaking so sweetly, so softly. He felt as if she had cast scalding oil over him and sliced him from midsection to groin. Ashley would be going away with them. Back where she belonged. She hadn't told him.

It didn't matter that she hadn't had much of a chance. It just suddenly hurt like all hell, and then he felt like a fool. He had known it all along. She was a beautiful gem cast down in the mud, and he had picked her up and cleaned her off—but now she was going back to her different world where she could shine in a black-velvet setting. He had been a fool to get involved.

Somehow, he just hadn't expected her to leave so quickly.

"I guess we'd better get on out," Tara whispered, taking his arm. She led him back to the living and dining room combination. "I did want to say thank you. You did so very much for us."

"I didn't do a thing. Wendy did."

Wendy heard him. She laughed. "I know all about birthing babies!" she teased with wide eyes. Then she came over to them, dragging Ashley along with her. "Isn't she just darling? Oh, Eric, she's just beautiful. All that hair! Josh didn't have that much hair until he was almost six months old! Come, let's eat."

They sat at the dining table, and the longer the meal went on, the more Eric wished that he had departed right after bringing Ashley. It wasn't that Wendy couldn't cook—she could. She and Brad had a generator, so she had been able to make a big tray of lasagna with canned spinach and tons of garlic bread.

And conversation flowed easily. Brad had lived in New York for a while, and he and Rafe discussed streets and buildings, theater and music and ball games in the park. Tara got Eric's attention by telling him how her labor pains started about two minutes after he had left them at Wendy and Brad's door, and now they had called the hospital only to be warned that the roads were already impassable and that she was best off staying where she was.

Ashley smiled at Eric, but it wasn't a warm smile. "You never mentioned any of this."

"I thought that they were well on their way out of the swamp," he said, looking at her. He smiled crookedly and took a long sip of burgundy wine. "You never mentioned, Miss Dane, that you were flying out of here in a helicopter tomorrow."

"I didn't have a chance."

She was hurt, and he knew it. He hadn't touched her, he hadn't gone near her, he had barely acknowledged her existence, and she was sitting right next to him.

She didn't understand. They were back in the real world. The Tylers might be the nicest people in the world, but theirs was still a different world, and pretty soon, Ashley would realize that. Wendy's table was set with beautiful linen and china and crystal wine goblets, but the table still sat in the middle of the swamp.

And Ashley was still a glittering gem, accidentally dropped into that swamp. Somehow, being here with Wendy made the past cascade down on him with great ferocity. He didn't want to, but when he closed his eyes, he could see Wendy's face when they had gone to the mortuary together to identify Leif and Elizabeth. He could imagine his own face. He could see the blood spilled all over his wife's white dress and Leif's white dinner jacket. His brother had died defending Elizabeth, and he had sworn then that he would always defend Wendy. Wendy had Brad now, but she and Eric would also always have their link. Stronger than blood, maybe. He knew that Wendy wanted him to have a future, but tonight, all he could see was the past. He suddenly felt wrong. He'd had women before, but he'd never felt the way he did with Ashley. Never felt the guilt, as if he were giving more than he had the right to give, as if he were taking more than he had the right to demand.

"So, Eric, how did the two of you manage during all those days of wind and rain and havoc?" Brad asked.

Eric glanced down the table. Brad had a mischievous and very self-satisfied look about his eyes.

"Fine," Eric said flatly.

"No television, no movies, no music! What on earth did you do to keep occupied?" Wendy questioned innocently.

"I can imagine what he wanted to be doing," Brad said not so innocently.

Eric heard a choking sound. It was Ashley. Brad patted her on the back, handing her a glass of water. "Sorry, Ashley. Are you all right?"

"I'm fine!" Ashley gasped.

"That was a guilty choke if I ever heard one," Tara said, then smiled sweetly.

"Still choking," Brad said, shaking his head. "I hope that she's all right."

"I doubt if she is," Wendy said sweetly. She looked at the Tylers with wide, innocent eyes. "He's such a son of a gun, my brother-in-law."

"Nasty as all hell," Brad agreed pleasantly. Then he looked at Eric again. "How did you pass the time? Ashley, was he decent to you?"

"Brad!" There was an edge to Eric's warning.

Ashley still looked as if she were strangling. Beautiful, pale, stunned and very ill at ease. "Of course, he was decent."

"A perfect gentleman," Wendy drawled.

"Wendy!" Tara piped in sweetly. "I'm sure that he was good to her, much more than good."

"Tara!" Ashley snapped.

"What were you all expecting?" Rafe asked pleasantly. "The man is very ethical."

"Well, you just never know with Eric," Brad said. "We had a bit of trouble down here a few years ago on our doorstep and Eric had one of the culprits convinced that he was about to be skinned alive."

"Finding a naked, red-haired beauty in the swamp, who knows what he did!" Wendy said sweetly.

"I was not naked!" Ashley protested. She looked at Eric, and her eyes shone brightly against the porcelain beauty of her flesh. He tried to smile but gritted his teeth instead and turned to his sister-in-law. "Wendy-bird, the great spirits might very well come out of the sky and get you for this," he warned.

"I'll take my chances," Wendy said with a laugh.

Eric stood, achingly aware of how he wanted to sweep Ashley into his arms, hold her against him and tell them all to go to hell and that he'd enjoyed every second of the storm. But the storm was over.

She wasn't admitting anything. Neither was he.

He decided he wasn't going to be very good company, not for the rest of that night.

He spoke, careful to keep smiling. "I've got to go."

"Go!" Wendy said.

"I want to check on Mary and Willie and the kids. I know that they went to Big Cypress, but I'm willing to bet that they're back at the village. I would have gone earlier except for... except for Ashley. But she's safe here with you."

Ashley was already standing. They all were. Eric reached into his pocket for the emeralds he had scooped off his side table. "Here, these are yours, right?"

Rafe glanced down at the gems and looked into Eric's eyes. "Thanks for returning them. But they aren't important. My wife is, Ashley is. If we don't get to see you again, thanks for everything you did for them. And if you come to New York, make sure you see us. Please. If there's anything you ever need..."

Eric nodded. "I do come to New York from time to time. Maybe I will see you. Tara, good luck with the baby." He faced Ashley at last. "And good luck to you, Ashley," he said simply.

He turned away quickly. He didn't want to see the widening of her emerald eyes when she looked up at him. He didn't want to think of her, and he didn't want to remember her. It was over.

He started to say goodbye to Wendy, then paused, frowning. He heard something.

Baby. She was screeching and growling, the way she did when some stranger came around. Then he heard a distant airboat motor.

"What is it?" Wendy asked him anxiously.

"Someone, something," he said.

Ashley felt a coldness settle over her. The three men were already moving. Eric pulled his .38 from his waistband and headed for the door. Brad reached in the hallway closet, took a gun and tossed one to Rafe. They were all ready for danger, Ashley thought. It was chilling.

Wendy's hands fell on her shoulders. "Come on, get down," Wendy said softly.

Eric was already out the door. She heard him explode with an expletive.

Then he stuck his handsome face back inside. She would never forget the way he looked at that moment. His black hair fell straight against his collar and his eyes were nearly lime against the dark hue of his face. His full mouth was curved in a wry smile. He seemed invincible, and yet terribly human. Strong, masculine... almost reachable and capable of laughter again.

"It's okay, guys. We can all stand up again."

"Who is it?" Wendy demanded irritably.

"Seems we don't have to go to the police," he said. "The police have come to us." He turned around, looking back outside. "Baby, stop that and behave. It's just Billy Powell and Mica. They're the good guys, Baby. Are you ever going to learn?"

Chapter 8

"Hey, Billy!" Eric called out.

Billy swore, hopping ankle deep into the muck and wading to the house. He looked at Brad, Rafe and Eric standing in the doorway with guns, and with Wendy, Tara and Ashley behind. Billy was a man of medium height with coal dark hair and eyes, striking wide cheekbones and broad shoulders. Mica, an older, leaner man, followed him. There was a tag on their airboat proclaiming them tribal police. Billy was wearing a light brownish gray uniform with insignias on the shoulder. The older man was wearing uniform pants with a brightly colored Seminole shirt. He nodded to them in silence, letting Billy do the talking.

"What are you all expecting, the holdup of Fort Knox?"

Eric smiled and shook his head. "We heard you found a body."

"Yeah, I found a body." Baby was sniffing his hands. "Leave off, Baby, I haven't got anything for you," Billy said, then looked directly at Eric. "I just went by your place and saw all the broken glass. I figured your window was shot to hell. Mind telling me what's going on?''

Eric shrugged. ''I was hoping that you could tell us. But about your body, well, we might know something.'' He pulled Ashley forward and introduced her to Officer Billy Powell, and Sergeant Mica Crane.

It seemed to Eric that Billy held Ashley's hand a long time and that it took him a long time to manage to speak again. ''Hi, Miss Dane. It's real nice to meet you. Real, real nice.''

''My pleasure, officer,'' Ashley said. Then she nodded to Mica. ''Sergeant Crane.''

''Mica. Just Mica,'' Wendy said, smiling at the older man. ''It's short for Micanopy, which means chief. And he is a big chief, very important on the council.''

''Mica.'' Billy released Ashley's hand. Mica took it. The old coot was flushing, Eric thought.

''Why don't you tell them what happened, Ashley?'' Eric asked her.

''Let's bring them inside first, hmm?'' Wendy said, and they all went in. Ashley found herself on the couch next to Billy with Eric behind her. Hesitating a bit, she explained about her walk with Harrison Mosby into the swamp.

Rafe exploded with anger. ''Mosby was harassing you! Why didn't you tell me?''

''I thought I could take care of it myself, Rafe,'' Ashley said softly, her lashes lowering. ''Anyway, then I was lost. I was just running blindly. Then I saw the three men—''

''Men?'' Billy asked.

''Well, the three figures. You're right—I've no idea if they were men or women. I never saw faces clearly at all. I never saw the victim.''

''But you know that they saw you?'' Billy said.

She nodded, trying to explain. ''They turned—the two living figures—and looked at me. And I ran again.''

''Into Eric.''

''Yes.'' She said the word so softly it was barely heard. ''Yes, I ran into Eric.''

"And today someone tried to kill you."

Ashley looked up. She felt Eric standing close to her.

"Someone shot my room," he replied for her.

"Your bedroom?" Billy asked.

There was a slight hesitation. "Yes," Eric said flatly. "It was one of the rooms where I had opened the shutters."

"What makes you think that they were aiming at Miss Dane when they shot into your bedroom window?"

"Because she was a guest in my house, sleeping in my room," Eric said smoothly. Then he snapped, "Hell, Billy, I don't know what's going on. Maybe someone was aiming for me. Who knows?"

"Yeah, who knows? Tomorrow morning, Miss Dane, we'll have you identify the body. We've got it in Mac's big freezer at the gas station. We still can't reach the city. Phone lines are down everywhere. Roads are flooded. Airboat and helicopter are the only way out, and we'll be airlifting him out tomorrow afternoon. If you don't mind, Miss Dane, I'll bring you to see the corpse and help me with a little paperwork before then."

"Of course I don't mind," Ashley said.

"You're staying here tonight?"

"Yes," Brad answered for her.

"And you, Eric?"

"I'm going out to check on the folks."

"Maybe you shouldn't—" Billy began.

"I can take care of myself, and you know it," Eric told him.

Billy looked at Eric for what seemed like a long time. Ashley longed to turn around and study Eric's face, but she didn't allow herself. She watched Billy's eyes instead, and he seemed to know that Eric could take care of himself.

"Well, one of us will stick around outside for the night," the officer remarked.

"That's good," Eric said.

"It's probably not necessary," Brad said.

Billy smiled. "No, it's not, G-man." He laughed. "But if I don't stay, you won't sleep, and with everything going on, you should probably have a decent night's rest."

Brad shrugged. "Suit yourself. I tell you what. I'll spell you."

"Sounds good."

"I'm moving on," Mica said. "Check on some other people."

"I'm going, too," Eric said.

"I'll need your statements, too, Eric." Billy told him.

"I'll walk you all to the door," Brad said.

Ashley watched Eric leave. He didn't turn to look behind; he walked cleanly away.

Outside Mica paused, looking intently at Eric. "John Jacobs is out," he said.

Eric inhaled sharply. "What do you mean, out?"

"Who the hell is John Jacobs?" Brad demanded.

Eric didn't answer; he couldn't. Jacobs had been one of the punks who had broken into the liquor store—and shot his brother and his wife.

He couldn't seem to find the words to explain, and he was glad that Mica was there, with his passive, lined face and onyx eyes telling nothing of emotion or pain. "Jacobs was in the gang that killed Elizabeth and Leif."

Brad's lips parted as if he were going to speak, but they closed. Then he blurted, "What the hell is he doing out?"

"Calm down, McKenna," Mica said. "It wasn't the state, and it wasn't the legal system. Well, all right, maybe he took a long, long walk down death row, but his appeal had been turned down and his death warrant had been signed. He escaped."

"How the—"

"He killed a guard. Switched clothing, and walked out clean as a whistle."

"I should have killed him," Eric said flatly.

"And you could have taken up residence at Raiford Penitentiary," Mica said flatly. "I just wanted you to know that he was out and that maybe those shots didn't have anything to do with your girlfriend. You keep your ear to the ground, huh, Eric Hawk?''

"Yeah. Thanks for the warning, Mica."

The tall old Indian walked down to the airboat, and Brad and Eric both watched in silence as he disappeared around the bend.

"Damn," Eric said. He felt ill. He couldn't believe that Jacobs was walking free again. Brad's hand clamped down hard on his shoulder.

"They'll get him back."

"Yeah," Eric said without much conviction.

"They will. You've got to have some faith."

"I do. I have faith in me," Eric muttered. He smiled, not wanting Brad to know how upset he was. Fires seemed to have been lit inside him. He ached; he hurt. He wanted to scream violently and tear someone to shreds. He swallowed the emotion and poked Brad lightly in the chest. "And you!" he accused Brad. "What were you doing in there?"

Brad laughed, relieved that the subject had changed, yet wondering if it really had. He kept grinning, leaning back against the closed door and folding his arms over his chest. "You deserved it, you know."

"Did I?"

"I'm surprised she didn't throw her lasagna on you."

"Yeah? Well, she's flying away tomorrow."

Brad shook his head. "Well, she isn't going to be able to leave with the Tylers. They're going out early. Ashley will have to stick around."

"She needs to get out fast. She could be in danger here."

"You're the one in danger now, Eric. Have you thought of that?"

Eric frowned. "You think that Jacobs—"

"I don't know about Jacobs. I don't know the man at all. I wasn't here then. But the person who pulled that trigger, whoever he was, knows where you live, not where Ashley is now."

Eric hesitated. "I really can take care of myself, and damned well. You know that."

"I know you're good. But I don't know a man alive who couldn't use a little help now and then."

Eric paused again. "Don't leave her alone anywhere, all right?"

"Hey! This one's your ball game, not mine!" Brad protested.

"Wait a minute. When you needed help—"

"You were around, yes. And I'll be around. I'll be wherever you want me. But it's your ball game. You want to keep her safe, you better plan on being around."

"I have to leave now. I have to see about the folks."

"She should be all right tonight. I'm here, Tyler's here, and now Billy's here, too. You can leave tonight. You need to leave tonight. Yeah, it'll be good for you. Purge your soul, my boy."

"McKenna—"

"Just remember that she's here."

"Don't worry. I won't forget."

Eric whistled for Baby. The big cat padded around the corner of the house. He was amazed that she came so quickly. Actually he was amazed that she had obeyed him at all. Training the panther had not always been a successful project.

He shrugged. "At least the cat listens."

Brad laughed and waved. "See you. Give the family our love."

Eric nodded and headed down to his airboat. He already felt as if here in knots. He was amazed to realize that it wasn't Jacobs he was thinking about. It wasn't even revenge.

It was Ashley. He felt empty and more alone than he had ever felt in his life. It was almost as if he had severed a hand and left it behind. It was insane, it was madness. They hadn't been together that long; he couldn't care that much. He wasn't in love with her.

But as he leaped aboard his airboat, he admitted that he was in something, even if it wasn't love. Love was something that grew. It came in little things—in smiles, in sharing a sunset, in sharing desires and dreams, and in building dreams. He couldn't love Ashley Dane.

Maybe it was fascination, maybe it was lust. He couldn't forget her. Not for a second. When he closed his eyes he saw her.

He didn't want to see her.

Jacobs was out.

He wouldn't come here, Eric thought. He would probably try to leave the country. There was nothing that Eric could do about it—finding Jacobs would be like finding a needle in a haystack. He could be almost anywhere in the world by now.

It gnawed at him.

But not as fiercely as the thought that he could no longer take Ashley into his arms and forget the whole world.

He could not forget her.

And as he motored away from her, he silently damned her a thousand times. He would bury himself that night in the swamp, where she didn't belong. And maybe he could forget her there.

Ashley sparkled.

She talked, she laughed, she insisted on helping in the kitchen, and she washed the dishes so swiftly that Wendy assured her that if modeling and designing ever failed, she had a sure shot as the McKenna housekeeper.

Tara, who knew her better, watched her in silence. Even Rafe—and Brad, who didn't know her at all—kept a wary eye on her. Every time she caught someone staring, that someone would smile, make no apology and keep staring.

She had to keep moving and talking and laughing. It was the only way she could stay sane. Eric's departure had been brutal, and she really wanted to hate him for it. She might have been okay if she could have just gone home, but she couldn't, not yet. She had to stay and talk to the police, and she had to go to the morgue and look at the body that had been found in the swamp. There hadn't been a single identifying mark on it, so Brad had been told. Maybe Ashley could help.

She didn't mind helping. She minded staying in the same section of the state as Eric. No, she minded being in the same part of the country.

She wanted to kick herself a thousand times. She'd known not to get involved, but she had done so anyway. Everything about Eric had fascinated her. Even while rinsing a plate to put into the dishwasher, she was barraged with memories—of his arms knotted with muscle, of his smooth and sleek chest a color between copper and bronze, of his eyes, of the tone of his voice, of his arms wrapped around her, of his body deep within her own . . .

"Wait a minute, Ashley!" Wendy pleaded. "I don't put the salad bowl in the dishwasher. Takes up too much room."

"Oh. Oh, sorry!" Ashley said quickly.

Wendy shook her head, perching on one of the bar stools. "It isn't every day that I have thousand-dollar-an-hour models to do my dishes!"

"I don't make a thousand dollars an hour," Ashley said, grinning. Wendy hadn't been offensive, though. There was nothing about her that could be offensive. She and Brad were charming. They had welcomed the whole slew of them to their home, and Ashley already felt as if she had known both all her life. They were warm and natural. "I don't even model any more," she said. "I design clothing with Tara. I only did this commercial because they both asked me to."

"That was nice of you then."

"Thanks."

Wendy was grinning and playing with a teacup. Ashley paused, salad bowl in hand, because Wendy was so nakedly and unabashedly curious about her.

"What have you been doing for the past few days?" she demanded.

Ashley almost dropped the bowl. She tried to smile and stammer some kind of answer, but then Wendy laughed apologetically and spoke. "I'm sorry. I really am. It's just that, well, Eric is my brother, in almost every sense of the word. I love him very much. I hope you'll forgive me, but I did have the most marvelous time torturing him." She smiled and shrugged. "He'd put me through a bit, if you can imagine. And it's so damned hard to reach through his reserve! I haven't seen him react to anyone the way that he reacts to you in...years," she said softly.

Ashley turned around, washed the salad bowl, then dried it carefully. "I don't think he reacted at all. He left."

"Umm. In a bit of a huff, too."

"I didn't see him 'huffing.'"

"And you never will see any of his emotions, especially a 'huff'!" Wendy said wisely. She looked past the dining room to the living area. Brad and Rafe were sitting with their heads low, deep in conversation. Billy had gone out for a walk around the property. Tara was in the guest room nursing the baby.

Wendy smiled sheepishly. "He isn't an insecure man, not at all. It's just that sometimes..." She shrugged and her voice went so low that Ashley had to set down the dishrag and come over to the counter to hear her. "Eric and his brother were a lot alike. Leif was like that. When he was really mad, he walked away. When he was upset, he walked away. Eric almost never raises his voice. I was thrilled to see him the way that he was today." Wendy nodded her head at Ashley, indicating the clothes that she was wearing. "I was startled to see you in Elizabeth's things."

"Well, that hardly means anything. He really couldn't allow me to run around with nothing."

"He might have tried tying you into a pair of his own jeans!" Wendy laughed. Then she sobered. "Does he mean anything to you, Ashley? I probably don't even have the right to ask this, but I like you, and as I said, I love Eric."

"I could, too," Ashley whispered before she realized what she was saying. Her face flooded with color. She moved away from the counter. "I . . . didn't mean that. I—"

"Didn't you?" Wendy asked. She sounded so sweet and so earnest that Ashley lowered her head.

"It can't work," she said softly.

"Why not?" It was a new voice asking the question. Tara had come out of the bedroom, looking sleepy and a little weak and pale, but somehow staunch as she smiled at Ashley.

Ashley lifted her hands to them both. "Because he doesn't want anything more to do with me."

Wendy looked at Tara. "I'm sure that he does want more to do with her."

"Right," Tara agreed. She surveyed Ashley from head to toe. "I mean, he couldn't just walk away, not from her, could he?"

"I don't think so. Where is he ever going to find that hair again?"

"Hey!" Ashley laughed. "Wait a minute, there's really nothing more to discuss here. He's gone. I'll see the police tomorrow, and then I'm going home."

"I'll take odds on that," contributed a male voice.

Startled, Ashley whirled around to see Brad. He had slipped an arm around his wife's waist and was resting his chin on her head. Rafe was there, too, holding Tara against him. "I'll say that he comes back here by twelve noon," Brad said.

"I don't know about twelve." Rafe said skeptically. "I'll say one on the nose."

"Oh, no!" Ashley moaned. "What is this! No wonder he ran out. I think that I would run, too, if I had half a chance!"

Brad came around the counter, helping himself to coffee from the pot. He winked at his wife and smiled at Ashley. "I know where he is. I can take you there if you want to go."

"I do not want to go," Ashley said firmly. "And really, I do hate the swamp. I hate the stupid sounds those rotten alligators make. I hate the mud and the muck. I hate mosquitoes. I love concrete—honest, I do."

"Hmm," Brad murmured. But he was watching her very closely again.

"Keep an eye on her. She throws things," Rafe warned.

"I do not!" Ashley protested.

"Okay, enough!" Wendy decided. She was studying her husband curiously.

"Is something wrong?" she asked him.

He shook his head. "No, of course not, what could be wrong?"

"I don't know, I just feel like you're torturing this poor woman to keep quiet about something else."

"No," Brad said thoughtfully, and grinned. "I'm torturing her for the sheer pleasure of it."

"Okay, okay," Wendy groaned. "Let's leave her in peace, shall we? Come on, Ashley, I'll show you to the women's quarters. It's kind of a small place, do you mind?"

"Mind? Of course not, I'm just grateful to be here!" Ashley said. Brad and Wendy looked at each other and smiled. Wendy led her down the hallway into the back bedroom, touching her finger to her lip when they walked past the drawer-crib with the sleeping baby. Ashley paused and knelt to look at the tiny life. Amy was so small and so perfect, and her coloring was already beautiful. Ashley's throat and her heart constricted. She had always known in a vague sort of way that she wanted children, but she had never realized until this moment just how desperately she did.

The years were ticking by, she thought. She had just passed her thirtieth birthday. Not much time left.

Women were having children in their forties these days, she reminded herself.

Yes, but dangers increased with each year.

"It's a wonderful age," Wendy whispered from behind her. "They sleep almost all the time, and they never, never answer back."

Ashley smiled but didn't reply.

"Is something wrong?" Wendy asked softly.

Ashley stood away from the baby and smiled. "Yes. I'm getting old."

"Not that old. How old are you. Twenty-seven, twenty-eight?"

"Thirty."

"Well, I'm thirty-five, and I'm not old, so that makes you a spring chicken," Wendy assured her.

"Thirty-five?" Ashley asked, stretching across the bed.

Wendy, putting a pillow into a new case, nodded. "You just made me feel eighty."

"No!" Ashley laughed. "I was just thinking about your son."

"You've plenty of time ahead of you," Wendy said, just as if she read Ashley's thoughts. "Not—" she added teasingly "—that I would want to waste any of it."

"Meaning?"

"Nothing. I'd just like to see you stay around for a while, that's all."

Ashley shook her head slowly. "I have to get out of here. And quickly. I was scared to death in the swamp when I saw the murder. And then when we were shot at . . ." Her voice trailed away and she shivered.

"And that's not it at all," Wendy said pragmatically.

Ashley sat up, crossing her legs Indian fashion beneath her. "What—what did happen to his wife?"

Wendy paused a long moment and then she sat down. "She was killed. Shot to death."

"Oh, my God!" Ashley gasped.

"With Leif," Wendy added, running her fingers over the pillowcase. "Eric and Elizabeth were having a wedding anniversary party, and he had ordered a very special wine from a friend who owned a liquor store. He was supposed to deliver the wine, but the party was right near Christmas, so he was very busy that night with customers and couldn't come. I was fixing some things in the house because I had insisted that Elizabeth wasn't to lift a finger. Eric was fooling around getting the barbeque going, and so Leif and Elizabeth went together to pick up the wine. She was so excited. Eric was quiet, even with her. He wasn't the type to say 'I love you' all the time, but he showed it in little ways.'' Wendy shrugged. ''She was really beautiful.''

''I've seen her. I've seen her picture, I mean,'' Ashley said.

Wendy nodded, as if that said it all. ''They were in white that night.'' She flashed Ashley a quick smile. ''Don't get me wrong—I'm happy now. I love Brad with all my heart, but until the day I die, I won't forget that night.''

''What happened?''

''There was a holdup at the liquor store and Leif and Elizabeth walked right into it. One of the men struck Elizabeth and Leif tried to fight him. They shot them both. Leif was killed instantly, one bullet to the heart. They shot Elizabeth four or five times. It was horrible, absolutely horrible. Friends on the tribal force came to the house for us, but I guess we both reacted very badly. It was terrible for Leif and Eric's grandparents, and the rest of the family, too, but I don't think that anyone could have understood how Eric and I felt, except Eric and me.'' Wendy fell silent then. She looked at Ashley. ''Think you understand him any better?''

Ashley looked at Wendy. ''I understand how very badly he must have been hurt. But...''

''But what?''

''I still don't understand his attitude toward me.''

Wendy shrugged. ''Fight him. He probably thinks you're a beautiful wildflower brought by the wind and soon to be swept away again. He's a hard man. There's only one thing sure about Eric.''

''What's that?''

"If you want him, you're going to have to fight for him."

Ashley was determined to salvage a bit of her pride. "I'm not sure if I want him or not," she said flatly.

"There's more that you should know," Wendy told her gravely.

"What's that?" Ashley asked.

"He went after the men who murdered Leif and Elizabeth."

Something seemed to lodge in Ashley's throat. "And—and what happened?" she said.

"Eric caught one of them."

"He—he killed that man?" Ashley said. "In cold blood?"

"It wouldn't have been 'cold' blood," Wendy murmured. "No murder would have been more violently hot. But he didn't kill the man. He turned him over to the police. He's still on death row up in Raiford."

Ashley exhaled. Then she smiled slowly. "I'm glad."

"I was glad, too. Once he passed that obstacle, he made an effort at living again." Wendy walked toward the door. "I'm going to check on Josh before I turn his room over to the guys. Help yourself to a nightgown—they're in the third drawer over there. Cotton-shirts to lace and frills. Take whatever you like and please don't be shy. There are towels and washcloths in the bath. Do you need anything else?"

"No. Thank you very much," Ashley said, smiling at Wendy and liking her very much. "You've already given me much more than I expected."

Wendy smiled in return and left.

Ashley lay back and wondered how she could have possibly come to care for Eric Hawk so deeply and so desperately and so swiftly.

And then, like Rafe and Brad, she began to wonder if he would show up the next day.

When she fell asleep that night, it was with a prayer on her lips that he would.

* * *

Five miles away, in a distant hummock, Eric stood atop a chickee in his grandfather's village and stared at the moon. It was a full moon, exceptionally big and beautiful and brilliant after the days of the storm.

Toward the center of the small village there was another chickee where a fire burned—the communal cooking fire. It was slowly dying to embers.

Eric heard night sounds. The occasional call of a crane or a heron, the whir of insects, the distant guttural grunt of a gator, all blending together in a strange and beautiful harmony.

Eric stood tall and straight and shirtless and let the night breeze wash over him and cool him. But it did little good.

He had come to forget her. Yet she was ever more present with him here.

He wanted to show her how the grass looked like a river in the moonlight. He wanted her to feel the air, and he wanted—he burned—to hold her beneath him, to make love to her in the moonlight.

She wouldn't need her Tyler jewels at all. And he would require nothing but the primitive earth and the sweeping beauty of her eyes.

She wasn't meant to be his.

One of the men who had killed Elizabeth was out, and Eric should be hating himself, because he was wishing that he could be with a woman other than his wife, instead of wondering if there was any way to catch the murderer.

There was not, he told himself, not tonight. But if God had any mercy, the murderer would be on death row again by tomorrow or the next day.

Ashley could be in danger.

Ashley would soon be gone.

But she wasn't gone yet, and she wouldn't be gone tomorrow. She was in the swamp, and she could be in danger.

He clenched and unclenched his fists at his sides. Not far away, his grandparents were surely sleeping. His whole

family was probably asleep, happy to be back in the village
where they spent their summers. Brad and Wendy even came
there sometimes. In the Seminole nation, a man joined his
wife's family, and so Brad had become part of the Hawks.
They were as close as any full-blooded relations.

But Ashley...

He wasn't going to think about her.

Great. He was going to spend his night with a tame and
half-trained panther curled up beside him when he could
have brought Ashley with him here.

Ashley? Here?

No.

He wasn't going to think about Ashley.

He stared at the moon a moment longer and felt the air
upon his bare flesh. It didn't help. It was a moon meant to
be shared. He turned away, unrolled his sleeping mat and lay
down on it. Baby crawled beside him.

"You're a poor excuse for company!" Eric charged the
cat. He closed his eyes, then opened them again. He had no
right to be worried about her. Brad and Tyler were with her.
She was safe.

He sighed. He knew that he would head back to Wendy's
first thing in the morning. Whatever happened, he was going to be with Ashley. Billy wanted to talk with him about
the shooting, so he had to go back. He should go back to
Ashley.

He would go back. Early. It wouldn't be for the police,
though. It would be for Ashley.

He sighed deeply. It was going to be one hell of a night,
lying there in a searing state of fury, longing to go back in
time—to strangle John Jacobs with his bare hands.

Eric had done the right thing. The law had dealt with Jacobs fairly. There had to be law; it was important for all
men, Eric knew. A half smile curved his lips. The Seminoles were one of the "Five Civilized Tribes."

Still he wished that he could get his hands on Jacobs
again.

There was nothing that he could do. Except, of course, dream of Ashley.

He sat up, swearing. Baby growled, annoyed that he had turned. He settled back down to try to sleep again. He would not dream. . . .

But dreams could not be denied.

And softly, slowly, hauntingly, Ashley came to him like an angel of the night and touched him with the gentle fingers of the breeze. In the darkness, she was there, an angel to sweep him into dreams.

Chapter 9

"Oh, my God!" Ashley gasped, staring down at the bloated face of the body. They were in a garage belonging to a nice old man named Mac, and the body, covered by a white sheet, was on a shelf in his back freezer.

Tara and Rafe were in Fort Lauderdale. They had been taken out that morning by helicopter. Brad and Wendy were behind her, Billy was next to her.

And Eric was there, too. He was leaning casually against the doorway, watching, waiting. No one got to see whether he would come to the house or not because Wendy had insisted on airboating to the little village to leave Josh with Willie and Mary, Eric's grandparents. Wendy wasn't taking her young son to see a corpse.

They had reached the village by eleven. Eric had been up and dressed, and had come down to the airboat, ready to accompany them. Wendy had run up to the chickees with Josh alone, and they had all waited for her in silence.

Ashley had wondered if Eric didn't want her to meet any other members of his family. It seemed that way.

Eric's appearance had given Ashley little comfort. He was cool and distant, so carefully polite. She hated it. He was with her only because he had to be, she knew. Because the police officer was going to question him again about the shots fired at his house. It would have been better if he hadn't come at all.

He was there, though, leaning against the doorway. He was wearing sunglasses that completely hid his eyes, a leather headband and a Seminole shirt in shades of red and green. His jeans fit snugly, and he looked so much like a renegade.

As much as his manner had hurt her, Ashley was more concerned with the body in front of her. She was stunned.

Bile rose in her throat. She was going to be sick. She'd never seen a corpse before, except for her grandfather's, and his body had been touched up by the mortician. He'd worn his best pin-striped suit, and he had looked as if he were sleeping.

The flesh on this corpse had gone gray. The time in the water had caused a hideous swelling. She didn't even dare think of the other things about the corpse that were just not human anymore. She knew she would feel sicker and sicker.

Because she recognized the man. She had known him in life. "Oh, my God!" she repeated, and turned around. She had to get away from the horrible stench that wafted to her despite the icy cold of the freezer.

"Ashley!"

She felt Eric's hands on her shoulder. He had moved at last. His touch was firm as he guided her outside.

"Leave me alone!" she begged him. "Please!"

"Look, it's all right, it's all right," he tried to tell her.

It wasn't all right. She managed to tear away from him and reach a patch of saw grass, and then she was violently ill. She fell down flat on the earth, afraid that she would pass out.

Eric bent down over her and smoothed a damp handkerchief over her face. She couldn't see his eyes, just her own pathetic reflection in his glasses. "Let me help you up. Mac can get you some water."

He didn't give her time to answer, but brought her to her feet. By that time, Wendy and Brad and Billy were out with them. And Mac was coming her way with a paper cup full of water.

She drank it gratefully. Wendy took over for Eric, grabbing the handkerchief, smoothing back Ashley's hair. "Are you all right now?"

"I'm sorry—" Ashley began.

"My stomach almost went in there," Brad assured her, smiling. Then he cast a quick glance at Billy. "Ashley, you recognized the body."

"Yes. It was Harrison Mosby. He was the director of the commercial we were shooting. He was the one who—who—"

"Who lured you into the swamp?" Eric finished softly for her.

She looked his way, but she could still tell nothing of his feelings. Those damned glasses hid everything.

"Well, then," Billy murmured, "at least we know who this stiff is. Sorry, miss, if he was a friend—"

"He wasn't a friend," Ashley said quickly. "But I wouldn't have wished this on a—on a—"

"On a dog!" Wendy supplied.

"On a dog," Ashley said without warmth.

"Billy, can we take her out of here now? That was pretty awful for all of us, and having to see someone that she knew . . ." Eric said.

"Yeah, sure, sure," Billy replied. "Eric, Miss Dane, I just need you to sign your statements, and then you're free to go."

Seconds later, Ashley was done, having scrawled her signature where Billy wanted it. He thanked her, telling her that without her help they might have spent aeons identifying the man. Now, thanks to her, they did have something—if very little—to go on.

"What will you do? How will you try to solve this?" Ashley asked.

"Oh, we'll check around. If he was from New York, we'll get cooperation from their police department. The storm washed away anything that might resemble a clue, but eventually, the top-notch detectives will make it out here and see what they can come up with. We're not at a dead end, so please, don't worry. Eric, she's still awfully pale. Why don't you all get going?"

"Yeah, we'll do that," Eric said.

"You're not going back to your house?"

"Not today. I'm going back out to Willie's."

"We all have to go back out to Willie's. Josh is there with Mary," Wendy said.

"All right. Take care," Billy told them.

He waved as Brad led the way toward their airboat, one hand gently on his wife's back, and the other on Ashley's. Eric followed at a slight distance, with Baby at his heels.

He caught up with them at the airboat, taking Ashley's arm and turning her around to face him. "Are you all right?" he asked softly. "You're still as white as snow."

She nodded, deciding that maybe he was not completely heartless. He swore slightly then, and she appreciated the protective gesture until he muttered, "This was wrong. You just weren't cut out for stuff like this."

"No one is cut out for murder!" Ashley protested.

Eric waved a hand in the air. "I mean all of this. The swamp, the storm, the place, what has happened. All of it."

She lifted her chin slightly and smiled. "Don't kid yourself, Tonto. I'm tougher than I look."

She didn't wait for a reaction from him but tossed her hair over her shoulders, and walked onto the airboat behind Wendy. She turned around and called to the big cat. "Baby, here, Baby, come here!"

To Ashley's astonishment, the graceful feline decided to be on her side, and padded silently away from Eric to leap up beside her.

"Damned cat!" Brad laughed. "We've done a great job with her, huh, Eric?"

"Yeah," Eric muttered, hopping onto the airboat along with Brad. He sat behind Ashley. She felt his presence there with all her heart. It was as if just his being near made fire blaze down her back.

"You'll like Willie and Mary!" Wendy shouted to her above the roar of the motor.

"I'm sure I will!" she called back.

"And the kids!" Brad added. He laughed. "Just be prepared to be tied to the stake. They like to play cowboys and Indians."

"Do I get to be a cowboy or an Indian?"

"Maybe a cowgirl," Wendy said. "Or a prisoner. Or if you're real lucky, they'll let you be a healer."

Ashley smiled. Then she noticed that Eric was staring into the distance and that his countenance was as hard as rock. He wasn't into games, not that day.

Ashley let her hand rest on the panther's head. She closed her eyes and opened them. Wendy nudged her, pointing out a half dozen blue herons standing at the edge of the water among the grasses. The birds were elegant and beautiful and stared at them for their impertinence in coming through. The sound of the motor didn't frighten them. They glared with regal disdain.

"They're not afraid of the motor," Ashley said.

"They're accustomed to the sound," Wendy shouted back.

"They're brave!"

"Not when it comes to the natural enemy!" Brad shouted back. He grinned. "Watch a gator move in there, and you'll see all the flapping and flying you could imagine."

Grim, Ashley thought with a shiver. The swamp was beautiful and deadly in so many ways.

She looked at Eric. He had not moved and was still staring into the distance. To the future, she thought. And she was not part of that picture.

Brad cut the motor at last and the airboat came to rest against the embankment. There was a path leading to the circle of chickees where the Hawk family lived. Baby went racing off first, then Eric stepped off. He started to walk on, but stopped and turned back. He offered Ashley a polite smile. "Here, give me your hand. Careful," he said stiffly. "The muck gets deep here."

He helped her down and then he started up the path again. Ashley caught his hand, pulling him back. "Why don't you want me here?" she asked him.

He looked her up and down, as if he'd just met her for the first time. His gaze carried disdain. "Because you don't belong here; it's that simple."

"Why not? Why does Brad belong here? Why does Wendy belong here? Why don't I?"

"Well, for one, Wendy doesn't drip with emeralds."

It was a low blow. She wasn't wearing the emeralds anymore, not even the ring that belonged to her. Tara had packed them all up to take into the city.

"Unfair. I wasn't born wearing emeralds."

"This isn't your world, Ashley," he said softly. "It just isn't."

"Why—?"

"Because we don't like pretty little white girls who like to play games. This is real life. If you want to drop in to study tribal ways, go to the open villages and the tourist traps. You can walk around and gawk to your heart's content. You can see the way that it was, and drive away in an air-conditioned car. This isn't a place to just drop in and make judgments and act condescendingly and then turn around and fly back to your penthouse."

"I don't live in a penthouse," Ashley said, and suddenly she was mad. She stepped forward, heedless of Brad and Wendy who had discreetly gone around them. She poked a finger hard at his chest. "You're acting like a martyr. As if you have some special hold on the evils of life. So all right, one of my best friends is married to one of the richest men in the world. So what? If you tried for a million years, you couldn't begin to imagine the world where she came from. Awful, awful, white American poverty, Mr. Hawk. It does exist. She grew up with no electricity and no plumbing and not because she wanted to live in the wilderness. There was no beautiful clean wilderness to run to. So quit judging people right now!''

"You couldn't make a single night out here!" Eric told her.

She straightened. "Bet me."

"What?"

"Bet me. I can make it."

"You hate the swamp. You've said so yourself."

"Bet me," she challenged. It was true. She hated the swamp. But she'd see him eat his own words if it killed her. She was staying.

He threw up his arms. "You're on. But you're on your own. No help from me on anything."

"Then I should definitely manage," she said sweetly.

He smiled pleasantly, then went past her. Ashley turned to follow him. Almost instantly she stepped into a hole filled with muck that reached nearly as high as the boots she was wearing. Elizabeth's boots. She swore softly, then pulled her leg out. While she was trying to clean the boot on the grass, someone spoke softly to her. "It's kind of a mess right now with the storm and all, but at least there's no quicksand around."

"Quicksand!" Ashley said, startled. She turned around to stare at a handsome young man with onyx eyes and black hair in a contemporary cut. He had on worn jeans and a T-shirt advertising a rock group. He offered her his hand. "Anthony Panther. Tony. I'm Eric's brother-in-law."

"How do you do?" Ashley murmured, taking his hand.

"Come on. Meet the rest of the family. They're all dying to meet you."

"Oh?" Ashley said curiously.

"Eric mentioned you last night."

"Did he say a lot?"

Tony chuckled softly. "It's what he didn't say that has us all interested. Let me take your arm."

They passed by the first of the chickees, and Ashley was startled to see just how high it was above the ground and just how low the thatched roof sat over the dwelling. "Height to keep creatures out, the slant of the roof to protect against the elements," Tony said, watching her gaze.

She smiled. "Thanks."

"There they are!" someone cried, and they were surrounded by a group of children who had raced down the ladder of a large chickee.

"Whoa, kids. Wait!" Tony commanded.

Suddenly they went still, all six of them, in jeans and T-shirts, except for the oldest girl, who was wearing a denim skirt and a wild print blouse, and was adorned with all the jewelry customary of any teenage girl. She had her long black hair tied up in a French braid, and she was very petty, her smile showing a set of deep dimples.

She had green eyes, like Eric.

She smiled shyly at Ashley, fascinated.

"This is Elizabeth," Tony said, indicating the oldest girl. "And here we have Michael, David and Dorinda—mine and Marna's brood—and these two are Charlie and Jemina. They belong to Eric's cousin, Tom, and his wife, Sharon."

"How do you do?" Ashley said, and shook all of their hands, one by one. By then Tony's wife was approaching. She was a tall woman with her eldest daughter's dimples and Eric's magnificent green eyes. She offered Ashley a beautiful smile. "Welcome, Miss Dane. We're delighted to have you here, and we're so sorry to hear about all the trouble. Wendy was telling me that you knew the dead man." Her voice was soft and musical.

"Yes."

Marna caught Ashley's hand and drew her along. "We won't let you think about it while you're here. Come on over and meet my grandparents. Mary is cooking. I hope you'll enjoy dinner.''

"I'm sure that I will," Ashley told her. She was delightful, just like Tony.

And not a thing like Eric.

Marna led her to the chickee's ladder, and Ashley quickly climbed the distance to the floor. Brad was there and helped her crawl inside. Wendy was there, too, with Josh in her arms. She smiled at Ashley. "We're in luck. Mary's catfish, koonti bread and wild turnips. I wasn't in the mood to cook and neither was Brad, and this far out, it's hard to call for pizza!"

"Ashley, this is Willie Hawk and Mary Hawk. Willie, Mary, Ashley Dane," Marna said.

The man took her hand first. Ashley was instantly fascinated. His face was wrinkled, yet somehow it was still beautiful. She imagined that as a young man, he must have been completely compelling and striking. And she imagined, too, that in the days of the war, such a face would have ignited terror within the heart of the enemy.

She murmured the right things as he looked her up and down with unabashed interest. Then he told her that she was welcome anytime as his guest. He drew his wife forward. Mary was small, and despite her age, she still had nearly ink-black hair. She smiled shyly and only said hello.

"She doesn't speak English very well," Wendy explained.

"Oh," Ashley said. She took the small woman's hand and squeezed it while smiling warmly. Mary smiled back, and she was instantly beautiful. She turned and said something to Willie.

A sudden noise came from the area of the far support pole. Ashley saw that Eric had been leaning there. He straightened and said something with anger.

His grandfather spoke back sharply. After a moment, Eric stepped over to his grandmother, kissed her cheek, then turned around to face everyone. "Excuse me for a bit, will you? I'll be back in time for dinner."

They were all silent as he crawled down the ladder. The children below called to him, laughing and clinging, as he walked away. He spoke softly to them, and they let him go. He strode toward the trees that grew high on the hummock.

Mary said something to her husband, then shrugged. After eyeing Ashley calculatingly, she smiled like the Cheshire cat.

Tony cleared his throat and asked Brad a question. Ashley turned to Wendy. "What was that all about? What did Mary say that got Eric all upset?"

Wendy grinned. "*Hoke-tee*. She called you Eric's woman."

"Oh," Ashley murmured, a dark flush creeping to her face. She lowered her eyes. Wendy, however, wasn't about to allow her any discomfort.

"You're safe here, you know. Whoever followed you to Eric's house couldn't possibly find this place. I myself have trouble at times. Are you worried still?"

Ashley looked around. "No, I'm not worried out here," she said softly. "Not at all. Honestly."

"Good. Because no one can find you here." Wendy tossed back her hair, changing the subject. "Have you tried koonti bread yet? It's from a root that grows in the swamp, and without it, the Seminoles—"

"And the Miccosukees," Tony interjected.

Wendy grinned. "Tony is a Miccosukee," she explained. "Anyway, none of the Indians would have survived without the koonti root."

Marna flashed her a beautiful smile. "And pumpkins. Years and years ago, we grew pumpkins. You won't find many in the swamp these days, though."

"Times change," Willie said. He sat down by Ashley, watching her curiously as he spoke. "That was one of the ways that the soldiers finally defeated many of the Seminoles. They found the villages and destroyed the food supplies. Many families moved west. There are many, many more Seminoles in Oklahoma today than there are in Florida."

"Out of the swampland," Ashley murmured.

"They were given a barren desert," Willie said dismissively. He shrugged. "I like my swamp. Do you like my swamp?"

She laughed. "Well, I guess I'm coming to like your swamp." She hesitated and glanced at the others. "I like the people in your swamp, Mr. Hawk. Very much."

He patted her hand. "That's good. People matter more than a place." He stood and walked over to his wife.

Marna caught her watching Willie, and smiled. "He's the greatest old man in the whole world. Beyond a doubt."

"He would have never surrendered," Brad said, laughing.

"Hey!" Tony protested. "The Miccosukees were the ones who never signed a treaty."

"Hmmf!" Marna retorted. "Those of us who stayed here didn't sign any treaties."

"Children, children," Willie said. He turned around, his eyes sparkling. "None of us were alive back then, so we didn't sign or not sign treaties!" He looked at Ashley. "And don't let them fool you. None of them live here full-time. Tony and Marna are here as often as they're not, but they have a nice house with a white picket fence. And Brad and Wendy—"

"Wait, wait, now," Brad dared to interrupt. "I surrendered the first time I came out here, bear that in mind."

They laughed and the conversation eased. Marna explained to Ashley that Miccosukees and Seminoles had been grouped together for years and years, though they weren't even from the same language-speaking groups. "Now, of course, we've melded a lot. We've been intermarrying for years and years. History is always fun."

Ashley smiled. "I know something about what went on. I read Eric's book. And—" she stopped.

"What?" Marna said.

"Don't tell Eric!"

They all looked at one another and shook their hands in conspiracy. Ashley grinned. "My brother is married to a Nez Percé. I've spent a fair amount of time with them out in Arizona, and Liz has a wonderful library, so I've done lots of reading."

Wendy burst into laughter and hugged her. "No, I'll never tell Eric!" she promised. "Never."

Ashley glanced at Marna. "I made a bet with him. He said that I wouldn't make it here one night. I said that I'd stay."

Marna's brows shot up. "Well, it isn't quite like camping in the Yosemite," she said. "I'll show you his chickee."

"No, I'm on my own."

"Ashley," Wendy warned, "maybe you don't want—"

"Wendy," Brad interrupted her. "Maybe it's the best place in the world for Ashley. You said it—nobody could possibly find her here."

"And we'll all be here," Marna said. "If she needs help, she can call on us." She stood. "Eric will be here, too. You know that. He may be rude at times, but he's never careless." She shook her head at Wendy. "That brother of mine! Ashley, come on, and I'll show you where you can sleep. Your place," she told Brad and Wendy.

"Fine," Wendy said.

Brad nodded. "Of course. Just don't let the kids tuck you in. They like to tie people up!"

"Thanks for the warning," Ashley said. She and Marna went down the ladder.

"You really will be all right," Marna assured her. "The storm has hurt us some, but . . ." She shrugged. "There's a clear pool through here. The water is good. Eric has a man out to check it once a month. We're in the wilds here, which has its advantages. Clean water is one. Even with the flooding, it's a beautiful area. I'll show you.''

Marna pushed through the brush, and they came to a small pool surrounded by pine trees and wild orchids. It was one of the prettiest places Ashley had ever seen. ''It's delightful,'' she told Marna.

''I'm glad that you think so. Come on, I'll show you the chickee.''

She led Ashley to one of two chickees that were far away from the others. ''Wendy and Brad's.'' She hesitated. ''It was Leif's, you see.'' She pointed to the second chickee. ''Eric's. If anything does go wrong, just scream like hell. I promise you that he'll be there in an instant. Go on, climb up.''

Ashley did so. She had expected the chickee to be empty, but it was not. There were mats rolled up in a corner and a large hardy trunk by the far pole. ''Anything here is Wendy's, and you're more than welcome to it. Wendy would insist. There's a pitcher and bowl in the trunk if you want to bring back some water from the pool. She has dishes in there, too, and clothing. Wendy is short, so I guess you'll need to keep Liz's jeans, but I'm sure there's a nice gown to sleep in. Want to take a bath down by the pool later?''

''Sure,'' Ashley agreed. Then she hesitated. Did she? Weren't there all kinds of slimy creatures in the pool?

Marna winked at her. ''Come on. Let's get back for dinner.''

Eric was there already eating when they returned. The Seminoles had a matriarchal society, but by custom, the men ate first and were served by the women. Wendy had helped Mary serve. When Ashley arrived, Mary served her next, then urged her into a seat beside Eric.

She didn't look at him, but she felt his eyes on her. He had stripped off his shirt and boots, and she was acutely aware of his chest. She was ashamed by the depth of her desire just to touch him. He didn't want her; he didn't even want her there accepting his grandparents' hospitality. But she couldn't forget the days that had come before yesterday, the days in which they had done nothing but touch. She suddenly gave her bowl a very fierce attention. She needed to get out and away as fast as she could. She was falling in love with him, and he was the one playing games.

"I showed your guest to her quarters," Marna told Eric sweetly.

His head shot up and he glanced at his sister. "What?"

"I showed her to her chickee," Marna repeated. "You did invite Ashley to stay, didn't you?"

He stared at Ashley. She felt the power of his eyes and she almost shivered. Then she longed to demand to know why he was casting something so wonderful to the wind.

"Yes," he said softly, studying her. "I did invite her to stay." He smiled. "So you think that you'll enjoy yourself?"

"Yes, I think that I will."

"Well, good." His eyes widened in mock menace. "Lots of creepy crawlies around here," he said pleasantly. "The mosquitoes will be out soon, too." He lowered his voice. "Remember, you're on your own."

"I remember," she whispered. "Do you mind if I'm sociable with your sister?"

"Not at all. But you curl up for the night alone."

"I'll try," she said. "But Baby is really beginning to prefer me, you know. She might come up, and I have to admit that I'm not at all sure about pushing a panther out of my bed."

"Funny," he assured her. He stood and kissed his grandmother's cheek, then excused himself to the others. "I'm going to wash up and turn in," he said apologetically. Brad and Wendy said good-night; the children kissed him. He started down the ladder.

"Excuse my grandson's rudeness," Willie said loudly. Ashley could hear that Eric's descent had ceased. He shook his head, making a *tsking* sound. "It must be the Viking in him."

"The Viking!" Brad laughed.

"Umm," Willie said. "And his mother was such a good woman, gentle and kind. I don't understand. But it is not the Seminole in him who is so rude. I want you to know that."

They all heard the soft expletive that left Eric's lips as he walked away from the chickee. "Cover your ears, chicks!" Marna warned her children.

"What's wrong?" David asked his father.

"Nothing, nothing. Uncle Eric is on the warpath again," Tony said serenely. He looked at Ashley. "You haven't even tasted the koonti bread yet. How is it?"

"Different," Ashley admitted. It wasn't a soft bread, and it had a nutty flavor. "Good!" she said. She wasn't going to worry about Eric, she determined. His family was charming, and she was going to have a good time with them all. "And the catfish is wonderful."

"Freshwater," Tony told her. "Freshwater catfish is always good. Stay away from the saltwater variety."

After a while, they finished dinner. Brad and Wendy said that they were going to take Josh home.

Ashley walked them down to the water with the others. It was hard to see them go. In the short time that she had known them, she felt as if they had become very good friends. She hugged them both, thanking them for everything. "Come back whenever you're ready," Wendy told her.

She smiled. "When they clear the roads, I'll have to get back. Tara is going to take time off with the baby, so I'll have to go into the office and see how things are going."

Wendy nodded. "It's important to you then, your work?"

"I like designing. I don't care about the office or administrative part very much, but after Galliard, Tara and I decided that we wanted to work for ourselves."

Wendy nodded. "Well, don't worry, we'll see that you get into the city when the time comes. And we'll be with you until you're safely away."

"Thanks," Ashley said, hugging Wendy again. Then the small blonde and her husband departed, waving to everyone.

"Well, this is it then!" Marna told her. "Come on. It will be sunset soon."

Marna led her back to the center of the village. She went up to her own place and came back with towels and clothing and her two girls at her heels. They stopped by Wendy's chickee and Ashley borrowed a long white cotton gown, a comb, brush and a bar of soap. They started down for the water. Elizabeth was entranced by Ashley and asked her dozens of questions about New York and modeling and all else. Ashley, equally entranced with the girl, combed out her hair and answered everything. "Would you like to live in New York?" she asked her.

"I'd like an apartment there," Elizabeth said. "But I'd want to be able to come home, too."

Marna had stripped and moved out into the pool with little Dorinda. "It's wonderful! Like a cool bath!" she cried delightedly.

Elizabeth took off her clothes and went dashing out to the pool. Ashley couldn't help but hesitate. The water looked black.

Marna laughed. "See the way that Elizabeth came? Run out that way, on the path, and you won't hit any muck at all."

"There's really nothing in there, is there?" Ashley asked. "A coral snake—"

"They don't like water; they like dry!" Marna assured her. "So do the rattlers. And we've yet to find a moccasin in here."

"Yet!" Ashley wailed.

"It's all right!" Elizabeth yelled.

Ashley stripped off her clothing and headed along the pine path. She closed her eyes, swallowed and dived in.

The water was cool. She didn't stand on muck, but on rock and sand. Still, she couldn't see below the surface very well, and she determined not to move very far. "It's all right!" Marna said, and swam away. Dorinda and Elizabeth followed, tried to make Ashley join in.

"Oh, what the hel—heck!" Ashley said at last, and squinting her eyes, she moved deeper into the water and swam with the others. Elizabeth splashed her, and she splashed the girl. It was fun.

She lost all awareness of time and place.

She even forgot Eric.

But he had not forgotten her. He had walked down to the pool and discovered the women. He was about to turn and walk away discreetly when he heard Ashley's laughter. Then he paused and came forward.

She was there, in the water, with his sister and nieces, as natural as Eve, and looking comfortable in the wilderness.

She played and splashed with the others, then climbed out and picked up a towel. He watched her standing there, still smiling, wet and slick and framed by the sunset. The dying light touched her hair with a spectacular radiance, and fell over her flesh, defining every beautiful curve and nuance of her body. She had never been more beautiful.

And he had never wanted her more.

With a soft groan he turned away and wandered back to the solitude he had ordered on himself. He indulged in his grandfather's potion, in the black drink, and he lay down, wishing it would release the tempest from his body.

It did not.

Ashley dressed in Wendy's long white cotton gown. She felt refreshed and clean. She went to Marna's chickee where Tony was reading to the boys by lamplight and brewing tea.

"Seminole tea?" Ashley asked him.

"Lipton's," Tony said with a grin. "I'm just a tea drinker at heart, what can I say."

Ashley laughed and sat down with them. She had a cup of black tea and brushed Elizabeth's hair again. Then she did Dorinda's. When it started to grow late, she yawned and said that she needed to get some sleep. Tony walked her back.

"There's always a fire burning in the center of the village. There's always light," he assured her at the bottom of her ladder.

"Thanks!" she told him.

"You're going to be all right?" he asked.

"Fine," she assured him.

He wished her a good-night and left her, and she wasn't at all sure that she would be all right. She had never felt so alone in her entire life. There might be a fire burning in the center of the village, but it didn't seem to reach her chickee.

There would be a lamp up there, she thought. Brad and Wendy would have something.

She crawled up, and suddenly the darkness seemed terribly menacing. She thought that the floor was alive with living creatures—snakes and spiders and cockroaches or palmetto bugs. She was afraid to walk.

"And I'm going to sleep here?" she asked out loud.

She hurried to the trunk, found a battery-powered lantern and switched it on, bathing the chickee in yellow light. She smiled to herself and breathed more easily. The place was swept clean. She was certain that everyone had seen to their property as soon as the storm was over. Surely she was in a far better place than a New York City delicatessen.

"I will survive this just fine!" she assured herself. She found a reed mat and unrolled it. Then she found a pillow in the trunk and laughed softly, glad that either Brad or Wendy still required a few comforts of the white world. She set the pillow down, found a blanket, curled up and tried to close her eyes.

She couldn't sleep with the light; it was too bright. She pulled the lantern close and turned it off. Then she lay back down.

It wasn't a hot night because of the wind that rushed past the chickee, bringing all kinds of sounds. Like a bird calling and crickets chirping. Like that peculiar stalking noise, as if something was moving through the trees by the pool.

She jerked up, reaching for the lamp. A scream rose in her throat. Someone, something, was moving up the ladder. She opened her mouth as a creature appeared in the doorway.

Her scream escaped—then broke off abruptly. She laughed and choked. "Baby!" she exclaimed. The panther had preferred her company to Eric's tonight.

"Bad cat, you scared me half to death!" she said. Baby snarled, them promptly curled up beside her. To her amazement Ashley found herself hugging the huge beast. "Well, you're safer than anything else around here!" she declared. Baby licked her arm; the cat's tongue was like sandpaper. "That's enough. We haven't decided that we're friends for life or anything!" Ashley announced, then turned out the light and lay down.

She had barely closed her eyes when tension streaked through her again. There was someone inside. He had come in silence, but she felt him now.

Her eyes flew open. There was a man towering over her, his skin completely bronze in the pale moonlight. Her scream died. She recognized him instantly. The muscle-rippled chest, the cock of his head, the way that he stood.

"Eric!" she gasped, shivering.

"Ashley!" His tone was harsh. "You screamed. Why the hell did you scream?"

She sat up, smiling ruefully. "I'm sorry. I thought I caught it before anyone heard me. I was just startled. Baby came up here."

"Oh." He looked at the cat for a long moment. "You're all right then," he said to Ashley.

She nodded. "I'm all right."

But still he hesitated. Then he reached down, urging the cat away from her. "Go, Baby, go sleep somewhere else!" Snarling from being disturbed, Baby waved her tail disdainfully and headed for the ladder.

Eric reached for Ashley, pulling her to her feet.

Ashley saw the pulse that beat furiously at the base of his throat. He held her against him, then caught the hem of her gown and stripped the garment from her body. She stood before him in the moonlight, naked and touched by the softest glow. His breath left him in deep and ragged sighs as he watched her in silence. Gently, he touched his lips to hers, then set his mouth on her shoulders, her collarbone and her breasts. Slowly he caressed the length of her, and where he touched her, she became molten. He moved his lips over her belly, trailing liquid passion across the bare flesh. Then he caught her buttocks in his hands and kissed at the juncture of her thighs, he sought every intimacy, stroking and teasing the very bud of her desire. She cried out softly and collapsed in his arms. He lowered her gently to the floor, shed his jeans and he was one with her.

There was magic in the night, Ashley thought, and in the power of the primitive earth. This was where she longed to be—with this man. His temper was fierce, his pride was ice, but he loved like fire, with all the fury and passion of life.

She strained and writhed and arched against him, and she whispered his name. The moon exploded with a soft and mystic glow, and she drifted down with it, to kiss the earth and lie upon it in naked splendor.

She drew his head against her. She felt his light kiss on her breast, and he held her close. Words hovered on her lips. I think that I love you, I think that I have been falling in love from the very moment that I first saw your face....

She didn't speak. He wouldn't want to hear her words; he would think that they were a lie. She couldn't say them.

Tomorrow he would probably be ice again. He would spurn her; he would forget tonight.

He didn't know how to believe in love anymore.

She had to let go completely; it was the only choice that she had. It was strange how very clear that seemed at that moment.

She would let go tomorrow. But tonight...

She held him close and savored his nearness. When his lips found hers again, she greeted them eagerly. She made love fiercely and savagely, knowing that she would take and hold dearly the memories of this moment between them and the moon and the breeze and the sky and the primitive earth.

Chapter 10

"Tell me something. Honestly. Have you ever seen a
more beautiful sunset?" Eric asked her softly.

It was very early evening and they were down by the pool
together, lying idly on the leaf-carpeted bank and watching
the coming of night. Ashley shook her head. No, she had
never seen a more beautiful sunset. Golden light fell on a
profusion of wild orchids, branches swayed in the breeze,
and far across the water a great blue heron stood on a single foot in a motionless vigil. She still considered the swamp
deadly, but it touched her that a place so dangerous could
also offer such peace and tranquillity. She was grateful to be
here.

And grateful to be with Eric.

For two days now they had stayed in the village. Almost
friends by day, parting by evening and coming together
again by the moonlight. It was his grandparents' home, and
they both respected Willie and Mary, but they were far away,
and here, privacy was deeply respected, too. She was comfortable in her surroundings. Eric was discreet, as was his

sister and Tony and the cousins and uncles and others she
was coming to know.

The second night he had played with her fingers and told
her that tribal law had nothing against consenting lovers.
Warriors and maidens had often dallied before marriage.
Adultery was the sin. Warriors and maidens alike could lose
their ears or noses for that offense. Marriage was sacred and
to be honored.

She liked that idea, but it left her wondering about his
feelings for her. She wasn't his wife. He'd had a wife whom
he had loved beyond all else.

But she didn't think about it long. She was there on borrowed time already. When the roads were cleared and the
downed electrical wires repaired, she would leave.

Until then . . .

Tonight, they had the sunset.

She had awakened alone that morning. Instinct had
drawn her to the pool, and that's where she found him. Like
the great blue heron, he had stood silently, watching the sun
rise. She had almost left him there with the peace he seemed
to need and to have found. But though he stood away from
her, with his back to her, he had heard her, and without
turning, had called to her.

He had faced her at last, and a smile had touched his features. He was content. She had walked into his arms while
the sun rose, drying the morning dew, warming them as they
lowered to the ground together. The breeze had whispered
soft encouragement, and she had learned in those moments
that no man or woman needed more than the primitive
earth, that everything else of value and beauty came from
within. In his arms she hadn't feared any creature of the
swamp, because she was with him.

She didn't think that there could be anything more beautiful than lying there together, watching the day awaken.
They hadn't spoken; they had just been together, and it had
been wonderful.

The rest of the day had been very full. Ashley had spent
the time with Marna and Mary, learning what a koonti root

was and just how hard it was to grind one to make bread. Her palms were blistered and every one of her nails was cracked and broken, and she didn't care in the least. She was just delighted that she had more or less survived the initiation.

Lying idle now on the bank, she thought of how Marna and Tony and the children were delightful, how Willie was both wise and funny; and she was almost sorry that somewhere else in the world was her apartment, her friends, associates and employees. She realized she didn't want to leave this place. Especially not when Eric was like this—his mood light, his eyes filled with laughter and a certain amount of pride in her, too. Maybe it was his pride in her that mattered the most. She wasn't sure. And even if she couldn't hold him forever, she would be able to cherish the memory of this time always.

She watched his face as he chewed on a blade of grass and gazed at the distant horizon. Then he glanced her way, and she couldn't begin to read his thoughts. He smiled, dropping the blade of grass, and planted a kiss on her lips.

"You've done real well, white squaw," he told her teasingly. He picked up her hand and gently rubbed his finger over a blister. "I had always thought that you wouldn't be able to bear a broken nail."

She pulled her hand away, looking with a certain superiority out over the water. "I've done exceptionally well for a featherbrained *hoke-tee*," she said sweetly, and he laughed. Then his laughter faded and he rose and walked some distance away from her. He leaned against a pine tree, still gazing out on the pool as the sun fell.

"I know I've been harsh with you," he said quietly. Then he faced her. "I meant to be. I meant to be cruel."

"Why?" Ashley asked him.

He smiled, turning back to the water. "Because It's a harsh and cruel world here."

Ashley shook her head, seeking the understanding that he was trying to give her now. "It's not a horrible world. Your grandparents prefer the wilderness. You live in a nice, comfortable house, and so do Brad and Wendy and the others. Actually you seem to do exceptionally well."

"I do well because my father did well. He was in the army during World War II and he learned a lot about the world. He met my mother during the liberation of Norway and brought her home. She loved being here, but she made him accept her life, too. My mother knew the importance of education, and my father remembered enough of the past. He said that most of America wasn't even aware that there was still a war being waged within the country. We might not have ever surrendered, but as Indians, we were never going to win a war against white America. If we wanted to win any battles, we were going to have to win as men, not Indians. Then, at the same time, we all know that heritage is desperately important." He shrugged. "Dad started buying land, as an individual. He sent us all to good schools. And he taught me that words were the weapons we had to use in this day and age, and that words were far more powerful than any ax." He paused, shrugging. "'More powerful than the sword.' But this isn't an ideal state. It's far from it. We do fight poverty, we do fight illiteracy, and it's my fight, I can't forget it."

"I understand—"

"No, Ashley, you don't," he said quietly. "Or maybe you do, but not completely." He walked back to her, smoothing his thumb over her cheek. "You really are so beautiful, wild and exciting with emerald eyes and flame hair." He sat down beside her, holding her hand. "Elizabeth—my Elizabeth, Marna named her oldest daughter for her—wasn't a Seminole."

"She was a Miccosukee."

"No." He shook his head. "She was a Cherokee, and her mother brought her family down to Miami when her father died. She was horrified when Elizabeth fell in love with me—because I was an Indian. I was part of the world that she had run from. No one had ever taught her to be proud, not where she came from. It was a harsher world then, people were very cruel. Indians weren't allowed to drink out of 'white' water fountains. It took her years and years to believe that she did have a heritage in which to take pride.''

Ashley looked at him and shook her head. "But your mother was Norse, and you're so very close to Wendy and Brad, and by the tone of your book—"

"What?"

"There's no bitterness in you with Wendy, and your outlook in the book is optimistic and humorous, and there's so much hope there! Why is the . . . bitterness only with me?''

"Maybe because it just suddenly mattered so much with you, and I just wasn't expecting it, and I didn't want it.''

She caught her breath at his admission. She was glad and reached up to him, placing her palm against his cheek. She knew with a certainty that she was in love with him, that she would be in love with him all of her life.

But it didn't really change things, she knew. She had to walk away. If he followed, then there was hope. But the final decision had to come from him.

Ashley looked down at her boot. "That's nice," she said quietly.

"That's nice?"

She looked at him and smiled. "Yes. It's much, much more than I expected from you.''

He swore with a sudden fury, grasping her shoulders as if he would shake her. "You still don't understand. This isn't all that it appears to be. I don't spend all my time in my nice air-conditioned house, or with Brad and Wendy, or even with my grandparents and sisters. Sure, it's a nice, normal life in a way. We have parties, we go to movies, I have good friends in Broward and Dade. But there's a lot more to it. There're kids down here who we fight to keep alive, we've got prostitution, orphans, old people who need help—and bingo. Where would we be without our bingo and our cigarette sales? Don't you understand, Ashley? It isn't always pretty. We're noble, we're proud, but you'd swear that a lot of our people just forgot about those virtues, or no one in the twentieth century remembered to tell them that we're supposed to be noble and proud. We have a council, and I'm

on that council, and I will always give the tribe my time and
my effort.''

"Eric—"

He seemed to realize just how tightly he was holding her
arms, and he released her abruptly. "It's close to a normal
life, Ashley. But don't you see—your life isn't normal.
You're accustomed to snapping your fingers and a secretary arrives. Hail a cab, send out for Chinese or sushi.
You're worried about the latest fashions from Paris while
we're just trying to keep decent clothing on all of our kids.
It's an uphill battle. It's my fight, not yours. You can't even
begin to see it. Life is like the lay of the land, Ashley.
Sometimes the rivers and the grass lie soft in the breeze, and
all that you can see for miles and miles is peace and beauty.
But always lurking, soundlessly like a jutting log, is the
deadly gator or the slinking coral snake or the rattler. I love
this place, Ashley. I would never, never leave it.''

She jerked away from him, leaping to her feet. She'd
meant it to be so very different, but he had the most awful
effect on her temper. "Who ever asked you to leave it?" she
demanded. "No one has asked anything—anything at all—
from you! And no one will, Eric. If there's anything that
you want, you'll have to come and get it.''

"What are you talking about?" he demanded harshly.

"You can't be that cold, that stupid, or that wrapped up
in your own little world! But you needn't worry about de-
mands being made on your life. I'm leaving. Tony said that
the roads would be cleared by tomorrow, and he and Marna
have offered to take me into the city. I'm flying out on the
first plane that I can get.''

He stood stiffly for a long moment, then frowned suddenly. "You can't just leave like that," he said harshly.

"I can't? You spent the entire week trying to get rid of
me. I'm going, and you stand there and tell me that I can't
leave?''

"You're in danger," he said softly.

"I'm in danger in the swamp," she corrected him. "I
won't be in danger in the city.''

"It was your friend who was murdered."

"He was not my friend."

"Sorry," Eric responded offhandedly.

There was something about the way he said it that clawed its way up her spine, irritating her beyond belief. She screeched something totally incoherent and threw herself against him.

For once, she caught him completely by surprise. He cast up his arms to catch her, but she had come too hard upon him, and they both fell to the ground. Not even that curbed her temper. She slammed her hands hard against his chest. Startled, he coughed at the blow. Then a fire sizzled in his eyes, and he shouted. "Ashley, damn it, stop it!"

She didn't listen. She hit him until he caught her wrists, and with a loud grunt, flung her beneath him. Still, she was seething. He straddled her, holding her down, and she yelled for all that she was worth. "You are just too much! This is it! You should be scalped yourself. I'm—"

"Ashley, stop it."

"I will not stop it!" With a burst of energy, she freed one hand and took a swing at him. He ducked, but the motion sent them rolling down the bank. To her horror, they plunged right into the pool, where there was mud and muck and who knew what else. She sank first, and gasping and gurgling she kicked against the muck to come to the surface.

"Here, take my hand," Eric offered. He was already out, and standing on the bank. Ashley ignored his hand.

"I can get out myself!" she sputtered furiously. But one step sent her sliding down. Eric came to get her, sweeping her into his arms. She didn't appreciate the effort. She beat against his shoulders. "Put me down! I don't want your help; it isn't worth it! A damned rattler is a friendlier creature! Put me down, and so help me, I mean it!"

His teeth grated. She heard the sound and saw a vein bulge in his throat, along with the muscles that constricted in his neck and bunched and rippled in his arms. "You want down?"

"Yes!" she snapped.

"Fine!"

He released her. She crashed back into the mud. He turned on his heel and walked away. Ashley found her footing. It wasn't easy, but she managed to make it to the bank. Eric was already moving along the path to the little circle of chickees. Ashley tossed back her hair and started the same way. Suddenly she heard a giggle, then laughter. Elizabeth and Marna came out of the bushes.

Marna tried to compose her features. "Can I give you a towel, Ashley?"

"Yes, thank you!" Ashley took the towel with a nod, following with her eyes the trail Eric had taken. Elizabeth giggled again, and Ashley smiled slowly, aware that she was covered with mud and that swamp grass was trailing down from her hair. But her smile faded suddenly. "Marna, I do need you to take me out of here in the morning, if you would, please."

Marna's grin faded, too. "Of course," she said sweetly. "We'll leave in the morning. We'll take the airboat up to Mac's garage. Our car is still there."

Ashley smiled her thanks, and Marna looked her over from head to toe. "Why don't you get rid of that muddy stuff, and I'll bring you some of my clothes? Take a bath in the clear water. You'll feel better, I promise."

Ashley shook her head slowly. "Nothing is going to make me feel better, but thanks, Marna."

Eric didn't show up in the communal kitchen chickee for dinner, or appear later. Ashley tried to enjoy herself, and she managed to laugh and talk with the others, and smile a lot, but she was wretched inside. She hadn't wanted it to end this way. Before she had dreams; she allowed herself illusions.

And now he wasn't allowing her any illusions.

She went to bed early, not disrobing, but lying down on her mat with her pillow in the beautiful and brightly colored Seminole shirt that Marna had given her. She stared into the darkness, with her lantern turned off. She could already make out sounds in the night. She heard a cricket, an owl, and from a distance—thankfully—she heard the pig-like grunt of a gator. The air smelled nice. There was the scent of the campfire, mingled with the gentle fragrance of wild orchids. She closed her eyes, torn apart inside, yet still feeling the peace around her.

She heard him when he came. She heard his footsteps on the ladder.

She had expected him to come, and she knew in her heart that he was every bit as torn as she. But there was a difference. She had faith in him—and that was what he lacked. He had no faith in her.

She thought that if she had any pride and dignity, she would walk away from this relationship. She would sit up, wait for him to arrive, and tell him to leave her alone.

But she had one more night, and she wanted it.

She kept her eyes half closed and saw him come inside and walk toward her. He stopped suddenly, inhaling sharply, his body silhouetted in the moonlight. His fists clenched. Ashley wanted to move, to say something, to discover what on earth was wrong. But then she knew, because he whispered a name.

"Elizabeth . . ."

His wife's name. In the dim light he had seen her in the beautiful blouse, her hair spread beneath her, and he hadn't been able to tell that that hair was red, not black.

He knelt down beside her, and Ashley still couldn't bring herself to stir. He reached out and touched her hair with trembling hands, and some harsh sound like a sob escaped him. The illusion had not lasted long. He had quickly realized who she was, and that the moonlight had played an eerie trick on him.

She wanted to open her eyes fully, she wanted to tell him that if he would reach out, she would be there. She loved him, and nothing about life mattered at all, if only she could live it with him.

The words would not come to her lips.

"Ashley," he murmured. "Ashley."

He lay down beside her and threaded his fingers through her hair. She should have turned him away, but she could not. He buried his face against her throat. "I'm so sorry. I never meant to hurt you."

She touched him at last, reaching out to stroke his face. "I have a bad temper," she said.

He smiled. "I shouldn't be here."

"Just whisper my name again," she told him softly, and he did. He whispered it again and again, and she clung to him. He moved his lips against her throat, and his fingers worked over the tiny buttons on the blouse. Moments later they were entwined in each other's arms, their clothing shed. He made love that night with a raw, near-desperate passion, his arms tight around her, his every stroke and thrust fierce and sweetly explosive.

"How is it possible to want a woman so desperately, and know that it's all so terribly out of sync and without rhyme and reason," he whispered to her. He had risen above her again. His fingers touched and studied her face, and lingered over her hair. "You are an emerald to me, Ashley, can you see that? A beautiful, exquisite gem, but one that I can't afford, one that isn't within my reach. I love everything about you so much. I love your eyes and your hair, and I love every line and curve of your body. I love your breasts and your throat, and sometimes I can't imagine that you're real, and that I'm touching you. I love to make love to you."

She wanted to say something, but inside she was aching. He loved her eyes, her hair... but he did not love her. He couldn't love her, or so it seemed. Maybe he couldn't allow himself to love her.

She stared up at him, wishing that he would leave, because she felt like crying. But he didn't move. He seemed locked in that straddled position over her, all bronze and sleek with sweat, a rawhide band holding back his black hair. In the night his eyes were luminescent, like a cat's. He brought his knuckle against her cheek.

She turned her head aside, choking on a sob. Gently, he held her face so he could see her eyes.

"What is it? What's the matter?"

She shook her head.

"What?"

"I—I love you," she said softly. "I—I've fallen in love with you."

He stiffened instantly, going as taut as a drum. From his throat to the lean rippled muscles of his belly, he went cold and straight. "No, you don't love me," he said. He stood quickly, walking away from her, restless as a panther. Ashley closed her eyes and fell back in misery. Telling him hadn't helped her.

Only leaving would help her.

He strode back to her and glared down at her angrily. "You don't love me. You're going to leave here. You're going back to New York."

"Yes! Yes, I'm leaving!" she cried.

"This has been fun and games. Dick and Jane in the jungle. Fall in love for a lark, and fly away to your next adventure."

"Stop it!" she yelled at him. "Just stop it." She was on her knees, challenging him. "You're an idiot! I told you that I love you because it's the truth. I've had one affair in my entire life, and that's it, so tell me about the world. I've learned to survive, too, even if my world's a bit different. I'm sorry about Elizabeth, damned sorry. And I'm sorry that the world isn't fair—it never has been, it probably never will be. I don't mind that you fight the unfairness. I would be happy to fight it with you—"

"It isn't your battle—"

"It is anyone's battle! Anyone can want to see it change! You fool! I can survive the swamp, and I can love the beauty, and I can deal with anything that you can create to hold against me. What I can't combat is you! I can't fight your belief that you can't love again because of Elizabeth, and I can't fight your total lack of belief in me as a human being!"

"What?" he said, startled, his eyes narrowing.

"Me, Eric, me. I don't understand how you could want me the way that you do, and not care in the least about the woman who I am! Yes, I own a Tyler emerald, a damned good one! Rafe gave it to me, as a friend, and I accepted it from him, as a friend. But I don't need jewels to survive. I don't even need New York to survive. But I am leaving, I am going home. Just as fast as I can!" Tears streamed down her face and she let them fall unchecked. She rose, naked and unaware of the fire in her hair, cascading down all around her, unaware that she was exceptionally proud and beautiful and more so for the truth and humility of her words. "I don't need the city, but I do need to be loved. I need to believe, and to be believed in. I can't survive without... faith. I do love you."

"Ashley!" He called out her name with fury. "You—you can't! I don't believe you."

"No, Eric, you don't believe in yourself anymore. And you can't let Elizabeth go."

He exhaled slowly. He came toward her as if he wanted to touch her, but he didn't. Instead he turned away. His shoulders stiffened, and a horrible sound, like a sob, escaped him. He stood very still then, tired, weary, almost as if he were defeated. "No," he said. "No, I can't forget her right now. You're right, I just can't. Not while her killer is on the loose."

He didn't touch her again or linger longer. He found his jeans and put them on. She couldn't rise to stop him, she couldn't even move. He was silent in the night as he left her, climbing down the ladder into the darkness, never once looking her way.

She lay awake, listening to the night and the sound of her own breathing. She closed her eyes and clenched her teeth against more tears. And she prayed that he would come back to her. She wanted him so badly, even though he had denied her. She wished that she had never spoken, that she could just lie with him and hold him in the darkness.

Where was Baby, she wondered? Tears burned at the back of her eyelids, and she hoped that the big cat would come back. She could cry into Baby's tawny pelt, and she wouldn't feel so terribly alone.

Then she heard motion in the darkness once again. She pulled the sheet over her. Eric was coming back. There was a God, and he had listened to her prayers. Eric was coming back. She closed her eyes, silently saying a prayer of thanks.

Then she felt the cold steel against her throat.

Her eyes flew open and she would have screamed, except the steel pressed more tightly on her flesh. She could feel the razor sharpness of the blade. She was certain that a trickle of blood had already formed on her throat.

She stared into the face of an Indian, but not one she knew, and not a full-blooded Seminole, but a man of mixed race. His face was dark and harshly lined, and there was a ragged scar that cut across his forehead.

She hadn't the faintest idea who he was. Or why he would want to kill her.

He smiled as he looked down at her. He was between thirty and forty, she thought, and yet he might have been any age. His eyes were nearly as dark as his hair, cut short, almost a crew cut. He wore a plaid shirt and worn jeans, and his lips were full. His eyes were icy cold. She knew instinctively that slitting her throat would mean nothing to him. He had killed before, and he would kill again very easily.

"That's right, don't scream, Ashley. My name is Jacobs. John Jacobs. Does that name ring any bells with you? It doesn't matter. Your name is Ashley, right? That's what he was calling you."

She didn't respond and he drew the knife down her body, pulling the sheet from her breasts to prick the shadowed valley between them. A little point of blood appeared.

"Careful, Ashley, I like you. You've got all kinds of fire and temper, huh? And you seem to be a smart girl. Be nice, and I may let you live."

"What do you want?" she demanded. The words came out in a harsh whisper because she barely dared to breathe.

"Eric Hawk," he told her. "That's what I want. I want that bastard half-breed. I've been sitting on death row because of him, and he's going to be the one to pay this time."

The night swam before her. She was going to black out, or be sick. This was the man who had slain Wendy's husband. The man who had killed Elizabeth so heinously, leaving her white gown a spill of crimson blood....

"Get up," he told her.

She exhaled, unable to move because of the knife. She had thought he would rape her, and she had known she would have preferred death to being touched by a man with so much blood on his hands. He smiled, seeing in her eyes all of her fears. "We may get to it later, baby, but I want out of here before Eric returns."

"But I thought you wanted him," she said quickly.

His teeth grated. "I want him on neutral ground. Not here."

"You have no right to be here. Anyone here would kill you with his or her bare hands alive."

"Smart, lady, real smart. Now get up and get dressed, and let's go."

"Where?"

"Don't ask any more questions. I'll start to reckon that it might be easier to leave you dead and let him come after me in revenge. Just get dressed. Now. Quickly."

He kept the knife tight on her body, and she hadn't the courage to move. He made a sound like a growl, pressing the point of the knife against her breast. She found courage and stood. She fumbled for her shirt, then the jeans—and Elizabeth's boots. She almost screamed when she pulled them on, thinking that they belonged to a woman this man had killed.

He made a sniggering sound, and she hated the look in his eyes as he stared at her. "Funny, ain't it? Here I am making you get dressed at knife point. Should be the other way around, huh? Excepting that I don't usually have no trouble with the ladies. Naw, they like me well enough." He flashed her a quick smile. "Thanks to Hawk, though, I've had me a dry spell for a while. Up in Raiford. It's a mean place, Miss Ashley, that it is. You should see it when they do get to an execution. The bleeding liberal hearts are all on one side of the fence, screeching about God's right to take lives. Then there are the bloodthirsty vamps on the other side, chanting 'Fry 'em!' Yep, it's a hell of a place.''

Ashley swallowed hard. "You murdered people. You were sentenced and condemned."

"I never wanted to shoot, Ashley. 'Specially not the girl. Damn, but she was a looker. I didn't hit her—it was Robbie Maynard did that. Then that half-breed Hawk—Leif Hawk, that is—steps in, trying to defend her. We had to shoot him, and then, well, she'd seen our faces. She had to die. It was real regretful, but..." He shrugged. "Only they knew who we were anyway. We had gloves on and all, but we peeled 'em off too soon. I had a record, so—" He paused again, looking her up and down in the dim light. "I could have gotten away with it. I was the one who knew the swamps, I knew where to run, and I knew where to hide. Except that Eric knew where to find me."

If he kept talking, Ashley thought, someone would come. Eric might, maybe to apologize to her. And if he did come back, what then?

"Let's go," Jacobs said.

"Where?"

"Down the ladder. Move."

She walked across the floor as slowly as she could. She wished desperately that she could think of something clever to do, or that she had the courage—or foolish bravado—to scream. She wished that she did belong in the swamp so she could plan some way to escape this man.

Where was Baby? The damned cat had run off when Ashley really needed her the most.

"I said move."

She started down the ladder, wondering if he was armed with only the knife. Maybe she could get ahead of him and run and start screaming.

"I've a nice-size Magnum in my waistband, and I can blow the whole of your head off with one bullet. So crawl down nice and quiet, huh?"

Ashley looked up—straight into the evil barrel of the gun. She no longer had to wonder just how well armed he was.

He smiled and followed her down the ladder. On the ground, he caught her arm. "This way!" he ordered.

He was leading her away from the pool and the village, toward the canal—into the absolute and horrible darkness of the swamp.

"Faster!" he said harshly.

She couldn't run any faster. Her heart was thundering and she could barely breathe. She tripped and cried out.

"Get up!" He jerked her arm.

She tried to get up, and touched something very soft. She looked down and a scream froze in her throat.

She knew where Baby was. The great cat lay silent and still beneath her.

"Oh, my God!" she whispered, and suddenly it all seemed more horrible than she could bear. He had killed that beautiful cat.

But then he had killed human beings, she reminded herself dully. What could the murder of the cat mean to such a man?

Tears stung her eyes as she stumbled to her feet. He started to drag her.

"You killed the cat. And you killed a man here, on the first day of the storm."

"Shut up and keep moving."

"You killed a man—"

"I didn't kill any man the first day of the storm. But if you don't shut up, I will kill you. I tried. I tried to reach the two of you at Eric's house after the storm. You got lucky then. Stay lucky, Ashley. Stay real lucky, and shut your mouth for now. Later, you can scream all you want. Yeah, honey, you can scream all you want."

Chapter 11

Eric cursed himself. If he wasn't so wrapped up in the past, he might have the good sense to worry about the present.

He couldn't go back to Ashley. He didn't know how to explain to her that Jacobs was out and that there was no way for him to find peace—or to escape the past—until Jacobs was behind bars again.

Or dead.

He walked down to the pool. Baby wasn't around, he noticed, but then she was more mobile than any of them. She had probably gone on to Brad and Wendy's. Eric mused that not even Baby seemed to like him very much these days.

The cat had good sense, he thought, staring out across the water. He wished that he could stay the hell away from himself.

Ashley Dane was like a star, fallen from the heavens, and she hadn't been meant to remain here. Not in his life. When she saw that, he thought, his heart hardening anew, she would feel like a caged beast. This wouldn't be a wonderful wilderness and freedom for her, it would become a prison cell. Maybe she even believed the things that she said to him, and she did know how to touch deeply. But she also knew how to wound, and she knew how to hurt. He had let her come close. He had wanted her to come close. He had played with fire, and now he was burned.

Suddenly he stiffened. He didn't know quite what it was that alerted him, but he felt that something had changed. Instinct pulled him, and he walked back to the cluster of chickees. He stared at his own and saw nothing—no movement, just the natural quiet of the night.

But something wasn't right. He knew because he felt the night breeze all along his spine and on his nape—and the breeze seemed to whisper of evil.

He paused below his brother's chickee—Wendy and Brad's now—and heard nothing but silence there, too. He looked toward his grandparents' chickee, far into the center of their small village. Someone was moving about.

He didn't think twice about running back to his chickee, where he strapped his knife to his ankle and shoved his .38 into his waistband. He climbed down and hurried to the center of the village.

Below Willie's chickee, flat against one of the corner poles, was a figure.

Eric circled, coming up on the figure from the back. He crouched low and moved across the earth in dead silence.

Then the figure sensed him and swirled around. Eric crashed into the figure, bringing it down with him before it could fire or throw a weapon.

"Son of a gun!" came a mutter. "Eric!"

Just about to throw a hard punch to the jaw, Eric paused and blinked against the darkness, the voice registering slowly in his mind. "Tony!" he gasped. He muttered an expletive and they got to their feet together.

"You scared the hell out of me!" Tony said. "My heart's still beating faster than the storm!" He dusted off his shirt.

"What are you doing here?" Eric demanded of his brother-in-law.

"I was worried about Willie and Mary. I thought I heard something. I could have sworn someone was around here. I heard Baby crawling around, and then I couldn't find her. I just thought that something was up, and I was worried."

"Are they all right?" Eric asked quickly.

"Yeah. I checked on Willie and Mary; they're sound asleep."

The two men both started when they heard Willie clearing his throat above them. He came down the ladder. "I may be old, Anthony Panther, but I'm not dead. I'm not sleeping. I heard you moving. What's going on here?"

At a loss, Eric shook his head, but the feeling that sent both ice and fire all along his spine was growing worse. "I don't know, Grandfather. Something." He turned to Tony suddenly, desperately. "My sister. Marna—"

"Marna's fine. The kids are sleeping, and she's wide awake and sitting up with the shotgun. No one's going to bother her."

They all swung around then, looking to the canal far away. They could hear the sound of a motor, and a pale light was coming out of the darkness.

"Airboat," Tony commented unnecessarily.

They started for the water, but Eric paused suddenly, looking down. His heart caught hard in his throat, then seemed to slam against his chest. He dropped to his knees.

It was Baby. Dead, he thought.

He clutched the huge cat into his arms, pulling her onto his lap. Her heart was still beating, he realized. He pulled open her lids and stared at her pupils. She was barely breathing, but she had no visible injury.

Poisoned. She was such a beggar. Someone who had realized that the cat could be more trouble than a pair of pit bulls had managed to see that she could spread no alarm.

Eric picked her up, staggering to his feet. Carrying her on his shoulders, he followed his grandfather and Tony. He heard Wendy's voice and realized that Brad and his sister-in-law had come.

It was late for a visit. Very late.

"What is it? What's happened?" Eric demanded.

The motor was already cut; Wendy was standing on dry land, and Brad was leaping over to join her. "Oh, Eric," Wendy began, then stopped. She stared at Baby; her eyes widened with surprise, then went damp with the threat of tears. "Eric, you tell me, what's happened? Is she—is she dead?" Wendy rushed forward, lifting the cat's head, opening her eyes as Eric had done.

"Poison, I think," Eric said.

"But why?" Wendy demanded blankly. "Baby needs a vet, but we'll never make it to one on time. We'll try to induce vomiting. Marna must have something for the kids. And it could be the wrong thing to do, but we've got to do something. Let's get her up to the cooking chickee. And get Marna. And—"

"Wendy," Brad interrupted his wife softly. "If Baby has been poisoned, there's a reason, and we've got to find it. And you've got to tell Eric the message we're supposed to be bringing, remember."

"Here, I'll take Baby," Tony said, and he lifted the cat from Eric. "Wendy, get Josh from Brad. He's sleeping, isn't he? Good, I'll get him over to Marna. And now, Wendy, you come with me. Brad, you tell Eric whatever it is."

Brad nodded. "The phones are working. Rafe Tyler called. Two of his chief management officials confessed to charges of murder yesterday when confronted with evidence against them. They were in a conspiracy with Mosby to heist the emeralds in the storm. They were after Ashley. Harrison had been given some big bucks to lure her into the swamp where they could get their hands on her—and the emeralds." Brad paused, watching Eric. "The body should have been Ashley's. They killed Mosby for losing her, for screwing up the deal. They probably would have killed him when they were done anyway." He shrugged. "They weren't the brightest crooks. Rafe has a half-brother who works covert operations and he was able to trace a few telephone messages and get his hands on some written material that clinched it all. Anyway, it's over."

Looking at Brad, Eric slowly shook his head. "It can't be over. Something is happening here. Baby—" he broke off in horror. He hadn't actually seen Ashley. He had gone to the chickee, but he hadn't seen Ashley.

An expletive escaped him like an explosion and he turned around and started to race toward where Ashley was sleeping. He berated himself furiously as he ran, his heart thundering against his chest. He took the ladder two rungs at a time, and then his breath escaped him in a ragged gasp.

She was gone.

There was no sign of a struggle. Eric hurried over to the mat and fell to his knees. He remembered how he had left her. On her knees, her hair streaming behind her. Looking almost as she had when he had first seen her in the swamp, and she had fallen wet and bedraggled in her tiger-striped bikini bottom at his feet in the mud. But there had been nothing wet or bedraggled about her tonight. She had been stunning, proud, her bare breasts beautiful and high in the glow of the moon, her eyes an emerald fire, her hair a river of flame. Her voice and words had seared his heart, and he had longed with all of his being to believe.

That was all that she had wanted—his faith in her as a woman.

And he had left her.

He dared not think of it now. She was gone, and time was passing. Someone had come here, someone who knew what he was doing. Someone who could come quietly, who could watch and wait. Someone who knew the swamp. . . .

He swallowed hard as bile formed in his stomach.

Jacobs.

He knew what it meant for blood to run cold then, for all of his limbs were constricted by ice. He breathed the cold, and he felt it around his heart. He stiffened and cast back his head, barely suppressing a savage scream. For in those moments, he could see it all again—walking with Wendy into the morgue, watching the attendant cast back the white sheet, then seeing Elizabeth's beautiful face, frozen in death, and the endless blood. The white dress that had been so beguiling against the copper of her skin was stained to crimson.

Jacobs was prowling the swamps with Ashley. He had taken her just as if he had dropped a calling card. Come on, get me, he was saying. It was a cat-and-mouse game. They were well matched. They both knew the swamp. They knew how to hide and move in silence.

Evenly matched! If Eric had had half his wits or his senses with him, Jacobs wouldn't have made it into the village. Eric would have heard him or sensed him before the damage had been done.

He stood quickly and came down the ladder. Brad was hurrying toward him. "She's . . . ?"

"She's gone," Eric said quickly. "I'm going after her."

"I'm coming."

"You can't."

"Eric—"

"Brad, you don't understand. This is a private thing between Jacobs and me. If he sees you, he'll kill her."

"He won't see me," Brad said firmly.

"But if he does—"

"Eric, four eyes have to be better than two. And if Jacobs does manage to kill you, he'll kill Ashley anyway. The man has no conscience. He's already condemned to death. Let me come. I'll be quiet. I'll stay low."

"He's going deep into the swamp, I'm certain—"

"I know the swamp real well," Brad interrupted him softly. "I had the best teacher in the world—you. And you're forgetting something else."

"What's that?"

"He killed your wife and your brother. But he also killed Wendy's husband, and I won't be able to go home if I don't get into this with you."

"Wendy wouldn't want—"

"*I* want."

Eric hesitated a moment longer. Brad was a good man to have on his side, and maybe what he was saying was true. Maybe it was personal for Brad, too. "Let's go," Eric said.

They started down toward the canal, then paused, hearing footsteps behind them. They turned around and saw Willie. His huge dark eyes were haunted. "Jacobs?" he asked Eric.

Eric glanced at Brad, then nodded slowly to his grandfather. Willie exhaled slowly, swallowing and closing his eyes, and Eric knew that he was thinking about Leif and Elizabeth.

Willie opened his eyes. "Last time, son, I told you not to kill him. I was afraid that your heart and soul would fester with the hatred, and that you could live better knowing that you'd had the strength to trust in the law. And the law was fair—the law of our state condemned him. I'll tell you the same thing now. Don't kill with hatred."

"Grandfather—"

Willie lifted his hand. "But if he threatens your life, or Brad's, or if he hurts that pretty woman in any way, then I say, blow the monster's head off and be done with it. Just remember—do what is necessary, and that will sit well in your heart."

"All right, Grandfather. I'm taking the canoe."

Willie nodded, and Eric and Brad walked on. The old man called out, "Wendy will save the cat."

Eric's lips curved in acknowledgement. "Yes, she will."

"Tell Wendy where I am," Brad said.

"Wendy will know where you are," Willie answered.

Eric pushed the canoe out from the shore and into the water, and they saw Willie, standing calm and stoic upon the land.

As they moved away from the village, darkness settled down upon them.

"I'll get the lantern," Brad said.

"No, just the flashlight. We don't want to advertise our presence."

"It's black as Hades," Brad reminded him.

And it was. The moon went behind a cloud, and the canal water and the saw grass seemed to be one with the sky. "I just need a pinpoint of light," Eric said.

"How do you know—"

"He's leaving me a trail, Brad. He wants me to follow him." To prove his point, he stopped rowing as they passed beneath a branch, and showed Brad the broken twigs and the bracken. "He's leaving a trail as broad as daylight. He knows that I'll come."

Eric sank his paddle back into the water in rhythm with Brad. The canoe glided on through the water.

Ashley stared out into the night as Jacobs sent his canoe skimming through the water. She could see very little, not even see his face. Yet he was moving through the darkness, sure of his way.

A cloud shifted, and a small amount of moonlight shone down upon them. When they had first left the village, she had thought about braving the water to escape him. He must have read her mind, for as soon as they turned around the first hummock, he had ceased to paddle and had brought his knife against her throat, demanding her hands. Now they were tied before her with thin strips of rawhide, which chafed and tore her skin. She hadn't a prayer in the world.

He smiled at her, seeing her face in the moonlight. "You didn't want to go swimming anyway, not here and not at night. Look over there at that log—only it's not a log. Put a juicy morsel like you into the water, and that log will come alive faster than you can spit. They're mean, gators are. Did your boyfriend warn you about that? Even if you made dry land, that gator could come right after you, and fast."

She shivered although she didn't want to. He leaned close to her, and he had that awful look in his eyes again. He might like women—he had said that he liked her—but he liked killing more than anything else, she was certain about that.

"Eric and I are old friends," he said. He waited for her to respond. When she didn't, he kept talking. "Leif and I went to school together, did he tell you that? Man, those Hawks, they just excelled at everything. Everyone knew that they wouldn't be sitting around in any kind of poverty.

When they were kids, all the adults talked about what the Hawks would bring to the council. They were the promise of our people. Kind of makes you a little bit sick, huh? They went off to college; they got to be football stars—and the nation don't give a damn about what color you are as long as you can carry a pigskin ball over a goal line! Then Eric went off to Vietnam, and he was a hero all over again. It wasn't that smooth for me. My old man was a no-account trash who had a night's fun with an Indian girl at a festival and then took off. Mom picked a last name out of the phone book—Jacobs. It has a good ring. It looked good the first time I was arrested. I never could get the right numbers in bingo, and so I just decided to take the pot without them. I wasn't loved by the tribe like the Hawks, so I went behind bars. Then I started up with Maynard and Fitz. They were in on a house razing deal. We got together real good when they found out just how well I knew the swamp—and just what could be hidden in it.

"You want to know something that was true? As much as I hated those Hawks, I didn't want to kill them on the night of the holdup. It was just that Leif Hawk wasn't going to let it be. And now—now there's Eric. And this is him and me. And he is going to die tonight."

Ashley laughed suddenly because she was so horribly nervous. "I think you might have missed your mark. We had a bit of an argument, remember? He'll probably stay away all night. And when he finds me gone in the morning, he'll think that I just left him. It's what he's been expecting me to do."

She felt a new chill seize her as Jacobs slowly shook his head. "No, I don't think so. He'll figure out that something is wrong right away."

"Why is that?"

"I killed the cat, remember?"

"Oh!" Feeling sick, she lowered her head. She swallowed and tried very hard to control her panic. She had been in rough spots before. Tine Elliott had kidnapped her at gunpoint to get to Tara. He had threatened her life, but she hadn't become a helpless victim. She had fought back—and help had come.

But this was different. This was the swamp. This was a darkness worse than anything.

Yet she didn't want Eric to try to rescue her. Because Jacobs meant to kill him. And then her.

"It's not much longer, Ashley," Jacobs told her.

She shook her head. "You're a fool. You escaped. You should have left the state, you should have sailed to the islands, you should have hidden—"

"It isn't easy for a half-breed Indian to blend with the rest of humanity, lady," he said dryly.

"Out west—"

"It doesn't matter. I'm going one way or the other. Florida is tough, if you haven't noticed. My death certificate has been signed. They'll get to me sooner or later. I didn't escape to live."

"Then—"

"I escaped for revenge. And I'm going to get it."

She lowered her head again and tried not to cry. There had to be some way out of this. Eric wasn't a fool, he wouldn't come alone.

"Ah, hope springs eternal in the human breast!" Jacobs laughed. "If he comes with a friend, count on it, the friend will die right along with him."

She tossed back her hair. "What if he comes with an entire S.W.A.T. team?"

Jacobs stopped paddling. He leaned forward. "S.W.A.T. teams are loud, even *if* one could get out here right now. You have to know the swamp, honey. But if he does come with a pack, well then . . ." His voice trailed off.

"Then what?"

He shrugged. "Then I kill you. Just like his wife. Four bullets to the chest. And he may not be dead himself, but life will be over for him. He'll know then that he's just hell on women, and that will be that."

He was going to kill her anyway, no matter what.

"We're almost there," he told her. "Just up ahead. That nice dry hummock there. See the little shack. For weekend hunters. White boys. They come out here and shoot up beer cans. Big men. They don't know the first thing about hunting." He hesitated. "But Eric does. That's why we're going to play real safe."

The canoe scraped the edge of the bank. In the darkness she could barely make out the tiny cabin and what was beyond it. There was water around them, and there seemed to be a bog of deep black muck and high saw grass to the left.

There was death in the darkness. Alligators were nearby, and deadly snakes. But Eric had been right when he had told her that there was still no creature as deadly as man.

"Get up careful—" Jacobs began.

But Ashley was already standing, causing the canoe to dip and sway. She had never been so scared in her life—and never been more blindly determined. She wasn't going to help him kill Eric. She'd rather take her chances with the swamp.

"I said—" Jacobs continued, but it was too late. The canoe capsized, and they both fell into the murky waters in the pitch-black of the night.

Eric suddenly stiffened where he sat in the front of the canoe. He raised his paddle and lifted his hand so Brad would do the same.

"What is it?" Brad barely mouthed the question.

"I don't know. Something," Eric said. He turned off the flashlight and sat very still.

They both heard it—a splash. Then, from somewhere not far ahead, a scream. It was high and long and shrill, filled with terror and pain. Ashley.

Eric's jaw constricted and his stomach went tight as a drum. He drove his paddle into the water and raced along the water.

Ashley screamed again.

This time, her cry was choked to a stop. Eric could hear the sounds of splashing water, of fighting in the long grasses not a hundred yards away.

He sank his paddle deeply into the mud, bringing the canoe to a halt. He turned to Brad. "Can you face him down? And I'll come around."

Brad hesitated. They'd worked together before, and they'd been a good team. Then, Eric had swaggered calmly out to do the luring. He had helped saved Wendy's life.

The waters here were deadly. Eric intended to plunge into the canal, Brad knew it. They could both figure what had happened. Ashley had tried to escape, and now she was struggling for her life.

"Go on," Brad said. "I can handle my part."

Eric nodded. "Thanks." Silently he stepped over the edge of the canoe and sank in the water.

"Hey," Brad said.

Eric surfaced, watching him.

"I was going to tell you to be careful, but you can be meaner than any gator I've ever come across when you've got the mind to be."

Eric smiled. He grasped Brad's hand for a moment, then plunged back in the water.

And he disappeared into the night.

"You stupid bitch! I should plug you right now, I should do away with you this very second!"

Ashley had barely dived into the blackness before he'd had his hands on her. His fingers gripped her hair, and he dragged her back to the surface. She came up gasping for air, then screaming for dear life.

Surrounded by the muck and the saw grasses, she kicked at him with fury and desperation, screaming again.

And he dragged her down deep in the water. Her lungs began to burn. She felt her head spinning and a blackness more complete than any other falling upon her. She nearly opened her mouth to inhale the water into her searing lungs when he jerked her up at last. This time, she kept quiet. She choked and coughed and didn't have the breath left to whisper, much less scream.

He jerked her against him hard, staring into her eyes. "Don't do it again. I don't have to kill you, you know. Plenty of people know my face. I die if I kill you, and I die if I don't. If I get Eric Hawk, I might feel generous. I might let you live. And then—" He paused, and Ashley wondered why.

Then she saw the snake.

It was slithering in and out of the grasses to their right. It was large. Desperately, she tried to remember what Eric had told her. Rattlers like hummocks. So did coral snakes. There were only four poisonous snakes down here, and one of them liked water.

The cottonmouth...

Neither of them was breathing. They both stared at the creature as it silently streamed through the water toward them. They both watched....

The snake ignored them. It continued moving. In another second, it disappeared.

"Nice place, the swamp. You like it here, Ashley?" Jacobs whispered to her at last.

She started to shiver. She couldn't help it. She desperately wanted to get out of the water.

Abruptly, Jacobs set his knife against her throat. "We're going to move now—" he began, but then stopped. He swung her around in front of him in the waist-high water. Ashley didn't understand. Then she saw the faint light and heard the dip of a paddle in the water.

"Playtime!" Jacobs whispered against her neck. "And I'm not quite prepared the way I wanted to be, thanks to you. Come on, now, move!"

He started dragging her to the shore. They didn't make it. A voice called out in the darkness.

"Jacobs!"

It wasn't Eric. It was Brad.

Jacobs swore furiously. "Get the hell out of here. You come any closer, and the girl is dead."

"How do I know that the girl isn't dead already."

Jacobs pressed his knife against her flesh. "Say something, sweetheart."

"I'm—I'm alive, Brad." She hesitated just briefly. "But don't come any closer. All he wants to do is kill us all and—" she broke off, screaming in pain as Jacobs knotted her hair viciously into his fist.

"You stay where you are because I want Eric Hawk. And I'll kill her if I don't see him out here alone in a matter of minutes. You got that."

There was silence out on the water. Ashley felt something move against her legs. She swallowed, terrified of the steel against her throat, wretchedly aware of the death that lurked in the water.

"I mean it!" Jacobs claimed. "You get that half-breed out here now—or she dies!"

She felt something sure and hard against her leg.

Suddenly the water beneath her exploded. She screamed as she was torn from Jacobs's grasp and sent flying farther out into the water. She sank low, then surfaced, thrashing and panicking. All around her, the water was still exploding, splashing wildly.

Then she realized why. No snake had touched her leg. It had been Eric. He had reached them from beneath the surface of the water and had wrenched her from Jacobs's grasp before the madman's knife could sink into her flesh.

And now he and Jacobs were engaged in deadly combat. She couldn't even tell who was who in the consuming darkness as the men fell and sank, then rose, gasping.

Ashley strained to see. Jacobs had Eric in a headlock and was pulling him down again. Eric locked his fingers on Jacobs's arms, dragging him forward. They sank together again. They rose, apart this time. Eric cast himself against Jacobs. They fell.

They moved closer and closer to the shore, fists flying. Jacobs caught Eric in the jaw, and he went down, splashing hard, his grunt of pain seeming to echo in the night.

Ashley screamed.

She heard the lap of the water and realized that Brad was coming up with the canoe. "Ashley, shut up!" he warned her.

"Brad, do something! He's going to kill him—"

"Ashley, just stay very still."

She stared at Brad in horror, then realized that something was slithering by her again. She stood very, very still, and tried not to hear the sickening crunches of the vicious fight taking place just yards away.

The snake was back. It was circling her and swimming around and around her.

"Dead still, Ashley. Do you understand me? Blink, if you do."

She blinked. She didn't move. The sounds of the fight faded behind her.

Eric burst from the surface a split second before Jacobs. It was the advantage he needed. He blinked once and saw Elizabeth, dead, in her pool of blood.

He slammed his fist into Jacobs's face with all the strength in his body. He heard bone crack, then Jacobs went down, his eyes closed.

Jacobs's jaw was broken, Eric thought impassively, but he wasn't dead.

He should go back to Brad and get a gun and blow Jacobs's head away.

He clenched his hands into fists at his sides.

He still believed in the law. He had bested Jacobs barehanded and should hand this murderer back to the police. He would meet his fate in the electric chair, or rot forever on death row. He wouldn't escape again.

Something hot and horrible inside of Eric wanted to kill Jacobs in the worst way. He knew that he had killed in the war. But he had never murdered.

And he had to believe in the law. His father had taught him that law was the dividing line, and man's belief in it made him civilized, and separated him from the savage. It had nothing to do with color or creed or race; it was about right and wrong.

Jacobs was dung, and he might be better off dead. He probably would be dead soon.

But it wasn't for Eric to be judge and jury—or play God. He exhaled slowly and turned around. He needed to call Brad over so that they could tie Jacobs up. Once he awakened, he wouldn't hesitate to try to murder Eric again.

But when Eric turned, he forgot Jacobs.

He saw Ashley in the water. She was dead still, and Brad was talking to her very quietly, his Magnum aimed at the water. But he seemed to be having difficulty getting a fix on his target.

A snake. With antivenom, she could survive a bite. Except that they were deep in the swamp, and it could take a long time to get back to the village.

"Ashley!"

He hadn't meant to speak; her name escaped him.

Ashley heard her name called out with a horrible anguish, and she realized that it was Eric. He was alive. There was no more motion in the water, just the silent, deadly dance of the snake.

She felt movement near her. Eric was making his way toward the canoe. Brad was speaking to him very softly. "I can't get a fix on it."

"Give me the gun."

"Be still," Brad whispered.

"Ashley, dead still!" Eric warned her, just as Brad had done.

And the water exploded all around her as a shot was fired. She screamed when pieces of snake carcass and snake blood splattered her.

Then she was pulled up, by strong arms. She looked up and discovered deep green eyes, full of care and anguish and concern, staring into hers.

One of Eric's eyes was already sporting a bruise. Blood trailed from his nose and his jaw. She wanted to ask him what had happened to Jacobs, but when she opened her mouth, no sound came. She wanted to smile, too, because

Brad was there, looking down at her with the same concern.

"Jacobs," she mouthed.

"He's worse than I am," Eric promised her.

Then her eyes widened suddenly, because she could see what they could not.

Jacobs might be worse than Eric, but he wasn't down. He was coming at them again, his knife poised high.

She screamed out the warning just in time. Eric ducked as Jacobs rose from the water. Eric turned around in the bottom of the canoe, Jacobs rose from the water. Eric turned around in the bottom of the canoe, ready to fling himself at the assailant.

But it wasn't necessary.

Another shot rang out in the darkness. Jacobs, stretching high with his lethal knife glinting evilly in the moonlight, suddenly opened his eyes and mouth wide. He looked down at the huge hole burning in his chest.

Then he pitched forward into the water.

Stunned, Eric, Brad and Ashley turned around.

Willie Hawk was balanced carefully on his knee in the canoe that now came toward them. He carried a shotgun, and the muzzle was still smoking. Wendy was behind him, rowing.

Willie nodded to them, then looked impassively down into the water. "Never kill in anger; it's bad for the heart. You can take a life only to save a life. And that's good for the heart. Come on, now. It's time to get back. Eric, you're going to need a hospital. Marna is at Wendy's—and Brad's house. The police will come soon enough."

He turned around and smiled at Wendy. "Let's go home."

They returned to the village with Jacobs's body.

Wendy insisted Eric had three broken ribs, maybe more, and made him lie down in the hut. She gave Ashley instructions on binding his chest. Eric protested, of course; he was a lousy patient. And there wasn't a moment for him and Ashley to have even a single moment alone together. Brad explained everything that had happened with Harrison Mosby, and she was sorry to hear that greed had brought about the downfall of so many. Then she was furious to hear that she would have been murdered herself.

She was also grateful to Eric. He had saved her from the jaws of death not once, but twice.

Eric didn't see it that way at all. Wincing as he lay on a mat on the floor of his grandfather's chickee, he caught her hand. "I'm so sorry. What a fool I was. I thought you were safer out here, when I was actually putting you in danger."

"You did save me, you idiot," she assured him. Her lips were suddenly chattering. She hadn't dried completely, but she didn't really care. "They would have killed me before the storm—if I hadn't found you."

He smiled and closed his eyes, and she was worried. She looked at Wendy and at Mary, who was surveying her grandson with grave concern. "Concussion, I think. That was one hell of a fight," Wendy murmured. "We can't let him sleep—" she began, but then they heard the arrival of the helicopter.

Eric was lifted in a stretcher, followed by Jacobs's body.

"Go with him," Wendy told Ashley.

She hesitated.

"There's room." Wendy sighed. "All right, I'll come, too. We'll both go, and Brad can come in the morning with clothes. Let's go."

Ashley wasn't sure if riding in the helicopter wasn't almost as bad as being in the black water with the snake. She closed her eyes, feeling the breeze, and she knew it didn't matter. That night she wanted to be near him.

It was almost dawn by the time Eric was admitted into the hospital. Wendy and Ashley took a cab to a nearby hotel, where they stayed the night.

Ashley barely knew that she had slept until she awoke to find herself still wearing muddy clothes.

"It's all right," Wendy said, laughing at Ashley's expression. "Brad came—the roads are fine—and he's left us stuff to wear. He's over at the hospital now."

"That's wonderful," Ashley said. She showered, and when she came out, Wendy was just finishing her makeup. "I'm ready whenever you are," she announced.

Ashley hesitated. "I'm not going with you, Wendy."

"What?"

Ashley hesitated again. "I don't know if you can understand this or not, but I need to go shopping. I'm—I'm going to fly back to New York tonight."

"But why—" Wendy began, then stopped speaking. She shook her head. "Never mind. It's none of my business. It's between you and Eric."

Ashley shook her head, too. Then impulsively, she kissed Wendy on the cheek and gave her a warm hug, which Wendy returned. "I'm in love with Eric, Wendy. I told him so. And there's nothing on earth that I wouldn't do for him. But he has to want me first. For what I am, not what he thinks I am. I'm going to see him before I leave. I'm just going shopping first."

"You have to do what you think is right," Wendy assured her.

Ashley called a cab and went down to the Bal Harbour shops where she looked for something that was ridiculously expensive. She took her time and bought a smart red suit with a tight skirt and a jacket that flared at the waist. She also bought a floppy, wide-brimmed hat, black heels, a black handbag and black gloves. She had her hair done in a chignon.

Then she took a taxi to the hospital.

Brad and Wendy were in Eric's room. One of Eric's eyes was horribly black. He was shirtless, his ribs were taped and a needle was stuck in his arm so fluid could drip into him from an intravenous tube.

Despite all that, her heart beat furiously and she could barely breathe. He was still the most striking, magnetic man she had ever seen. The dark slash of his hair against the sheets and the bronze color of his body all added up to the man she loved.

He had been talking animatedly, but when he saw Ashley, he stopped.

So did Brad and Wendy. They stared at her open-mouthed. Ashley smiled sweetly, drawing off her gloves as she came in, a large box of chocolates in her hand.

"Ashley!" Brad gasped at last.

Wendy laughed then and tapped his jaw. "Shut your mouth, my love, before you drool. And come on, let's leave them alone together for a minute."

Ashley cast her a grateful glance. Brad winked, and he and his wife left. Ashley took the chair that Wendy had vacated. Eric just kept staring at her.

"You look great," he finally told her.

"Thank you." She crossed her legs elegantly. "It was nice to have a hot shower. But I shouldn't have said that, right? That means I'm not suited for the swamp."

Eric breathed slowly. "You're not suited for the swamp, Ashley. I'll never forget—"

"Forget what?"

"Your face when the snake was moving around you."

"Oh, I see. If I was suited for the swamp, I would jump up and down and say, 'Oh boy! A cottonmouth. What fun!'"

He flushed, then glared at her. His hand shot out and his fingers closed around her wrist with startling strength. She looked at his hands and remembered the way they felt on her and how they looked against her flesh. She swallowed. She had to go. She had known it for some time.

"They're going to release me tomorrow morning," he said somewhat irritably. "Talking about this will be a heck of a lot easier once I'm up and about."

"No, it won't. Because I'm leaving this afternoon."

"You're what?"

She snatched her hand away quickly. If he decided to hold on to her, there wouldn't be a prayer in the world for her to escape his strength.

She stood and looked down at him. "I've told you how I feel. And I made a fool out of myself."

"Ashley, wait a minute. You don't understand. I knew last night that Jacobs was out. I had no idea where he was, but Mica had told me that he had escaped. I couldn't begin to think of a future when—"

"No, you couldn't think of a future, but you could make love. Well, I want more than that. My cards are on the table, and they have been there, faceup, everything naked for you to see. You have to bury Elizabeth, Eric, once and for all. And you have to do more than that—you have to want me. If you do, you come talk to me. You know where I live."

With that, she turned around to leave.

"Ashley!"

She heard him jump out of the bed and swear because of the needle in his arm.

She stepped outside. Brad was there, smiling. "I'll handle Tonto for the moment," he said. Then he kissed her warmly on the cheek and went back into the room.

Wendy didn't say anything at all. She just gave Ashley a big hug.

Ashley started down the hall and ran into Willie Hawk. He was very handsome and dignified in a business suit and a cap with an egret feather.

"Goodbye, Willie. Thank you for everything," Ashley told him.

"You're leaving?" he asked.

She nodded, then said, "I have to."

He nodded, too. She didn't know why she kept speaking, but she did. "I'm in love with him. He doesn't love me. Not enough."

Willie smiled and patted her arm. "Do you know there are many roads? They wind around and around. And maybe there are many roads that lead home. It doesn't matter which one you take, just as long as you get there. Goodbye, Ashley. We'll miss you."

He kissed her cheek and hurried toward his grandson's room.

She left the hospital. And though tears clouded her eyes, she didn't look back.

There were many roads . . .

And many of them lead home.

She could only hope and pray that she had set upon a course that would bring her home.

Chapter 12

Four weeks later Ashley stood at her window and looked down at the human traffic in front of Rockefeller Plaza. She arched her back, trying to do away with the little cricks and pains caused by her hunching over her desk.

When she had first returned, she had wondered how she would ever settle down to work. She had believed that Eric would come. She had wanted to believe so desperately that he loved her enough to come for her. But days had passed, and then weeks, and still there was no sign of Eric Hawk. She began to give up hope.

Then she discovered that all that she cared about was her work. So she sat for hours and hours over sketches, and she drove the staff crazy demanding more and more fabric samples.

She was even driving Tara crazy by calling all the time before making decisions. Because of the baby, Tara wanted nothing to do with work.

"Fly back to Florida," she told Ashley irritably.

"No!"

"Then come over for dinner. Rafe's having a few old friends over to see the baby and—"

"No, I don't want to come to dinner. Thanks anyway." She hung up quickly. She didn't want Tara to do any matchmaking for her. She just wanted to be alone—with her work.

But it seemed that she had been working just too much. She looked out into the hallway and called her secretary. "Jennifer! Make me lunch reservations at the Plaza, will you, please?"

"Are you going alone?"

"Yes. And don't tell anyone where I am, please."

"Whatever you say, Ashley," Jennifer promised.

It wasn't lunchtime, but Ashley left the office anyway. She took a cab partway, then had the cabbie let her out. The air was just a little bit cool, and the leaves were beginning to turn. She loved the park in the fall.

As they did every so often in a most annoying way, tears burned against her eyelids. They had no fall in the swamps! she told herself. And it would be awful for Christmas. There was probably very little ice skating down there.

But her assurances rang hollow in her ears. She had made the mistake of falling in love with the right man. And autumn didn't matter at all, neither did the beautiful color of the leaves. Where she lived didn't matter at all. Who she lived with mattered tremendously.

At last she left the park behind and started across the street for the Plaza. She checked her coat and the maître d' gave her a secluded table in the corner. She ordered a glass of white wine, sipped it and leaned back in her chair. She closed her eyes.

Seconds later, she heard a stir around her, and curious, opened her eyes. People were looking around, staring and trying not to look as if they were staring, the way they did when a celebrity was present.

Ashley wondered who it might be. Several big stars were in town, appearing on Broadway or filming movies.

She caught a glimpse of a man's back. He was tall, broad shouldered and dressed in a very handsome tailored black suit. His hair was very dark and very straight, just over his collar.

He was the man who had turned all the heads, she realized. And he was seated right by her. Only an oak pillar separated them.

She sipped her wine again, forgetting the attention-grabbing stranger. She shouldn't have come, she decided. It wasn't restful at all.

She ordered lamb and began to sketch on her napkin. Suddenly she realized that the waiter was hovering by her table.

"Yes?"

"*Madame.*" With a flourish he set a package wrapped in white tissue paper before her.

"What—" Ashley began.

"A present," he said with a broad grin, turning away.

"But who—" The waiter had already disappeared between the tables. Someone had tipped him well, she thought with annoyance.

Then her curiosity got the best of her and she started to open the package. The tissue fell apart, and the contents—a little ball of material—fell on her lap.

Amazed, she stared at the material, then picked it up.

Her breathing stopped. It was the tiger-striped bikini bottom she had been wearing when she ran into Eric Hawk in the swamp. She gasped.

Then she looked up.

Eric was standing in front of her.

He was the man in the black suit, she realized, and he wore it well. His shirt was white and startlingly attractive against the hue of his skin. His hair still fell, over his forehead.

But he was elegant, too—sleek, handsome, virile. He smiled slowly, his green eyes flashing, his full lips curving, as he reached for the chair opposite from her. "May I?"

She nodded. He sat.

"I thought maybe I should return those," he said, indicating the bikini.

She swallowed. Her teeth were chattering and her fingers froze. "It's, uh, very, very rude to surprise people in restaurants," she told him.

"Oh. Sorry. Well, I may need help in New York, you know." He lowered his head. "I'll try real hard to be civil."

She nodded. "Good."

He reached across the table and took her hand. "Forgive me?"

"What?"

"I couldn't believe that you could love me. And now, well, I'm still as scared as a high-school kid, but I just can't stand being without you. I had to come and tell you that. I love you, Ashley. Did you mean what you said, that you loved me?"

She nodded again, still not believing that he could be there.

His fingers moved over hers. "I'm not easy to live with, you know that already. I've a bad temper. But then, yours is horrible, so we're about even there. I had thought that maybe you could keep up your work. The mail service is incredible these days. I wouldn't want to take away anything that is you, and I think that you like to design. Do you?"

She nodded once more.

He reached into his pocket and produced a little jewel case. He popped it open. A beautiful diamond was inside. It was huge; it was a wonderful cut, and even if it had been just glass, it still would have brought tears to her eyes.

"Tara gave me the size," he told her.

"Tara!" she gasped.

He nodded, and a teasing light touched his eyes. "I'm pretty good at picking up a trail, but in a city of eight million people, I thought I should get a hold of her to find out where you might be. I tried to get you at work. You weren't there, but thankfully, Tara was—showing off the baby—and she assured me that this was a very good place to look for you. I'm glad that she knows your habits well." He cleared his throat. "Will you marry me, Ashley? I was trying to find a few good points to sell myself, and all I could remember was that I was pretty hard on you. Let's see. I don't snore. I take out the garbage. I'm a fair to middling cook. I like to make love. I'm fairly handy with the plumbing—and I love you. I love you with all of my heart, and I believe in you. Ashley, say something, please."

She did. She shrieked so that every head turned, and she jumped up, knocking over everything on the table, and she kissed him.

He kissed her back, then he turned to the startled old couple beside him.

"She's just a little savage at times!" he said, shaking his head. He tossed some money on the table and lifted her into his arms. With the whole restaurant staring at them, he carried her out to the street.

"My coat!" she told him.

"I'll go back for it," he promised, his eyes locked on hers.

"I love you. I'll live with you anywhere," she told him. She touched his hair with her fingertips.

"I love you, too."

"People are watching us."

"So they are."

"Where are you taking me?"

"To your apartment. It's been a long four weeks!"

Seconds later she was deposited into a horse-drawn carriage, and Eric was giving the driver her address.

"Tara?" she asked.

"Tara," he agreed, holding her hand. "Now, I've figured it out. We can always spend a season here—"

"Fall," she said.

"Fall, it's my favorite. Oh! Until we have children. Then we'll have to settle down because of school. Fall until we have children, then the summer."

"Fine."

"And Christmas! Maybe we'll come for Christmas."

"Maybe. Now and then."

The carriage stopped in front of her building. Eric paid the driver, and holding hands, he and Ashley hurried past the doorman, who received a beautiful smile from her. Then they were in the ornate elevator heading up to the fifteenth floor. "Nice," Eric commented.

Ashley laughed. "You hate it."

"I love it. For fall."

The door opened. She hurried along the hallway to unlock her apartment, and he followed. She was suddenly nervous. She wanted him to like her place. It was furnished with antiques, the window opened to a view of Manhattan, and the tile and carpet were soft beige.

"Well, what do you think?"

But he wasn't looking at the apartment at all, he was looking at her. He walked across the room and swept her into his arms again. "It's beautiful. Where's the bedroom?"

She whispered the answer into his ear and he carried her to her bed with its comforter and satin sheets. "We can be married down in Florida. Tara and Rafe and the others can come."

"Umm," he murmured. He tugged off her shoes while she stared at the ceiling, floating on clouds. She felt his hands on her shirt. "Oh, we have to be here for Amy's baptism next week. I'm a godparent."

"That's wonderful," Eric murmured. Her clothes seemed to be melting away from her, and he was up again, tossing pieces of his elegant suit all over the place.

"And I'm keeping my emerald ring. I'll be very happy to live with you in the swamp, but I am keeping my one Tyler emerald."

"Good for you! I'll try very hard not to be jealous of your one Tyler jewel," Eric assured her, and laughed. He stretched out on top of her, and his eyes filled with fire and mischief as he moved his hands along the length of her. Her breath caught and he frowned suddenly, looking down at her. "Is there something else you need?" he asked.

She loved the tone of his voice. He did love her, and he believed in her. He didn't question any longer that their worlds could be combined.

She offered him a dazzling smile and threw her arms around him. "There's nothing...nothing," she said softly, sensually, "that I need. Nothing but the primitive earth—and you."

He cast back his head and they laughed. Then he kissed her until they could laugh no more.

Epilogue

Three months later they were married. The wedding took place at sunset, and it was as if nature had made everything spectacular for the occasion.

Ashley told Eric that she didn't mind having the ceremony in the south if he didn't mind having a wedding with all the frills. He told her to go right ahead and plan it, and she did.

It was a big wedding. Ashley had two sisters-in-law and three very close friends, including Wendy, for bridesmaids; Tara, of course, was her maid of honor. Brad was Eric's best man, and by the time the wedding day arrived, Rafe had become a good friend, and so he was an usher. Tony Panther, an old army buddy and two friends from the council rounded out Eric's lineup. The wedding-guest list was huge, and as the time for the ceremony drew near, Eric realized that he hadn't even begun to meet Ashley's relatives. They had been arriving all day, up to the last minute.

He saw Ashley running into the church's nave. She laughed, seeing him, and he would have laughed in return, but she was so breathtaking a bride that his breath caught and he reached for her hands. "This is it," he whispered. She had chosen a soft cream color for her long gown. It was traditional in cut, almost a Renaissance style, and had a fabulous pearled train. She wore a tiara with a sweeping veil, and beneath it, her eyes were stunning. He was suddenly very humble, thinking that God had granted him this angel, not to be borrowed, but to be cherished forever.

"This is it," she repeated. "You're sure, right?"

"More sure than I have ever been in my whole life about anything." He forgot her dress and her veil and his own tuxedo and he drew her against him, kissing her deeply.

Someone cleared a throat loudly. "Ashley!" It was Tara. "He's not supposed to see you in the gown and Father O'Neill's saying that we must come into the chorus room and get ready!"

They separated, though their gazes remained on each other. They both smiled with tremendous happiness.

"For heaven's sake, Eric! You'll be married soon, and you can stare at each other all night!" She grabbed Ashley's hand and pulled her away. Eric, still smiling, turned around to walk outside for one more moment before taking his place by the altar.

He was startled to see a very pretty girl of about thirteen come racing up to the church. She paused, just as startled to see him.

Her hair was ebony and fell down her back in blue-black swirls. Her complexion was deeply tanned, her eyes a soft hazel. She was an Indian, and yet he didn't think that she was a Seminole or a Miccosukee. He was almost positive that she wasn't related to him. He didn't think that he had any long lost relatives.

"Hi! You're—you're him, right? Eric? Oh, thank goodness, if you're here, then I'm not late. I had to wait for the sitter for the baby. Mom said that he was just too young for the ceremony. It was tricky finding the right person to come to the hotel room. I'm talking too much, right? I'm sorry, I'm nervous!''

She paused, gasping for breath and just staring at Eric with a beautiful smile on her face.

He smiled himself. "You're not late," he told her. "And, yes, I'm Eric." He hesitated just a second. "Who are you?"

"Leah. Leah Dane. I'm Ashley's niece." She stuck out her hand, flushing again. "And you're almost my Uncle Eric. If that's all right, of course."

After a moment, he started laughing. Leah just stared at him, and he tried to sober quickly. "Leah Dane, I'm delighted to make your acquaintance. And I'll be quite delighted to be your uncle."

"Thanks," she said. "But what's so funny?"

"Your aunt," he assured her. He set his hand on her shoulders and turned her toward the church. "I think I should be getting down to the altar. There's Brad motioning to me. You'll meet him soon enough. By the way, what is your tribe?"

"Nez Percé," Leah said. She glanced at him slyly. "Aunt Ashley never told you, huh?"

"She never told me," he said solemnly. He smiled and pushed her ahead. "We'd better get on. We'll get a chance to talk more later. And maybe you can help me get one back on Aunt Ashley, huh?"

She flashed him a dazzling smile and walked into the church.

Brad called softly to Eric, and minutes later, Eric was standing by the altar. An organ, a harp and two guitars were playing, and the last of the attendants had walked down the aisles. Ashley came toward him at last. He saw the emerald fire in her eyes beneath the veil, and he saw her smile. Though night was falling, he felt as if the sun's radiant beams were shining down on him. He smiled, remembering Leah.

We are going to have beautiful, beautiful children, he thought. Then he took Ashley's hand in his hand, and turned around to face the priest. He vowed his love, and all of his life, to her.

* * * * *

MILLION DOLLAR SWEEPSTAKES (III)

Stories that capture living and loving beneath the Big Sky, where legends live on...and the mystery lingers.

This November, meet more MONTANA MAVERICKS in

THE ONCE AND FUTURE WIFE
by Laurie Paige

Back in his passionate embrace, she wondered if a second go-round would bring love for better or for worse?

And don't miss a minute of the loving as the passion continues with:

THE RANCHER TAKES A WIFE
by Jackie Merritt (December)
OUTLAW LOVERS
by Pat Warren (January)
WAY OF THE WOLF
by Rebecca Daniels (February)
and many more!

Only from *Silhouette*® where passion lives.

Don't miss these additional titles by favorite author
DIANA PALMER!

Silhouette Desire®

#05733	+THE CASE OF THE MISSING SECRETARY	$2.89 ☐
#05799	*NIGHT OF LOVE	$2.99 ☐
#05829	*SECRET AGENT MAN	$2.99 ☐

+Most Wanted series
*Man of the Month

Silhouette Romance™

#08910	*EMMETT	$2.69 ☐

*Long, Tall Texans
*Fabulous Father

Silhouette® Books

#48242	DIANA PALMER COLLECTION	$4.59 ☐
	(2-in-1 collection)	
#48320	LONG TALL TEXANS	$5.99 ☐

Best of the Best

#48292	SOLDIER OF FORTUNE	$4.50 ☐

TOTAL AMOUNT	$
POSTAGE & HANDLING	$
($1.00 for one book, 50¢ for each additional)	
APPLICABLE TAXES**	$_____
TOTAL PAYABLE	$_____
(check or money order—please do not send cash)	

To order, complete this form and send it, along with a check or money order for the total above, payable to Silhouette Books, to: **In the U.S.:** 3010 Walden Avenue, P.O. Box 9077, Buffalo, NY 14269-9077; **In Canada:** P.O. Box 636, Fort Erie, Ontario, L2A 5X3.

Name: _____

Address:_____ City: _____

State/Prov.:_____ Zip/Postal Code:_____

**New York residents remit applicable sales taxes.
Canadian residents remit applicable GST and provincial taxes.

Silhouette®

SDPBACK8

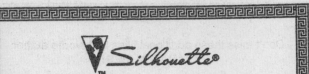

Don't miss these other titles by
New York Times bestselling author

HEATHER GRAHAM POZZESSERE!

Silhouette Intimate Moments®

#07416	HATFIELD AND McCOY	$3.29	☐
#07499	BETWEEN ROC AND A HARD PLACE	$3.50	☐
#07525	THE TROUBLE WITH ANDREW	$3.50	☐

Silhouette Shadows®

#27001	THE LAST CAVALIER	$3.50	☐

Best of the Best

#48279	DOUBLE ENTENDRE	$4.50	☐
#48280	THE GAME OF LOVE	$4.50 U.S.	☐
		$4.99 CAN.	☐

TOTAL AMOUNT	$
POSTAGE & HANDLING	$
($1.00 for one book, 50¢ for each additional)	
APPLICABLE TAXES*	$_____
TOTAL PAYABLE	$_____
(check or money order—please do not send cash)	

To order, complete this form and send it, along with a check or money order
for the total above, payable to Silhouette Books, to: **In the U.S.:** 3010 Walden
Avenue, P.O. Box 9077, Buffalo, NY 14269-9077; **In Canada:** P.O. Box 636,
Fort Erie, Ontario, L2A 5X3.

Name: _____

Address: _____ City: _____

State/Prov.: _____ Zip/Postal Code: _____

*New York residents remit applicable sales taxes.
Canadian residents remit applicable GST and provincial taxes.

SHGPBACK3